All That Remains

Melva Haggar Dye

iUniverse, Inc.
Bloomington

All That Remains

iUniverse books may be ordered through booksellers or by contacting:

iUniverse
1663 Liberty Drive
Bloomington, IN 47403
www.iuniverse.com
1-800-Authors (1-800-288-4677)

Because of the dynamic nature of the Internet, any web addresses or links contained in this book may have changed since publication and may no longer be valid. The views expressed in this work are solely those of the author and do not necessarily reflect the views of the publisher, and the publisher hereby disclaims any responsibility for them.

Any people depicted in stock imagery provided by Thinkstock are models, and such images are being used for illustrative purposes only.

Certain stock imagery © Thinkstock.

ISBN: 978-1-4697-9621-5 (sc)
ISBN: 978-1-4697-9622-2 (hc)
ISBN: 978-1-4697-9623-9 (e)

Library of Congress Control Number: 2012904488

Printed in the United States of America

iUniverse rev. date: 3/28/2012

For my husband, Charles Lewis Dye,
the best part of my day.

The US Department of Justice reports

that 797,500 children (individuals younger than eighteen) were reported missing in a one-year period, an average of 2,185 children being reported missing each day.

Andrea J. Sedlak, David Finkelhor, Heather Hammer, and Dana J. Schultz
US Department of Justice

"National Estimates of Missing Children: An Overview" in
National Incidence Studies of Missing, Abducted, Runaway, and Thrownaway
Children
October 2002, page 5

Acknowledgments

My friend, Robin Good, for believing in my writing.

The sister of my heart, Barbara Georgia, for believing in me.

In loving memory of my dad, Melvin Allison,
for encouraging imagination and demanding achievement.

Prologue

The view from the grimy, cracked window yielded little. Two old trucks sat on their cinder-block foundations, their rusted-out bodies soon to be overtaken by weeds. Broken bottles and tin cans lay scattered on the ground, circling smelly trash barrels. The man paid scant attention to the litter. He was supposed to keep the area clean, but no one ever came back to where he was—hardly anyone.

The four boys rounded the corner of the dilapidated shed and climbed nimbly over the stack of rotten wood that had once served as a privacy fence for the next-door housing project. These same boys came most afternoons to wander through the deserted back lots behind the man's home. They came to rummage through the piles of debris and to pilfer anything not nailed down. The three younger boys looked to be around eight or nine years old. They plodded along at a respectful distance behind their leader, a scrawny, orange-haired youth who couldn't be a day over thirteen but who already carried himself with the swagger of a street thug.

The man watched the boys intently as they began to poke a dead rat with sticks, the younger boys jumping and squealing when the older boy flipped the carcass too close to them. Their shrill voices annoyed him. The boys annoyed him in general, especially when they ventured too close to the woods and out of his view.

"Get away from here, you little peckerwoods!" His raspy, seldom-used voice carried through the partially open window. The younger boys ran, while the older one turned to stare defiantly at him for several seconds. Then, after slowly raising his hand and extending his middle finger, he turned to saunter off after his friends.

"Good riddance," the man muttered. He turned from the window and closed his eyes. The peaceful image of her came to him immediately. He had wanted to be gentle, like with the baby bird so many years ago. Wanting only to touch it and feel its tiny heartbeat, he must have squeezed too hard. The Woman always told him he did everything wrong, said he was stupid! Maybe she had been right.

No, no, no! He would not think about The Woman now. He would think only of his girls, especially the last one. How long had it been—three, four months? Time played tricks; it seemed like only yesterday. He breathed deeply and pressed his fingers tightly against his temples, trying to quiet the whispers inside his head.

He savored the memory of the little girl for a long time. As his eyelids fluttered open, he half expected to see her, still lying there on his bed, so quiet and so peaceful with her blonde hair surrounding her head like an angel's halo. But only the gloomy silence of his room greeted him.

It had pleased him to see the fear slip from her face, from all their little faces. His girls were safe now, in heaven. Never would they grow up to be whores, like The Woman. He had saved them from that fate. Yes, that's exactly what he'd done! Just like that man, Jesus, he had saved them!

It was a good thought.

What next befell me then and there
I know not well—I never knew.
First came the loss of light and air,
And then of darkness, too.
— "The Prisoner of Chillon,"
Lord Byron

Part I

Part I

1

"So you're leaving after all." He spoke in the tight, clipped manner that sparked her annoyance.

"I'm not leaving, Joe," Thea replied tiredly. *Or was she?* "I'm merely going on a trip alone. You know I've dreamed of going to Mexico City for years."

"Why now? Why not wait until I finish the Beckerman project? We could go together then. I'll take some time off after the first of the year, and we can—"

Thea cut him off. "Joe, we don't need to go together. We need—okay, *I* need—space. Besides, you said yourself you won't have the final blueprints ready for Mr. Beckerman for another two months at the earliest." She wished for that same all-consuming passion in her teaching that Joe had found in his architectural designs. Maybe then the dreaded images wouldn't invade and torture her so. *Yes, they would.*

"I could drive you to the airport, you know. I'd like that." He wouldn't let it go.

"Max is coming at seven in the morning. I've already arranged it with her." That was all she said. It was kinder than telling him the truth, which was what? That the less time they spent together these days, the better? "Thanks, anyway," she added, guilt nibbling at her.

"I see. While you're away, perhaps Teresa could pack up the room. I think it's time," he said.

"Well, I don't!" Thea responded sharply. She turned her back to her husband, making a pretense of rearranging her suitcase, wishing he'd leave the bedroom. He wouldn't leave, though, and warned by his deep sigh, she tensed at what came next.

"Thea, it's been over a year." Joe's voice was thick with emotion. "Can't you put it behind you?"

"Can you?" She turned to face him squarely. "Can you honestly tell me you can't *feel* her still alive? In here, Joe," she said as she pounded her chest where a heart had once brimmed over with love. "In here, I feel it! In here, I know she's out there somewhere, waiting for me." Spurred on by her own intensity, she continued. "And please, Joe, stop telling me it's been over a year. I know exactly how long it's been! Thirteen months, eleven days, and, let's see," she checked the bedside clock pointedly, "three hours. I was here, remember?"

"Oh, and I wasn't here, so I'm to blame? That's it. That's what you're saying! If I had left work a little earlier—"

"That is not what I'm saying, Joe." Thea bit her lip. She was so tired of talking and so tired of him. When had it become so tiresome being with the man she'd loved half of her life? "If anyone's to blame, it's me," she went on. "So please stop reminding me how long it's been."

His deep voice cracked with the agony of the moment. "I'd give my life to have her back, you know that. The two of you were my whole world. It's the future we need to work on now, though. We can get it back, Thea. Together we can do anything!"

Poor Joe—he tried awkwardly to embrace her and to soften the sting of his words. But those strong arms she had once loved, that embrace that had cradled her in safety for so long, now threatened to smother her. She pushed firmly against his chest, creating a distance between them. Heartbroken as she was over the cracks in their marriage that threatened to become chasms, she felt powerless to repair the damage. "No, Joe, we cannot do anything together, not anymore."

Thea turned away from the hurt in his eyes and moved to the window seat, dismissing him. It wasn't in her nature to be deliberately cold and insensitive. The realization was troubling to her. Sometime later, the sound of the car's engine broke through her reverie. She watched his car disappear down the driveway into the gathering darkness. "Oh, Joe," she whispered, "not only have we lost our daughter, we have lost *us!*"

2

The Plaza de la Constitución pulsed and throbbed with energy. Here the imagination soared to limitless heights, as both life and death were celebrated. Adorned now with the festive trappings of *Feliz Navidad*, the ancient plaza embraced the throngs of people who filled her.

Thea Kelly felt herself being drawn into that embrace, experiencing a deep reverence for what her eyes beheld. "This is the second-largest city plaza in the world!" she marveled aloud.

She became conscious of her surroundings as the slightly embarrassed taxi driver cleared his throat and spoke. "*Senora, por favor?*"

It was her turn to be embarrassed. How long had she been sitting in the taxi, mesmerized by the sights and sounds of the plaza? She laughed—a forced and hollow sound—as she paid the friendly driver and stepped from the taxi.

Earlier anxieties hovered. Perhaps coming to Mexico alone hadn't been a good idea after all. Thea had looked forward to this trip, but the moment the bellman had deposited her bags and left her in the silence of her hotel room, that familiar curtain of depression threatened to descend once more. She had hurried downstairs to engage a taxi.

Standing now in the historic *Zócala*, in a land whose peoples and cultures she so greatly admired, she took pride in having fought off her depression and once again felt a hunger to consume the sights and sounds all at once. She was eager to travel back centuries in time and immerse herself in the art of Mexico through its world-famous museums and to gain a deeper understanding of past civilizations. God willing, she would find some measure of peace to sustain her throughout the rest of her life—a life that now held little appeal.

For a time, Thea wandered reverently through the wonderful old Metropolitan Cathedral, marveling at architecture that had withstood the ravages of time. And the art! She would never tire of gazing at the larger-than-life images of the Virgin and Christ Child, Jesus as a man, the disciples, and the angels. In her mind's eye, she could see clearly the ancient hands of the craftsmen at work still. The wood carver, the stonecutter, and the painter all came alive to her.

As she emerged from the cathedral later in the afternoon, her tear-streaked face and grave expression gave mute testimony to a ceaseless agony. *What a sight I must be*! Thea loosened the combs that held her hair and allowed it to fall in a silken black cascade nearly to her waist. Even in her disheveled state, she drew admiring glances. This attention puzzled her as it always had. Joe often said her feelings of inferiority resulted from an only-child complex, but Thea didn't buy into the analysis; she was well aware of her flaws. She was too tall, her eyes were too wide set, and her nose was much too prominent.

To the casual observer, she looked to be a native of Mexico; but on closer inspection, her olive skin, almond-shaped eyes, and chiseled features were unmistakably Mediterranean. In spite of her wretched mood, the jovial atmosphere began to have an uplifting effect on her. She found it impossible to keep her body from swaying in rhythm to the mariachi bands and was soon returning smiles and nodding greetings.

Distracted by the frivolity around her, Thea very nearly bumped into the little girl standing before her now—eyes riveted on her. Oh, those eyes—solemn black pools, they were! Even amid the gaiety of the plaza, her Spanish eyes remained secretive, knowing, perhaps resigned to accept whatever life held in store.

Thea guessed the child to be about five or six. Without warning, the image very nearly blinded her with its brilliance, and she fought its possession. She fought it but lost.

Alexa will be six in two months. Alexa, skipping without a care, lifting chubby arms to be embraced. Alexa with dark and rolling eyes, hair curling in damp ringlets against her neck, mahogany hair, black like Thea's and that of her Greek mother's, but shot through with red highlights inherited from Joe—

"Alexa!" With her own anguished cry, the image receded, leaving her wounded and alone. Thea saw that the little girl had not moved, those intense eyes unwavering in their study of this strange, sad lady. A woman, most likely the mother, seized the child's hand and quickly pulled her away.

She spoke tersely as she hurried across the plaza, no doubt admonishing her daughter not to stare, perhaps warning her not to get too close to strangers.

Thea wanted to run after them and tell the mother that she, too, had a beautiful little daughter and to reassure her that no harm would come to her child. But how could she make the mother understand? How could she talk of reassurance, of protection against harm? She had failed to protect Alexa. Everyone had failed.

In spite of her comfortable hotel room and delicious dinner, Thea endured a sleepless first night in Mexico City. Even with the flight, long taxi rides, and hours of walking in the *Zócala*, the escape she had sought in sleep had not come. She had risen early and, after a light breakfast, wandered into the park.

Even in December, the weather was pleasant. She soon found a bench to her liking and began to leaf through the various brochures she had picked up in the hotel lobby, attempting to keep her mind occupied. She figured that it might be a good day to visit some nearby villages noted for their crafts, mainly Metepec for the pottery.

Thea's dream of one day becoming a successful potter had been shared with her best friend, Maxine Lindel. A sad little smile crossed her face as she recalled Max's words: "You're going to be famous one day, kiddo. Believe me!"

Now, the excitement of that dream was gone. Thea still enjoyed teaching to some degree and enjoyed the young people. After seven years, though, the familiarity of her classroom and school had left her weary. She longed for a more creative role as well as a new direction in her career and in her life. She just didn't know how to go about achieving it yet.

She and Max taught at the same junior high school in the Dallas, Texas, area. Max taught physical education and coached the girls' swim team, while Thea was head of the Arts Department. They had met shortly after Thea and Joe had moved to Texas, and the bond that had formed between them was precious.

The two women had become almost inseparable—"traffic stoppers," Joe often called them. Max's height matched Thea's five feet, eight inches, but the similarities in their appearance ended there. In contrast to Thea's dark features, Max's short blonde curls framed an impish, freckled face and piercing aquamarine eyes. Wild, witty, wonderful Max! She had been the one person who did not attempt to dissuade Thea from believing that Alexa was still alive and would be found and returned to them one day soon.

"Sorry I can't tell you what you want to hear the way Max does!" Joe's words had stung, driving the wedge between them even deeper.

Being several years older, Max also helped to fill the void left by the untimely passing of Thea's mother many years earlier. In retrospect, Max was the only real friend Thea had, except for Mike, of course. She had called him Daddy when she was a child, but he had become widely known as 'Big Mike' and Thea thought it fit him so well that she took to calling him by his name. He hadn't objected. It had been tough growing up without a mother, but Thea could not have wished for a more wonderful and loving parent than Michael Chandler.

Long-ago words echoed in her mind: "Stay close to your father, Athena, and be strong. You are all he will have left when I am gone." Mary Poulos Chandler's final words had fallen heavy on the shoulders of ten-year-old Thea. But they had risen to the occasion, she and Mike.

In spite of Mike's doting, growing up in the rural Ozark Mountains had been lonely for Thea. But then came Joe, and her loneliness had ended. Thea smiled. How out of place the gangling, freckled-faced, forever blushing fourteen-year-old boy had looked that first day of junior high school! Joe had always said it was love at first sight for him; Thea couldn't remember. She realized she'd never given much thought to her relationship with her husband until recently. The marriage, while far from perfect, had been good, hadn't it? Having Alexa had made it good.

Again they lured her, those haunting images of her life and her child before the nameless, faceless horror had struck.

"I named her Mary Alexa, Mike," Thea had murmured, slipping into her drug-induced sleep as the nurse gently removed her newborn daughter from her arms. Groggy as she was, she couldn't miss the smile that lit up her father's face. Tears of happiness filled his shining eyes as he simply nodded his approval.

The years following Alexa's birth were truly blissful for Thea. Over time, Joe had mentioned more children, but his dream of a gaggle of freckled faces spilling out onto a huge front porch was not her dream. For Thea, one happy, healthy, beautiful child was enough. And beautiful Alexa was! Her olive skin would glow golden in the summer sun, highlighting those dark, luminous eyes. At birth, she had had a small red birthmark just behind her left ear, shaped exactly like a strawberry. It was this strawberry that caused much delight among the three of them.

Many nights, the child would come bounding into her parents' bedroom. Smelling of Ivory and clean cotton and with a bedraggled and one-eyed teddy in tow, she would scramble under the covers between them. After much giggling and tickling, Thea would hold the squirming child, kiss her neck, and ask, "Whose berry is this?"

Alexa would throw tiny arms around Joe's neck and delightfully squeal, "Dat Daddy's berry!" And "Berry" she came to be—

A tiny whimper escaped Thea's lips as reality returned. The kaleidoscopic images began to fade, and a multitude of feelings and experiences that bound her to Joe drifted in and out of focus. As desperately as she had resisted their invasion, she now fought to hold onto those images, fearing that when they were gone completely, no more would she feel the loving touch of her husband; no more would she taste the sweet, wet kisses of her child.

4

"Paul, darling, there she is again, the young woman. She is so beautiful but so sad! She's been alone every day. Do invite her to join us."

"Elena, has it occurred to you that she may prefer to be alone?"

"Nonsense. No one should be alone during the Christmas holidays. Besides, she can always decline. Now go ask her, just for a drink."

Thea couldn't help but overhear the hushed voices of the couple at the nearby table. She had noticed them as well during the past week. The woman looked to be in her mid to late forties; the man several years older. Their traditional Spanish dress and flawless mastery of the language made it obvious to Thea that they were Hispanic. A shy smile crept over her face as she gladly accepted their invitation to join them.

Soon, the three of them were laughing at her attempts to speak Spanish. "With my fascination with Mexico and the culture here, wouldn't you think I would have taken time to learn the language?" Thea shook her head and made a wry face. "That's my next project." Being fluent, her new companions proclaimed the immediate beginning of lessons.

"The two of you are from Mexico, then?" Thea asked soon after joining the Ramirez couple.

"Actually, no," Paul answered. "Elena and I are natives of Santa Fe, New Mexico. But this is the birthplace of both of our families. We visit often and especially enjoy Christmas here."

The cocktail hour progressed to dinner, and Thea realized as she climbed into bed hours later, exhausted, that it was the first truly enjoyable evening she had spent in a long time.

During the days ahead, with the three of them spending so much time together, the chord of friendship was struck. Paul captured Thea's interest when he spoke of their home and his real estate business.

"Our city is the art capital of the Southwest, dear." Elena contributed to Thea's education of Santa Fe. "With your background and interest in art, you must come for a visit!" Elena was an accomplished artist herself, successful in marketing her jewelry creations throughout the Southwest.

In the company of her new friends, Thea began to believe some purpose might once again exist in her life. She found herself looking forward to each day when she awoke and constantly bombarded the couple with questions about Santa Fe.

"I wonder what it would be like to live in a city such as yours, surrounded by beautiful mountains and with more art galleries than I can visit in weeks! It sounds like the perfect place to live," Thea said.

Paul and Elena seemed to be just what the doctor ordered. They were obviously a happy couple, with Paul's composed demeanor complemented by Elena's high spirits. *Some of their happiness is bound to rub off,* Thea reflected. When asked about family, she had only briefly mentioned Alexa's disappearance. It was impossible for them to feel her pain—for anyone to feel her pain, for that matter. But she drew comfort from their presence when her tears would come without warning.

"Thea," Paul said several days after their first meeting, "Elena and I would never intrude, but sometimes sharing grief with friends can be a solace. We truly hope we are such friends."

The three of them were enjoying lunch at a wonderful little outdoor restaurant when, in spite of her efforts at self-control, Thea began to sob. As she dried her eyes and fought to regain her composure, she looked at Elena and saw her own anguish mirrored in the other woman's eyes.

"Yes, Paul," Thea replied. "You two are such friends."

"Dear," Elena fretted, "please don't feel that you have to tell us anything."

Thea held up a hand, silencing the other woman. "It's time."

The couple sat with hands clasped, their hearts aching for their young friend, as she quietly told them of her loss. Paul almost wished he hadn't asked as he sadly watched Thea's face become a veiled mask and her eyes grow dull. Her normally lilting voice dropped an octave as she calmly began to recount her daughter's disappearance thirteen months earlier and the frustrating dead end the police had run into in their search for her and four other missing little girls. No ransom notes had been sent in any of the disappearances. The members of the police department, as well as the media, were of one accord: they were looking for a pedophile.

"No one has mentioned serial killer yet, but we know that's on everyone's minds." Thea paused and took a deep breath. "But so far, no bodies have been found."

The community of Hampton Woods, where Joe and Thea lived, had the reputation of being the safest community for miles around. An approximate forty-five-minute drive from Dallas, it provided the amenities of shopping centers, medical and dental facilities, day care, kindergarten, an elementary school, and a junior high school, with the local high school only a few miles away. Nearby were two private day care and preschool centers.

"We enrolled Alexa in Ascension. The nuns were forever telling us how they enjoyed her and how smart she was." Thea smiled at the memory. "They would say, 'Mrs. Kelly, she'll be reading before you know it.'"

Just a few months shy of five years old, Alexa already knew the alphabet and had memorized their home telephone number and address. "Joe and I made sure of that, just in case. We would tell her: 'Don't talk to strangers, Alexa. Don't get in cars, Alexa!' Our neighborhood and the golf course have always been gated and manned twenty-four hours. We just felt so damned safe," she finished flatly.

It had happened quickly, with no warning and no clues. That had been the most maddening aspect of the disappearance for the local police department. "Oh, I can't fault the police," Thea stated emphatically. "How do you start a search for a missing child with no clues whatsoever?"

As she chillingly told her story, she relived that day as if it were still happening. It seemed, she told her friends, as if she were caught in some vicious time warp, with events happening over and over from which there could be no escape.

"Fridays were always special for us. Joe would leave work early, usually by two o'clock, and since my school has art classes only four days a week, I don't work on Fridays at all. That was always my time with Alexa."

That particular Friday, Thea had decided to stay home. An upcoming rummage sale at Alexa's preschool prompted her to spend the day cleaning out the garage and tagging items to be donated. Just an average, ordinary Friday it was, with the weather a bit nicer than usual for November.

"It was cool and sunny, and I knew Alexa would love being outdoors with me. She could ride her tricycle and play with her dolls in the drive while I worked in the garage," Thea continued. "Well, she soon became bored and wanted to help me. Paul, Elena, I never had a moment's hesitation when she begged me to let her take some rubbish to the curb. I was proud of her for wanting to help." She closed her eyes tightly, with the scene still fresh in her mind. So fresh, in fact, she could almost reach out and touch … *the half-skipping, half-stumbling four-year-old, dragging a bag larger than she, talking to herself as she made her way down the drive and around the curve* …

Thea's eyes flew open as she voiced aloud for the first time the words that had echoed in her mind for thirteen months: "That was the last time I saw my little girl!"

The next thing Thea became aware of had been the sudden panic that rose up inside her. For the first time in her life, she experienced fear as something she could actually taste—when she realized that Alexa had been gone from her sight for fifteen minutes. "I remember screaming for our housekeeper. 'Teresa! Teresa! I can't find her! I can't find Alexa'!"

The elderly housekeeper had tried to reassure her employer that the child was only playing a game, but she would later tell the police of the deep sense of foreboding that had crept over her at that moment.

The Kelly home had been built on an acre lot, and while most of the trees in the estates were not yet very large, the vegetation was thick. Pines, live oaks, and dozens of ornamental trees and shrubs had been planted and would one day afford maximum privacy. The landscaping had been done in such a way as to block the view of the house from the street, and vice versa. Thea, Teresa, neighbors from next door, and Max were all outside calling, walking, searching when Joe arrived home a little after three that afternoon.

"He knew something was terribly wrong the minute he got home. I'd never seen him so upset. He kept running wildly through the neighborhood shouting for her. I can still hear him, 'Please answer Daddy, Alexa! Please! Berry, can you hear Daddy'?"

Elena gently interrupted Thea at this point, offering her a dry tissue and suggesting she drink some of her iced tea. "There were no clues whatsoever for the police to go on, dear?" she inquired.

"Relatively none," Thea answered. "The only thing they found was—" Here the recounting of that horrific afternoon almost became too much for her once again, and she sat unmoving, unspeaking for several minutes. After a time, she swallowed her tears and continued.

"A few months earlier, Alexa had wanted her ears pierced. We went to a jeweler in our shopping mall that specialized in piercing little girls' ears.

You wouldn't believe how brave she was! Her eyes got so big, but she never cried or even moved. I was so proud of her. When the jeweler showed her the earrings, she picked a pair of tiny gold hearts with a ruby chip in the center." Thea's face clouded. "The police found one of them lying at the end of our drive. That earring coupled with the fact that the trash bag was left in the middle of the drive and not in the receptacle were the only signs that anything was out of the ordinary."

Telling her story had evoked many memories for Thea, memories of the helplessness she had felt and of her frustration over the seemingly inane questions repeatedly asked by the police. But most of all, memories of her husband's plaintive cries for their daughter echoed in her mind. Sharing her loss with friends was therapeutic, though. She realized that part of her problem was the dreadful burden of guilt she carried on her shoulders.

"Not only do I blame myself entirely for letting Alexa out of my sight," she said as she finished recounting her story, "but I'm also to blame for the miserable state of my marriage."

Indeed, Thea knew that it had been her aloofness and inability to bond with Joe in their hour of grief that had created the rift between them. Sadly, with this realization came the awareness that while she accepted the blame, she had no desire to make things right with her husband.

5

Thea darted through the hotel lobby, drawing inquisitive glances along the way. She hadn't been this excited in a very long time. During her two weeks in Mexico City, she had taken several day trips to sites outside of the city. She had climbed the Pyramid of the Sun and experienced a thrilling view from the top as she learned of the Teotihuacan culture. And would she ever forget the huge stone carvings resembling giant totem poles at Tula or the breathtaking views of the endless mountains and valleys? The three-day side trip she had just returned from, however, had fascinated her far more than she could ever have imagined.

Her guide had arranged for a trip to the Mitla archeological site and provided her with a brief history of the Zapotec culture she would be visiting. Before this trip, names of cities and villages were but descriptions in textbooks and travel folders for Thea. The imagery of Mexico's ancient civilizations aroused her interest, but the history and romantic past of the country had not truly come alive for her in the pages of books.

But now, after walking the cobblestone streets and seeing not just ruins but art, Thea could actually glimpse life as it had been centuries ago. She could hear the voices. She knew that most artists possessed this mystical imagination, but she was not prepared to be so overwhelmed by Mitla's finely carved stone forms and patterns that so closely resembled the Greek key designs. She marveled as to how these ancient craftsmen, with only primitive tools at their disposal, had managed to fit their stones together so exactly. It had been this likeness to Greek designs found here in Mexico amid the remains of an earlier culture that had planted the seed of an idea to sprout in Thea's mind. She was eager to share her idea with Paul and

Elena and could hardly contain her excitement as she hurried to shower and dress for dinner.

She thought fleetingly of Joe. She had purposely not telephoned home since her arrival in Mexico, except to call when she knew he would be at work. She had given Teresa the number of her hotel room but left no message for her husband. The realization that she was avoiding him had been foremost in her mind over the past two weeks, and Thea took a moment to examine these feelings as she finished dressing.

Studying her reflection in the mirror, she pondered words that, up until a few months ago, were foreign to her: *loss, separation, divorce.* She drew a deep breath as she left her room to meet her friends downstairs. A familiar longing filled her. It was a longing not for her husband, though, but for what had once been.

The three of them had reservations for dinner at the Hacienda de los Morales. Paul and Elena had been there many times, and their description of the beautiful, old Spanish colonial house and the excellent menu had Thea looking forward to the evening with much anticipation. She was smiling as she entered the cocktail lounge to join them.

~

"Your ideas for pottery designs are fascinating!" Elena said. "Combining the Greek symbols with replicas of pieces produced during the Zapotec culture would be stunning. Oh Thea, you're going to be famous!"

Elena spoke spiritedly, with the trademark animation that drew people to her. She had an elegance that commanded attention. As she gestured with beautifully manicured hands, silver and turquoise bracelets jangled and rings sparkled—jewelry she herself had designed. She sipped her martini and continued.

"Please come to Santa Fe and talk to some of the potters in our area. As a matter of fact, I have some friends who would love to meet you, maybe even have you join them in their shop. No, wait; you'll want to be entirely on your own. That way when you're famous, no one can say that they had a hand in it—no one but Thea Kelly herself!"

"Slow down, Mama," Paul said, flashing his dazzling smile at both women. "Thea has some terrific ideas, I agree; but all good things take time. She's here on a vacation, and she's going back to her home in, what, Thea, another week or so? Anyway, my dear, do some more research and a great deal more soul searching. If a new career and a new location are indeed what you really want, then, by all means, do it! Life is short—remember that."

Paul quickly realized that the last statement had been a careless thing to say and felt like biting his tongue off. Nervously, he continued. "And Elena and I will, we hope you know, be there to help you and advise you all the way."

"That is true," Elena added, also trying to soften Paul's tactless statement. "I just get so carried away when I really believe in something. Thea, I do believe in you. You're young, beautiful, and talented. And you have a dream!" Elena's voice softened, but her exuberance remained. "Dear, don't let that dream go. Don't ever let your dreams go!"

"What good friends you two are!" Thea said, becoming misty-eyed. "I was so alone when I first came here; now I feel as if I've known you all my life. If your invitation to visit you in Santa Fe still stands, I'd love to come. I have so much to sort out first, though; it's going to take time. I don't know what to do about my marriage, my teaching. I—" Her voice trailed off, the excitement over her new ideas momentarily fading as she once again thought of Joe. How could she ever make him understand what even she, herself, did not?

"To answer your question," Thea continued after a brief pause, "I'm going back home on the twenty-third. I do want to be there for Christmas. Mike's flying in for the holidays, and I need to spend time with him. And I miss Max. You're going to love her when you meet, but I warn you, Max is unique."

"Thea," Paul said as he took her hand in his, "Elena and I are not pushing you. We are just at such a terrible loss as to how we can help you. You see, you are quickly becoming the daughter we never had. Isn't that right, Mama?" Paul's voice was comforting. "Please rest assured that we will do whatever we can to help you personally and, should you decide to pursue your new ideas, professionally as well. Hell, what's the use of being in real estate if you can't sell some property to a friend?" he concluded, making both women smile.

Thea studied the handsome couple in front of her: married twenty-five years, successful, but, more important, enjoying their success. And they're still so in love! *It would have been that way with Mama and Mike*, she thought; but it would not be that way in her marriage. The enthusiasm generated by merely considering change was an omen. It was a new life, a new career, and new surroundings that she needed. She would begin this new life soon.

"Thank you, my friends," Thea said from her heart as she lifted her glass in a toast. "To us and to our friendship."

"And to your healing spirit," Paul said, touching his glass to hers. "We all have one within us. May you find yours soon, Thea Kelly."

6

"That was the most delicious dinner I have ever had," Thea said as the three of them walked slowly into their hotel lobby several hours later.

"Wine wasn't bad, either," Elena slurred happily. "Do we dare a nightcap?"

"If you wish, my dear," Paul replied, steadying his wife lovingly. "After all, tonight has been something of a celebration, I'd say. Not only have we been gifted with the ideas of a soon-to-be-famous potter, but we have been equally gifted with her beautiful smile!" He concluded his speech and bowed from the waist.

Both women pretended to swoon and collapsed on a nearby couch, chuckling. Indeed, it had been a heady night. The food and wine were grand, as was the Hacienda itself. At that moment, Thea realized she was as contented as she could be without Alexa.

The women chatted quietly, wondering if a late-night drink was entirely in order. "Where's Paul going, Elena?" Thea asked, seeing him walk briskly across the lobby.

"Oh, I believe I heard the concierge call to him a moment ago," Elena replied. "He probably wants to know if any of us will require a taxi and guide tomorrow. By the way, do you have plans? Maybe we could get in a little shopping in the afternoon."

"I haven't given it much thought, but I am a little tired. Maybe I should just take it easy tomorrow." Thea suppressed a yawn. "Elena, is Paul calling me or you?" she questioned, seeing her friend's husband motion rapidly with his hand.

Moments later, Thea stood flanked by her two friends. "Did my husband say *why* he was calling? Did he leave a message?" she asked the concierge anxiously. The man spoke little English, and it was maddening to endure translation.

"Dear," Paul spoke somberly to Thea as he took her by her shoulders. "He says that the only message is for you to call your husband immediately and that it is of great importance."

"Dear God, please—please, let it be Alexa! Please let Joe say she's been found!" Thea prayed aloud, her hands shaking as she dialed the number and waited for Joe's answer.

She didn't wait long, as the telephone was answered on the second ring. "Joe?" Thea said loudly.

"No, ma'am. Wait just a minute." Thea heard muffled voices, and after what seemed an eternity, Joe's voice came on the other end of the line.

"Thea, is that you?"

"Joe, what is it? Is it Alexa?" Is there news?"

The pause on the other end of the phone seemed to last a lifetime. "You need to come home right away, Thea—tomorrow, or even tonight, if possible. Do you understand? We need you to come home now." Joe's voice was flat and lifeless.

"Yes, Joe, I'll be on the first plane out of here. Now tell me what's happened?" Thea spoke slowly, with enough calm to make her husband tell her exactly what she wanted—or didn't want—to hear.

"Thea, the police have arrested a man. Uh, he's a truck driver or a delivery man—oh, I'm not sure! They—" His voice cracked. "They believe he's the one that took Alexa and the other little girls, too. Thea, they … they—"

"Damn it, Joe! Spit it out!" Thea said harshly, her frustration mounting.

"They found two bodies buried near where he lives. They have the man in custody. Oh, Thea, come home now!"

Joe's painful sobs were audible to everyone in the small office behind the concierge's desk as Paul gently took the phone from Thea's shaking hands. He turned away to speak quietly into the receiver. She barely heard Paul's voice as she buried her face in her hands and allowed herself be cradled by Elena. She was only dimly aware of the agitated behavior of the concierge as he stood by, helplessly wringing his hands. Finally, Paul put down the receiver and turned to the young man. Thea caught a few words in the hurried Spanish, and she realized that Paul was arranging for her to be on the next plane to Dallas.

Her mind was in a fog. Her movements were stiff and unfeeling, like those of a mannequin, as she went through the motions of packing her suitcases. Paul and Elena had not left her side throughout the remainder of the night, and Elena even helped her bathe and dress for the plane trip.

"Listen to me, child," Elena said gently. "Paul talked with the policeman at your home last night, and he said—wait, Thea. Don't pull away. Please listen to me." Elena's tone of voice was firm yet loving as she turned Thea once more to face her. "He said that no identifications had been made yet. He also said that the description of Alexa that Joe gave did *not* closely resemble the ... the findings." She chose her words carefully. "If you fall apart now, Thea, if you lose hope, you will be no good to yourself or to anyone."

"It's so easy for us to tell you to be calm and stay positive." It was Paul's turn to try to reassure her. "All we can do is to offer our support. Elena is right, you know. You must remain strong."

Thea pressed the wet tissue tightly to her swollen eyes. "I know. I guess I'm crying for the parents of those two little girls they found. I'm crying for all the lost children, for all the monstrous inhumanities! How could someone murder a child?" Her composure once again threatened to crumble. "But you're right. I've got to get a grip. You see, I *know* that neither of the bodies is Alexa's." Her sobbing stopped. Drying her eyes one final time, she turned stiffly to face her friends and met their gaze squarely. "I know Alexa is still alive. I just know it!"

"There, now. That's our girl." Paul spoke with an assurance that masked his misgivings. He hugged the young woman while his eyes met his wife's, both of them sensing the pain that their young friend was yet to endure.

~

The plane lifted off three hours later, and Thea sat gazing numbly out of the window at the receding mountains of this land she had grown to love. As they soared higher and higher, she closed her eyes and tried to summon positive thoughts: the beautiful places she had visited and the smiling faces of her new friends.

The images flickered and then vanished, only to be replaced by the devastating reality her husband's words conveyed: "They've found two bodies.... They have a man in custody."

Thirteen months earlier

The man drove the truck faster, causing it to slip and slide over the icy road as his mind raced. He cast a furtive glance across the seat at the object of his frustration—so little, so young, and yet so goddamn bossy, just like The Woman! And this one, she didn't cry, didn't whine like the others had. She just stared at him with those black eyes of hers, those devil eyes! He hated black eyes, and black hair, too, for that matter. They reminded him of The Woman.

"No! I won't think about her. I won't!" The sound of his own coarse voice startled him, almost like it was coming from someone else's mouth.

The man had not touched this Dark One. In his mind, she was a child of the devil for sure. And now, in his agitated state, he wondered what in hell had prompted him to take her in the first place.

The little blonde-haired girl was the one he had gone looking for. Oh, she was so beautiful, so bright and shiny. She would have been all clean and pink and soft to his touch—so smooth, not with that awful hair on her body. That's when they became whores, he had decided years ago: when they grew up and got hair on their bodies like The Woman.

In spite of his resolve not to think about The Woman and his hatred of her, there she was again, crawling around inside his head with her fat, ugly body; glaring, black eyes; and huge red mouth. She had been loud, too, always yelling, and her breath had smelled bad. In fact, she had smelled bad all over.

Thinking about The Woman made his head ache, his teeth chatter, and his hands sweat. Sometimes he missed time, too. A lot of things happened that he couldn't remember—bad things—but he was used to that. Bad things had been happening to Hurley Dobbs most of his twenty-four years on earth.

The Woman had been his mother. He knew this even though he had never been allowed to call her that. "You think I want ever'body knowin' I gave birth to an ugly, stupid little bastard like you?" she had said.

Hurley's thoughts rambled back to his early years, the years he'd spent with The Woman in the dirty little two-room garage apartment. The small windows had provided little light, and their dismal home had seemed even darker with the constant fog of cigarette smoke pervading its interior. Hurley remembered, too, the never-ending stream of grubby, mean men who frequented his dismal home. He was never allowed inside during these visits. No great loss, he had thought at the time; he would rather have been by himself anyway. He hated everyone—The Woman, the men, everyone!

Hurley continued his erratic driving, becoming slightly hypnotized by the steady *thwack, thwack* of the truck's windshield wipers. He was unable to stop his thoughts from dragging him back to the tormented years of his childhood.

If the men gave The Woman some money, she was a little nicer to him and would even allow him to sleep on one side of the only bed they had. All too frequently, though, the men would leave without giving her anything. They would stumble out of the door, calling her names while being pelted with anything in reach. After these episodes, The Woman would walk the floor, drinking from the bottle, smoking cigarettes, and cursing loudly. After decreeing all males to be sorry, no-good bastards, she would turn on Hurley—for being male, he guessed—and a beating would ensue. Then, he would have to sleep on the floor or on the battered old kitchen table with only his coat to cover him.

One night came to mind when The Woman did allow Hurley to sleep in the bed, or rather she didn't stop him. As he recalled, she had been too drunk to object. Passed out and snoring loudly, she never moved when he lay down on the other side.

Several hours later, Hurley awoke in panic to find himself on the floor, his head pounding. He looked up and saw The Woman, completely naked, standing over him. His ears rang with her screams and curses, like he'd never heard before. He barely heard her words, though. He barely felt the repeated slaps across his face or the repeated kicks to his bony body as she continued to berate him.

"Filthy little brat! You're just like that miserable, lying, son-of-a-bitching daddy of yores! Goddamn little pervert. Whaddya mean getting in bed with me? I'll beat you to death, that's what I'll do! Be one less mouth to feed then!"

On and on her tirade continued. Hurley stopped feeling the blows completely after a while, but he never stopped looking at The Woman's body. What an ugly sight she was to the child of eleven! In fact, he had never seen anything as ugly—sagging tits, protruding belly, bulky thighs, and pasty white legs covered with black stubble. The memory still sickened him.

It had taken Hurley the better part of a week, lying very still on the floor, before he could walk without gasping in pain. He had heard of broken ribs, and he guessed he had several. And his head hurt for a long time—a funny kind of hurt, like a buzzing going on in there.

The Woman wasn't home very much during that time. She had brought some food home, though, the kind he liked. She'd muttered something about being sorry, saying it had been for his own good.

It had seemed like the most natural thing in the world when it happened. Hurley shivered, fully aware once again and enjoying this particular memory. One morning, a few weeks after the bad beating, The Woman had gone out of the door and was standing on the rickety landing at the top of the stairs. Just a tiny little nudge it had been, not really a push or anything—

The child, clad in his forever-dirty jeans and shirt and the tattered coat-blanket, stepped over the crumpled form at the bottom of the stairs and made his way down the street to school. He thought dimly, *One less mouth to feed.*

8

"Shit!" Hurley yelled loudly. He sat bolt upright in the truck's seat and turned the steering wheel just in time to avoid a collision with—what, a deer, maybe? Had he skipped time again? He couldn't stop himself from thinking about The Woman, but now he remembered where he was, more or less.

He had left Dallas, heading west on Interstate 20. He soon became tired of the monotonous four-lane highway, exited, and turned north, finally veering slightly west into Colorado. How long had he been driving—two, three days, now? Concentrating on time messed up his mind, but he knew it had been several days. He had stopped only to put gas in the truck. The thought flashed through his mind that it was a good truck. It made him a good living when he could get hauling jobs away from them goddamn Mexicans.

He had stopped, too, for hamburgers and coffee, lots of black coffee. He liked the way the little white pills made him feel when he washed them down with the strong black coffee he got at truck stops.

Nobody looked twice at him. He became just another face in the crowd to the scores of weary waitresses at the dingy diners along the way. He was just another loser ordering the same thing, leaving no tip. There wasn't much to notice, anyway. Hurley Dobbs was of medium height, with dirty-blond hair brushing his collar. He had pale gray eyes and a rather large nose, obviously broken before, that dominated an acne-scarred face. If he had smiled, teeth badly pitted with cavities would have been visible. Hurley never smiled, though. He never warranted a second glance.

No one saw the child, either—the Dark One. No, he'd been very careful of that! Tied her up, he had; made her lay on the floorboard, too!

The one night he had stopped at a dilapidated motel somewhere just south of Amarillo, he had made sure no one saw him carry her into his room. He'd kept her hands and feet tied and made her sleep on the old couch in the corner, facing away from him. He couldn't stand to have those eyes looking at him. Devil's eyes, they were!

Oh, he fed her from time to time, and he let her go to the bathroom. Finally, she stopped talking so much. Finally she stopped asking for her mama and daddy. It made him sick to hear her grown-up little voice calling for Mama!

"You ain't got no goddamn mama and daddy, do you hear me? Why? 'Cause I killed them, that's why!" He had screamed the lie at her. That had been the morning after their stay in the motel. Hurley had made sure he woke before daylight, carried his bundle to the truck, and left unseen. He'd thought she might still be asleep; she had been so limber and unmoving. But then, several miles down the road, she had startled him.

"Are you taking me home now? I want my mama *now*!"

That's when he had almost lost it. The brakes of the truck locked as he slammed them on, making the vehicle skid dangerously to a stop on the icy road. It had unnerved him mightily to see the change come over the child's face when he told her he had killed her parents. He'd been glad for the silence, though. It gave him more time to think, more time to remember—

The weeks following The Woman's "accident" were confusing. Everyone seemed to think Hurley was deaf the way they always talked over him as if he wasn't even there. "Poor little boy. He's obviously been abused! It's a blessing, that's what it is!"

"Now, maybe he can get some help. Oh, no, we certainly can't take him, but, well, surely someone will want him."

"He's a polite, quiet boy, don't you think? Especially after having been raised in that sort of atmosphere and all. I mean, she had men in, don't you know!"

Hurley could still hear the words of neighbors, teachers at the school, and the social workers.

"He's got no family—nobody."

"Sad is what it is. There aren't many folks willing to care for an older child; they want babies and toddlers while they're still cute."

But someone did take Hurley. Rupert and Callie Johnson said God had spoken to them, and He said to take this pitiful boy and make a difference in his life.

"They will make a difference in your life, Hurley, if you'll just be a good boy and do as you're told," the social worker from Child Protective Services said stiffly the morning she drove him from the center to the Johnsons' home. "They're fine, Christian people, Hurley, and you must make an effort to get along with them. After all, son, you might not get a second chance to have a good home."

Hurley soon realized that it wouldn't be very hard to get along with the Johnsons. They were a middle-aged couple with no children. Their parenting skills consisted mainly of Mr. Johnson's endless readings from the Bible in his slow drawl and Mrs. Johnson's nervous hand-wringing as she went about cooking the most delicious meals Hurley could ever have imagined.

He had his own room. He couldn't believe it—a bed complete with sheets and blankets and a pillow! The boy was amazed at the bathroom, as well. It was always so clean, not constantly stopped up. But the grandest part of all was the food—plates and plates of good food. Mrs. Johnson said he could eat all he wanted.

Of course, Hurley quietly hated the Johnsons. But then, he still hated everyone: the Social Services lady, his teachers, the neighbors, other children, everyone. Even though loathing for all around him clouded his mind, stupid he was not. He had never before in his life been clean, warm, and well fed, not to mention that he was never beaten in this new place. He certainly had no intention of screwing up.

So, for the next seven years, he did as he was told, performed his chores, and went to school. He brought home mostly failing marks, never really earning promotion to the next grade. His teachers would shake their heads worriedly, realizing something was "very strange about that Dobbs boy," and reluctantly pass him on to become some other teacher's worry the next year.

Hurley did learn to read and write passably and would always regard the day he received his driver's license as the happiest one of his life. It had taken him three tries to pass the written test, but at age seventeen, he was filled with the first true sense of accomplishment he had ever known. He could relax while driving, and it became the one thing that he could do well.

Old Mr. Johnson himself said Hurley was the best driver he had ever seen, a real natural. He had said this with quiet pride since he had been the boy's instructor.

A feeling of exhilaration filled Hurley the first time he sat behind the wheel of Mr. Johnson's ancient station wagon and deftly piloted it down the narrow gravel driveway. Glancing in the rearview mirror, he saw the frail form of Mrs. Johnson standing on the front porch wringing her hands. How he longed for the day when he would see that sight no more, when he could get away from the constant Bible reading and hand wringing, live alone, and just maybe, have his one dream come true: to drive a truck.

Hurley quit school at seventeen. No one cared—not Mr. Johnson, who had never finished high school himself; not his teachers, who breathed a sigh of relief at his leaving; and certainly not his fellow classmates. Hurley had no friends. He had joined no clubs, and he detested sports, believing them to be a waste of energy. He vaguely remembered a couple of homely, white-trash girls in high school who had smiled at him and tried to make conversation. The thought of them with their hairy bodies turned his stomach. They were whores, he had decided, just like The Woman.

The Johnsons worried and whispered to each other their fears for the boy. They had grown quite fond of him, as he had always been so polite and helpful. Yes, they had done their Christian duty in bringing him into their home. They did admit, however, to being sorely disappointed that Hurley had not turned out to be a more sociable boy. It would have been nice if he had brought friends to their home, maybe even a girlfriend now and then.

"Always hoped he'd find a nice Christian girl and settle down," Mr. Johnson remarked one evening as the old couple sat on the porch watching Hurley drive away in the station wagon. "Maybe we'd be Grandpaw and Grandmaw one day, huh, Mama?"

"Never happen, Rupert," Callie replied stoically. "It'll never happen." She had wanted to have motherly feelings for the boy. She'd wanted to love him, but she could not. Oh, she had tried as best she knew how to break through that cold, hard shell that surrounded Hurley, but she had failed.

As she sat rocking quietly in the twilight, Callie knew something dark lived within her foster son, something evil. She suppressed a shudder as she realized that in all the years he had lived with them, she had seen him smile only once: the day he'd gotten his driver's license. "No, Rupert," Callie continued as she voiced her fears, "there'll never be any happiness for that boy."

9

There had been happiness for Hurley, though; when he was driving he was happy. And shortly before dropping out of school, he had discovered another kind of happiness—a sweet, aching, frustrating, confusing kind of happiness. At times, these wondrous feelings would wash over his body, making him weak and hot.

He had been drawn like a magnet one afternoon to the preschool center not far from his own school. What a wonderful afternoon it had been! Hurley sat on the cool grass shaded by huge live oaks and watched the little girls on the playground. They were so pretty, and they looked so clean. He became mesmerized as he watched them at play. Sometimes he could see their panties—pink, white, and lacy—as they climbed on the swings or sat in the sandboxes. What, he wondered dreamily, would it be like to touch them there, in their panties? The thought made him groan. God, he wanted to touch them, to look at their smooth bodies! That had been quite an afternoon for Hurley. He would go back again and again.

Most afternoons, when the old man didn't have something for him to do around the place, Hurley sat entranced by the little girls. He loved the blonde-haired ones. They looked cool and unsoiled. He knew one day he would have to touch one of them; merely watching them couldn't last him forever.

Hurley knew all about sex. He had sat through the disgusting films in his physical education classes, shutting his eyes most of the time and listening to the insipid snickering of the other boys. He hated it! It reminded him of The Woman, the whore. He hadn't thought of her in years, but the films had brought it all back. And with his recurring memories came the nightmares, the headaches, and the lost time. He had stopped going to school completely soon after the sex education classes began. He knew all he needed to know. He knew what he wanted.

Hurley did odd jobs from time to time to earn spending money after he quit school. He didn't need much money, as the old couple provided all his necessities. Gas money for when he was allowed to drive the car and candy bars were his chief expenses. He hated going to the movies; he couldn't concentrate on the plot and soon became frustrated. It didn't take much money to drive around for a few hours or to go down to the playground.

Hurley told Mr. and Mrs. Johnson matter-of-factly one evening after supper that he needed a truck, with four-wheel drive, to be specific. He wanted to get a job, he said. He had seen a sign at a local landscaping company advertising for drivers to haul sand, gravel, sod, small trees, and so on. He could do this, he told them emphatically; he knew he could! The only hitch was that the drivers had to have their own trucks. Well, he wanted to know, could they buy him a truck?

"We'll have to sleep on it, son," Mr. Johnson had said. "It's a lot of money and a powerful big decision. But if it's going to help you build some sort of life for yourself, well, maybe we can swing it down at the bank."

The next morning had dawned bright for Hurley. He had been pretty sure the old couple would spring for his truck, and he had been right. After listening to a stiff speech about the responsibilities of owning a vehicle, Hurley was further subjected to a lengthy prayer for "God to lead young Hurley here into a bright future in his chosen profession." This had been accompanied by much hand-wringing from Mrs. Johnson, but it had all been worth it. The Johnsons signed a paper at their bank, and the next day Hurley was the proud owner of a two-and-a-half-ton Ford truck with four-wheel drive.

Before he drove away that afternoon to apply for the job, Mr. Johnson awkwardly broached the subject of making payments. Hurley merely looked at him.

Not only did Hurley get the job as a hauler for Santos Landscaping, but Mr. Santos called him the best driver he'd had in a long time. Most of his young drivers drove too fast—trying to impress their girlfriends, he said—but not this boy. No, sir! This one really knew how to take care of his truck, too.

Hurley hated the thought of working for a Mexican, but he nodded politely and asked for all the work he could get. He loved driving, and actually getting paid money to do it was terrific. He decided it would not be very long before he would move out of the Johnsons' house for good.

His wish came true sooner than he'd expected. On the back lot of Santos Landscaping stood a plain but sturdy garage with an efficiency apartment built above, much like Hurley's first home. The apartment was indeed sparse, comprising one large room serving as both living room and bedroom, with a kitchenette in one corner.

"Well, Hurley, whatcha think?" Bob Santos asked him one afternoon after mentioning that the company needed a watchman of sorts. "You interested? I need someone to just be here and more or less look after the place when we're closed and feed the dogs on weekends. You'd mainly just keep an eye out for any mischief at night. If you see or hear anything suspicious, just call me or the police. Oh, and you can park your truck in the garage. Think about it, boy, and let me know in a day or two."

Hurley certainly didn't have to think about the offer very long. Of course he was interested! This was his chance to be away from the Johnsons. Not that they weren't nice enough, he reasoned; they never yelled at him or hit him. But Hurley wanted to be alone—alone with his thoughts.

"Don't have to think 'bout it, Mr. Santos," Hurley answered before this golden opportunity could vanish. "I'd like it real well!" Hurley always had trouble looking folks straight in the eye, especially someone with authority like Santos, but this time he made himself meet the older man's gaze. "I'll do a good job," he said with as much respect as he could muster.

The next morning at breakfast, Hurley told his foster parents about his new duties at the landscaping company and of his new home. He'd be leaving that afternoon, he informed them.

Mr. Johnson allowed that he sure would miss Hurley around the place. "Always be welcome here, son! Ain't that right, Mama? And now, let's read a few words from the good book and wish our boy here luck. Why, son, we're real proud of you, getting such a fine job!" Mr. Johnson patted Hurley on the shoulder as he rose from the table to get his Bible.

Mrs. Johnson had remained at the sink with her back to the kitchen table. Neither man saw the faint smile that spread over her tired face, nor did they notice the complete absence of hand-wringing.

10

Hurley's palms stung from pounding the truck's steering wheel. Blinding goddamn snow! Why had he driven so far? And what in the hell was he going to do with *her*?

Oh, the buzzing was starting again in his head, bringing with it the bad headaches. And time—he must be losing time again. Maybe not. Maybe just too much thinking, too much remembering. The day he took this Dark One came to mind now, a day he wished he could live over.

Mr. Santos had told him to take a load of sod to the new house he was working on, but Hurley had forgotten, or lost time, maybe. Santos had said to take it on Thursday, and suddenly it was Friday. If he lost this job, he didn't know what he'd do! It was hard enough getting driving jobs away from the Mexicans, and now he had forgotten something. Stupid—that's what he was. Just plain stupid!

Maybe he could take it over a day late and no one would notice. After all, no one had said a word to him about the sod not being delivered when the workers had returned to the office Thursday evening. Just maybe he could get away with taking it over on Friday. Yeah, Friday afternoon would be good. The boss never worked then anyway.

Hurley loaded the sod on his truck by himself and drove out the back gate, using his key. He had boasted to the Johnsons that Mr. Santos gave the gate keys only to his top men, and that's just what he was. Hell, Santos might chew his ass for forgetting to make the delivery, but he wouldn't fire him. Hurley was sure.

In spite of his bolstered confidence, he quickly decided it would be better to not get paid for one lousy haul than to tell the dispatcher where he was going and risk getting yelled at. Hurley wanted to go back to that subdivision anyway. Maybe he'd get to see that pretty little blonde-haired girl again. He had seen her walking with a woman several times. He liked her even more than the others.

~

Corliss Watkins was by nature not a patient man, and today was near to being the most exasperating day of his entire life. Being a gate guard at the Hampton Woods Estates and Country Club was usually an interesting job. His bad back, stemming from a truck accident years before, made it difficult to find work he could do on a part-time basis without endangering his Social Security disability income. And at only fifty-two, he needed to do something.

Corliss had been employed by the Hampton Woods community for six months, and this was by far the slowest day he had seen. With three new homes under construction and constant deliveries throughout the estates, there seemed to always be traffic at the gate and people he could talk to. He thought of the country club, too. With nice weather like today, where were all the golfers? Oh, well, he surmised, today was just a slow day for once.

The main reason the security guard was edgy today concerned Carmen. Last night he had gotten up his nerve and asked her to marry him. "Baby, I know I'm fifteen years older than you," he'd told her nervously, "but, well, damned if you ain't the finest thing I ever had! Carmen, will you marry me? I got a little money put back, and with my check and the job and all, we can make it. Well, what do you say?"

Corliss fretted. It was close to one o'clock. Carmen had promised him she'd call on her lunch hour and give him her answer. He couldn't imagine what he'd do if she said no. Corliss was lonely, and he was in love.

"Afternoon to you," Corliss said as he grinned and tipped his cap to the driver. "Thought I knew all of Santos's drivers. You new?" he asked, glancing at the landscaping company's sticker on Hurley's windshield.

"Been with 'em a while," Hurley replied curtly.

"You're the only one of Santos's trucks that's been through here today. Thought maybe you guys took a long weekend," Corliss continued.

"Yeah, well, I don't know 'bout that," Hurley replied. "I just drive the truck. Guess if nobody else is here, I'll have to unload it, too. If it's a holiday, they didn't tell me," he quipped as the gate began its slow swing open. "Have a good 'un."

"Thank you. How long you reckon you'll be?" Corliss was interrupted by the shrill ringing of the phone in his guard shack. "Hello? Oh, Carmen, honey, I've been waiting on your call!"

He never heard Hurley's answer to his question. In fact, Corliss Watkins quickly became oblivious to everything around him except the voice he had longed to hear all morning. Leaning back in his chair and smiling, he closed his eyes. He'd log this guy in later, after he finished talking to Carmen. He wouldn't forget.

~

Hurley was pissed. "Now ain't that a bitch!" He muttered under his breath. "All that worrying and nobody's even here to do the unloading."

After finding the job site and unloading the sod, Hurley rested in the shade of a large tree for a few minutes and then decided to drive around a bit before leaving the subdivision. After all, he didn't get much free time during daylight hours.

It had just happened! He certainly hadn't planned it, but there she was, dragging that bag down the driveway. *More or less cute*, he'd thought at the time. But that was before he saw those eyes.

It had been real easy and quick, too. He could tell no one was around—never were this time of day. He'd just stopped the truck, walked around like he was checking his tires, and opened the door. It took only seconds: one quick, stunning blow to the side of the head, in the truck, and head for the gate. *Now, where's that idiot of a guard? Probably taking a leak*, Hurley assumed as he glanced around quickly and eased his truck through the open exit gate.

Hurley did not learn the reason for quite a while, but when he returned to the landscaping company that afternoon, a sign had been posted on the main gate notifying all workers that the company would be closed for the next two weeks. All drivers were to call the dispatcher at that time for their haul assignments. If he had checked in with the office that morning, he would probably have found out why, but who gave a shit. He could use a vacation. As he used his key to unlock the back gate and drive unseen to his garage apartment, Hurley knew that luck surely was with him this day. He needed time to figure out what he was going to do about things.

The child had walked like a zombie as Hurley roughly guided her up the stairs to his apartment. He never released his grip on her thin shoulder.

As they entered the door, however, it became evident to him that he would not control her.

"I don't live here! Why are we here?" she asked, staring at him intently. "I want to go home now. My head hurts."

"Stop whining, kid."

Hurley had wanted to appear superior to this child, but in reality, she unnerved him more than a little. He had wanted to touch her soft little body, but he was scared to death of her! Tying her hands behind her back had been as close to physical contact as he had been able to get, and that had brought about a tingling sensation throughout his body like an electrical shock.

"I gotta get rid of this one!" he had muttered over and over to himself while pacing the confines of his small apartment as darkness descended.

11

"But now what, damn it?" Hurley yelled as he pounded the steering wheel again. "Now what are you going to do with her?" Oh, why hadn't he just driven by and left her standing there on the side of the street? And then, he had gotten the bright idea to simply drive her out of town somewhere and get rid of her.

"But why did you drive so freakin' far, you stupid piece of shit?" Again he cursed himself frantically. He continued cursing not only his own stupidity but the continuing snowfall, the child, everything that had contributed to his present predicament.

Fueled by too much coffee and too many white pills, his body and mind ravaged by a desperate need for sleep, Hurley teetered on the brink of paranoia. In his fragile state of mind, fear became an animate object. Taking form before his very eyes, she rose up slowly, emanating from the small form lying on the floorboard. The more he shook his head, blinked his eyes, and slapped himself in the face, the more real his vision became, like—"Oh, God, no," he groaned. It was The Woman!

Hurley's arms flailed out, trying to strike his ghostly adversary. But she grew larger, coming closer to him, encircling him now with those flabby arms, mocking him in whispers, breathing her stale breath on his neck. As he fought desperately to keep control of the truck, he knew that this thing threatening to suffocate him was surely The Woman, and in his mind she radiated from the Dark One. This must be what they meant by reincarnation!

In spite of the truck's heater blowing full blast, Hurley was freezing. His teeth chattered, and his knees shook. Finally, with great concentration, he managed to free himself from the imaginary clutches of The Woman and bring the truck to a stop.

His ragged breathing had exhausted him. How long he sat there, eyes tightly closed, hands locked on the steering wheel in a death grip, he did not know. After a while, he mustered up the courage to open his eyes. To his relief, The Woman was gone. She had gone back into the body of the child.

Hurley suddenly knew what he must do. He had to get as far away from this child as possible and soon, before she turned into the dreaded form of The Woman again. An idea came to him in a flash, and the cruelty of it made him giddy with pleasure. He had not been able to bring himself to touch this one, not even to make her die, and it was the realization of his own weakness and fear that had brought him to the brink of madness.

He climbed from the truck's cab on legs as weak as a kitten's. "I gotta get away from her, gotta get rid of her, now, get far, far away," he muttered in a sing-song voice. With ever-quickening breath and glazed eyes, he made his way around to the passenger's side, holding on to the truck for support against the swirling wind and snow.

Moments later, the deed done, he skillfully turned the truck around and headed south. His face was awash with a smile that mirrored insanity. He cast a fleeting glance in the truck's rearview mirror and giggled gleefully at the receding form in the middle of the snow-covered road.

The bitter wind began to slow its assault, the snowfall gradually diminished to mere flurries, and the moon peeked from behind clouds. Hurley failed to take notice of these changes, so occupied was his mind with relief.

"Soon, soon," he murmured aloud as he rocked back and forth in the seat. "Soon she'll be in hell with the devil and The Woman, gone forever!"

His anxieties lessened as he continued driving. Gradually, he grew calm and began making soft, tuneless whistling sounds. Soon he would stop, maybe at a motel, and get some sleep and some food.

Hurley was at peace once again. With his serenity came the stirrings of the familiar pain-pleasure that started in his loins and quickly spread all through his entire body. With it came images of small, smooth bodies and shiny blonde curls.

12

The Monday morning sky dawned gray, accompanied by a cold and drizzling rain so common for Dallas in December. Captain Cal Evers's bones ached as he made his way from the parking lot to the suite of offices occupied by the members of the special task force.

"Let's get to it!" He barked his orders to no one in particular and everyone collectively as he entered the office. It had been their ritual every Monday morning to gather around the conference table and go over each missing child's case separately, reviewing each report word for word. Everyone had them memorized by now.

Cal had never been a man to mince words or waste time, and since being named head of the task force created to find the missing girls in the area, he had had precious little time to waste. He and four carefully chosen detectives had worked almost round the clock for the past eighteen months since the first little girl had been reported missing from just outside the town of Irving.

Cal thought now, as he had so many times during those eighteen months, that it had been by far the most frustrating time in his entire police career. The proverbial needle in a haystack would have been easy to locate compared with what his people had come up against over the past year and a half. Most of that time had been spent trying to placate those assholes down at city hall as they constantly whined about the lack of progress being made on the missing girls' cases. Lately, there had even been talk of dissolving the task force.

Their Monday morning routine was boring, maybe even pointless, Cal knew. But what else could they do? Maybe, just maybe, some tiny shred of a clue would jump out at them. Cal's contention was that someone, somewhere, had to have seen something.

~

Detective Manny Garza knew the message that he held in his hand this morning was wrong, no mistake about it. "Sir, this phone message that the desk sergeant took last night—no way. Can't be." Manny kept staring at the message and shaking his head in disbelief.

"Well, you gonna tell us what's wrong?" Cal sounded disgruntled with his young detective. "We're not here for you to play twenty questions, Garza."

"Sorry, Captain, but this is real confusing," Manny continued, ignoring the exasperated groans around him. "Sir, this message says a Mr. Corliss Watkins, gate guard at Hampton Woods where the fourth little girl—let's see, Alexa Kelly—lived, says he remembers somebody else coming through the gate that day." Manny's voice trailed off.

"Spit it out, Detective!"

"Yes, sir, Captain. He—Watkins, that is—says he remembers a driver from Santos Landscaping coming through the gate that afternoon, even though it was over a year ago. He doesn't know how long the guy stayed, didn't see him leave 'cause he guesses he was in the men's room when he left."

The other four task force members continued to stare mutely at Manny, waiting for the punch line.

"And your point is?" Cal asked menacingly, his patience with his young detective nearing its end.

"Well, sir, that can't be. You see, Bobby Santos, the owner of Santos Landscaping, is my brother-in-law, my sister's husband. I remember distinctly that he closed the whole company that morning for a couple of weeks. Bobby had to go down to Corpus 'cause his mother had died suddenly. Well, you see, sir, there couldn't have been a delivery made that day. They were closed." Manny grinned and drew a deep breath, finally getting his story out.

"How can you be sure it was that particular day, Detective?" Lieutenant Lois Castle asked. Lieutenant Castle was second in command of the task force and Cal's right hand as well as his best friend. "That's a long time ago. Couldn't you—or Watkins, for that matter—be wrong about the day?"

"No, Lieutenant," Manny answered calmly and with confidence. "You see, my wife and I kept the kids while Bobby and Maria drove down to Corpus. He brought them over early that morning. It was a Friday, and I was supposed to be off for a long weekend. But when the Kelly girl was reported missing that evening, I had to come back down here. Remember? We worked through the night. My wife, Lita, she was scared to death. Wouldn't let those two babies out of her sight."

Manny turned to Cal and continued speaking. "Sir, I'm positive. If a Santos Landscaping guy was in Hampton Woods that day, he didn't have no authority from Bobby to be there. That's a fact."

As he digested this bit of information, Cal looked around the table at his people—people he'd spent more hours with during the last year and a half than he had spent with Sophie and their three boys. He knew these people, their habits, their strong points, and their failings. He never doubted that they were the best.

Now, as they all sat quietly, each one savoring this bit of information in his or her own way, Cal could almost feel their pulses accelerate along with his. He sensed their collective juices flowing. He realized how alike they all were, the bottom line being that they were cops. They had a job to do, and now they had a lead!

"Why in God's name didn't that stupid bastard remember before now?" Cal said, his frustration making itself known. "It took him a whole year to speak up? I ought to arrest the son of a bitch for obstruction, that's what! Get him in here, now!"

13

To anyone who had known him thirteen months earlier, which Cal had not, Corliss Watkins was a mere shell of the man he had been. He smoked far too many cigarettes and had the perceptible shake of a man who drank more than he should. And he was a sad and lonely man, too, Cal discerned. He had noticed the tan line on his left ring finger immediately, most probably indicating a wedding band recently removed.

So the son of a bitch had woman problems, Cal thought. *Big deal!* Cal was interested in Watkins solely on the basis of what he saw or didn't see the afternoon of Alexa Kelly's disappearance. It was this single-minded objective that prompted Cal to regard his potential witness with scathing dislike.

"Suppose you tell us, Mr. Watkins, why it took you over a year to remember something that could possibly have prevented one, or even two, kidnappings? Maybe you don't think missing children are a very important cause?"

Cal bit his tongue, realizing that his feelings of contempt for the former security guard could hamper the questioning. He was grateful for Lois's intervention.

"Mr. Watkins, no one's blaming you for anything," Lois said, smiling at him in what she hoped would be construed as a sincere act of friendship. "We are, of course, curious as to why you didn't come forward with this information before now. But we are grateful for anything you can remember that will help find out what happened to these little girls."

"I—I'm so sorry," Corliss replied. "I just purely forgot about that landscaping truck. But as soon as it popped into my mind, I phoned you guys, you know? I sure do want to help. Me, I got no kids, but I love 'em. I'm just so sorry!"

Corliss was near tears, and Cal realized that Lois's approach was the right one. It obviously wouldn't take much provocation to send this poor slob over the edge.

"All right now, Corliss—can I call you Corliss?" Cal's voice lost its caustic edge, and at Corliss's eager nod, he continued. "Corliss, I'm going to record our talk here on this recorder if it's okay with you. I'd like for you to start at the very beginning of that day and tell us everything you remember, no matter whether you think it's of any consequence or not. Is that okay with you?"

Again, Corliss nodded profusely. He was eager to not only cooperate with the police but to absolve himself in his own mind of the terrible guilt he felt for failing to do his job properly—a failure he knew could very well have led to a child's death. "Yes, sir, Captain, I'll tell you all I remember. Again, I'm sure sorry about forgetting and all."

"Corliss, would you like a cup of coffee before we get started?" Lois asked him.

"Yes ma'am. Thanks." After taking an inordinately deep breath, Corliss related to the task force the events, such as they were, on the day in question. After going over each entry in his logbook that the police had obtained from Hampton Woods' Director of Security, Corliss told them in a rather embarrassed fashion what had led to his forgetting to log in the Santos Landscaping truck.

"Sir," Corliss's voice cracked. His eyes met Cal's, and the police captain was momentarily taken aback by the pleading he saw there. It was a pleading for some measure of understanding, man to man, for a situation that had so obviously ruined his life. "I'd give anything to just go back and do my job right. There's no excuse for my breach of security, I know."

Corliss related how he had quickly forgotten the landscaping truck that afternoon when Carmen phoned him. The news that she would, indeed, marry him had blotted everything else from memory. She had wanted to leave that night for Las Vegas, where they would get married and stay for a week or so to have some fun.

"Hell, I'd never been to Vegas, so I said, 'Why not!'" he told the silent detectives. "We had a great time, although I didn't go much for gambling. I didn't want to risk our savings, you know? But Carmen sure did like it, and I sure did want to please her."

For all his previous loathing of this man, Cal gained a measure of respect for Corliss while listening to his story. He realized, as did the other detectives, that a lesser man would never have spoken up at all. They owed the former security guard a debt of gratitude, and Cal made sure he told him so before he left that afternoon.

"Corliss, I apologize for my earlier attitude. We appreciate your help, and we'll certainly keep you informed if anything from this information pans out. Thanks again, pal. Oh, I hope things work out with you and your wife."

"Thanks, but she'll soon be my ex-wife. We separated right after we got back from Hawaii. She wanted to go there, too. No fool like an old fool!" Corliss smiled grimly as he shook Cal's hand. "Do let me know if you find out anything."

Cal watched the broken man leave his office, probably heading for a bar somewhere. "I will, Corliss. I'll call you soon," he said.

Corliss had chronicled for the task force his activities since the day in question. Carmen had not wanted him to work for the security company any longer; she said it wasn't exciting enough. He had taken a part-time job as a bartender at one of her favorite nightspots soon after they had returned from the wedding trip to Las Vegas. He hated the long hours and the night work. Worst or all, he had started smoking again, after having quit three years earlier. He had also admitted what Cal knew from the onset, that he drank too much. When he quit the job after a few months, Carmen was so angry that he had agreed to the trip to Hawaii to appease her. And, as each member of the task force had guessed long before Corliss admitted it, when his money ran out, so did Carmen.

It had been quite by accident that Corliss had remembered the Santos Landscaping truck at all. As he told the detectives, he knew he had forgotten to do something that day. But when the recollection didn't come to him immediately, and with the excitement of leaving for Las Vegas and marrying Carmen, he dismissed it as being unimportant.

He always turned in the logbook at the end of his shift to the guard who relieved him, and he in turn would pass it on. Everyone was part-time on the gate, and since Corliss was already en route to Las Vegas by the time the police were called in, and the logbook itself held no questionable entries, he was never interviewed.

Just one of those oversights on everyone's part, Cal concluded as he summed up his report that evening after questioning Corliss. There was no point in belaboring the issue. They had a lead now, and it wouldn't be too difficult to identify the driver of that landscaping truck on the day in question.

According to Detective Garza, Santos employed only three drivers, two gardeners, and a dispatcher, in addition to himself. With the dispatcher's help and Corliss's description, Cal figured they wouldn't have any problem pinpointing exactly who had made a delivery to Hampton Woods that fateful day thirteen months ago.

"Manny, first thing tomorrow morning, you and I are going to Santos's place, you hear me? And not a word to anyone. You got it?" Cal knew each and every one of his detectives would want to be present if an arrest was indeed imminent, but his youngest would have that distinction.

"I got it, Captain!" Manny replied proudly.

14

"Somebody check and see what time Mrs. Kelly's plane gets in from Mexico City, okay? You, Manny, check on that for me. Oh, and be sure to arrange for a policewoman to meet her at the gate, escort her home, wait for her, and then bring her down here, pronto! Understand?"

Cal didn't wait for answers. He spoke with barely contained excitement before closing the door to his office for what would most probably be the only quiet time he would have for a very long while. He needed this time to gather his thoughts before meeting with Thea Kelly later in the day. Mrs. Kelly was the last of the parents to be interviewed since the arrest of Hurley Dobbs. Cal wasn't looking forward to facing her any more than he had the other little girls' families.

He leaned back in his chair, closed his eyes, and thought of his early years as a beat cop. Were all young rookies as idealistic as he had been? Of course they were. Each of the young men and women fresh out of the academy believed that he or she would be the one to change the world.

Cal hadn't wanted to end up a cynical, depressed, overworked old cop with nothing more to show for all his years on the force than a meager pension and a sour attitude. So he had kept up his education, stayed squeaky clean, and advanced through the ranks rapidly. For the most part, he had enjoyed his time on the force. He enjoyed the camaraderie with his fellow officers, and from time to time, he luxuriated in the knowledge that they truly did make a difference.

But then, there always had to be that one case to deflate even the most positive outlook, the one that made cops waiver in their belief that good does outweigh evil. How many times, Cal pondered now, had he sat here in his chair staring at the wall in front of his desk? How many nights had the faces on that wall permeated his dreams? He knew their names and the details of their disappearances by heart: Erin Stevenson, age five, vanished from a playground; Jennifer Wilder, age four, at a shopping mall with her grandmother—gone; Tara Kingsly, four and a half, disappeared from her own backyard, for God's sake; Alexa Kelly, would've been five years old in three months, disappeared from the most protected neighborhood around; Kate Somersby, age five, nearly six, taken from another playground. All of these little girls were there one minute and gone the next, leaving no clue—until last week.

~

Thea's plane touched down smoothly the afternoon of December 21. She realized that in spite of the turmoil in her mind, she had slept most of the flight. It wasn't surprising, however, since the night before had been spent almost entirely in worry and tears. "What in the world would I have done without Paul and Elena?" Thea whispered under her breath as she gathered her coat and carry-on bag and stood to depart from the plane.

Mike Chandler almost didn't recognize his beloved daughter as she entered the gate area. The dark circles under her eyes and sad expression were to be expected, but what he observed now to be entirely foreign in Thea's appearance lay in her presence. Never had Mike seen her so dejected, never had he seen her walk with so little grace, so little enthusiasm. Her shoulders sagged, and her eyes were downcast. *Where*, he thought sadly, *is the aristocratic presence so like that of her mother? Where is the poise with which this beautiful woman has moved before?*

Countless times over the years, Mike had fervently wished that Mary could see the happy, well-adjusted, and, in his opinion, magnificent person her Athena had become. But now, along with his sadness, came a small measure of relief that his wife had, by her untimely death, been spared the heartbreak of witnessing their child's utter despair.

Mike, of course, adored little Alexa. But unlike so many grandparents, the center of his heart was occupied not by his grandchild, but by his daughter. After Mary's passing, Thea had been all the happiness he'd needed to sustain him for the rest of his life. "Please, God," he prayed softly as tears misted his vision. "Please comfort my child."

"Oh, Mike," Thea cried out when she saw her father in the crowd. "You're here. You're really here!"

"Of course I'm here, baby. I'll be here as long as you need me. Let me look at you. Thea, how tired you look, and how thin you are! Have you been eating at all?"

"Now, Mike," Thea said with a smile, in spite of her mood. "Don't be a mother hen. I'm okay. Let's get my bags and go home. I want to shower and change before talking to the police. Do they know anything else?"

The two of them walked rapidly, keeping up with the crowd of people moving toward the baggage claim area. Thea tried unsuccessfully to blot out the holiday merriment around her. She held only resentment toward anyone who exhibited even the slightest measure of happiness at this moment.

"All I know is that Captain Evers wants to see you as soon as you have time to catch your breath," Mike replied.

As they neared baggage claim, Lois Castle recognized Thea from their meetings during the previous months. She had volunteered to meet her at the airport and escort her to the task force's office later in the day. As soon as she caught sight of Thea, her heart went out to the younger woman.

"Mrs. Kelly," Lois said as she caught up with Thea and her dad. "I don't know if you remember me. I'm Lieutenant Castle with the special police task force. Please call me Lois. I'm here to escort you home, and when you're ready, Captain Evers would like to see you. Sorry I wasn't at the gate when you arrived, but traffic was the pits."

"Yes, I remember you, Lieutenant—I mean, Lois," Thea answered. "This is my father, Mike Chandler. Please call me Thea." As the two shook hands, Thea continued speaking. "Have they made identifications yet on the two bodies?"

"They're working on that now. We'll know before long. Come on. Let's get your bags and get out of here."

Once in their cars, Lois followed Mike and Thea through the maze of airport traffic and finally out into the suburbs, where the pace was slower and calmer, to the Kelly home in Hampton Woods. *Just how much safer could a family be?* Lois thought, shaking her head ruefully, as she emerged from her car to help with baggage.

The peaceful beauty of the home's setting only partially masked the tension Lois immediately encountered. The policewoman had seen her share of family crises, with most of them bringing the surviving members closer to one another. All too soon, however, she realized that was not to be the case here. While Thea clung to her father and to her best friend, Maxine Lindel, she barely touched her husband, Joe.

"It's so sad," Max whispered to Lois. "Just when they need each other the most, they seem to have drifted even farther apart than before Thea left for Mexico City. She's my dearest friend, and I'm at such a loss as to what to do."

"We all are, Max," Mike said as he joined the two women. "All we can do is be here for her. She's always been the strong one in this marriage. Did you know that?"

"Oh, I knew it, all right," Max answered. "But how long can she hold on to that strength, Mike?"

"As long as I need to," Thea replied quietly from behind the group. "I have to stay strong to find my daughter."

15

Cal Evers studied her as she sat quietly across the desk from him. He realized he was thinking the same thing he thought each and every time he saw her—that Thea Kelly was one of the most graceful and attractive women he had ever met, even with the obvious toll her loss had taken on her.

"I wish with all my heart, Mrs. Kelly, that I had more news for you—more positive news of your daughter. What we do have is a suspect in custody, and we're 99 percent sure he's the one who took Alexa. We believe he's the one responsible for all five disappearances. I don't think we'll have any trouble at all proving it; in fact, we may not *have* to prove it. His court-appointed lawyer is with him now, as we speak, explaining everything to him. He's going over all the evidence we have, telling him what he can expect with the required psychiatric exams he'll be going through, and so on. Mrs. Kelly, what I expect is a plea of guilty but insane."

Cal spoke awkwardly and rapidly, trying to stall the barrage of painful questions that he somehow knew this woman was going to ask.

"Captain Evers, do you have a positive identification on the two bodies yet? And where exactly were they found?"

Cal had been right. She wanted all the information he had. The veteran policeman drew a deep breath. This would be a long afternoon, he surmised. "Please, Mrs. Kelly, turn around, if you will, and look at the wall behind you. I know you've been over every detail dozens of times, but let's go over a few things once more, okay? Now, I'm sure you notice in looking at these photographs that your daughter is the only missing girl with dark hair and eyes."

At Thea's nod, he continued. "Does anything else different about Alexa come to mind?"

"I see nothing else different, Captain. They were all approximately the same age, were they not?" Thea asked.

"Yes. The girls' ages range from just barely four to almost six. All of them lived within an hour's drive of Dallas, and all of them, except your Alexa, were blondes with either blue or green eyes."

Thea rose from her chair and began slowly pacing back and forth, probably to calm herself, Cal thought. "Are you sure—I mean, *really* sure— that the same man took all the little girls? Perhaps someone different—"

Cal held up his hand to silence her. "Yes, ma'am, Mrs. Kelly. I believe we have the right man. To answer your earlier question, the two bodies were identified positively just a couple of hours ago, and the parents have been notified." Cal shuffled some papers on his desk. "Tara Kingsly was taken from her own backyard in a subdivision north of here. And the latest child reported missing, only a month after your daughter's disappearance, has been identified as Kate Somersby. She was last seen at a municipal playground.

"I sure don't want to put you through any more pain than you've already suffered, but I will tell you that our men found these two bodies buried in shallow graves in a wooded area about fifty yards behind where our suspect lives. Mrs. Kelly, do you know a Hurley Dobbs?" Cal asked the question and simultaneously presented the mug shot.

Thea thought for several moments that she would vomit. Yet, she could not make herself look away from the image in front of her. She felt the shaking of her own hands as she reached for the photo. She swallowed the bitter bile in her throat and continued to study the face of the man who, according to the police, had taken Alexa.

She stared at the photograph for several minutes, memorizing every detail of his hated image. Finally, when she could speak again, she looked up at Cal. "No, Captain Evers, to my knowledge I have never seen this man before. I would like, if possible, to hear all the evidence you have against him. Do you think it would it be possible for me to speak with him?"

"Absolutely not, Mrs. Kelly. No way!" Cal was emphatic. "In my opinion, not only would it be harmful to you personally, it just might jeopardize our case. We plan on a formal interrogation of him tomorrow morning, with his attorney present, of course."

"Could I at least listen to the interrogation?" Thea asked. "I just have to know, Captain. Please."

Cal sighed and looked at Thea. "I don't think it's a good idea. It could get rough, and you might hear something you don't want to hear."

"I can handle it," Thea replied. "It can't be any worse than what I've imagined all this time."

"Well, I'll see what I can do. I guess I could arrange for you to watch from an adjoining room, through the one-way glass. He wouldn't be able to see you. But you can't try to talk to him or let him know you're there. And I can't control what you hear. Do you understand?"

"Yes, Captain, I understand," Thea said, holding his gaze. "I might hear how he sexually and physically abused those two little girls before he killed them. I might hear him tell of where other bodies are buried. I might even hear him tell of brutally raping my Alexa. But what I *won't* hear is Dobbs telling where he buried her because I know my daughter is alive. I can feel it!"

"How can you be so sure about that, ma'am?" Cal asked. "Lord knows, I want to believe it, too. I've wanted to believe it about all five of the missing ones. Hell, maybe there are others from years ago that we don't even know about. But how—" Cal's voice trailed off. What could he say to this tortured woman?

Thea stood and began putting on her coat. "Do you have children, Captain Evers?" she asked him quietly.

Cal nodded thoughtfully. "Yes, ma'am. I've got three boys. They're thirteen, eleven, and five. The youngest one snuck in on us," he finished, smiling at her.

Thea smiled back. "You may not understand intuition, but I'm sure your wife does." Her gaze drifted from his and became momentarily locked on some intangible object for her eyes only. Swiftly, her eyes met his again, and she straightened her shoulders. "I don't know how I can be so positive, Captain, but I am. I'll see you tomorrow morning."

She paused with her hand on the doorknob. She kept her back to him as she asked one final question. "How, Captain Evers?"

It was the question all of the parents had asked, the question Cal dreaded answering most of all. "Strangulation."

16

She was gone. His office felt strangely empty, and Cal himself felt strangely alone. He was still in this detached state an hour later when Lois entered his office.

"How'd it go with the Mrs. Kelly?" Lois asked as she helped herself to a cup of coffee. "How'd she take the news of Dobbs's arrest?"

"Huh? Oh, she was calm enough, I guess. Wants to view our interrogation tomorrow morning. I agreed, even though I know it could prove to be a bad idea. Somehow, I think she can take it, you know? She strong, that one. I don't believe she'll fall apart. She's positive her kid's alive, Lois, and I—well, let's just say I wouldn't be at all surprised."

"Why, Cal Evers," Lois teased. "You mean to tell me that you believe in women's intuition? What would the rest of our rough and tough team say?" Being his best friend, she could give him the kind of grief he wouldn't tolerate from anyone else.

"The rest of the team ain't married to Sophie," Cal responded with a wry grin. "Damn woman's a witch," he continued. "I mean it, Lois. She knows things—maybe senses things—about our boys." Cal chuckled as he thought about his wife. "Hell, she senses things about me, too, for that matter!"

"Yeah? I'll just bet she doesn't *sense*, as you put it, that her husband's got the hots for one Thea Kelly. Or am I wrong, my friend?" Lois suddenly became serious.

"You're dead wrong, lady, and don't let me hear that crap again!" Cal rose from his chair and began putting on his coat and hat.

"Mrs. Kelly's a fine woman, and I admire her," he continued. "That's all. And I want to help her and all those other parents, too! Maybe that crazy bastard'll tell us tomorrow what he did with those other little girls. Hell, Lois, I think about my boys. The hardest part would be not knowing, don't you think?"

"No, Cal," Lois answered sadly. "The hardest part would be the burying. Then there's no hope left."

Cal pressed a dry kiss on his friend's cheek. "Get some sleep, sweetie. Tomorrow will be rough."

As he made his way out of the building and started down the street toward the parking lot, Cal pondered Lois's words. "No, I ain't got the *hots* for her. For chrissake, Lois," he muttered under his breath. In truth, there had been no other women in Cal's life since marrying Sophie sixteen years earlier. Tempted constantly for many years, especially when working as a beat cop, he had never strayed, not even once.

Having reached his car, Cal started the engine and waited for the heater to come on. It had been dark for over an hour now, and the cold was penetrating. As he rubbed his hands together, trying to shake the evening chill, Cal's thoughts were on Sophie. Oh, the many nights he had gotten home in the wee hours, exhausted both physically and emotionally from the grim and brutal realities he faced in his profession! Would he ever become immune to the killing, the drugs, and the malignant forces at work, destroying all he valued?

With these thoughts eating away at him, he would slip, exhausted, into bed beside Sophie. As he lay against her sleeping form, softly caressing her ponderous breasts, listening to her steady breathing and her drowsy murmuring, he would feel the anxiety and the sickness of his life gradually slipping away. During these times, the poison would be drawn from his body and, in its place, a soothing balm applied. That's what his woman did for him with her mere presence. Yes, Cal realized as he began the drive toward home and Sophie, she was so much more than a wife, a mother, and a companion. She was his comfort.

He reached his destination and saw lights on throughout his house. He knew that Sophie would be in the kitchen attempting to cook something marginally edible. She would smile, glad to have him home at a decent hour for a change.

As he turned into the drive, Cal saw the ever-present bikes, skates, and wagon blocking his entrance to the garage. For some reason, this didn't irritate him tonight as it usually did. Instead, the somber thought of how blessed he was that his kids were here to leave this mess came to mind.

No, sir; he would never do anything to tarnish what this family shared together, what they gave to one another. But, oh, that Kelly woman—she did lay sweetly on a man's mind!

17

The morning dawned cold and dreary, with a carbon-copy drizzle of the preceding day. Thea sat in the morning room sipping coffee, trying to quiet the uncertainties that raged within her. This room, with its southern exposure and decor of subtle earth tones, had always been her favorite in the house. It was close enough to the kitchen to be cozy, and with its high ceiling, large windows, and slate floor, it took on an easy elegance befitting the woman of the house.

She closely studied the room now, recognizing it as her place. Her presence was truly everywhere—in her pottery pieces displayed in corners and on low tables, in her charcoal etchings adorning the walls, and reflected in the smiling faces in photographs perched on bookshelves. Even with the past year's turmoil eating away at her and after the miserable night she had just endured, this room could still quiet her and make her feel welcome. Truthfully, Thea realized it had become the only place in the entire house where she felt at home anymore.

"I wish I had an entire house designed and decorated just like this room, Max," she said as a way of greeting her friend as she entered from the kitchen.

"Um," Max grunted, sipping the much-needed coffee. "It does reflect the inner you. Maybe you should give some thought to redecorating. The way you love the Southwestern themes, I think it would look stunning. I'd be glad to help."

The two women entwined arms and walked to the low-slung leather couch in front of the fireplace. "How about some breakfast before we leave to meet Captain Evers?" Max asked.

"*We?*" Thea raised her eyebrows in surprise at her friend. "You have classes to teach, Max. You can't baby-sit me forever. I'll be okay, believe me. I still haven't definitely decided to view the interrogation. I've been thinking about what Mike said last night. He's so against it, you know."

"Nobody's trying to baby-sit you, kiddo," Max replied, turning to face her friend. "You, Joe, and Alexa have been the only family I've had for a very long time, and I want to be with you. Besides, if the PE Department can't get along without me once in a while, then I deserve a big, fat raise! Now, what's it going to be—stay or go?"

Thea studied her best friend. "That's a question I've been asking myself quite a lot lately."

"Huh? What are you talking about, girl?"

Rising from the couch, Thea tugged Max to her feet and led her toward the kitchen. "Let's get some breakfast, and then we'll dress and go meet Captain Evers." She turned toward her friend and, seeing the confused look on her face, continued speaking. "Max, I'm on the verge of making some big decisions. We need to talk later on today, maybe at the pub or some other quiet place, okay?"

"Sure thing, Thea. Wherever you say, I'll be there."

The wheels were turning in Max's head. She had worried that spending last night at Thea's house would be a mistake, but everyone including Thea had insisted. It had been late when they had finally wound down after dinner and conversation, and no one had wanted Max to drive the thirty minutes to her house. Being so close to Thea, she had sensed her friend's misgivings when it came time to retire for the night. Of course, no one even suggested using Alexa's room, and with Mike in one guest room and Max in the other, that left Thea and Joe in the master bedroom. To anyone else this would have been looked upon as the normal, even expected, arrangement. But Max alone knew that Thea had not shared Joe's bed for the last six months.

Max had constantly prayed for the safe return of little Alexa and also for her friends' marriage to somehow survive this upheaval. But Thea had made it painfully obvious to everyone last night that she wanted nothing to do with her husband. Now, with her friend wanting to talk, Max knew it was just a matter of time.

~

Cal awoke with a start, his heart racing and his head pounding. He was sweating profusely, and for several moments he didn't know where he was. It was still dark, but he could see the digital clock's illuminated numbers; it was four in the morning. As he swung his legs over the side of the bed and slowly sat erect, he realized it was only a dream. Dream, hell—it had been the worst nightmare of his life!

"You okay?" came Sophie's groggy question as she reached to rub his shoulders.

"Yeah, I guess. Damn nightmare," was all he could say.

Stumbling to the bathroom for a drink of water, Cal shuddered violently as he remembered how real his dream had been. Hurley Dobbs was running through the woods, just like the woods behind his apartment at Santos Landscaping. All around him lay corpses of little girls, corpses with their eyes open, horror frozen on their little faces. In Dobbs's hand, limp as a rag doll, he carried Tim, Cal's youngest son.

"Dear God, Sophie," Cal said weakly as he climbed back in bed. "It's just a nightmare for me; I can wake up. For those families, though, their nightmares won't ever end."

"Maybe not, but they'll take comfort in knowing you got the son of a bitch! I know I would. I'd want to be sure he'd never be free to hurt another little girl, ever." After several minutes of silence, Sophie asked, "That will happen, won't it, Cal? I mean, Dobbs will be put away for life, don't you think?"

"Yeah, in some mental facility with three squares a day, medical care, TV, and all the comforts of home."

Sophie had realized some time ago what her husband had not yet admitted, probably not even to himself—that this case had really gotten to him. He had never been so distant with her or so impatient with his boys, and he looked haggard. He had not mentioned the results of his latest physical, which led her to believe the news had not been good.

She wouldn't raise the subject until after the Dobbs case was finished, but Sophie fully intended to suggest early retirement to Cal. With his degree in criminology, he could always teach or do private investigating work. She could go back to work, and the boys—well, they'd just have to get scholarships. Nothing mattered to Sophie Evers as much as protecting this man she loved—nothing!

"So, you want to talk about it, or do you want to get up? I'll make hot chocolate."

"Neither," Cal replied as he drew her close, feeling her calming influence flow over him, slowly blocking out the horrific images of his nightmare.

They lay quietly, not moving for some time; Sophie didn't know how long. She stayed there when her husband finally rose and made his way to the kitchen. She would wait until he had made coffee and had a little more time to himself, and then she would join him in their morning routine. They would speak of his dream no more.

18

"Good morning, Captain Evers. You remember my friend Maxine Lindel, don't you?" Thea smiled at Cal as he rose to greet the two women. "Max wanted to be here with me today; it's all right, isn't it?"

"Of course. How are you, Mrs. Lindel?" Cal responded warmly.

"It's *Miss*, Captain, and please call me Max. I'm not used to formality."

Thea said, "Captain Evers, I've brought the most recent photo of Alexa. I couldn't remember if you had this particular one or not."

She produced an eight-by-ten color portrait of the pretty little girl. She was a miniature version of Thea, smiling back at Cal. Her long, thick hair was held back from her face with blue ribbons. Her hair was black and streaked with red, and her dark eyes sparkled for the camera. Posed on a garden seat in the Kellys' backyard, she wore a long, white, lacy gown. In her hand she held a single long-stemmed red rose.

Cal's heart quietly broke as he studied the still image. He finally managed to speak after the painful silence, saying, "We'll find out what happened, Mrs. Kelly. I promise you."

"You have the description of what Alexa was wearing that afternoon, don't you, Captain?" Thea asked. She was in control this morning, Cal noticed, and he was glad for that. He desperately hoped they could all keep their emotions in check throughout this day.

"I have the file right here, ma'am. Let's see, now: blue corduroy jeans; light-blue, long-sleeved blouse; red-and-blue knit pullover sweater; white socks; and white tennis shoes. Is that it?"

"Yes, that's it," Thea replied, her resolve wavering. She was determined to remain calm this morning, allowing herself no tears. She needed to stay detached, but seeing the effect Alexa's picture had had on the seasoned police captain and remembering how her little girl looked in her new fall play clothes that fateful day almost dissolved the emotional barriers she had erected. She swallowed hard. "When do we get started?"

"Dobbs and his lawyer will be here at ten thirty. It's almost that now. Let's get some coffee, and then Lieutenant Castle can show you both the ladies' lounge and the observation room." Cal hit the intercom button on his desk. "Lois, come in, please."

After Lois had escorted the two women from his office, Cal left word that he did not want to be disturbed until Dobbs arrived and had been placed in the interrogation room. He wondered what it would feel like to not be tired all the time, to have a job that he could actually leave at the office when he went home at night. Cal closed his eyes, remembering countless family outings and backyard barbecues that had been planned and then called off, baseball games he had missed, their last vacation cut short—all because of Hurley Dobbs and men like him.

He opened his eyes as his intercom crackled, announcing the arrival of their suspect. His gaze rested briefly once again on the face of Alexa Kelly as he gathered her picture and file together with all the others and prepared to leave his office.

In just the few short minutes he had spent in solitude, Cal had come to a decision, though not an easy one. This case, when closed, would be his last; he was quitting the force. He wondered what Sophie would say when he told her.

~

Cal had been giving serious thought during the past three days to exactly how he would handle the formal interrogation of Hurley Dobbs. The evidence against the man was staggering in the two deceased girls' cases, and Cal knew the police held all the cards.

"Lieutenant Castle, gentlemen, good morning," Cal spoke formally as he looked at each person sitting around the conference table. "This is an official questioning of Mr. Hurley Dobbs with regard to the disappearance and subsequent deaths of Tara Kingsly and Kate Somersby. Our conversation will be taped." Cal placed a tape recorder on the table in front of him and switched it on. "Mr. Dobbs, have your rights been fully explained to you?"

Hurley nodded, and when Cal instructed him to give a verbal answer, he replied, "Yeah."

"And are you represented by counsel, Mr. Dobbs?"

"I'm Mr. Dobbs's attorney, Captain Evers. I'm Franklin Tate, sir."

Cal looked at Tate, the court-appointed counsel for a child murderer. *The poor slob likes being here about as much as I do*, the police captain thought. He held sympathy for anyone whose job it was to defend scum like Dobbs.

"Fine, Mr. Tate. Mr. Dobbs, are you satisfied with your attorney?"

"Yeah, I guess," Hurley replied, becoming sullen.

"Mr. Dobbs," Cal said, his voice rising slightly, "are you satisfied with the attorney provided you by the court, or are you not? Give me a decisive answer, and speak up. Do not mumble. Am I clear?"

"Yes, I'm satisfied! Okay?" Hurley's gravelly voice cut the silence like a knife. He hated this man, all these men—everybody here! Especially that colored woman, looking at him like he was dirt, thinking she was better than him because she's a cop. Well, he'd like to show her! Hurley's head was buzzing and hurting again; it had been ever since the cops came to his apartment. How many days had it been? He couldn't remember. All he knew was that he wanted to die and he wished he could take everybody here with him.

Cal stood up and walked to the counter along the opposite wall. He poured himself a cup of coffee. "Mr. Dobbs?" he said, holding the pot toward Hurley.

"Captain Evers, my client doesn't want any coffee. Can we get on with this, please?" Franklin said. After seeing how agitated Hurley could get, he certainly didn't want him pumped full of caffeine. The attorney had spent a modicum of time coaching Hurley to remain calm. "Don't let 'em get you riled, boy," had been the extent of his professional advise.

"Very well, counselor," Cal replied. "We'll get on with it." Cal sat again and in one swift motion spread a collage of photographs on the table for viewing. The photos ranged from glossy, colorful, posed eight-by-ten portraits taken by professional photographers to family groupings, amateur photos taken at picnics, candid shots of little girls at play, and finally the stark black-and-white shots taken by detectives at the crude burial sites.

Also in the group of photos were the ones taken by the coroner and his team—a bleak contrast to earlier images of smiling faces and golden hair. Cal leaned back in his chair and lit a cigarette. No one spoke for the entire time it took him to leisurely finish his smoke. During that time, Cal's eyes never left the face of Hurley Dobbs.

"Do you have questions for my client, Captain?" Franklin's weak voice finally broke the silence.

"No, counselor," Cal answered. "I have no questions for this man." After another pause, he continued. "What I do have is a mountain of evidence against your client—evidence that I will at this time lay out for you."

For the next half hour, Cal methodically recounted the evidence he and his task force had compiled against Hurley Dobbs. He spoke in monotone as he reviewed the dates and approximate times that the Kingsly and Somersby girls had been reported missing.

Using Santos Landscaping Company's dispatch logs, Cal offered proof that Hurley had, indeed, been in the vicinity at the times of not just the murdered girls' disappearances but of *all* the disappearances.

He talked of the latent fingerprints found in Hurley's apartment—fingerprints belonging to both the murdered girls. He passed around the lab's report on blood stains found on Hurley's mattress. There were a lot of blood stains, some of which were inconclusive, but one in particular was the same type as Tara Kingsly's.

Cal took his time with the reviewing of this evidence, letting it sink in and watching Dobbs's face for any sign of a reaction. In fact, Cal never took his eyes off the suspect except when he had to reach into his files for more evidence.

Cal Evers knew people. He had spent his entire adult life studying human reaction, and he could recognize guilt or innocence with uncanny accuracy. Of course Dobbs was guilty. He had the proof! But Cal wanted more. He wanted to crack this man wide open, allowing whatever evil boiling inside him to be spilled out. He wanted to leave him no private recesses into which he could escape. He wanted to not only prove beyond a reasonable doubt the depth of depravity that lived inside Hurley Dobbs but also hear Dobbs admit his sins and his perversion. Cal's intention was to take away his pleasures and his secrets, to strip away the disguise of normalcy, and leave him exposed and naked with no place to hide. Then Cal knew that Dobbs would destroy himself.

"The graves, Hurley—the small graves were right behind your house!" Cal's voice became soft now, soothing and hypnotic, as he once again spread the police photos in front of Dobbs. "Oh, and your fingerprints alone are on the shovel handle, Hurley. Now, I ask you, Mr. Tate, what possible questions would I need to ask your client?" Cal finished with a flourish.

Cal saw that Hurley was beginning to sweat, and by the way the suspect kept crossing and uncrossing his legs, Cal knew he probably needed to use the bathroom. He also had the shakes again, and his teeth were starting to chatter.

"You—you don't know nothin' 'bout me!" Hurley uttered gruffly, half rising out of his seat before being calmly restrained by his attorney's hand on his shoulder.

"Really, now, Hurley." Cal's lips parted in a mirthless grin as he addressed the man. "Well, let's just see what I do know about you. Your mother was Fannie Mae Dobbs, right? I just happen to have a picture of her right here. Is that her?" He produced one of the few known photos of Hurley's mother. The police mug shot taken after one of her arrests for prostitution depicted a puffy face, slack jaw, and large lips, all covered with too much streaky makeup.

As soon as Cal slapped the picture down on the table in front of Hurley, he knew he had hit upon a nerve. "That is your mother, isn't it, Hurley? Or, I should say, *was* your mother. She died when you were eleven, didn't she? It was an accident—a fall, I believe."

Hurley couldn't answer; he couldn't take his eyes off the picture, either. Her awful face had been in his mind often over the years, but he had never before seen an actual photograph of her. All he could do was stare at the hated image. For a while Hurley couldn't hear the voice of the policeman, although he knew he was talking to him. Finally, blessedly, Cal removed the picture from the table.

"Now, what else do I know about you, Hurley?" Cal continued. "I know you were raised by a foster family, Mr. and Mrs. Rupert Johnson. You lived with them until you were eighteen, and then you moved into the garage apartment on the Santos Landscaping lot.

"You drive a truck for Santos, or you did until you were arrested. I don't think you have your job there anymore. Mr. Santos told us you were a good driver and a good employee, but he won't want you back, Hurley.

"And the Johnsons—well, I sure hate to break it to you like this, but they don't want to see you, either. Neither one of them is willing to be a character witness for you.

"But we do have some folks willing to speak, Hurley. It seems like you've been seen hanging around playgrounds quite a bit lately. So, you see, I do know something about you, Hurley. I know more than enough!"

19

The interrogation room had grown quiet, with the only audible sound being Hurley's ragged breathing and the chattering of his teeth.

"Excuse me, Captain," Lois said quietly. "I have a few questions for Mr. Dobbs, if you don't mind."

"Certainly, Lieutenant," Cal replied. "Be my guest. Uh, Hurley, you don't mind talking to Lieutenant Castle, do you?" Cal asked pleasantly.

Hurley appeared to be beyond answering. His eyes warily followed Lois as she rose from her seat at the opposite end of the table and began to slowly walk toward him.

"Hurley," she said softly as she drew close and perched herself on the corner of the conference table just inches from him. He was sweating profusely now, his scent pervading the room. In barely visible movements, he pulled away from Lois. "Do you like women?" she asked.

After noticeable effort, Hurley answered, "I ain't no queer, if that's what you mean!"

"I didn't say you were. Certainly not." Lois continued speaking calmly. "I just wanted to know if you like women. What type of woman do you like, Hurley? Do you like young women or older women? Do you like me?"

Lois ignored the man's grunt in reply to her questions. She inched closer to him, allowing her thigh to brush his arm.

"I don't think you like me, and I wonder why, Hurley," Lois continued. "Maybe you just don't think I'm attractive. Or maybe it's because I'm an African-American woman. Or maybe—" At this point, Lois stood abruptly, surprising Hurley and forcing him to look up at her. "Just maybe, Hurley, the reason you don't like me is that I am a woman, period! You hate all women, don't you, Hurley? Just like you hated your mother. You can't get it up with a grown woman, can you? Well, if you hate women and you're not homosexual, then exactly who does turn you on?"

Lois had not discussed questioning tactics with Cal, but he trusted her enough to never second-guess her. She was going to serve this bastard up on a silver platter; he would bet on it.

Up to this point, no one had noticed the slide projector sitting on a small table in one corner of the interrogation room. It had been covered by a cloth, which Lois now removed as she switched the machine on.

"Hurley, you don't mind if we dim the lights just a bit, do you? These pictures are so much clearer in the dark. Okay?" No one expected an answer from the trembling suspect as Lois proceeded to start her show.

Cal did notice the look of apologetic regret on Lois's face as she turned toward the one-way mirror, through which she knew Thea was watching. He saw the hurt in his friend's eyes as she mouthed silently, "I'm sorry." The room went dim, and the first in a series of heartrending images exploded on the screen.

"How about her, Hurley? Did you like her?" Lois asked in her soothing tone. "Or, maybe you liked her?" She continued her questions in time with the *click-click* of the slide projector.

The air in the interrogation room was becoming stale after so much time with the doors closed. Legs were cramped, feet were asleep, heads ached, mouths were dry, bladders were full, and bellies growled for lunch. In spite of the collective discomfort, though, no one moved a muscle as Lois presented slide after slide of the missing little girls in various stages of play—all except for Alexa Kelly, Cal noticed.

Lois suddenly began to speed up the slide changes—*click, click, click, click, click.* The different faces of the four little girls seemed to mesh together into one. Cal was able to see Hurley's face in the light cast by the projector. He had become drenched with sweat; his face, hair, and shirt were soaked. And the man was shaking, so much so that the legs of his chair made a *rat-a-tat-tat* noise on the tile floor. Cal smiled to himself. *She's got the bastard. By God, she's got him!*

As the slides whizzed by on the screen, Lois's voice rose, becoming louder and louder. Her questions changed, too. Now, instead of merely asking Hurley if he liked her, or her, or her, she asked with each click of the projector, "Did you touch her, Hurley? Did you rape her? Did you kill her, Hurley? Did you? Tell us, Hurley. What did you do with her? Did you put your filthy hands on her little body? Tell us. Did you?"

Lois was on a roll. Cal knew she wouldn't stop until she had him, until he told everything about what he had done with the other girls—if he remembered, that is. When Cal thought she had no more to hit the man with, Lois shocked even him.

"And how about this one, Hurley? What did you do with her?" And there on the screen appeared the smiling face of Alexa Kelly. But there was more: superimposed dimly behind the child's photograph was the image of Fannie Mae Dobbs.

Lois had hit a nerve, all right. Of course everyone connected with the case knew that Alexa Kelly was the only missing child with dark features. Hurley's mother, while certainly not pretty, had possessed the same coloring, and Lois was milking this similarity for all it was worth.

And it worked. Hurley became completely unglued. He seemed to lose all muscle control and had to be held in his chair by two of Cal's detectives. As Lois turned the lights up, the evidence of his madness was visible to everyone.

Hurley's eyes were wild, still locked on the now-empty screen before him, obviously still seeing the faces that were there no more. Had it not been for Thea, Lois would probably have left the faces of Alexa and the Dobbs woman in view. Cal realized, however, that it wasn't necessary. Hurley still saw them in his tortured mind.

Everyone waited silently for the suspect's sobs and screams to stop; not even old Franklin Tate could speak. Finally, when Hurley seemed a little more in control, when his eyes became focused, he was bombarded once again. Lois now placed before him a photograph of Alexa Kelly.

"You don't like little girls with black hair very much, do you, Hurley." Lois made more of a statement now rather than asking questions. She expected no audible answers as she continued.

"Maybe you don't like black hair because your mother had black hair, huh, Hurley. You hated her, didn't you? Did you hate this little girl enough maybe to kill her?" Lois paused briefly now, retrieving photographs of the other missing children.

"But, oh, you loved her, didn't you, Hurley? And her—how those blonde curls shine! Did you touch her, Hurley?" Lois's voice had taken on a singsong tempo, reminding Cal of a metronome.

"What did you do with them, Hurley? Where are they now? Can you tell us?" She leaned closer, whispering in his ear but loud enough for the others in the room to hear: "You killed them, didn't you, Hurley?"

Hurley slowly raised his head, finally tearing his gaze from the myriad of photographs on the table before him. His eyes, blazing with the gleam of madness, met Lois's directly. "Fuck you, bitch!"

Lois's hand flew to her mouth in feigned shock. "Language, Hurley! Language!"

"They're all dead!" he screamed. "They're all dead! I—I saved them!"

"Saved them, Hurley? How did you save them?" Lois asked, successfully masking her shock at his words. "Tell us—if you did, in fact, kill these girls, then how did you save them, Hurley? I don't think we understand."

We've won! Cal thought. *Or rather,* she's *won. She broke him!* He remained silent as he, along with the other members of his task force and Franklin, watched the defenses of Hurley Dobbs shatter.

"They're saved 'cause—'cause they won't never grow up and be whores, that's why! That's how come I saved 'em!"

"So, Hurley, do you now freely admit to abducting and killing these five little girls, whose photographs are before you now and who have been previously identified by name?" Lois spoke sadly as she slowly walked to the other end of the table.

"Yeah, yeah. They're all dead! I—I saved them. All but her," he said, motioning to Alexa's picture. "She's dead, too, but not like them others! No, sir. That Dark One—she's not dead like them! I couldn't save her. I couldn't! Get it away now. Get away! Get away!" Hurley's screams reverberated against the concrete walls.

Cal leaned forward, closely observing Hurley as he stared wildly at the photograph of Alexa Kelly. The man began waving his hands, trying to push the image from him, but he was unable to bring himself to actually touch it.

The stench in the interrogation room suddenly became unbearable. Cal noticed his detectives sitting tight-lipped and momentarily closing their eyes as they fought nausea. The reason was all too obvious: in his near-convulsive state, Hurley Dobbs had lost complete control of his bowels.

Cal rose stiffly to his feet and spoke hoarsely to the man seated at his right. "Detective Erskin, please have a couple of uniforms escort Mr. Dobbs here to the showers and then to the infirmary. I want the doctors to check him out thoroughly before he's put back in his cell. Thank you, Detective."

As soon as the shaking suspect had been half carried from the room, Cal continued speaking. "Mr. Tate, I'll have the tapes of this morning's session transcribed and get a printed copy to your office later this afternoon, if that's agreeable to you. Do you wish to confer with your client further today?"

"Tomorrow will be fine, Captain. Thank you." All Franklin wanted was to get the hell out of there. He needed to obtain the necessary documents for the psychiatric exams and prepare his client's plea. But right now, what he needed most of all was fresh air.

"Brilliant, Lieutenant Castle," Cal said. "You were simply brilliant!" Cal was proud of his best friend, proud of them all. "Let's get out of here now. We'll meet back in the conference room at three o'clock. Thank you, all of you."

As they filed out of the room, no one spoke. Cal realized gratefully that it was for the most part over. Only formalities and paperwork remained now, just routine odds and ends to be cleaned up. He felt positive there would be a plea of guilty but insane entered with no trial, just a sentencing. It would be better on the families that way.

What was it that son of a bitch had said? "She's dead, too, but not dead like the others"? Cal swiftly exited the offices by means of the fire escape. He couldn't face Thea Kelly—not right then, anyway.

20

Thirteen months earlier

"Charlie, it was grand, truly grand! The play, the ballet, the stores—I loved it all. I thank you for giving me so much! I love you, Charlie. I do!"

"And I love you, Peg. I only wish I could give you more. It's been hard on you, I know, moving so far from your home and living where we do, so remote—" He hesitated, momentarily taking his eyes off the snow-covered road and slowing the progress of the vehicle ever so slightly. "I pray to God you've not regretted marrying me, Peggy. If I could make life perfect for you, you know I would. Why, there's not a day that passes that I don't say to myself how lucky I am to have you."

"Charlie O'Malley, don't you dare think I'm regretting our marriage! Sacred it is, and sacred is our love—will be forever and ever!" Peggy turned sidelong on the Jeep's seat, drawing her legs up under her as she faced her husband. "What do I have to do to make you believe you're my happiness, Charlie? I wouldn't trade you for the world's gold. I wouldn't!" She inched closer to him, nuzzling his neck just above his turtleneck sweater, making him groan. She smiled to herself as he warned her not to make him wreck the Jeep.

As she snuggled down to rest her head on his shoulder, she thought again of the wonderful weekend they had enjoyed in Denver. It was true: she did miss the cultural advantages a big city offered, and she missed her many friends back in Cleveland. But most of all, Peggy Sullivan O'Malley missed the Catholic Church. Throughout her life, she had attended Mass regularly, taking comfort in the scripture and gaining peace from the sacraments.

"You know, the best part of the trip was going to Mass again. I have missed it so much!"

"I know, love. I wish we had a parish nearby. But," Charlie breathed a deep sigh, "Deer Run isn't exactly the center of Catholicism."

Deer Run wasn't exactly the center of anything, in Peg's opinion, except of course hunting, fishing, and tramping through woods. Oh, and don't forget gossiping—the primary pastime of the womenfolk of the community. Peg continued to snuggle comfortably against her husband's shoulder. He was right in saying that the move here had been hard for her, although she was careful never to complain. Regrets—there were none. This big, quiet, ruggedly handsome man was the only love Peg had ever known. Deep down in her heart, she knew he would be the only love of her life.

Peggy's thoughts wandered back in time, back to the day she and Charlie had met almost five years earlier.

Charlie's aunt, Fiona O'Malley, was a patient of Peg's in the extended care wing of St. Francis Hospital in Cleveland. And what a grand lady she had been! The two women had gotten on fabulously, in spite of the difference in their ages.

Fiona was relatively healthy at eighty-five years old, her only complaint being arthritis, which made walking unassisted almost impossible. Her body was simply wearing out, according to her doctor. But her mind had stayed razor sharp. How her eyes sparkled when her late husband's nephew, Charlie, wrote to say he was coming for a visit. Fiona had been widowed at a young age, had never remarried, and was childless. Her life, she told Peg often, had been a happy one. Not one thing would she change, except to make Charlie her own son. Of all the nieces and nephews in the family, Charlie was her pick, and now she would see him soon.

It was obvious that Fiona was trying her hand at matchmaking when she introduced Charlie to Peg. "Charlie, my boy, have you ever seen such a lovely young woman in all your life?"

Peg's cheeks had flushed a bright red as she'd tried to avoid the twinkling blue eyes of the handsome man standing across the hospital bed from her. "Fiona O'Malley," she had said, "if you don't stop your foolishness right now, I'll not be your nurse anymore!"

"Now, Miss Sullivan," Charlie had said after a conspiratorial wink in her direction, "let's you and I just humor the old girl here and have a late supper together; just for the sake of my dear aunt, you understand."

Fiona loved it. In her weakened state, she could still enjoy her surroundings. Peg had witnessed this with pangs in her heart for her failing patient and friend. She'd known that the mischievous glint in the old woman's eyes as she looked back and forth from Charlie to her was born out of genuine affection for them both.

"Would have to be a very late supper, Mr. O'Malley," Peg had replied. "I don't get off my shift till midnight. I think that's a bit late for dining."

"Midnight, late?" Fiona had said. "Young folks sure are sissies these days. Why, in my day, we were just getting started at midnight!" Fiona, enjoying her role as instigator as well as being the center of attention, continued speaking, her voice growing softer and more serious. "Peg, you have made my stay here so much more than bearable. I've actually been happy here. I know I'll be going to a nursing home soon, so please do something for me. Take my sweet Charlie here out and see that he has a nice time and doesn't get mugged in the big city. I'm not sure he knows how to act out of his woods, you see."

Fiona had had a way about her, for sure. Even though she didn't speak of it, she must have sensed that her time was short because she'd confided to Peg a few days later that she hoped Charlie would find true love and happiness. "He's such a good man, dear, and caring, too."

Peg became convinced of this on that first night after they had left the hospital together. Their late supper had flowed easily into breakfast following a night of talking about everything from their own childhoods to her nursing career and Charlie's job as police chief of Deer Run, Colorado.

Actually, Peg had soon realized that Charlie was a lot of things in his beloved little town. "Oh, I know with my law degree I could do quite well just about anywhere. I sure would make a lot more money in a big city," Charlie had told her. "But I guess I just like being a big fish in a little pond. I like being a help to folks and knowing everyone by name. You see, in the winter months, we're just about snowbound there, and it's sure nice to know you can count on your neighbors to check on you. We sort of look out for each other, you know what I mean?"

Peg didn't know, not exactly. She had been raised in Brooklyn and had moved to Cleveland when a job at the hospital was offered to her. Her thoughts had turned to her own neighbors. They were pleasant folks, but could she really count on them? Charlie's Deer Run had sounded nice and homey, like a Christmas card.

Fiona had been right, Peg decided—Charlie was nice. She could tell right off that he was the kind of man a girl could depend on, as was evidenced by the loving way he treated Fiona. It had become obvious to both Charlie and Peg that the old woman was fading fast, and Charlie was determined to spend her last days with her. The two weeks he'd spent in Cleveland were the happiest of Peg's young life. She was twenty-four years old and had never really been in love before. Oh, there had been many boyfriends, but none to stir her heart as this man did. She wasn't one bit surprised when Charlie asked her to marry him on their fourth date.

Fiona wasn't surprised, either. "Knew it from the start," had been her proud response to the couple's news. She had, in fact, observed the immediate physical spark between the two and had somehow known it would grow into a deep and lasting love, the kind she had always wished for her nephew.

Charlie had returned to Cleveland six weeks later, and he and Peg were married in the beautiful little chapel at St. Francis with only Fiona in attendance. That's the way Peg had wanted it. She knew that Charlie had only a few cousins left, and although she had scores of relatives, none were very close. Fiona had passed on peacefully soon after that, and Peg realized the loneliness her husband must feel knowing he was one of the few remaining O'Malleys.

Family—the very word conjured up images in Peg's mind of a house full to the rafters with laughing children and huge holiday dinners around the dining room table—an image that would never become a reality for her.

21

If two people's thoughts could be simultaneously examined, Charlie's would have mirrored his wife's during their drive home that cold, snowy night. He, too, had been luxuriating in the quiet time and reflecting on the happiness Peg had brought into his life. She never expressed it, but Charlie had seen the hurt in her eyes many times since her move to Deer Run. Peg had not been—and Charlie feared never would be—entirely accepted by the townsfolk, especially the women. He had witnessed their polite but cool rejection of her at the monthly covered-dish suppers held at the town hall. And he had heard the whispers from time to time.

"She's Catholic, you know."

"I wonder just how much they could possibly have in common. She's so much younger than Charlie! I guess our local women weren't good enough for him."

"Do you suppose that red hair of hers is natural?"

Oh, Charlie heard all right, and it galled him mightily to think that the folks he had grown up with and worked alongside—even helped to deliver babies to two of these women—could be so spiteful. He supposed he could understand some of the jealousy that abounded. He had been considered the best catch around these parts. And he'd had his share of lady friends, but none he'd wanted to spend his life with until Peg. His beautiful Peggy! No wonder the women of Deer Run took an instant dislike to her and most probably gave their husbands strict orders not to be too friendly.

Peg's golden-red hair hung past her shoulders in natural curls, framing a face of exquisite beauty and highlighting soft brown eyes. She was indeed a vision, but much of her beauty lay within. She was one of those rare individuals who seemed to regard life with a childlike wonder. She was always positive and eager for what lay ahead. Peg loved people and never seemed to meet a stranger. Charlie knew she had previously enjoyed her role as life of the party, and it pained him to see her excluded from the town's social life, limited though it was.

Her handmade quilts and embroidery work were by far the finest around but were ignored at the many arts and craft festivals. Finally, she stopped entering them. She had tried to be a part of the activities at the congregational church, but her offers of help were shunned.

Charlie knew, however, that Peg's failure to be accepted into Deer Run's community life paled in comparison to her heartbreak at remaining childless. She had wanted to start their family right away, not only because of her strict Catholic upbringing but, as she put it, "Giving you children, Charlie, would make our love complete!"

Her despondency worried Charlie. He saw his beloved wife slip a little further each month into a melancholy state that he feared would one day claim her completely. One pitiful little baby, born much too early to survive, and three miscarriages had taken their toll on Peg not only physically but emotionally as well. He prayed that she would take the advice of the specialists in Denver and even in Cleveland, where she had flown for help last year.

That advice was simple: "Mrs. O'Malley, it is highly unlikely that you'll ever be able to carry a child to full term. If, however, you did, it might very well cost you your life."

"We'll try no more, Peg," Charlie had told her firmly. "I couldn't bear to lose you." They had stopped even speaking of children for a while, but Charlie knew that his wife prayed fervently each morning and night, rosary beads in hand, for pregnancy.

Lately, she had hinted at adoption, an idea Charlie would wholeheartedly agree to, but there were drawbacks. He knew the state agencies would frown not only on the difference in their ages, Charlie being forty-two now, but also at the remote area in which they lived. He had very quietly looked into private adoption as well, but money was the problem there. So, Charlie lived each day in an attempt to make life pleasant for his wife. That's what this trip to Denver had been all about. It seemed to have worked, too.

He felt her stir in the seat next to him. "Did you sleep, darling?" he asked.

"Umm, I think so," she answered. "I feel so rested." Peg looked around to see where they were, her eyes still adjusting to being awake. Then she turned to face her husband with a serious look on her face. "Charlie, I must talk to you about something. Please don't interrupt me, okay? I know you don't want to discuss it anymore, but we need to." Peg hesitated, not knowing exactly how to explain her feelings. "The last thing I want, my love, is for us to argue, but Charlie, I want a child! I love you so, but I'm empty, and I have prayed so hard for so long! Anyway, last night at Mass, well, I can't explain it, but a feeling of peace came over me. It did. Never have I had a feeling like that in all my life. Do you understand? Somehow, it's as though everything's going to be okay, almost as if I heard the Blessed Virgin speak to me, telling me I'm to be a mother!"

"Now, Peg, we've gone over and over this. You know what the doctors said. I will not risk losing you."

"Charlie," Peg's voice grew calm, the effervescence of a moment ago quieted. "I'm not saying I actually heard voices from above; it was more of a feeling. What I am telling you is that I know things are going to be—how shall I say it—complete? That's it. We're going to be complete!"

Oh, this passionate woman! He drew her close to him, breathing her scent. If anyone on earth deserved to be surrounded by a loving circle of family and friends, it was his Peg. And yet, here in this mountain wilderness where she had come willingly for his sake, she had found neither. Charlie vowed that she would always have him and his love.

"Whatever it is that's in my power to make you happy, Peg, I'll do it. This I promise you!" he whispered hoarsely against her soft hair. To be sure, whatever it took to drive away her despondency, Charlie O'Malley would do it. And all he would ask in return would be to bask in the bright, youthful glow that was his wife.

The snowfall lessened a bit, and Charlie began seeing signs that were familiar to him, bearing nice names of nice little towns and communities: Bear Creek, Wolf Pass, Cascade. Soon they would see the sign for Deer Run. The weekend had been good for Charlie, as well, but he was ready for home. He had especially enjoyed the shopping. With all the new Christmas decorations Peg had bought, their home would look great.

Charlie loved the Christmas season. Maybe this year they would throw a party. He had mentioned this to Peg, and she was all for it, still determined to make friends. *Who knows*, he thought absently. *Maybe it just takes longer to break the ice in small towns.* Charlie's thoughts were interrupted by Peg's rising from her place against his shoulder.

"We're getting close to home, huh, Charlie. I'm sure needing to stretch my legs," Peg said, suppressing a yawn.

"Won't be too much longer, hon. It was a good trip, but it's good to be getting home, too." Charlie had increased the speed of the Jeep slightly, not realizing they were approaching a curve in the narrow road.

Suddenly and without warning, they were upon it. "Good God almighty!" Charlie shouted as he threw an arm across his wife's shoulders, frantically trying to restrain her from being thrown against the dash as he swerved to the right. "Hang on, Peg! Hang on!"

Charlie silently prayed that the Jeep would stay on the wide shoulder of the road and not end up in a ditch, and his prayer was answered. Even he did not know how he'd managed to stop so quickly on the slick roads, but he was grateful.

"Are you all right, Peg?" he asked.

"I—I'm fine, Charlie. What in the world happened?" Peg asked, rubbing her shoulder absently. "My shoulder bumped the door, but I'm okay. I should have had my seat belt on. Was that an animal in the road?"

It happened all the time in that area. Deer would come bounding across the roads in front of vehicles, especially at night, drawn and then blinded by the headlights.

"Stay here, Peg," Charlie said.

"Not on your life," his wife replied. He noticed that she had already pulled on her boots and parka as she opened the passenger's door.

"All right, but step carefully. We're near the ditch. The snow could've drifted, too. It didn't look like an animal—looked more like a big rock. Whatever it is, we'll have to move it, if we can. If not, I'll put a flare out."

Charlie was talking as much to himself as to Peg. His long strides brought him to the object well ahead of her, but he now stood dead still, unable to speak, staring down with unbelieving eyes at what was centered in the golden halo of his flashlight.

Peg approached and dropped to her knees. Shock registered on her face as she looked up at her husband and spoke in a whisper. "Sweet mother of God!"

22

Thea and Max emerged from the observation room shortly after Hurley Dobbs had been hauled away. Neither woman spoke, each engrossed in thoughts of what they had witnessed. But silent as they were, they walked in unison, each sensing the other's destination.

As they entered the small restaurant a few blocks from the task force headquarters, it was Thea who spoke first. "How can I possibly feel pity for that man, Max? He took my baby, and I actually found myself feeling sorry for him! I guess we never know exactly how we're going to react to a situation."

"No, we don't." Here, Max thought it best to throw in as much positive thinking as possible. "I know you caught, as I did, Dobbs's remark about Alexa not being dead like the others. I've always wanted to believe she's alive, and now I truly do!

"Thea," Max continued after more mutual silence, "I'll do whatever you wish, but let's wait until tomorrow to go back and talk with Captain Evers. You said this morning you needed to talk to me. Let's just stay here, order drinks and lunch, and talk. I'll call the captain and tell him we'll be in tomorrow. How 'bout it?"

Thea looked at her friend and, after a time, nodded thoughtfully. "Good idea. To tell you the truth, I wasn't looking forward to walking back in that building so soon, anyway. Go ahead and call Captain Evers. He's probably at lunch, but you can leave him a message that *I'll* be in tomorrow. *You* have to go to work! While you're gone, I'll order the Bloody Marys, and then we'll talk."

Max could see the determination on her friend's face when she spoke of going alone the following day, and she knew it was the right decision.

She nodded, and as she rose to step outside and make her call, her thoughts were of her best friend. *If anyone can survive a nightmare such as this, it will be Thea.*

After the waiter brought their drinks, both women relished the quiet atmosphere of the restaurant. They made small talk at times, but mainly they enjoyed the periods of silence as only two people comfortable with each other can. After the second round of drinks arrived, Thea leaned back in her chair and looked at her friend. Max knew that look.

"Max, I'm going to tell Joe I want a divorce as soon as possible, and I'm most probably going to move to Santa Fe, New Mexico. There, I've said it aloud! I've thought it so many times, even whispered it to myself, but that's the first time I've actually spoken it to another person."

"Well, how does it sound to you after hearing yourself actually say it?" Max was quite proud of herself at this moment for keeping her normally explosive reaction in check.

Thea closed her eyes and remained silent for a time before answering. "It sounds sad, Max, and lonely, but at the same time, it's exciting. It's the right decision, my friend—the only decision."

Thea had mentioned to Max only briefly the evening before of meeting Paul and Elena in Mexico City, and now she fully described her feelings concerning her new friends. "I know most people will think I'm just running away from my grief, hoping a new life in a new location will make the pain go away, but that's only partly true. I've never had many what you could call real friends, just social acquaintances. I guess until you, I was pretty much a loner—with only Mike, Joe, and Alexa." Thea's voice broke as she spoke her daughter's name. "Anyway, now I have two more people that I know already are true friends. And I've got some pretty great ideas, too!"

Thea expounded for almost another hour on her tours in and around Mexico City. She couldn't help but become a bit animated when she described her ideas for a line of pottery she would most definitely introduce.

"Oh, I know it's going to be tough for a while," she continued, "but I still have the life insurance my mother left me. Mike and I have never touched it. And," she hesitated as she took a deep breath, "I'll have my share of the equity in our house and our savings."

On and on, speaking more freely and seeming more relaxed than Max had seen her in months, Thea outlined plans for her move and what type of house and studio she would tell Paul to find for her. Finally, they decided that they needed to order some food. After the waiter left, the conversation worked its way around to Thea and Joe and the sad state of their marriage.

"I feel emptiness and loss, but nothing more. Have I changed so much? Has Joe changed? Or did *this* change us?" Thea held her hands out and looked imploringly to her friend for answers.

"To answer you, yes, *this* has changed all of us: you, Joe, Mike, me, and all those other families. We're all different now, Thea. But change, no matter what the reason, isn't always bad. I'm sure you've given a lot of thought to what you're going to say to Joe. I'm not going to ask because that's personal. But I do have some questions. Have you given any thought to what you'll do if your new business idea is a flop? What will you do if your pottery doesn't sell and no one comes to you for lessons?"

Thea looked at her friend thoughtfully before answering. "Yes, I've given that a lot of thought. The only answer I can come up with is that it won't be a flop. I'm going to be a success at this!"

"Good enough, then," Max replied, her eyes twinkling. "The only other question I have is, When do *we* leave for Santa Fe?"

23

Cal Evers had tossed and turned all throughout the night, wondering what Dobbs had meant by his remark that Alexa wasn't "dead like the others." He finally rose at five o'clock and talked with Sophie until the time came to wake the boys.

"Cal, what *could* he have meant? You think maybe he sold her? Does white slavery still exist today?" Sophie agonized along with her husband over the fate of Alexa Kelly, as well as the other two little girls who were still unaccounted for.

"Oh, it exists all right, babe," Cal answered, rubbing his sleep-starved eyes. "A more believable scenario, according to Lois's research, would be black market adoptions. In those kinds of cases, though, it's mostly infants that are in demand. Quiet honestly, I doubt if Hurley Dobbs has got sense enough to carry out any sort of organized plan. I know nobody would initiate buying a kid through him. They mostly use shady lawyers for adoptions like that."

Cal rested his head on the kitchen table as he fell silent. Sophie knew what he was thinking, and she shared his helplessness. They would most probably never know what happened to the missing girls. She sat quietly stroking her husband's head until sounds from upstairs prompted her to rise, and she began to mechanically prepare breakfast and pack lunches.

～

Cal had been greatly relieved when he'd read the message from the previous afternoon informing him that Thea would not be in to talk to him until sometime this morning. God, what anguish that poor woman must have gone through watching that pervert confess to killing those little girls.

He remembered again with a tiny glimmer of hope Dobbs's words that Alexa wasn't dead like the others.

"Send her in the minute she gets here," Cal barked to no one in particular as he entered the office's reception area. He barely acknowledged Lois as he strode by her desk and into his office.

No one had to ask who he was referring to; they knew. Everyone dreaded the upcoming meeting with Mrs. Kelly, knowing that there was no way she could have endured the interrogation without being physically and emotionally shaken.

None of the detectives and few of the clerks had slept very much the night before, and they weren't even the little girls' parents. Lois dreaded seeing Thea most of all this morning. She'd agonized all through the night, wanting to phone Thea to apologize but not wanting to interfere. Her calls had instead gone to Cal.

"Hell, Lois, you're the one who broke the bastard!" Cal had said. "You were brilliant. We all think so, and so will Mrs. Kelly."

Having been somewhat reassured by Cal's words, Lois rose from her desk immediately as Thea entered the building. "Thea, I'm so glad to see you. I wanted to phone you last night, but I just didn't know what to say to you. I still don't."

Thea took the other woman's hands in hers and smiled a tired but genuine smile. "I'm certainly no expert on the subject, Lois, but I'd be willing to bet your colleagues have told you that you gave new meaning to the word 'interrogation'! You managed to get that monster to admit to enough to put him away for life."

Cal had seen Thea enter and, like Lois, had come forward to greet her. "Life, hell," he said. "I for one would like to see him fry. Texas leads the country in executions, especially for guys like him. Of course, his lawyer will go for insanity. That means a life sentence."

Thea entered Cal's office, took the seat he offered, and studied him before responding. "Captain Evers, the last thing I would want is for Hurley Dobbs to die. My personal feelings concerning the death penalty aside, as long as he's alive, there's a chance he'll tell us what he did with Alexa. Don't you agree?"

Cal ran a hand through his hair and regarded the woman before him. "You're quite a lady, Mrs. Kelly. Of course, you're right. I just hate the thought of the taxpayers having to warehouse someone like Dobbs for the rest of his life. Hell, he could live to be a hundred and all the while get room and board, free medical care, and protection—all at our expense."

Cal continued thoughtfully. "There are degrees of crime, and in my profession we tend to view child molesters and cop killers at the very top of the list. I apologize for my outburst, Mrs. Kelly. What I wanted to say to you this morning is that all of us here admire you. I sure do hope yesterday wasn't too hard on you." Cal finished his short speech while feeling the telltale blush creep upward from his neck to cover his checks.

In one respect, he was very comfortable talking with this woman, while another part of him felt like a schoolboy in her presence. That would be what Lois called having a crush. Cal recognized it simply as being at a total loss as to how to explain to this mother that, although he shared her belief that her daughter could very possibly be alive, the evidence told him it was highly unlikely that she would ever see her again.

After Lois had brought in two typed transcripts of the interrogation, Cal and Thea sat for the remainder of the morning going over pertinent facts that had been brought to light.

Thea confessed that while she was shaken and horrified at Dobbs's reaction to her daughter's photographs, she was also intrigued. "Of course, I'm just a layperson here, Captain, but don't you believe that Alexa's dark features brought to mind his mother—a mother he obviously hated?"

"Absolutely, Mrs. Kelly. That was our thinking from the beginning. It became quite evident, I might add, when Lieutenant Castle started her show. Of course, Dobbs is insane. That doesn't make it any easier to deal with, does it?"

Thea shook her head sadly as her gaze fell on the partially open file folder on Cal's desk. A portion of an exposed photograph held her gaze: a tiny hand holding a red rose. When she could finally tear her eyes away, she rose stiffly and made a last request.

"When you get the psychiatric evaluations, will you phone me? I'm going to be making some rather detailed plans for the future and may be out of the house. If I am, please leave a message. And thank you again, Captain."

As he watched her leave the office, Cal knew what "plans for the future" meant. He'd seen it before: a lost child so often resulted in a lost marriage.

24

She didn't spring it on Joe all of a sudden and not until after New Year's. Thea had told Mike, though. He'd been sad, but he was not the typical father who believed it was his duty to constantly give unsolicited advice. If she wanted him to stay longer, he would stay. If she needed his help, she would have it.

Thea had all she needed, she'd reassured her dad. She just needed to know that his faith in his daughter was strong enough to trust her judgment where her own life was concerned. Of course she wanted him to stay longer, but she knew he missed his home and his friends. It was apparent that he was growing fidgety in the strained atmosphere of his daughter's house.

"I'll call you the minute they let me know about the evaluations and what they mean," she had told him. "Go home. Go be with your friends, go hunting, and don't worry about me. I'll be fine."

"I know you will, baby," Mike had said lovingly as he embraced his daughter. "I've always loved Joe—you know that—but you're mine. You're all I have now. I'll support whatever decision you make."

Then Mike was gone, and Thea was alone with her husband. She was alone with a complete stranger in a house that had become uncomfortable and much too big. They hardly spoke, and they never touched. Their eyes never met.

~

Joe wasn't surprised when Thea quietly informed him one evening that she thought a trial separation would be good for them. They both had a lot of thinking to do, she said. She vaguely murmured that maybe things would work themselves out. Could he possibly take the following day off from work and look for a place to move?

Oh, she was kind, Joe thought as he watched his whole world slowly walk away from him and go upstairs to the guest room. She still had enough feelings left to be kind, but he did not want her kindness. What he wanted was the love they had shared for fourteen years. Joe mourned. He mourned for his lost little Berry and for his lost Thea. He mourned, knowing that he would never again hold either of them.

Shortly before dawn, Joe trudged upstairs to shower and dress. There were plenty of places he could stay temporarily, but he had no doubt that he would find a suitable apartment before the day was over. As he walked by the guest room door, he heard stirrings and knew she was awake. He fought the urge to knock, enter, and beg her to love him once again. Instead, he made his way heavily back down the stairs, stopping to scratch the head of Peaches, their Persian cat, who sat purring contentedly on the newel post at the bottom of the stairs.

Joe took his time leaving. As a sick form of self-abuse, he toured the entire downstairs one last time, burning the images of happy times into his memory, hearing the carefree squeal of a child's laughter ringing in his ears.

~

Thea heard the car slowly pull out of the garage and watched from the window as her husband drove out of sight. She had slept little during the night and now felt more alone than ever before in her life. The jangling of the bedside telephone caused her to jump, interrupting her melancholy mood for the moment.

"Hello, Thea, this is Lois Castle. Sorry to call so early, but Cal wanted to catch you before you left for the day. Can you come down to the office this morning?"

"Of course, Lois, and you didn't wake me. I'm not sleeping much these days. I'll see you around nine."

25

Cal didn't stand as Thea entered his office. Over the previous several weeks, they had started using first names, and a relaxed and friendly rapport had developed between them.

"Glad you could make it, Thea. I won't waste time. We received the psychiatric evaluations on Dobbs late yesterday afternoon. Here they are, and by three different doctors, too."

Thea hesitated for an instant before taking the thick manuscript from Cal's hand. "I'm not much for medical jargon, Cal. What do they say?"

"In short, the man's crazy as a loon. That's something we all already knew. I have talked at length this morning already with the District Attorney and with Dobbs's attorney. A plea of guilty but insane will be entered sometime tomorrow by the defense. The state will accept it and will request life in a top security mental institution." Cal shrugged his shoulders. "It's the best we can do, Thea. It's all we can do."

Thea nodded thoughtfully. "Oh, I heartily agree, not only with the opinions expressed here," she said as she scanned the opening pages of the evaluation, "but I also agree with the punishment. Tell me, is there any chance he'll ever be released?"

"I guess that could happen, especially if a bunch of them bleedin' hearts get a hold of his case, but I doubt it. I know for sure it won't happen as long as Dobbs is in his present state."

"And that state is?"

"Didn't I tell you? Hell, guess I didn't or you wouldn't be asking, huh?" Cal shook his head, making a mental note of how forgetful he was becoming. "Why, Thea, Dobbs has been practically catatonic ever since the interrogation. The guards walk him to the bathroom where he *usually* makes it, they tell me. They also walk him to the mess hall, where he eats very little. When they walk him to the showers, he just stands under the water till they turn it off. And when they walk him to the exercise yard, he just stands there, too.

"It's real weird, to say the least. Guards say sometimes they hear him snoring softly at night, you know, breathing regularly. When they check on him, though, his eyes are wide open. I've seen some fakers in my time, and I don't believe he's faking at all. For one thing, you have to be real smart to fake a condition like I've just described. Hurley Dobbs is just not that smart."

Thea rose and strolled to the coffee pot in the corner, poured herself a cup, and moved over to the window, where she stood lost in thought. After a time, she spoke.

"Cal, I want to see him in person, face to face. Before you say no, think about it. Whether he's faking or not, don't you agree that seeing me could shake him loose? Because of my dark features and Alexa's looking so much like me, it just might do the trick."

Cal pondered this for several minutes while they sipped their coffee and studied each other. "Very possibly it could loosen him up. Tell you what, I'll consider it only if both his defense attorney and the DA give permission. Is that fair enough?"

"That's fair enough. Cal, changing the subject a little, do you think Alexa could have been the victim of an illegal child-selling operation? Is that a far-fetched idea? Max and I were wondering."

"That's not far-fetched at all, but it is unlikely. My wife and I were discussing that very possibility some time ago. Of course it happens, although most people want an infant. There are folks, though, who have a lot of money, can't have kids, and desperately want one but don't want to go through the colicky months or the potty-training time. Lois has toyed with that angle quite a bit and has done some research, so you might want to talk to her."

After a brief silence, Cal resumed speaking. "We all know that children's memories go way back, certainly to age four, four and a half. But I want you to remember something, Thea," he paused for emphasis. "A lot of things can happen—horrible things that can wipe the memory slate clean as a whistle."

26

Charlie O'Malley thought for a while that the child would surely die from exposure. Clad only in lightweight pants, shirt, and a sweater and with only cotton socks and tennis shoes on her feet, her little body already held a blue tinge when he and Peg arrived home with her. Peg had been the one to act quickly, while Charlie remained in a state of slow-moving disbelief at what they had found. Peg had immediately wrapped the child in her down parka and carried her quickly to the warmth of the Jeep, speaking softly and rubbing her all the while.

In fact, Peg didn't stop cuddling and crooning to the child all the way home. Her voice held a soothing quality that would calm anyone—if they could be calmed. Charlie had seen frostbite many times—blackened toes, fingers, and noses mostly—suffered by the amateur hikers and mountain climbers he had helped rescue over the years. He knew upon examination that the child could not have been outdoors very long as she had no frostbite. But he and Peg both knew that just a few minutes more and she would not have escaped it. Most probably, if they had stopped for coffee as they had debated earlier, they would have found her dead. Time was that crucial in this weather.

She was deeply in shock, though. Charlie wanted to call the doctor, even bundle her up and head for the nearest hospital some ten miles away, but Peg would have none of it.

"I'm a nurse, Charlie, remember? Besides, whatever this wee one's gone through, she doesn't need another strange place and more strange people poking at her. Once she gets warm and comforted, she'll come around. You'll see."

He had to agree with her. The child didn't need to be subjected to more strangers, at least not until she was well enough to tell them how on earth she got in the middle of a road in below-freezing weather, clothed as she was, and miles from the nearest dwelling. The only plausible answer to that question lay heavily on both their minds for days. Finally, Charlie brought up the subject of getting in touch with authorities from all the surrounding towns and cities in an attempt to establish the child's identity. Peg was horrified at his suggestion.

"Don't you realize what you're saying, Charlie? If you do find out who she is, can you live with giving her back to the very people who most probably threw her out like—like a sack of garbage? How else would she get there? She can't be from around here since nothing's come over the radio about a child wandering off. Why, you yourself said she couldn't have walked from any of the homes in the area—she would have died from exposure. No, Charlie, we'll tell no one. When she's better, she can tell us herself."

His wife was adamant, and Charlie knew that she was most likely right in her assumption that the child's own family had simply left her there. *My God,* he thought, *a wild animal doesn't even leave its young defenseless!* He had considered the possibility of an automobile wreck and of the child being thrown out. This, too, he dismissed after realizing that, while there were cliffs and deep ravines in the area, none were within a mile of where they had found the child. He doubted she could have walked that far in the dark. Unfortunately, the snow had obliterated any possible footprints or tire tracks.

"It's almost as if she just appeared, Peg, right out of nowhere!" Charlie told his wife one evening as they sat before the fire, the child sleeping between them with her head on Peg's knee.

"I know, darling. I know," Peg replied as she gently and lovingly stroked the child's face. "Maybe she did just appear."

Charlie looked guardedly at his wife. She was smiling, and her eyes gleamed with a strange light. He was frightened not only by what he saw in her expression but by what he knew she was thinking. Did she hunger for a child so desperately that she could believe the improbable? No, not his Peg! She was too stable, too sensible!

~

The child did not speak for an entire week. She slept, ate, and seemed to respond to Peg's loving caresses. The first words she uttered were the unintelligible screams borne of her nightmares. For a while, they occurred nightly. During these times, she would reach her tiny arms upward, not to embrace Peg but to cling to her frantically.

The first nightmare had been the worst for all of them. The look of sheer terror on the face of one so young made Charlie's blood run cold. As she clung to Peg, Charlie stroked her hair, which was wet with perspiration, and spoke ever so gently to her. "It's all right, little one. It's all right now. Can you tell us your name? What's your name, darling?"

On and on, he tried. Peg tried, too, when the screams and tears had subsided into weak little sniffs. When her eyes lost some of their fright and as Peg softly crooned to her, Charlie tried again. "What's your name, darling? Can you tell us your name?"

Her gaze never wavered from some distant speck only she could see. Weakly, she whispered over and over words they could not understand, until finally she fell into a deep sleep.

"Could you make out what she was saying?" Peg asked Charlie as they tiptoed from her room, making sure to leave the lamp on in case she woke again.

"No, it sounded like she was trying to say Debbie or Darby. She was probably trying to say her name. I expect she'll be remembering very soon."

Charlie stepped aside for Peg to enter their bedroom. He was again chilled by what he saw written in her expression. His wife did not look forward to this child remembering; in fact, she dreaded it.

27

Charlie supposed it had been the Christmas tree that had brought things to a head between him and Peg. They had always had a tree during the holidays. They both loved the decorations and the smells of the season. Because of the horrendous wind and large amount of snow this year, Charlie had been late in getting out and finding a suitable tree. With the weather finally breaking, he was able to venture into the nearby woods to cut and bring home a rather full spruce of about six feet.

Oh, he and Peg had such fun stringing lights and bantering over which ornament would go where. It did seem, though, that his wife was more animated this year than ever before, and he knew why. Having a child in the house, a little girl like she had always wanted, had put a spark in Peg that he'd not witnessed before.

Darkness was gathering as they finished trimming the tree. After they had cleaned up the clutter, Peg made drinks and put a holiday tape on the stereo while Charlie stoked the fire in the fireplace. It was a wonderful, quiet evening. That's when it happened—when the child spoke distinctly for the first time.

They were sitting on the sofa enjoying their togetherness when a sound came from the hall door behind them.

"Sweetheart, you're awake!" Peg said. "How was your nap?" She went quickly to the child and spoke lovingly as she stroked that incredibly beautiful long hair. Charlie noticed on many occasions that his wife always asked the child questions as if she expected a sensible reply. "And what do you see here?" Peg continued speaking as she guided the child forward to stand near the Christmas tree.

They both could see the child's expression reflect an immediate understanding, something that had heretofore been missing. Gone was that vacant stare. Out came the small hand to hesitantly touch the lit tree, fingering first one ornament and then another. Finally she turned to face them, smiled slightly, and uttered in a shy and hoarse little voice: "Santa!"

Charlie thought at that moment that his heart would break. She was stronger than he had given her credit for being. With what the little girl must have been through, it seemed a miracle she still had a mind left. Down on his knees, he went to her, speaking softly; Peg knelt, too. There they were together, the three of them, beside the Christmas tree.

"And who's this, sweetheart?" Peg asked as she pointed to an angel hanging on a branch near the child's head.

The answer was whispered this time, still with much mental effort: "Angel." On and on, Charlie and Peg continued the guessing game, both of them enthralled by the starry-eyed wonder they saw reflected in the child's expression.

"Now, darling," Charlie said when he felt the time was right, "what's your name? Can you tell us?"

Nothing. Blank. Stars gone. The child slipped visibly back into her mute shell and clung to Peg's leg with a near death grip. Had he pushed her too hard and too soon? The thought struck Charlie that perhaps she did not remember her name because she did not want to remember.

"She'll come around again, Charlie. See? She's still looking at the tree. We just mustn't rush her anymore."

Charlie wasn't disheartened in the least. It had been a step forward, and there would soon be others. It came sooner than he thought.

Peg continued to carry on a one-sided conversation with the child as she went about cooking dinner, cleaning up the kitchen, and drawing a bath for the little one. Throughout the evening, Charlie noticed that the child would get no farther from Peg than an easy arm's reach. He also noticed how totally enchanted his wife was with the child's dependency upon her.

He automatically looked at the bedside clock when sounds woke him in the early morning hours. "Two o'clock? God almighty, what's wrong?" he murmured sleepily and rose to stumble through the house. "What happened, Peg?" he asked, fully awake now as he stood in the doorway of the child's bedroom.

"She had another nightmare," his wife answered. "Not nearly as bad as the others, I'm glad to say. I think she's just about asleep again. Let's see if we can get some more sleep ourselves."

As they began to tiptoe back to their own bedroom, the child uttered the single word that would forever change all three of their lives: "Mama!"

Before Charlie could even turn around, Peg was at the bedside on her knees. "Shush, baby. Shush. It's Mama. Mama's right here. Mama will always be here for her little girl."

Charlie watched from the doorway, horrified, as his wife continued to croon softly to the child until her even breathing signaled sleep.

"Have you gone completely mad, woman?" Charlie demanded as soon as the couple returned to their bedroom. "What on earth are you thinking by telling that child you're her mother! My God, Peggy, she unstable as it is! What will she do when she has to go away from here?" He continued pacing the floor and shaking his head in disbelief. "We have to contact the authorities. You know that!"

Peggy calmly sat down at her dressing table and began brushing her hair. Her eyes finally met Charlie's in the mirror. She stared at him for what seemed an eternity. Finally, she stood slowly and turned to face her husband. She spoke calmly.

"There's not been another man in my life, Charlie, and there never will be. I'll love you and care for you the rest of my days. I hate this miserable little town of yours, but I try not to complain. If it's here you must live, then I'll live here with you. I'll never leave you, unless you force me to. Whatever you ask of me, I'll gladly give it, except one thing."

Peg slowly moved nearer to him, her eyes never leaving his shocked gaze. "There is one thing I cannot do, Charlie. I'll not be giving her up!"

And so, for the remainder of that sleepless night and throughout the following day, Charlie and Peg talked about and planned what they would do. Rather, Charlie listened in abject silence to the plans his wife had for their future with the child. "Charlie, did I ever tell you my grandmother's maiden name was Reagan? It's beautiful, don't you think?" She spoke as if her scheme made all the sense in the world.

It was Peg's idea that Charlie should go see Titus. "After all, Titus is an attorney and a notary. He has the run of the entire courthouse—you've said so yourself. And we *know* he'll keep a secret, now don't we?"

It made sense to talk to Titus, Charlie had to admit, as much as he despised the man. Titus Peebles had for years been the only attorney in Deer Run. He never even used a clerk or secretary, choosing to do his own research and file his own briefs. Charlie knew the old reprobate had complete access to birth and death records. No one ever questioned anything Titus did or where he went, for that matter. Why, anything, Charlie supposed, could be slipped into the files. But Charlie knew the question of paperwork would be only a small part of their problem.

"And just how do you think we're going to explain a four- or five-year-old daughter, Peg? The goddamn winter wasn't that long!" Charlie shouted at his wife in anger for the first time in their marriage. "I feel like, like—I don't know—like I'm suspended in midair! I feel like I'm falling but never landing! Peg," he said in one last effort to reason with his wife, "it's not as though a stray pup found its way to our door! This is insane!"

On and on Charlie ranted, pacing like a caged animal in the small confines of their living room until, finally, he collapsed in his favorite chair by the fireplace, silent and brooding. Peg left him alone and went about her preparations for their dinner in relative silence, the only words she spoke being those of comfort to the child when she woke from her nap. Finally, as the light was fading outside, she came to Charlie and knelt at his side.

"This was meant to be, Charlie," she said matter-of-factly. "If you'll only calm down and think about it, you'll understand that a power greater than us made this decision." The light was bright in Peg's eyes again as she continued speaking. "The child belongs with us, Charlie. We saved her!

"Now, what I want you to do is to take a position elsewhere, in Delaney. They've been after you for months now to take the job as chief of police there. You like the town; you've said so many times. It's a larger town with more to offer—" Her voice trailed off as she searched for the right words. "I know it would be hard to sell this house, you being the one who built it and all." Peg's voice finally broke, the agony of their situation becoming too much for her to bear.

"Peg, Peg, come here, my love." Charlie held her close, stroking her hair, smelling the sweetness of her, feeling the heart inside of her break into pieces. He knew at that very moment that he loved this woman beyond all reason. As twilight blanketed them, he continued to hold her and listen to her plans. He felt his resolve waver, even as his mind filled with painful questions that would haunt him the remainder of his days. Can something good and honest and true ever grow from a lie? Can a dream be borne of a nightmare? Charlie O'Malley doubted it.

28

Charlie drove the Jeep slowly. Up until this afternoon, navigation of any kind had been virtually impossible. Snow had fallen by the foot ever since *that night*. He tapped the vehicle's brakes gently as he rounded the last curve before starting down the slight grade into the town square of Deer Run.

He wanted to be going anywhere in the world but where he was headed. In truth, Charlie would choose this moment to visit the devil himself rather than make a call to the dismal home office of Mr. Titus Peebles, attorney-at-law.

As he entered Main Street, he saw ahead the rambling two-story residence that had been home to the Peebles family for far longer than most of the other families had lived in Deer Run. He brought the Jeep to a stop in front of the old rail fence and sat for a time, dreading having to get out of the warm vehicle—not that it was especially cold. The wind had died down a couple of days earlier, and the snow had stopped.

The cold wasn't causing Charlie's discomfort this morning. It was the reason for his visit with Titus that had him on edge. He closed his eyes and leaned forward to rest his head on the steering wheel. He prayed, as he had done almost constantly over the past few days, that God would forgive him for the outcome his actions would shape.

It was almost a superhuman effort, but Charlie managed to switch off the Jeep's engine, open the door, and get out. He even managed to walk—stiffly, with legs of an old man—to the front door and ring the bell. During his drive into town, Charlie had played over and over in his mind just how he would ask—or rather, demand—a favor of a man who, for lack of a better word, sickened him.

Charlie was ushered unceremoniously into the parlor by the sour-faced housekeeper and realized that he didn't even know her name. He, as well as most of the townspeople, simply referred to her as old man Peebles's maid.

"Mr. Peebles is indisposed at the moment" she informed him. "You want to wait?"

"Yes, ma'am, I'll wait," Charlie answered politely, imagining the old pervert upstairs getting off to his photograph collection.

Charlie shuddered with disgust as he remembered an afternoon nearly two years prior and the events that led him to discover certain facts about Titus he had always suspected. Titus had suffered a serious heart attack at the courthouse, and Charlie had hurried to his house in search of the name and phone number of the sister that Titus visited several times a year. All he'd ever said about her was that she lived in Los Angeles. When Charlie found no name in the Rolodex in Titus's office downstairs, he'd made his way upstairs to the living quarters.

The only telephone in that portion of the house sat on the bedside table, and Charlie reasoned that a list of personal numbers would be in the drawer.

They had almost jumped out at him when he picked up the plain white envelope. There were eight of them—Polaroid shots of the most disgusting acts Charlie had ever seen. Certainly the *Playboy* magazines he had disinterestedly thumbed through on occasion in his youth did not compare with these.

There he was—Titus Peebles, in all his glory. His short, fat, white, sagging body was nude and surrounded by three very young, hard, glistening, equally nude male bodies. Of course, there had to be at least one other person in the room, stark and unfurnished save for the big four-poster bed. Someone had to have taken the pictures.

Charlie had been appalled. "Guess this explains all the trips to LA to visit the sister, huh, Titus?"

He had put seven of the eight pictures back in the envelope and left them in the drawer. He was no blackmailer, but just in case the old bastard survived the heart attack, Charlie wanted him to know that he knew.

"Well, now, Chief O'Malley," Titus said, breaking through Charlie's reverie. "What brings you here this morning? I figured the weather's been too bad for anybody to be committing crimes around these parts. What can I do for you?"

"Need to talk to you in private, Titus. You got time this morning?" Charlie tried to be civil, but he wasn't a very convincing actor. Titus was aware of his loathing. After bestowing a sidelong glance at the police chief, Titus walked through and closed the door of his office after instructing his housekeeper not to disturb them.

"Alone!" he said, gesturing with arms outstretched and beaming a nauseating smile in Charlie's direction. "Now, what's on your mind?"

"This ain't easy. Just bear with me, and I'll get it out, Titus."

Charlie did get it out, eventually. He told the attorney everything. He left out no details from the time he and Peg had come upon the child, mute and in shock, lying in the middle of the snow-covered road, her little body filthy and covered with bruises. He included all pertinent events leading up to the reason for his current visit.

"Sooooo," Titus said, licking his thick, red lips—lips that reminded Charlie of raw chicken livers—and studied the man before him in a rather condescending fashion. "What I do believe you're asking me to do, Chief O'Malley, is to commit a felony. I am to somehow enter an obscure birth certificate into the county records. Am I right?"

"You know damned good and well that's what I'm asking, Titus! It's what's best for a child someone obviously abused and doesn't want! More importantly, it's what's best for my wife!"

Charlie rose suddenly from his chair and leaned across the wide expanse of the antique desk, behind which a surprised Titus sat. Gone were the smug expression and superior attitude of a moment ago. In their place, a look of surprise, maybe even a touch of fear, registered on the attorney's face.

"You will do this for me, Peebles! You will do it, and you will keep silent! And I, in turn, will keep my silence!" Charlie's eyes remained locked on Titus's, conveying his unspoken threat.

Only the ticking of the grandfather clock broke the silence of the room, as each man wrestled with his particular demon: Charlie, trying with all his might to rationalize this masquerade, and Titus, wishing yet again that his life had been spared the sickness and ugliness over which he had no control.

The room had grown hot, the air stale. The words hung heavily between the two men. After a time, the attorney said hoarsely, "It'll be handled."

"Here's all the information you need—names, dates, everything," Charlie said as he dropped a manila envelope on the attorney's desk. He collected his hat and gloves and left the office without another word.

Outside, the air was clear and clean. The sun had popped through, making the snow almost blinding. Charlie stood still for a time, surveying the town—*his* town. He savored the memories of a lifetime. "They've got mountains in Delaney, too," he whispered.

He climbed in the Jeep and started the engine. During his drive back up the mountain, Charlie realized that even though he hadn't been gone more than a couple of hours, he was anxious to get back home to his family.

29

What fun the past few days had been! Charlie sat enthralled in front of the fireplace and watched his wife put finishing touches on Santa's parcels under the tree. A pillow, intricately embroidered and so soft for a little head, storybooks to delight the imagination, desperately needed clothes, a patchwork teddy bear—all waited to be cuddled by tiny arms.

"When have you had time to do all this, Peg?" Charlie asked in awe. "You do amaze me, my love."

"Thank goodness she still sleeps a lot," Peg replied, smiling at her husband's compliment. "Though I expect she'll not be sleeping so much now that she's more active. Have you noticed, Charlie, how she follows you with her eyes and looks out of the windows so much? She pays attention now to sounds as well. Oh, I forgot to tell you something! The other day she was looking at some of the Christmas cards, and she pointed to a picture on one and said 'cat.' She's going to be fine, Charlie. Just fine!"

Charlie had indeed noticed the change in the child lately. "Umm, we need to begin taking her out some now. Walks in the woods would do her good."

"We will after we've moved." Peg reminded Charlie of her fear that someone would see the child. There wasn't much danger of that, though, he reasoned. Their twelve acres were mostly wooded, and the house was not visible from the road. Even in good weather, the O'Malleys didn't have much company.

Charlie thought of the few social gatherings the couple had been invited to this Christmas season, but excuses of bad weather and Peg's having the flu seemed to placate the hostesses. Peg had telephoned the folks they considered friends and made her apologies for not entertaining during the holidays, so no one seemed suspicious.

It had been especially difficult for Charlie to give his notice to the town council that he was leaving Deer Run—not that they would have any trouble at all appointing a new police chief, as several younger fellows thought the job a snap and stood waiting for their chance.

The Delaney council was elated. Everyone who knew Charlie liked and respected him, and his reputation for being a good neighbor and always giving more than was required to the job preceded him. The pay was better, too.

It wasn't only the job Charlie felt sadness at leaving, though. He had spent his life here in this community, and he would miss it. But he and Peg had made this decision together. They would leave soon after the first of the year for their new life. In a lot of ways, life in Delaney would be far better for them. A few hours' drive to the west, the town sat surrounded by national forests. It offered more advantages than they were accustomed to here, but it was still small enough to give that hometown feeling.

"Any regrets, Charlie?" Peg asked timidly, almost dreading his answer, as they climbed into bed later that night.

"None, my love," was his reply as he cradled her in his arms. "There'll be no looking back now."

~

Dreamily, she began to wake. What a wonderful feeling it was to drift on this cloud-like perch of hers! Oh, she felt so warm and so happy! Through half-closed eyes still heavy with sleep, she saw dimly that she was surrounded by a beautiful halo of light, all red and gold. Here in this halo, she was safe, warm, and comforted.

Slowly, very slowly, out of the fog she was drawn toward that light and away from the dark place. It was a bad place back there, with sounds she couldn't exactly hear, words and names that held no meaning, and shadows she couldn't exactly see. There were things back there in the fog that she didn't want to see and whispers that she didn't want to hear.

So, we just won't look or listen. That's all!

There, that's better; that's safe. Out of the murky fog, she came toward the golden glow that was waiting for her. Fully awake now, the child saw the glow for what it was: beautiful red-golden hair, close to her face, surrounding her. Somewhere, back there in the fog, there was hair like that, somewhere, like—

"M-M-Mama?"

"Good morning, my darling! This is Christmas morning! Come, let's go join Papa and see what Santa brought you!"

The fog, with its dark places and frightening whispers, still lurked somewhere just behind her.

So, we just won't turn around. That's all!

~

Charlie's heart was near to bursting from his chest. Tears of happiness welled up in his eyes as he watched his wife and child enter the living room. He watched in silence as the child's face gradually took on a smile. Slowly she inched closer to the precious little possessions lying beneath the tree.

Peg beamed with more happiness than he had ever seen as she watched tiny hands tentatively reach forward to caress first one thing and then another.

"S-Santa!" she whispered.

~

At last she was standing in front of that fog, and the frightening shadows were slipping farther and farther away. The only whispers she heard now were gentle murmurings of love. The only visions she saw now were of smiling faces.

So, we just won't ever, ever go back there again. That's all!

The murky fog thickened, swallowing all that remained in that dark place in her mind. Both good and bad memories, both happy times and chilling horrors meshed together, becoming more and more distant by the moment.

We'll only look at the light now!

Ever so slowly, the child turned toward the beaming couple standing before her. She took a deep breath and, with a smile as bright as day, entered willingly into the warm and loving world of Reagan O'Malley.

30

The rain fell in torrents as it had for the past four days. The entire Dallas area was under flood warnings. The rescue squads, fire departments, and scores of volunteers were all near the point of exhaustion.

Thea stood in the morning room by the large windows sipping her morning coffee. Looking out at the pitiful remains of her south lawn and once-lush flower gardens made the day seem even more dismal. The rain would stop; it always had, she reasoned. But would it stop in time for her scheduled departure? The moving van would be there at nine the following morning, and the thought of loading her possessions in a downpour was depressing. Equally depressing, though, was the thought of delaying her move by even one more day.

Rains of this magnitude weren't uncommon for Dallas in early June, but Thea desperately needed to get this final step behind her. Any reason for prolonging the departure was making her fidgety and fretful.

"Why can't things go the way I planned just once!" she spoke aloud in frustration.

"Because then we wouldn't appreciate the smooth times," Max said as she entered from the kitchen door. "Even the ducks are miserable in this mess," she added, removing her soggy raincoat and pouring herself a cup of coffee. "What's left to pack today?"

Thea responded, "I've packed everything but a few odds and ends. I've already gone through the trunk upstairs and boxed up some things to take with us in the car. The movers should be able to load everything tomorrow, if they get here at all. You and I can head out the next day. How about things at your place? Do you need any help?"

"Are you kidding?" Max answered, grinning. "I told you, I don't do sentimental. I've sold practically everything except my clothes and books. I'll buy whatever else I need when we get to Santa Fe. Travel light—that's my motto!"

Thea studied her friend and thought again how alike they were in so many ways, yet they were different enough to truly solidify the relationship. "I'm keeping very little, considering this big house and everything we've accumulated over the years," she said. "I'm taking just enough to fill the house Paul has found for me. Oh, Max, this move is going to be good for me. I can tell!"

Thea had been pleased with the photos that Paul and Elena had sent the previous month of the delightful one-story adobe on Canyon Road in Santa Fe that they said was perfect for her. It was an older dwelling but had been completely refurbished. Paul said he knew the former owner, and it was a steal. Being in the midst of the dozens of art galleries lining Canyon Road, the location was ideal.

The house even had a tiny garden in back and was surrounded by an adobe wall for privacy. Thea and Max had pored over the layout and photos, deciding that the front part of the house would be used as a gallery and the back part as Thea's living quarters. Her potter's wheel and kiln would be in a separate, small structure adjacent to the house.

Thea was eager to begin her life in Santa Fe. She knew that recognition and success in the art community would come slowly, but she would be patient. Success was secondary to her, anyway, her first priority being her own emotional and mental health. New surroundings and new activities would do much to dispel the gloom that continued to overshadow her life here.

"This move will be good for both of us," Max said to break the silence and handed the photos back to Thea. "By the way, I talked with Paul last night on the phone, and he's got several condos lined up for me to look at. I'll know more about what I want when we get there."

At first, Thea had been shocked that Max would actually give up her job, sell her house, and move to Santa Fe with her. She was, of course, delighted and realized as time went on that Max was suffering, too. Her friend desperately needed a change in her life as well. The timing was perfect since their school year had ended two weeks earlier. Max was selling her car along with most everything else, and the two women decided to take stock of what would be loaded in Thea's station wagon for the long drive to New Mexico.

"Let's see, I'll have a small suitcase, my golf clubs, and a cooler for drinks. How 'bout you?" Max began listing items on her notepad.

"Not much more for me," Thea answered. "One small suitcase, Peaches in her kennel, and that box over by the door."

The box—Thea thought poignantly of its contents. There was a photograph album, bulging with mementos from a happier life: old love letters from Joe, graduation and wedding pictures, before and after shots of the new house, "Baby's First Picture," a tiny footprint, a lock of hair, photos of a face gooey with "First Birthday Cake," scores of vacation shots, "First Christmas," "Second Christmas," "Third Christmas," more birthday shots, and then blank pages. No other photographs had been entered. *But there's room for more*, Thea thought. *Someday there'll be more.*

On top of the photograph album laid a beautiful christening gown sealed in plastic. Thea's aunts in Greece—her mother's two sisters, whom she had never even met—had made the gown when Thea herself was born, and she had saved it for Alexa. Teddy was there in the box, too, his one eye still missing. That was all. *That's enough. I need nothing else tangible. It's all here in my heart!*

"Then we won't be crowded at all," Max said as she finished making her list. "Peaches is sure gonna be pissed, but she'll calm down after a while, don't you think?"

"I hope so," Thea replied absentmindedly, her mind lingering on the day she had packed that box. It was the day she had returned home alone from the courthouse, the day Hurley Dobbs had received his sentence.

Cal had told her the sentencing would be only a formality and wouldn't take long. He'd said it wasn't even necessary that she be present in court that day. Did he think she could possibly stay away? Of course she would be there, she *and* Joe! Perhaps it would be the last thing they would ever do together, the last time they would ever lean on each other.

Then, when Joe had stoically informed her that he would not be attending the sentencing, she couldn't believe her ears. "There's absolutely no use in either of us being there, Thea. We would only be torturing ourselves more," he had said to her matter-of-factly the evening before the scheduled sentencing.

"No use?" she screamed. "Maybe you don't see the use in being there to see that monster put away for life, but I do! If you don't care enough about my feelings to be there for me, then you can just go to hell!"

The couple had been having dinner at their favorite Italian restaurant when the argument erupted, drawing attention from other patrons. Before that, they had been so polite to each other, each one careful to keep the other informed of any plans. They were so civilized! But that was before Joe's refusal to attend the court proceedings. Thea hadn't known she could become so enraged with anyone, let alone the man she had once loved.

She had related to Max the following day the details of their argument and of her abrupt departure from the restaurant. "I wanted this divorce, Max, but until last night, I still had feelings for Joe. Now, there are none. It's over."

She went alone the next morning to the courthouse. Several of the other parents, grandparents, and family friends were in attendance as well. Of course, Cal had been right; there hadn't been very much to see. Since Dobbs had pled guilty but insane, there was no need for a trial. He had been led into the courtroom in restraints and seated at a table alongside his attorney, Mr. Tate. Cal, Lois, and the district attorney sat at the other table.

The judge had read the affidavits presented to him, read the state's charges against the man, read Hurley's confession, and after a brief sidebar with both attorneys, read his verdict. The court had, on the expert testimony of three psychiatrists, determined Hurley Dobbs to be insane. The judge thereby sentenced him to life, without possibility of parole, in the state mental institution for the criminally insane. Dobbs had been led out of the courtroom and it was over.

But it would never be over for Thea. The finality of Dobbs's sentence, even the part about no parole, paled in comparison to the punishment she felt had been inflicted upon her. A lifetime without Alexa was her sentence! ...*talking to herself as she made her way down the drive and around the curve...*

Stung by the mockery of justice, Thea's carefully constructed dam of control had burst at that point, spewing forth a flood of tears. They were tears not only of loss and sadness but of frustration as well.

Later, when she had managed to gain control of her emotions, she tasted the bitter bile of resentment. Joe should have been there to comfort her, but he hadn't. Her tears had fallen instead on the shoulder of a complete stranger, a kindly old man who attended all the court proceedings simply because he had no place else to go.

"You'll never forgive me, will you, Thea?" Joe had asked later that evening when he'd stopped by the house. When she did not answer, he made one final plea.

"I have loved you ever since I first laid eyes on you, and I still do. Before we go through with this divorce, do you think we could try to put it all back together again? I know I'm willing."

Thea couldn't believe what she was hearing from this man, this stranger. "Try again, Joe? Suppose you tell me how we would begin to try again!" With that, she had walked swiftly into the living room and poured herself a drink from the bar in the corner before turning to face her husband squarely, waiting for his reply.

"Counseling, of course, would have to come first. We were so happy for so long! We could get it back!" Joe's voice had softened. "Thea, we can have more children."

She could not breathe. For a moment, Thea could not imagine where the warm fluid seeping into her mouth was coming from. The faint metallic taste was foreign to her until she realized that it was her own blood she tasted—blood from her lip that she could not stop biting. Had he actually spoken of another child to her?

"Oh, I understand, now, Joe." Her voice had been mocking as she had walked toward him with a vicious sneer on her face. "It's sort of like, 'By the way, honey, the canary died. We'll get another one tomorrow'!"

Instantaneously, she'd sensed rather that felt the blow from his open right hand. She heard the *swoosh* long before the stinging pain caused her eyes to water. Dimly and without emotion, she had stared at her husband and saw the horror at what he had done slowly register on his face. He had left then, without another word. From that day on, they had talked only briefly over the telephone. Mostly they communicated through their respective attorneys.

"Incompatibility, Your Honor," her attorney had said. Thea had sat silent, wanting desperately to interrupt him. *It isn't like that, Your Honor. We were compatible! Something just got lost, got taken away. That's all!*

But she didn't speak, and it was over soon. The house had sold quickly, and Joe had sent word for her to take whatever she wanted. She chose very little. She would take her clothes, her art collection, enough furniture to fill her new home, the cat, and, of course, *the box*.

"Earth to Thea. Come in, please!" Max was standing before her, peering anxiously into her friend's huge black eyes. She smiled cautiously now, seeing Thea finally come out of the self-imposed trance. "I've been talking to you, but you wouldn't answer. You okay now?" She gently embraced her friend.

"I'm okay, Max. I've just been indulging in a little nostalgia," Thea replied. "I'm fine, really."

Max was grateful for the sudden ringing of the telephone and threw a worried glance back at her friend as she went into the kitchen to answer it.

"That was Cal," she informed Thea after the short conversation. "He wants you and me to have drinks this afternoon at the pub with him. He said Lois Castle will be there, too. Of course, I said yes. Never turn down free booze, right?"

"Right!" Thea answered, perking up at the prospect of spending her last free evening in Dallas with two people who had become good friends. "I'm glad we've become so close these past few months. Cal doesn't just go through the motions of being a cop; he truly does identify with the victims. He's certainly been honest with me, even when it hurts."

"What do you mean? Doesn't he believe that Alexa's still alive?" Max inquired.

"Yes, Cal believes she most probably *is* alive." Thea drew a deep breath and began sorting through a large stack of books on the floor. She had learned that busy hands were a good form of emotional defense. "He also believes that we'll never see her again. That's what I meant about his being honest. Of course, he's wrong, you know, but I can respect his opinion. And neither the DA nor Mr. Tate will give permission for me to visit Dobbs. That's a disappointment, but I'll live with it."

Thea turned her head away from Max, flicked away the sudden tear, and then continued. "Here, I'll pack these books for the move, and we'll donate the ones in this stack to the neighborhood rummage sale. There, that's done!" she said as she finished with mock cheerfulness.

"Well," Max's voice broke. It was her turn to blink away the tears that appeared so often without warning. "It'll be nice seeing Cal and Lois. He said he had some personal news to share with us. Wonder what's going on— probably something to do with his job. They're disbanding the task force, aren't they?"

"Yes, they are. Look, Max, the rain's stopping! Let's walk outside in the garden just a bit. It'll be my last chance."

Even with standing water that all but covered the stone patio, the beauty of the garden was still visible. Life remained, as evidenced by the profusion of color that had withstood days of pelting rain.

Azalea and Indian Hawthorn bushes, their heads hanging low, still displayed an abundance of new growth. Thea's roses, frequent winners in the Garden Club's annual judging, lay flattened but thick with buds. Beds of begonias and other perennials peaked in clusters through pools of mud and leaves.

There had been many times in the past when a contemplative stroll in this garden had resulted in confusing issues being resolved. Now, Thea suddenly became aware of a presence ever so gently stealing over her. She surveyed the garden again. No longer did it appear crestfallen and destroyed. It was tired and weak, perhaps, but alive nonetheless.

"This garden is going to live, Max! In spite of the beating from the rain and wind, everything's going to be fine. Why, just look at all the new growth!" Thea smiled wistfully as she looked around for the last time at the results of her labor. The garden hadn't been work at all—more like an adventure. She considered her garden another form of art, the results of her handiwork bringing pleasure.

A breeze refreshed the air with an enticing scent of jasmine, evoking smiles from the two women as they took a cleansing breath. "With all that's been heaped on it, this garden will continue to live and flourish. So will I, Max. So will I."

Thea surprised even herself with the positive about-face in her attitude since that morning. She knew that she had been touched by something unseen and had taken that first tentative and painful step in becoming whole again.

Conversation became unnecessary. The two friends strolled in the gentle mist, arms entwined, souls entwined, giving way to their tears. No longer were they tears of sadness and frustration but cleansing tears that bespoke new beginnings.

31

"You're really leaving the police force, Cal?" Thea asked her friend. From the first day she had met him, Cal Evers had struck Thea as the perfect example of a policeman. She was truly shocked.

"That I am, ma'am, and glad of it! After all these years, I've finally realized the stress it's put on Sophie. Now, I could be gallant and tell you that's my main reason, but it isn't."

Cal drained his vodka and signaled the waitress for another. Smiling faintly at the three women at the table, his eyes met Thea's, and he spoke again. "Of course, I want to spend more time with my wife and boys, but the main reason I'm quitting is a more selfish one. It's an old cliché that there's always one case a cop never gets over, and this one's been mine. For the life of me, I can't get those little faces out of my mind. And Dobbs, well, I—" Cal's voice broke noticeably as he buried his face in his hands. "The nightmares just won't end!"

Just as Thea had been tortured by her feelings of guilt for Alexa's disappearance and her failed marriage, she now, too, felt strangely responsible for her friend's turmoil. It was this self-reproach she fought against every day. Now, she must help Cal fight it as well.

"Cal, listen to me," Thea began as she laid her hand on the big man's shoulder and waited until his composure returned. "It wasn't my fault, and it wasn't your fault. Hurley Dobbs was responsible, and he's been put away. We must tell ourselves every day that we did all we could."

"I know that. I'm trying." Cal smiled at her. He had begun to notice a subtle difference in Thea but couldn't quite put his finger on it. She seemed to have more self-assurance than he had noticed before.

Max broke the silence. "What will you do, Cal?" She was troubled that their evening was in danger of becoming gloomy. "Have you made any definite plans yet?"

"That's the good part," Lois interjected. "Not good for me, since I'll be losing my best buddy, but good for you guys."

Cal and Lois laughed at the two puzzled faces before them. "Sophie has a brother in private investigation work, and he also does special assignments for the police department from time to time. He's got a terrific reputation and needs a partner. That's where I come in," Cal explained as his mood brightened. "From now on, you can reach me at Bascombe Investigations in Albuquerque, New Mexico!" He finished his announcement with a flourish, arms spread wide, grinning at the two shocked faces before him.

"Albuquerque? Well, hot damn, Cal! We'll be neighbors!" Max shrieked with delight. "Now this calls for a celebration!" She got the waitress's attention and called, "More drinks, please!" Turning back to the group, she continued, "Then, it's steaks on me at Del Frisco's! I won't take no for an answer."

"You've got no argument from me," Lois chimed in, relieved that the evening had taken on a happier, more festive tone. "With the three of you in New Mexico, my phone bills are gonna be out of sight!"

~

Several hours later, the four friends decided reluctantly to call it a night. Thea reminded Max about the movers' arrival the next morning. All in all, the evening had been a success. Max, after quite a few margaritas, had kept her compatriots howling with endless recitals of her past escapades, some bringing a flush to Cal's cheeks.

Although Lois's marriage had ended tragically in the death of her husband during his rookie year as a cop, she and Max discovered that they did indeed have a lot in common. As the two women became absorbed in comparing notes on their lives—Lois vowing not to marry again and Max swearing to *never* take the plunge—Cal was able to have a few moments of quiet conversation with Thea.

"Now, I don't mean to depress you tonight, but I want you to know I'll never, ever stop searching for answers. I'll never stop trying to find out what happened to her. This new job—it can get me in touch with a lot of influential people. I hope you believe me. I won't forget Alexa."

The look of determination on his face and the sincere tone of his voice warmed Thea's heart. "I do know that, my friend. I wasn't going to bring up the subject tonight, but—" Thea hesitated only momentarily, knowing she had to ask the question. "Has there been any change in Dobbs? Is he communicating with anyone?"

Cal ran a hand through his already tousled hair, relieved that these questions had come late in the evening after so much frivolity. "There's been no change to speak of. The chaplain has started meeting with him daily for a few minutes, and Dobbs seems to respond favorably to the man. So far, though, he isn't talking. Thea, you'd best hear this from a friend: they've closed the files on all five of the cases. The department's of the opinion that the other three girls are dead and that their bodies may never be recovered."

There, he had told her. But where was the reaction he had come to expect from Thea when they talked of her daughter? Where were the tears, the faraway look in those beautiful eyes, the self-induced trance he had seen her enter into in the past? What was it that was so different about her tonight?

The evening wound down, and the four friends strolled to the parking lot to say their final good-byes. As they made small talk and promised to stay in contact after their moves, Cal once again took time to study Thea. He decided he'd been right—there *was* something different about her. Not only were her reactions different, but her bearing and her behavior had changed as well.

～

"Of course she's different, Cal," Lois remarked to him later as they discussed Thea. "She can't change the past, so she's concentrating on the future. But don't think for one minute that she's giving up. That lady's just getting started!"

Only the soul that knows the mighty grief
Can know the mighty rapture. Sorrows come
To stretch out spaces in the heart for joy.
— "Victory in Defeat,"
Edwin Markham

Part II

Part II

32

The mere mention of Santa Fe had for months summoned a myriad of images in Thea's mind. The practical side of her nature recognized the vast opportunities that came with moving to an important art center. Maybe she would continue with her teaching, but what she really longed for was to sit at her potter's wheel and produce a craft worthy of recognition as Santa Fe art.

As Elena had pointed out, many new ideas and ways of life had been brought to Santa Fe over the years, but the history of the region had not been lost. The beauty remained, as did the spirit, making the city the very heart and soul of the Southwest.

Thea knew she had chosen a place where the sometimes-harsh elements of nature blending with the natural beauty would get her artistic juices flowing. With the vast stores of Native American and Spanish history to explore, the design possibilities open to her were limitless. Her Greek heritage would have its say as well. Thea felt confident that in time she would achieve a distinctive style of pottery easily recognizable as hers.

Despite the fact that she had not yet set foot in Santa Fe, the visionary in Thea could see clearly the beautiful Sangre de Cristo mountain range that surrounded the city. She looked forward to winter snows, when a blanket of white would soften the bold landscape. And when the snows melted, she would witness the subtle hint of color as cactus blossoms spotted the desert. Summer would bring not only the gentle rains but a profusion of flowers to her garden and the rich reds and purples of the rare double rainbows. The desert sunsets Elena had spoken of so reverently would soon be real for her. Indeed, Thea saw it all each time she closed her eyes. She saw the peace that she hoped would touch her soul. She saw home.

Ever since they had left Albuquerque, the boredom of the long trip from Dallas had disappeared. Both Thea and Max were enchanted with the countryside. "You haven't stopped reading from those brochures for over an hour," Thea good-naturedly chided her friend. "I'll be an expert on the ancient Anasazi by the time we reach Santa Fe!"

"It's all so fascinating. I didn't realize what a splendid heritage those people left behind," Max responded.

"I know what you mean. Did you look at the literature Elena sent on Pueblo vessels? Oh, I can't wait to get moved in so I can concentrate on my pottery!"

"I did see it," Max replied. "There are so many different styles and colors; they're wonderful. And yours—they'll be dynamite!"

Thea smiled and fell silent again, concentrating on her driving. Soon, she began humming pleasantly in tune with the radio.

~

Max offered up an unspoken prayer of thanks that her friend was in better spirits than when they'd initially left Dallas.

She had witnessed a rise of hysteria that almost overwhelmed Thea as they had begun their drive on Interstate 20. She would not be consoled as her paranoia worsened. It had taken every ounce of fortitude Max possessed to keep driving as Thea had begged and pleaded through tears for her to return to Dallas.

"Max, I feel so close to her—to Alexa! It's—it's almost as though she's calling out to me!" And then the self-reproach had set in. "I'm deserting her. I'm leaving Alexa! It's as if I'm giving up, running away. I know what I need. I need to go back and talk to Joe. He'll know what to do, won't he?"

For the better part of that first dismal day, with rain still falling, Max had continued driving as Thea's sorrow ran its course. Finally, exhausted by her own sobs, she had fallen asleep. Hours later, Peaches's yowling had awakened her. To Max's relief, Thea had suggested they find a motel for the night so they could let the cat out, have a nice dinner, and regroup for the next day.

"That way, we won't be so tired when we get to Santa Fe," Thea had said calmly. But Max had wondered how much of her horror still lay just under the surface and what would bring about another attack of remorse.

Max would never mention her worry, though; she would simply be there. "That's a great idea. We can phone Paul and Elena tonight and let them know approximately what time we'll be getting in. Hey, instead of going to Paul's office, why don't we get directions and meet them at your house? They'll probably be there finishing up with the moving van, anyway," Max had suggested.

"My house!" Thea had spoken the words thoughtfully, a smile lighting up her tired features. "Do you realize that it's always been *ours*, never *mine*? I'm starting over, Max, and to be honest with you, I'm scared to death!"

"It's okay to be scared, Thea. Just remember that you're not alone," Max had reassured her gently.

~

"Hey, wake up and help me look for street signs." Thea's excited voice brought Max back to the present.

"Okay, where are we?" Max was suddenly very anxious. Up until now, this move had simply been like any other. Max's life had been a series of changes; this one would be no different. She was merely comforting her best friend and she could do that in one place as well as another.

But all of a sudden, things *were* different. Max sat erect in the seat and surveyed the outskirts of Santa Fe. Her pulse quickened, and her nerve endings sparked with a long-forgotten excitement. "I can't quite put my finger on it, Thea—but, well, I feel like this is the place!"

They had exited I-25, skirted downtown Santa Fe, and soon found their way to Paseo de Peralta. This was the street leading to Canyon Road, where Thea's house was located.

"We're not too far from the house, I don't think. Paul said if we crossed the river, we've missed Canyon Road. Wait—there it is. I know exactly where to go from here," Thea chattered excitedly.

She could not have designed a more lovely setting for her new home. The tree-shaded front boasted a circular drive that afforded much more parking than most of the galleries and studios along the narrow Canyon Road. A freshly painted sign hung ready for lettering, and a gleaming new mailbox proudly displayed Thea Kelly's name. Most importantly, the beautiful and intricately carved front door stood open, beckoning them to enter.

"You're right, Max," Thea whispered as she brought the car to a stop. "This is the place!"

Paul and Elena walked hand in hand through the open front door at the sound of the car's engine and delightedly embraced the exuberant Max as she jumped from the car. "Ahh, Thea was right," Paul said warmly. "She said we would know you and love you immediately!"

"Welcome, Max," said Elena. "Welcome to New Mexico." She turned quickly toward Thea, but Paul's gentle pressure on her arm restrained her.

"Let her be for just a moment," he said. "She needs time to herself."

The two women realized he was right as they silently watched Thea emerge from the car. Even Peaches cooperated by ceasing her insistent mewing to be let out of her kennel.

Bedazzled, Thea slowly began to walk the expanse of her front yard. A young boy stopped his assault on the bramble of briars and weeds infesting the flower beds and shyly whispered a good day to her. Continuing to scrutinize her new home, Thea wandered through the open gate and into the backyard. There, the garden was almost completely overgrown with wild vegetation, but she could easily envision how spectacular it would be when cleaned and properly tended. A bronze fountain surrounded by a flagstone patio was being cleaned and repaired by an older man, and a smiling woman bid her good day in Spanish as she deftly pruned a small tree.

The house itself was larger than Thea had first thought. The adobe had been freshly painted a soft terra cotta, with the wooden shutters and doors stained dark brown in contrast. She immediately noticed the separate building, probably once used as a guest house. Its large windows with southern exposure would make it ideal for her wheel and kiln. It was all so perfect!

As she returned to the front of the house, her three friends stood anxious for her reaction. "Paul, Elena, this is wonderful!" she exclaimed. "How can I ever thank you for arranging all this?"

"Our reward is having you here, Thea," Paul said, his voice husky with emotion as his wife hugged Thea tightly.

"How many times have we wanted to come to Dallas to be with you, my dear. We knew it was best that you have time to yourself, though, to handle things in your own way. This," Elena said as she spread her arms, indicating the house, "this is our way of helping."

"I want you to know something," Paul said brightly as he patted his wife's shoulder. "This lady here has talked of nothing else since you called to tell us you were moving here! She's even planned a housewarming for you in two weeks. So we'd all better get busy and get this place shipshape."

"We are so happy you both are here," Elena said, beaming. "Excuse me, we're happy *all three* of you are here," she added, as Peaches set about making herself known once more.

"And one of us is especially glad this trip is over!" Thea said as she hurried to the car to fetch the impatient cat.

"What is this beautiful hanging?" Max asked moments later as they entered the front door for a tour of the interior. A large round circle framing finely woven netting festooned with many feathers hung just inside the doorway.

Thea and Max both admired the piece as Paul explained. "That is called a dream catcher, and it is given as a gift of love. The Native Americans used to hang them in the doorway of a tepee or near their beds. It is said the net will catch bad dreams, holding them tight. Only the good dreams can pass through the center of the net, bringing wisdom and peace."

They absorbed the beautiful story in silence. Elena spoke: "May we all receive these gifts, yes?"

33

The cluster of trees lining the banks of the Santa Fe River provided the walkers a shady respite from the morning's suddenly hot sun. Thea breathed the clean air deeply and realized she would soon experience her first crisp, crackling, Southwestern autumn. A slightly cooler breeze now wafted through the trees. The sun, hanging a bit lower in the sky this time of year, glinted through the fragile aspen leaves and cast dappled patterns upon the ground.

Nowhere was the clarity of light and colors more pronounced than in Santa Fe, particularly now as September began her enchanting visual assault upon the senses. The contrasting values of yellow and green of the chamisa, cottonwood, aspen, and pine formed an easy alliance with the blues and purples of thistle and aster and gave the color spectrum new definition.

As her daily five-mile trek neared its end, Thea shook her head and smiled at the good-natured grumbling of her fellow walkers. "If you think this is hot weather, you should try walking in Dallas, Texas, in September," she told them.

Soon after her move nearly three months prior, Thea and a group of her neighbors had begun these daily walks. Not only did it provide much-needed exercise after hours spent hunched over her potter's wheel, but it had also been a terrific way to learn her way around the twists and turns of the city streets. Thea soon realized that while most streets led to the plaza, it could certainly prove to be a circuitous trip.

"Well, this is certainly hot enough weather for me. Thank goodness we walk early!" Thea's new friend, Yolanda Cisneros, replied as she dropped to the ground.

Thea stopped, too, bending forward to rest her hands on her knees and catch her breath. The daily jaunts had helped to firm her thin body. Her newly developed muscles, instead of appearing masculine, added much-needed dimension.

"Ahh, I am jealous, my friend," Yolanda panted. "You actually enjoy this, and I walk only to keep away the extra pounds!"

"Enough talk and enough rest," Thea said as she pulled the reluctant woman to her feet. "Another half mile and we're home. You can make it!" As the two women rounded a curve in the road, Thea's house became visible, and she spoke again. "Look who's already back. And why am I not surprised?"

Max had walked with the group this morning, soon leaving them in her wake, and now stood waiting for Thea and Yolanda.

"How do you do it? Why, you're not even out of breath!" Yolanda exclaimed, hands on her hips and a mock frown creasing her pleasant face. "I'm going home now. The sopapillas await!" The women laughed at her reference to the sweet pastries.

"I'll be along soon, Yo," Max called after their new friend as she watched her slowly climb the stone steps to her studio and home. Max presently rented rooms from Yolanda until her new house was completed. Soon after arriving in Santa Fe, she had abandoned the idea of a condo, deciding to build a house just outside of the city on a high ridge. "I simply must have that view, Paul," she had said. "Build me something ultramodern with huge windows."

For Thea and Max, this morning began serene like most mornings since their move to Santa Fe. After Yolanda left, the two friends sat in Thea's garden, lazily watching the progress of a couple of bumblebees and talking of nothing in particular. Finally, Max stood.

"I've got to run—job interview at one this afternoon. See you tonight."

"Good luck," Thea said as she watched Max trot effortlessly up the stone steps to Yolanda's house. She felt confident that her friend would land the teaching position at the high school.

The morning sun was mesmerizing. Thea succumbed to a bit of laziness, which was a rare treat in her busy schedule. Since her arrival in Santa Fe, she had been welcomed warmly into the community and included in many art council meetings. She knew this was due in no small part to Elena's influence, and although she received many positive comments on her pottery, she held no illusion. It would be a very long time before she would produce a quality product.

She had, in fact, spoken despairingly of her own work weeks earlier during Indian Market. The weekend event was held each August and brought the very finest Native American craftspeople and artists to the Santa Fe Plaza to exhibit their wares. It was a lively time, as bustling crowds of collectors and those who simply appreciated beautiful art filled the city. And it was a time of fierce competition for prizes among the artists. Winners in the various categories could expect their works to escalate in value and their names to be applauded in art circles throughout the country.

"Yolanda, when I see the quality of the Native American pottery, I wonder if I'll ever produce anything to compare," Thea had moaned to her new neighbor and friend after the first day of the market. "Maybe I'm just dreaming the impossible!"

"Nonsense, child," Yolanda had chided her. "Do you think I, or any other artist for that matter, became successful overnight? Of course not! It takes dedication and self-discipline to achieve your goals. To some of us, recognition comes early; to some, later. You will not wait long for yours, believe me!"

Yolanda Cisneros was herself an accomplished painter, widely praised for her beautiful watercolors celebrating scenes of Santa Fe life and her own Hispanic heritage. Her latest work depicted a potter poised over the wheel, hands caressing clay, in the creation of a ceremonial vessel. Thea was deeply honored to have been the artist's model.

With Yolanda's encouragement and Elena's well-meaning prodding, Thea had joined the Museum of New Mexico and several community groups. It seemed that her life was a never-ending circle of research, work, and meetings, with precious little time left for relaxation and sightseeing.

One trip she and Max had managed to take was to the Anasazi cliff dwellings in Mesa Verde. Thea had begun the trip jubilant, but as they got closer to their destination in southwest Colorado, she had once again surrendered to depression.

"I can't explain it, Max!" she had practically screamed as she paced the confines of their hotel room. "All I can say is that I feel like I'm going to jump out of my skin!"

Her mood had brightened somewhat while visiting the masterpieces of the national park, and she was impressed with the influence these ancient cliff dwellers still maintained on Santa Fe architecture.

"We know so little about the Anasazi" she had said to Max during their excursion. "I suppose they'll always be clouded in mystery. What happened to them, I wonder? Were they wiped out due to disease or wars with other tribes?" We'll probably never know. As with my Alexa, we may never know."

Their return to Santa Fe had banished some of her melancholy, and Thea had been grateful for her hectic schedule. Their days melted into an easy, comfortable pattern, with mornings spent walking with the group and running errands. Max usually spent her afternoons shopping for her new house or watching its progress while Thea closeted herself at the museum library studying designs or sat mesmerized by her wheel—therapy in motion, she called it. It was then and only then that the anxieties would slip from her; tensions would be eased, and horrors would be momentarily blotted out. Everything dark and ugly would be transformed by the sheer artistry of molding a lump of clay into what would one day, hopefully, become a piece easily recognized by the one word marking it—*Thea*.

Thea's plans to continue teaching quickly dissolved when she realized how addictive her art had become. She had on several occasions expressed worry to her father. "I know I need an income to pay my living expenses and Cal's retainer, but I simply cannot tear myself away from that wheel!" But as always, Mike had soothed away her anxieties with his reassurance that nothing would make him happier than investing in her future.

Thea had sat idle long enough. She left the tranquility of her garden behind and began to prioritize the remainder of her day. She had come to realize just how big an investment her father might be making in her future if she didn't get busy.

34

Because she had not arrived until half of the peak tourist season was over, Thea had not seriously attempted to sell any pottery. However, a number of visitors wandering Canyon Road had stopped in and purchased several pieces. She had managed to turn out a quantity of bowls of all sizes, pitchers, coffee cups, and vases. Now, with the long, quiet winter not far ahead, she would be able to dedicate almost all of her daylight hours to refining her technique and producing a line of artistic storage vessels.

After her phone call to Cal to get an update on his progress from the prior week, Thea had intended to spend the remainder of the day working on her designs. But Cal's "nothing new" report had left her in the doldrums. She paced the small studio, wondering if their efforts were indeed pointless. No, she would *not* give up! And neither would Cal, she knew. Since moving to New Mexico, he had widened his circulation of fliers showing Alexa's picture. He'd even rented billboards and placed ads in area publications. But the few slim leads and vague recollections that trickled in continued to prove worthless.

Would her healing ever begin, she wondered, when wounds could be so easily ripped open by the smallest of disappointments? Would the rare joyful moments of her days continue to be beaten down by cruel reality? ...*talking to herself as she made her way down the drive and around the curve...*

Thea decided she could either muddle through another day of doubt or try and recapture some of the early morning's tranquility. Her wheel beckoned and very soon she was lost in her work and in the quiet strains of Mozart emitting from the stereo. Believing she would be totally alone this afternoon, she had dressed carelessly in cutoff jeans and a halter top.

Her lustrous hair was pulled back into a loose ponytail, and she wore no makeup. The open windows allowed an occasional bird's twittering to be heard. Once in a while, the faint voice of a neighbor was audible. Aside from the slight tickle as Peaches rubbed her leg, nothing else invaded her world.

Artist and wheel became one as she was drawn deeper and deeper into her creation. Slowly her hands moved together in what she hoped would be her final pull to bring the pot to its full height. Here was the crucial part. The hands could not move too quickly and the grip could not be too loose, or the height would not advance. On the other hand, a grip too strong might cause the already saturated clay to collapse.

With precision, her hands moved upward. "There, not bad. Now compress the top, and you're almost done." Thea talked to herself as she worked. This piece had turned out better than she'd hoped.

As she carefully sponged away the water and soupy clay that had gathered at the pot's base, she heard, "Pardon me. I believe I have your clay."

Luckily, Thea had just slowed the wheel and her sudden flinch at the unexpected sound did nothing to damage her work.

"I—I beg your pardon?" She turned toward the door, toward the voice. "You startled me!" She reached for a clean towel and, after wiping her hands, instinctively ran a hand through her hair. She was a little hacked at being taken by surprise, but she was getting used to having people stop by on the spur of the moment. Maybe this was a customer.

Then she saw him clearly. He filled the door, from top to bottom, side to side. And his presence filled the small room. It was a compelling presence. They both remained perfectly still, each one studying the other.

"It's very good, I think," he stated quietly.

"Huh?" *Simpleton,* Thea silently cursed herself. "I mean, what's good?"

"The pot, your work—it's very good." He moved cautiously, like a panther. "It appears you have modeled it after the Cochiti Pueblo. It's a fine likeness."

"Uh, thanks. Thank you." *Why can't you speak sensibly?* "I apologize. I'm quite sure I sound deranged. You startled me. What were you saying about clay?" *Well, that's a little better!*

"I had a large order of clay delivered yesterday to my studio in Taos. The delivery men had to unload yours to get to mine, and they inadvertently left yours behind. I brought it in my truck today. I had to come to Santa Fe on business anyway. Where shall I put it?"

He had turned to face her as he spoke, and Thea was able to study him even more closely. He was tall, at least six-three, she judged. He was muscular, but not overly so. He was dressed in jeans and western boots. A vest made of soft-looking leather with intricate beading was his only shirt. He was quite obviously Native American, with skin the color of burnished copper. His hair was as black as coal and had been neatly fashioned into a single long braid wound tightly with more beading. Thea continued to be transfixed as she studied him.

"Well, where shall I put it?" he repeated.

"Put what?" she responded dully. "Yes, the clay, of course! We'll take it around back. I hope it hasn't been an imposition. You could have just kept it. It wasn't that big of an order."

"No trouble at all. As I said, I had to come to Santa Fe on business anyway, and I can't use your clay. I sculpt, and my work requires a different type of clay from potter's clay."

Thea tagged mutely alongside him and somehow managed to direct him with points and nods to the storage building housing her clay. *Am I suddenly unable to converse with another human being?* she thought.

"Thea—it is a nickname?" He broke the silence after he had finished stacking the blocks of clay.

"Athena is my name. It seems strange to say it, though. I've been Thea for as long as I can remember."

"Athena is a beautiful name. Are you Greek?"

"My mother was from Greece." As she responded, Thea suddenly realized that she was very self-conscious in the presence of this stranger, and she knew the reason. How long had it been since she had had a one-on-one conversation with anyone other than her dad and her small circle of close friends? *At least I remembered my name!*

"Thea, I'm Monty. It's a pleasure to meet you at last." He shook her hand firmly. "I've heard good things about you from Paul and Elena."

Moments passed. Thea was oblivious to the fact that she was still holding on to that strong hand, still staring into those eyes. *Now, exactly how would one describe those eyes?*

"You know Paul and Elena?" she asked. "Oh, of course you do. You said so! Have you known them long?"

"I've known Paul all my life. He and I are cousins. My maternal grandmother was from Mexico and a sister of Paul's mother." He gently extricated his hand from Thea's and continued speaking thoughtfully as his gaze wandered to the garden area. "You've done a fine job bringing life back to the garden. It was in shambles when I saw it last. And the fountain—she's holding up well, I think."

As he spoke he walked to the center of the garden—to what Thea considered the focal point—and stood gently caressing the beautifully sculptured bronze figure of a woman rising from the fountain's center.

"You—you've been here?" Thea asked, quite taken aback. "And you've seen my fountain?"

"Seen it? Yes, Thea, I've seen it. As a matter of fact, I made it," he informed her with quite pride. "This lady was my first sculpture." His hands continued to examine the patina surface of the bronze. "I remember that it was the proudest moment of my life when I finished her. I was proud but sad as well to finish her." He continued speaking, almost as though he were talking to himself. "It's that way with all my work. The pieces I spend the most time on seem to be the hardest to part with. After a while they become a part of me. But art must be shared, don't you think?"

He faced her now, and sudden recognition caused Thea to blush. "Please forgive me," she began. "I didn't recognize you! You're Montana Arroyo, the sculptor!"

No longer was Thea completely tongue-tied. And no longer did this man who had so suddenly interrupted her work seem a stranger. Here in her garden was a fellow artist, the most successful sculptor of Southwest art today, a man whose work had indeed made him a legend.

"I saw your latest piece last month during Market. You won first place again in the bronze category." Thea smiled and extended her hand once again. "I am honored to meet you, Monty."

"I have been very fortunate," he replied. "Sometimes I think of it as a crime to make money from work I enjoy so much."

Thea replied, "I agree with you completely—art must be shared. It must be enjoyed by others. I yearn for the day my pottery receives a fraction of the praise given to that of other artists. To me, art is like—well, it's like love. It feeds our senses, yet we never become full. Our eyes never tire of looking at it, and touching a beautiful piece never gets old.

"I suppose I view my art as an extension of my life," she continued after a brief pause. "It will be what I will leave behind in this world. It will be all I leave behind. That's why I'm so passionate about it and why I long for success."

Thea realized with chagrin that she had been babbling with breathless excitement and had drawn a beaming smile from Monty. His smile was contagious, and soon they were sitting on the stone benches flanking the fountain, talking and laughing as if they had known each other forever. How good it was to talk to another artist! She felt a pang of regret when, an hour later, Monty stood to leave.

"My apologies, Thea, I've kept you from your work and made myself late for my appointment, as well."

"You haven't kept me from work at all," she said. "I needed a break. I've truly enjoyed our visit. Thanks again for bringing my clay."

They left the garden and walked slowly back through the studio where Monty once again examined a piece of pottery, exacting a blush of pride from Thea with his compliments. "I predict accolades for your first art show!" Monty's eyes met hers, and he smiled sincerely.

"You flatter me. Praise coming from you is an honor," Thea replied warmly. "Tell me, did you receive an award for your first piece?" She gestured toward the garden as she spoke of his fountain there.

Instinctively, she knew she had touched on a sensitive subject when his face clouded ever so slightly. After an obviously painful pause, he answered her. "I did not enter the fountain in competition. It was a gift for someone I—for someone," he finished with a quiet finality that ended the conversation.

Thankfully, Peaches chose that instant to announce her approval of Monty by rubbing against his legs and purring loudly, and the awkward moment passed. As they stood in her doorway once again conversing easily, the thought occurred to Thea that she did not want this man to leave. "I'm sure we'll see each other again, Monty," she said.

His head brushed the delicate feathers of the dream catcher as he turned to meet her gaze. "Yes, we will," he replied.

Alone once more, Thea wandered back outside to her garden. After careful examination of Monty's bronze lady, she realized that what was lacking in so much of the art she saw today—her own included—was the essential quality of life. She was certain he had had a live model for this piece. How else could she appear so real, so alive? Without actual inspiration, how could he have captured so exactly the vulnerability of youth reflected in her expression? Who was she, and what was she to him, that she could inspire art such as this?

"He's a genius and unequaled!" Thea marveled aloud as she returned to her studio and prepared to dismiss Montana Arroyo, the sculptor, from her thoughts.

~

Later in the evening, she sat again at her wheel and, seemingly without effort, threw the finest and most detailed pottery to date. Piece after piece, she mechanically pulled, compressed, and trimmed to near perfection. Almost without thinking, almost without seeing, she controlled the speed of the wheel with an exactness not exhibited before. As the gathering darkness blurred her vision, she brought the wheel to a stop and deftly sliced free the final vessel. She was dimly aware of the pieces that sat waiting to be wrapped in plastic for the drying process. Her hands instinctively performed this function before she began her nightly cleaning routine.

Thea was exhausted. With her day's work behind her, she sat in her rocking chair and stared vacantly at her handiwork. It was not pottery she saw, but instead eyes—eyes the color of smoke.

35

The telephone's incessant ringing brought Thea out of a deep sleep. Who could be calling her so early? She fought her way through covers, pillows, and cat to the bedside table.

"Um, hello?"

"Oh, have I phoned too early, dear?" Elena's lilting voice was apologetic. "I am so sorry. I just assumed you'd be up and about. It's after nine. Shall I call back later?"

"No, no, it's all right," Thea replied. "Is it really after nine? Guess I've missed my walk, huh?" Falling back across her bed and stretching languidly, Thea realized now why she had slept so late. "I didn't get to bed until after two this morning, Elena. I worked until dark at the wheel and then did some glazing on the plates I made last week. Time simply got away from me. I have no idea where my burst of energy came from, but I'm paying for it now!" she concluded, suppressing a yawn.

"Well, dear, the reason I'm calling is to invite you to a little impromptu dinner party this evening. Nothing formal, just a few friends. You know most of them, I believe. As a matter of fact, you met our houseguest yesterday. And from what I hear, the two of you had a delightful visit!"

"Oh, you're talking about Monty." Thea was suddenly fully awake, her interest piqued. "He delivered my order of clay to me yesterday. I didn't realize Paul had such a celebrity in the family!"

"Yes, Monty and Paul are as close as brothers. They had some business to attend to yesterday that didn't get finished, so he's staying a couple of days with us. And," Elena paused briefly, "I have been promising the Arts Council president a formal introduction to Monty for months now. We thought a dinner party would be a good idea. I plan to invite Max and Yolanda, you—oh, maybe six others. Can you make it, say, around seven?"

"I guess so. Now, let's see, what shall I wear? Just how informal is this, Elena? I don't want to show up looking totally out of place." Thea was unaware of the note of anticipation her voice carried. "How about my red dress? Is that too forward, too loud?"

"The red will be perfect, dear. See you at seven." Elena had to muffle a delighted giggle as she quickly ended the phone call. Matchmaking was her specialty, but after listening to Monty speak of Thea the previous evening, she realized that her skills at bringing people together might not even be needed for the two artists. Soon after Monty's arrival at their house yesterday afternoon and all during dinner, both she and Paul had noticed a rare bit of animation in Monty's countenance. A half-smile found its way to his face often during their conversations, a welcomed contrast to his seemingly ever-present scowl.

"A woman!" Paul and Elena had simultaneously whispered excitedly to each other in the kitchen after dinner. Upon returning to the dining room with dessert and coffee, they'd found out just who had put a much-needed spark into this troubled man.

"I met your friend Thea today, Paul," Monty said. "A shipment of her clay got left at my studio. Since I was coming to see you, I dropped it off to her."

"So that's why you were late for our meeting! Well, if a man's going to be late, I can't think of a better reason than Thea Kelly. She's a lovely woman, don't you think?" Paul was teasing, prodding—in a good-natured way, of course—and Elena had to excuse herself from the table to hide her grin. Emotional and passionate as she was, it was all she could do to appear cool when she returned to the dining room a few minutes later.

"Pardon me, Monty. What were you saying about Thea?"

"Just explaining to Paul why I was late for our meeting. We had a very nice visit, Thea and I. She has some real talent. I was quite impressed with her pottery." Monty sipped his coffee and continued thoughtfully. "I was impressed also with the garden. I don't ever remember it looking so inviting. I found myself not wanting to leave. The memories there were good, for a while—"

"I know, my friend. I know," Paul interrupted, gently laying a hand on his cousin's arm. It broke his heart to witness the cloak of sadness and frustration that still hung heavily on those broad shoulders.

After a time, Monty continued speaking. "I must remember that I am not the only one who has experienced sadness. From what you've told me about Thea, it is truly remarkable that she has been able to move forward in her life. Her work will help. For a time it will be all that will matter to her." He spoke from experience, the couple knew. "I suppose there are still no new clues in her daughter's disappearance?"

"None. I am afraid there will be none," Paul answered. "The authorities have closed the case. But she's not giving up. As a matter of fact, she has a good friend who is a private investigator. He stays busy following every lead on missing children that comes his way. It is devastating for her, but she knows she must go on with her life. She has made good progress since moving to Santa Fe, I think." *Yes, devastating indeed,* Paul thought. *The crosses that two such fine young people as Thea and Monty should have to bear!*

Elena managed to regain the evening's earlier pleasant mood by suggesting a dinner party the following night. "Monty, you know how long Mrs. Carson has wanted to meet you. She and her husband are two of the biggest promoters of Santa Fe's art festivals. A dinner party would be a fine way to recognize her efforts. We would keep it small, of course." Elena continued speaking thoughtfully, remembering Monty's aversion to large, boisterous parties. "We would invite a couple of local artists, as well. You know, it might be good for Thea to get out. How about it, Monty?"

Both Paul and Elena noticed the almost indiscernible straightening of the shoulders as Monty replied, "Sure, Elena. A dinner party would be nice. A small one, you said."

"Of course, Monty. I'll get right on it in the morning."

~

"Max, be honest. Which one should I wear?" Thea was exhausted from trying on dress after dress. She had begun early in the afternoon after suddenly realizing that she had not worn any of her dinner dresses in over two years. With the weight she had lost, they were bound to hang shapelessly on her.

"That's the one—definitely!" Max answered with conviction, referring to the simple column of white silk that hung from a golden clasp at one shoulder to flow freely and end just above the ankle. Max studied her friend as she turned first one way and then the other in front of the full-length mirror in her bedroom.

With a worried frown on her face, Thea critically judged her reflection. "Is it too formal? Elena did say informal. Maybe I should wear the short red one. It—"

"Absolutely not," Max interrupted sternly. "You want my opinion, you've got it. The white is perfect! Besides," Max rose from her perch on the foot of Thea's bed to hug her friend, "it's the only one that still fits you properly. My God, kiddo, you're practically skin and bones!"

Thea finally smiled at her reflection. "It does look good, doesn't it? This was always my favorite dress, but Joe never liked it. That's why I hardly ever wore it." Thoughts of Joe intruded only momentarily. She was determined not be a wet blanket tonight! "What shoes? And jewelry?"

"My gold sandals. I'll bring them down after I'm dressed, and *no* jewelry! Oh, and by all means, wear your hair down." She playfully tousled her friend's thick black hair before departing to get herself ready for the evening. "Yolanda and I will pick you up at about a quarter of, okay?"

"That's fine. I'll be ready," Thea answered absently, still absorbed in her own reflection. *What's happening to me? Is it possible to be attracted to another man so suddenly? Is it so farfetched an idea to think he could be attracted to me, as well? What if he has a lover—a wife, even! And who is the woman who inspired his fountain? Someone he obviously cared for. Someone he broke up with or who jilted him, broke his heart?*

"Would you just listen to yourself? Thea, don't be juvenile!" she berated herself aloud, shaking off her daydreams. "He probably hasn't given me a second thought! Why should he? I'm nothing to him." Finishing her conversation with herself, Thea disrobed and ran water for her bath.

Ever since that morning when Elena had phoned with the dinner invitation, she had thought of little else. In vain she tried to dismiss Monty from her mind. She needed no more dashed hopes and no more shattered dreams to deal with. And she pursued no pipe dream that life would ever again bring her happiness. There would be enjoyment in her life, and satisfaction would come from her craft. But there could be no happiness. Certainly, no thoughts of romance entered her mind. From now on, her work and her friends would be her life. She certainly didn't need a man to complicate matters!

But no amount of rationalization could blot him from her thoughts. She sank slowly into the steaming bath and felt the warm water begin to ease her tensions. The fragrant aroma of bath oil reminded her of how long it had been since she had even bothered with perfumes. *It's no use. Who do you think you're kidding?* Thea silently rebuked herself. In the span of one afternoon, she had become completely captivated by, what—his looks, his quiet, almost majestic manner, and his eloquent speech that hinted at years of formal education? Maybe it was just the attraction of an accomplished artist that drew her.

Maybe, she thought later as she stood once again in front of her mirror gazing at her reflection, *maybe it's those extraordinary eyes!*

36

Max did not have to hear it from her friend to know something special was afoot this evening. They were truly sisters at heart, and whatever one was feeling, the other sensed. More than anyone else, Max knew how long it had been since anything other than Alexa's disappearance had occupied Thea's thoughts—far too long!

Max watched her friend walk toward the waiting car. Thea had taken her advice almost to the letter. The white silk draped her body beautifully and emphasized her dark features. She was void of jewelry except for two wide gold cuffs worn on each wrist that Max knew had been her mother's. As she nimbly knelt to fasten the gold sandals on her feet, her two friends exchanged knowing glances. With wry smiles they acknowledged that they would take a backseat at the party tonight.

"Damn, I might as well go back home," Yolanda muttered good-naturedly, drawing a laugh from her friends.

The threesome arrived at the dinner party right on time and was ushered into the airy and spacious living room by the Ramirezes' housekeeper. Several people were already there, sipping cocktails, talking in hushed voices, and admiring the many works of art that adorned the elegant home. It was a warm and loving home; this was immediately obvious. Thea loved coming here. Paul and Elena had always made her feel welcome, and never more so than tonight.

"Thea, darling, we're so glad you could come!" Elena came forward to hug her warmly. She whispered into her ear so no one else could hear: "My God, you are a knockout!"

Thankfully, Elena had not embarrassed the younger woman by calling undue attention to her. In an uncommonly subtle way, though, she gave

Thea the reassurance she needed. "Max, Yolanda, thank you for coming. Let's get the three of you a drink."

Soon the doorbell announced the rest of the evening's guests—almost. Where was he? Thea wondered. With everyone talking at once, she was caught quite unaware by the voice behind her.

"Hello, again, Thea."

She turned quickly in response, and her sharp intake of breath let Monty know he had once again startled her. "I assure you," he said warmly, "I do not intend to make a career out of taking you by surprise. I apologize."

"That's quite all right," she replied. "I'm glad to see you again. Did you get your business taken care of?" Thea was suddenly very thankful for the drink Paul had brought her a moment earlier; holding it kept her hands from shaking. She tried with all her might to appear cool and composed when in truth her stomach was in knots.

"For the most part. One more day should wind things up," he answered. "I was wondering if perhaps—"

"Monty, dear," Elena interrupted. "You've met Thea. Let me quickly make formal introductions all around, and then we'll go in to dinner, okay?" She whispered a quick apology for her interruption before whisking him away.

Thea took advantage of her moments alone to study the other guests. Everyone appeared jovial and seemed to be enjoying the relaxed atmosphere Elena had created. Two handsome, middle-aged men were noticeably enchanted with whatever Max was saying. It was obvious, though, that Monty was the main attraction this evening. Thea continued to watch him closely.

Gone now were the jeans and leather vest. In their place he wore a pair of close-fitting black pants that resembled those of a matador. Black boots and a ruffled white shirt, open almost to the waist, completed his attire. His long hair was again neatly braided, and his only jewelry was a leather belt, laden with silver conchos and turquoise.

His voice, rich and vibrant, carried across the room as he graciously accepted a flurry of compliments on the magnificent bronze sculpture that occupied the sole position atop the room's huge coffee table. The piece was obviously one of Monty's works, and Thea listened intently as he the explained his inspiration for it.

"My father passed away when I was a young boy, but I never forgot his genius for wood carving. I used to sit and watch him for hours as he carved kachina dolls and ceremonial masks." Pleasant childhood memories were reflected on Monty's face as he continued speaking.

"He taught me to carve, but later on I realized I was much more comfortable with clay as a medium. That's how I began to sculpt, but he was always my inspiration." He finished speaking and directed his gaze downward to rest on the bronze depiction of a Native American, regal in presentation, his hands poised above his carving tools.

Thea was drawn more and more toward this man, as was everyone else within earshot, she observed. Mrs. Carter's eyes were misty with emotion, and Yolanda was, in a word, spellbound. Thea returned her attention to Monty only to find his eyes riveted on her. She had certainly received her share of admiring glances in the past, but none equaled the intensity of his gaze. Those smoky eyes seemed to bore straight through to the center of her soul, demanding her attention. Oblivious to others around him, he continued to hold her eyes. Thea had no wish to disentangle herself from that gaze, and had Paul not broken through her trance, she might never have.

"May I have the pleasure of escorting you to the table, my dear?" Paul asked.

Thea realized that Elena had announced dinner some moments ago, and most of the guests were already making their way into the formal dining room. She took the strong arm offered her and smiled at her host. "My pleasure, Paul," she answered with a fleeting hope that no one would notice the breathless quality of her voice, spoken through what felt to be swollen lips.

～

As with all of Elena's social events, the dinner party was a total success. The food, Southwestern fare, was delicious, and the complement of several excellent wines made for a stimulating evening. Topics of conversation throughout the dinner ranged from politics, understandably so, with Santa Fe being the state capital, to everyone's passion—art.

Thea could not help but notice how skillfully Elena skirted the subject of children and grandchildren. Each time the topic arose, she deftly turned it elsewhere so as to avoid any awkward situation should Thea be asked about family.

The expansive dining room seated the twelve diners comfortably, and Thea was almost sorry when Paul stood to announce brandy on the large patio outdoors. This was a signal that the party was nearing its end, and since they were seated several places apart at the table, Thea had had no chance to talk to Monty further.

It was a complete surprise to her when he gently took her elbow during their stroll through the French doors into the cool night air. "Will you have dinner with me tomorrow night, Thea?"

He had caught her off guard, and she was amazed at her presence of mind to remember a previous obligation. "I can't, Monty. I have an Arts Council board meeting tomorrow."

"Then the next night. I'll stay over." It was a statement, rather than a question, and was accompanied by the slightest increase in pressure of his hand on her arm.

"Yes." It was all she could say.

"Good. I'll call you tomorrow." His eyes locked once again with hers briefly before he left her side to formally toast their hostess for the delightful evening.

Soon afterward, the guests began to leave. Monty said his good nights and retired to the guest quarters upstairs, leaving just Paul, Elena, Max, Yolanda, and Thea. They lounged comfortably on the moonlit patio, making small talk, until Yolanda yawned sleepily. "I'm going to the powder room, and then we should really be going, girls."

"Yes. Elena, Paul, it was a wonderful dinner!" Thea warmly thanked the couple as she rose to leave. "I don't know when I've had a more enjoyable evening!"

"You made quite an impression, my dear." Elena couldn't help but show her enthusiasm as she lovingly teased her young friend. "Why, Monty was positively livid with me for not seating you next to him at the dinner table!" she continued playfully.

"See?" Max said. "Always listen to your old buddy, Max!" She pointed to herself in mock bravado. "I told you that white dress was a winner!"

"You certainly do look lovely this evening, Thea," Paul said, joining the conversation. "But you need not have gone to any trouble to impress a certain man. That was accomplished yesterday."

Yolanda returned to the group, and after more good-natured teasing, the three women prepared to leave.

Elena drew Thea aside and whispered, "He is a man like no other, Thea—a good man. Indeed, everyone noticed that he could not take his eyes off of you!"

The rush of embarrassment brought about by the ribbing of her friends rendered Thea totally speechless. She simply smiled her good-byes with her cheeks burning and her thoughts spinning.

37

Thea awoke the following morning to a monstrous headache. Too much wine coupled with regrets from the previous evening did not mix well. She wished she had not agreed to have dinner with Monty, but how would she get out of it? She didn't want to hurt his feelings, and she certainly couldn't offend Paul and Elena.

Gingerly, she sat up in bed and looked around her bedroom. Her dress and shoes lay in a heap on the floor where she had dropped them before falling into bed. She hadn't even brushed her teeth! She groaned as the telephone rang, jarring her senses. Something told her it was Max calling.

"I need coffee," Thea pleaded moments later as her premonition proved true.

"I'm on my way," Max responded, laughing at her best friend's obvious misery.

"Max, tell me I did *not* agree to go on a date with Monty!" Thea lamented a short while later as sat huddled on her couch, sipping the much-needed caffeine.

"What's wrong with going to dinner with him, Thea?" Max asked. "It's high time you began going out. And don't tell me you're not attracted to him," she added. "He's gorgeous!"

Thea's chin began to quiver, and Max saw that she was on the verge of tears. Sooner or later her friend would have to confront that old nemesis of self-doubt that stalked her. Maybe now was the time, though. Max moved closer to Thea and laid a comforting hand on hers. "Talk to me, kiddo," she said quietly.

Thea drew a deep breath. "Max, last night I felt like I was sixteen years old again," she confessed. "No, wait—I didn't feel this way when I *was* sixteen!" Thea realized that in truth she had never felt this way about a man, not even Joe. "Joe and I knew we were going to get married when we were in junior high. There was never any doubt for either of us. And for a long time it was good—and then it wasn't," she finished flatly.

Thea rose from her cross-legged position on the couch to wander across her small living room to the window. "But," she continued thoughtfully, "I never felt this, this—I don't know—this excitement for Joe. Maybe 'cause he was always there, always steady."

For Thea, there had been no other relationships. Her few escorts to college dances when Joe couldn't get away from his schoolwork to take her had been her only dating experiences. She reminded Max of this fact.

"Even then, I always made it clear that I was engaged to someone. I always told them it was just friendship—" Her voice trailed off, her mind once again in a whirl.

"What exactly do you know about Monty?" Max said, breaking the brief silence.

"Not much, actually. Only what's here in this brochure." Thea handed her friend a color pamphlet featuring several artists from the Taos area. "Look on page five. There's a write-up on Monty."

"Let's see." Max began skimming the article, reading aloud. "Says here he owns a ranch with horses, he loves to ride, likes the mountains, born and raised in Taos, Native American and Hispanic—obviously. We knew that. Navajo tribe, been sculpting since his teens, won best bronze category six years in a row, terrific. Okay, where's the good stuff?"

She skimmed further down. "Here we go: thirty-five years old, single—good, good. Lives alone except for the couple who work for him. Kiddo," Max said as she dropped the brochure on the table. "He sounds perfect to me!"

"He does to me, too," Thea replied. "And that's the problem."

"Am I missing something?" Max asked. "What's wrong with a little perfection?"

"I'm just not ready to enter into another relationship, not that he's offering one," Thea answered. "He could be showing me some attention merely as a favor to Paul and Elena. We'll go to dinner tomorrow night, and that will be the end of it. We'll be just a couple of friends having dinner together, talking about our art." Her voice trailed off again as she lapsed into silence, her eyes losing focus. "I'm only imagining something that doesn't exist!" she finished matter-of-factly.

"And you really believe that's all there is to it?" Max asked her incredulously.

After more silence, Thea responded bleakly, "No, Max. I guess I don't."

38

As arranged, Monty arrived the following evening promptly at six o'clock. "Come in, please, Monty." Thea hoped she sounded calm. "Would you like a cocktail before we go?"

"I drink only a little wine, sometimes a brandy," he informed her as he graciously declined her offer. "Perhaps we could have a nice wine at dinner?"

"Sounds good. Before we go, I wonder if you'd mind looking at some more of my pottery. The last couple of days have been quite productive," Thea said.

She watched nervously a short while later as he carefully examined first one and then another of her vessels. Finally, he turned to her and smiled—a little sadly, she thought.

"I do hope you're completely ready for success." His voice held a note of concern as he gazed from her to her work and then back again. "I know pottery, and these pieces are among the finest I've seen in a very long time."

"Oh, Monty, do you mean it?" Thea bounced up and down with exuberance. "I—I don't know what to say! Thank you! You've no idea how much it means to me to have your approval!"

Thea realized she had grasped both of his hands and continued to hold them tightly. Suddenly self-conscious, she attempted to pull away only to be restrained with increased pressure from his strong grip.

Compelled now to meet the smoldering depths of his gaze, she felt herself becoming weak and lost within his presence. *Slow down, girl!* Her inner voice finally broke through the mist to recapture her sensibilities. "Should we be going now?" she asked as calmly as possible.

A bit of the luster receded from his eyes as he lifted her hands to his lips for a touch as fleeting as a butterfly's. "As you wish," he answered quietly.

They both remained silent, walking side by side until they reached Canyon Road, but Thea knew that volumes had been spoken between them.

"It promises to be a beautiful evening," Monty said. "Do you mind walking to the restaurant?" His question ended the moment that Thea wished could last forever.

"Of course not. I love to walk. Where are we going?"

"La Plazuela, the dining room at La Fonda, the oldest inn in Santa Fe. It's one of my favorites. I hope you'll like it."

"I'm sure I will," she answered, calmer now that their easy conversation seemed to have returned.

The walk was a pleasant one, and soon they were seated in the historic courtyard dining room. It became obvious to Thea almost immediately that she would have to share her famous escort with quite a few admirers.

"I do apologize for these interruptions," Monty said, reacting with both pride and boyish embarrassment at being recognized so often. "I have many friends here in Santa Fe, and I haven't had a chance to visit with them very much lately. Now that my latest work is at the foundry, I hope to have more time to socialize."

He stopped speaking to taste the soup and then continued. "I want to see you again."

Caught off guard once more, Thea flinched as her soup spoon clattered loudly against her bowl. "I'd like that very much."

She forced herself to look away and was relieved when he began speaking matter-of-factly about his home and studio in Taos.

Time raced by as the two of them finished their meal and sat sipping wine until almost eleven o'clock. *How interesting he is to talk to. Still, I know no more of him now than I did before tonight,* Thea thought in bewilderment as their evening neared its end.

"Monty, what did you mean when you said you hoped I was ready for success?" she asked as they neared her driveway.

"Success can change people drastically, Thea," he answered thoughtfully. "Sometimes it can enhance a person's life by bringing about a much-needed maturity and happiness. You must remember, though, that with success comes responsibility, not only to your following but to yourself. Sadly, many people do not realize this until it is too late."

Thea looked at his handsome face in the moonlight and was confused by the sadness she saw reflected there. "Surely your success has made you happy."

"I was not necessarily speaking of myself." He turned to her, and she saw the tragic expression of a moment ago slip from his face. "We will talk more another time. I have to go home tomorrow, but I'll call you."

They had reached Thea's front porch and stood together, their features obscured by the shadows. Expectedly, his hands rose to cup her chin, tilting her head slightly back. There was not the slightest bit of doubt in her mind that the thundering of her heartbeat could be heard throughout the city as velvet lips left their gossamer touch on the corner of her mouth.

"Good night, Thea."

Sometime later, she wandered indoors and absently prepared for what would no doubt be an achingly sleepless night.

39

True to Thea's expectations, winter introduced a new element of artistry to New Mexico. The trees, stripped of their fiery autumn cloaks, now stood naked against the brilliance of the snowy landscape, and sagebrush and rock were transformed into frosty little mounds. Santa Fe snoozed.

Christmas lights had been strung throughout the city square and twinkled in the early dawn as Thea walked alone. Her group of walkers had dwindled in the cold winter months, and she welcomed the solitude. It gave her a chance to reflect on the changes in her life during the past year.

Could it be December already? She shook her head in amazement. How the time had flown since she and Max had moved here, especially since she had met Monty. The expected sadness and depression of the holiday season that had begun last month still hung over her, but it had been eased somewhat this year. The ache within her heart was just a little less painful.

And he'll be here tonight! Her pulse quickened at the thought. The two of them had had only brief, rushed visits since their first date nearly three months earlier. Besieged by invitations ranging from artist's receptions at galleries showing his works to lecturing at the art institute, Monty's free hours were rare. "Remember, I told you success has its responsibilities," he had reminded Thea after countless broken dates.

"One day, dear, you'll have the same hectic schedule," Elena had comforted her the previous day after listening to Thea bemoan the fact that she might never truly get to know this man who had piqued her interest and, she feared, captured her heart. "When you are a world-famous potter, Thea, your friends will see less and less of you."

Elena herself had been busy for weeks preparing for a jewelry show in Los Angeles. Monty was planning to stay at the Ramirez house, but with the couple out of town and Max on a skiing trip, Thea realized just how alone she and Monty would be that weekend.

After her walk, she spent the day aimlessly puttering in her studio, accomplishing nothing. She tried working, but concentration was impossible. Her emotions were a constant scrimmage of anticipation and misgivings as she moved toward the evening with frazzled nerves.

~

Her schoolgirl jitters yielded to a woman's desire when, promptly at six o'clock, she opened her door to his smoldering gaze, warm smile, and maddeningly brief embrace. After each of their rushed visits or phone calls, Thea would close her eyes, romanticizing, imagining the taste of his mouth, the feel of his embrace—

"How've you been, Thea? You look wonderful!" Monty stepped past her to warm himself before the fire in the kiva. "I don't think we'll be walking to dinner tonight. The weather is freezing," he continued. "Do you mind going to La Fonda again?"

"No, of course not," Thea replied. "It's lovely there." She shook off the dizzying effects of his presence and managed light conversation as she proudly showed her latest pottery pieces.

"I'm quite proud of these, Monty. What do you think of them?" She studied him now as he critiqued her replicas of Grecian urns. *He handles them as if they were newborn babies!* As she listened absently to Monty's praises, Thea realized she wasn't nearly as concerned with his opinion of her pottery as with her personally.

"I'm sorry," she apologized, embarrassed by her inattention. "What were you saying?"

Monty laughed. "I merely said that you're going to be the most famous potter Santa Fe has seen in ages. And the most beautiful, too," he told her quietly. He then added, "We should be going. Are you hungry?"

"Starving," she answered him, gathering her coat and gloves. "Now, I want to hear all about your latest bronze. Did you bring sketches?"

~

It was obvious to Thea throughout their dinner that Monty was most relaxed discussing art. He proudly showed her his drawings of the Indian warrior on horseback, poised for battle, his current work in progress. He shared with her his thoughts on emerging new talents in the art world. And with her permission, he intended to mention her name to several writers he knew who were interested in doing pieces on Santa Fe art.

Their conversation was lively without a doubt, but Thea longed to know more about Montana Arroyo, the man. Discretion and restraint, however, kept her from bombarding him with personal questions. She told herself to be patient; in time he would certainly share more of himself with her.

"I have a very fine bottle of brandy Paul gave me last week," Thea said as the waiter cleared their table. "Would you like to go back to the house for a nightcap?"

"Sounds wonderful," he replied. "We can decide how to spend the rest of our weekend. If you like, we could pack up and go to a ski lodge. It's a beautiful drive. You do ski, don't you?"

His sudden exuberance was contagious. "I don't, but maybe you could teach me," she answered.

They smiled at each other and left the restaurant, arms entwined, laughing and making plans. Thea would remember in the days ahead, her hopes dashed, how an evening that had begun so perfectly could have ended in such disaster.

40

"This *is* a good brandy!" Monty proclaimed, swishing the amber liquid in the snifter, savoring the aroma as much as the taste. "I must see if Paul has another bottle around someplace that I could sneak back to Taos."

Thea added more wood to the fire and then moved to the couch to sit beside Monty, sip her own drink, and study his profile in the firelight. They were comfortable with silence for several minutes.

"Tell me about yourself, Monty," Thea finally said." Do you have family?"

He turned sidelong on the couch to face her. "You first. I want to know everything about you."

Thea remembered Elena's words of advice several weeks earlier in answer to her questions: "Monty's tremendous talent has made him the center of attention almost everywhere he goes. He handles that well, dear, but let's just say his personal life is another matter. I'm sure he'll open up to you in time."

"I'll go first, then," Thea said. "I was born in the Midwest, the Ozark Mountains of Missouri, to be exact. Oh, it's a beautiful place! I don't go back nearly as often as I'd like. My mother died when I was ten, and my dad raised me. He's still my best buddy. You'll like him, I know. He's planning a visit here in the spring." She paused and took a sip of her brandy before continuing.

"I had a wonderful childhood; Mike saw to that. But I see now how sheltered and naïve I was. If I hadn't been, I'm sure I would have married someone stronger, someone I could have counted on. Yes," she went on, a bitterness creeping into her voice, "someone who would've been there for me when I needed him most."

Thea rose abruptly from the couch and began poking at the fire, sending a flurry of sparks up the chimney. Monty allowed her a moment's solitude and then rose to stand behind her.

"Thea," he breathed her name softly as he gently turned her to face him. She lifted her eyes to his, and he saw the fire's flames reflected in those ebony pools. He saw something in her eyes, too, anguish that few people could identify with. "You are thinking of your little daughter, of Alexa. I know. Paul and Elena told me, and my heart weeps for you."

Moments later she was in his arms, her tears moist upon his neck. He held her close for a long time until she lifted her head and turned away to dry her eyes. "Monty, I'm embarrassed. Just when I think there are no more tears left—this time of year is so hard! I didn't mean to put a damper on our evening."

"There's nothing to apologize for. Come, sit back down and talk to me." He led her back to the couch and continued to hold her hand. "Tell me, did your husband leave you? Is that what you meant?"

Thea sniffed, took another sip of brandy, and regained some of her composure. "Oh, no, I wanted the divorce. You see, our marriage was over almost from the time Alexa disappeared because Joe simply gave up hope. He never believed as I did—as I *do*—that she's still alive. He became so dispassionate! He was a wonderful father and loved her so much, and then he just gave up!"

She paused and shook her head. "All he could say was, 'We have to get on with our lives. We can't live in the past.' Can you believe he actually had the nerve to suggest another child to me? Joe and I had a good marriage for a long time, or at least I thought we did. I guess I never really knew him."

Monty watched her, breathless from emotion, still shaking her head and wiping away the last vestige of tears. Of course, her loss was still too recent to mirror anything but pain. And he knew about pain.

"We all grieve in our own ways, Thea. It sounds like to me that your husband held his suffering deep within himself." Monty spoke slowly, choosing his words carefully. "Perhaps he was afraid to even hope that Alexa was still alive. So he put emphasis on you and your future together."

Thea stood abruptly and began turning on the lamps in the living room, dissolving the warm, romantic ambience.

"I hardly think," she said deliberately as she turned squarely to face him, "that you're qualified to analyze a man whom you have never laid eyes on. Let's just drop the subject, shall we? I mean, what could you possibly know about my loss?" She gathered the glasses from the coffee table and walked into the kitchen.

Monty saw all too clearly the path their evening was taking. Wanting to avoid a full-scale disaster, he followed her. "I'm sorry. I didn't mean to upset you. Of course I don't know Joe, but I'm sure as the husband and father, he felt directly responsible for anything that might happen to his family. It's a heavy burden for a man to bear when he cannot protect his loved ones. This I do know."

Thea remained motionless with her back to him, hands planted firmly on the counter in front of her, shoulders rigid. Finally, she spoke.

"You don't need to apologize, Monty. I suppose I expected too much of you. I expected you to feel my pain. But how could you?" Her voice still held its caustic edge as she continued. "There's no way you could know how I felt or how I still feel. People who haven't lost someone as I did can't possibly know—"

"You certainly cannot believe you're the only person who's ever lost a loved one or ever grieved for someone!" Monty cut her off, his own voice rising. "Believe me, Thea, you will in time come to realize what your ex-husband probably realized early on. When one door is closed, another one opens. I was only trying to comfort you!"

"My daughter is *not* a closed door!" Thea's voice rose in anger. She was furious at his calm manner in the face of her tears—tears drawn as much from embarrassment as from remembered pain. Was she ashamed of her outburst? Yes, but she was beyond realizing how out of control her emotions were as she continued her scorching verbal attack.

"And just what do you know of loss, Monty?" Her voice continued to swell with fury, barely controlling the tremor that threatened more tears. "I suppose when you speak of loss, you're referring to the loss of some girlfriend! Am I right? Maybe she jilted you. Is that it? Is that what happened to your precious lady in the fountain? Was she some beautiful young thing that modeled for you and then left you? How dare you even think of comparing whatever tragedy you think you've suffered with the loss of my daughter?"

Breathless and drained from her harangue, Thea turned to walk away only to find herself jerked into an about-face and anchored by his vice-like grip. Huge hands that might have caressed her lovingly now imprisoned her shoulders painfully. She was firmly pinned against the kitchen counter by the rock-hard muscles of his torso and forced to look into his face. He was so close now that she could feel the breath from his mouth—a mouth she knew for its fleeting touch that was soft and warm and teasing, but not now. Now that mouth wore a sneer of contempt, and the sound of a low growl escaped his lips. Those eyes no longer held her captive within their smoky depths but burned with a white-hot rage that frightened her. She knew her words had triggered emotions raw and primitive within this man. Frightened as she suddenly was, however, she could not look away.

Finally his grip on her lessened, and he spoke in a slow, measured monotone. "You are way off base, Thea. You are selfish, and you are self-centered!"

"I—" She tried to interrupt him, but he would have none of it.

"Can you possibly think you have a monopoly on grief? How many of your friends, me included, have silently grieved for your loss and have given you our hearts? But you want more, don't you? Poor little Thea—no one hurts like you do! Is that what you think? You're so wrapped up in your own self-pity that you can't see a whole beautiful world out there, a world full of people who admire you." His head dropped and his voice softened almost to a whisper as he continued. "You are blind to a world full of people who care for you."

He released her. They both fell silent, their anger dissolving into regret for words that could never be unsaid. Moments passed, and Thea realized he was preparing to leave.

"Monty, I—"

"Good-bye, Thea."

The front door closed firmly. She stood for what seemed an eternity listening to the silence broken only by the hum of the refrigerator and the creaking of tree limbs as a cold winter wind blew. He was gone.

41

Thea sat at her wheel, ignoring the incessant ringing of the telephone. Outside, twilight had crept in and would soon put an end to her day's work. It had been a good day's work—productive, like yesterday.

She had spent the entire weekend in total silence and work. Now it was Sunday evening, and she didn't have to answer the telephone to know who was calling. Max wasn't due back from her skiing trip until much later, so it had to be Elena calling to inquire how the weekend with Monty had gone. Thea needed a little more time alone before speaking with other people, even close friends.

How strange it was to realize that the more time she spent alone, the less she liked herself. It was a bitter pill to swallow, admitting her selfishness, but it was true. And it had taken someone standing outside of the cocoon she had built around herself since Alexa's disappearance to shake her into reality.

Poor Joe. She could see the hurt on his face even now when she closed her eyes. Joe hadn't known how to point out her faults, Max wouldn't, and Mike—well, he didn't think she had any. It had taken someone like Monty.

After cleaning her work area, Thea grabbed a heavy woolen shawl and went outdoors for a short walk before dark. The cold stung her cheeks and made her eyes water, but it felt good. Breathing the frigid air cleared her head. When she returned to her house half an hour later, darkness had fallen and the telephone was again ringing.

"This time, I'll answer it," she said aloud. "Hello? Elena, how was your trip—profitable, I hope?" She attempted to sound in good spirits but didn't quite pull it off.

Elena's voice carried worry. "Thea, was everything all right this weekend? I don't mean to pry, but it doesn't appear that Monty was here at all. I—"

"Well, he wasn't here, either, Elena." Thea interrupted, realizing at once how tired her voice sounded. "Look, can we talk in the morning? If you and Paul don't have plans, I would like to come over. Is it okay?"

"Dear, of course. We'd love to have you. Please tell me you're all right." The concern in Elena's voice was genuine.

"I'm fine, Elena. I'll see you in the morning."

~

"You said *what* to him? Oh, Paul, I knew we should have warned her! We should have told her!" Elena was beside herself. Holding her head with both hands, she paced back and forth across the living room. Paul and Max remained silent, obviously astonished at Thea's recounting of her evening with Monty.

"Tell me what? What's the big dark secret surrounding him?" Thea demanded loudly. Silently cursing herself, she lowered her voice to plead with her friend. "Please, Paul, help me to understand him. I've been such a selfish fool! I hurt so badly, and I guess that deep down I wanted everyone else to hurt just as much."

Paul leaned back in his chair and studied the young woman for a long time before finally speaking. "Thea, my cousin is a very private man, possibly the most private person I've ever known. He holds his sorrows deep inside and would never want pity. I will tell you part of what happened to him; the rest will have to come from him."

"If he ever gives me the chance," Thea replied despondently. "Go on, Paul. Please tell me what happened to him."

"You've heard Monty speak of his father, the inspiration for all his work? Well, he passed away when Monty was only fourteen. His mother, however, died four years earlier in childbirth. The baby was a little girl." Paul stood, walked to the fireplace, and lit his pipe before continuing.

"The doctors had told Kyle and Shauna that they would never have another child after Monty. But there she was ten years later, little Tondra, the most beautiful baby I've ever seen. Shauna was not a young woman, and the birth was simply too much for her. She died after holding her daughter for only a few moments."

"Monty was always his father's pride and joy," Elena said, taking up the story. "And with the pain of losing his wife, well, Kyle seemed to shower even more attention on Monty. Poor little Tondra—she became his forgotten child."

"Elena is right," Paul said. "Had it not been for young Monty, I dare say the family would not have been held together. You see, he practically raised that little girl. And did he love her! With each passing year, Monty loved her more. She finished high school at seventeen, and I don't think I've seen many fathers who were as proud of a daughter as Monty was of his sister.

"But I'm getting ahead of myself. When Kyle died, the two children went to live with a wonderful couple in Taos, Clayton and Lydia Johns. As a matter of fact, they now live with Monty and help take care of his ranch. But Monty was the one who always cared for Tondra."

"Yes," Elena murmured. "He worshipped that child! She was so beautiful and so happy!"

"What happened to her? Where is she now?" Thea asked, silently dreading the answer.

"I don't want to go into the story. The details need to come from Monty," Paul replied with resolve. "We have discussed his personal life enough."

"Oh, my God," Thea said as she buried her face in her hands. "The cruel things I said to him—*she's* the woman in his fountain, isn't she?"

"Yes, Thea. Your house once belonged to her," Elena said quietly before being silenced by her husband.

"Go to him, Thea. His heart is not hard—believe me. He will listen to you; and when he decides the time is right, he will tell you the rest," Paul said as he smiled and patted Thea's hand. "By the way, my wife is the family's resident matchmaker, but I will say this: you and Monty belong together!"

"I wouldn't know what to say to him." Thea said, still trying to absorb the impact of what Paul and Elena had told her.

"Start with a telephone call," Paul suggested. "Apologize to him, and ask if the two of you can talk. You could offer to drive up to Taos to his ranch."

"Max, will you go with me?" Perhaps we—"

"No," Max interrupted her. "I've got my hands full with the holiday programs at school and moving into the new house."

Thea knew how much it hurt her friend to deny her request as Max averted her gaze and prepared to leave. "You're right. I need to do this on my own. I'll call him tonight. He may never want to talk to me again, but I must try."

42

Thea drove the winding highway slowly. She took her time, not as much to avoid the patches of snow and ice that clung to the road but to enjoy the beauty of the scenery.

To her left, the Rio Grande cut through the rocks like a silvery thread. The river sparkled crystal clear in the morning sun. It looked entirely different from the lazy flow of dark, murky water it became after reaching Texas. On the highway's right, sheer rock faces rose skyward. Thankful she had borrowed Yolanda's Jeep for the trip, she skirted small piles of fallen rocks here and there along the way.

There were few vehicles on the road this morning, and Thea was surprised to realize how much she had enjoyed the solitude of her drive. By her calculations, she had about another forty-five minutes to an hour of driving time to reach Taos, depending on the road conditions.

Time had dragged these past four days, since she had phoned Monty on Monday evening after her visit with Paul and Elena. She remembered now how her heart had pounded, how dry her mouth had felt as she heard the telephone receiver being lifted.

"Yes?"

"I wouldn't blame you if you hung up, Monty, but I hope you won't," she had responded.

He had hesitated only a second. "Hello, Thea." His voice had held no emotion.

"I don't know what to say to you, except I'm so very, very sorry! Monty, if I could start over and take back all I said, I would. I was so wrong!"

"We were both wrong, Thea. I should not have lost my temper. My behavior was inexcusable."

"No, no, everything you said, I deserved." It had been hard to keep her voice from breaking as she continued. "Monty, please, can we talk? I have a great deal to learn. Will you help me?"

"Perhaps we could help each other," he had said.

Thea had been relieved. The heavy cloak of shame had been lifted from her shoulders, leaving her feeling clean and reborn.

Monty had indeed seemed flattered when she volunteered to drive to Taos, expressing her desire to see his ranch and studio, and especially his latest sculpture.

"You're sure you don't mind the drive? There's more snow here than in Santa Fe," he had said with concern.

"I'm pretty good at driving in bad weather, and I'll bring Yolanda's Jeep. She told me to use it whenever I needed it while she's away."

So it was settled. They'd planned her trip for the weekend. "I'll get you a room at the Taos Inn," Monty had offered, his voice becoming a bit warmer. "It's just past the town plaza. You can't miss it. Call when you get there, and I'll give you directions to the ranch."

~

Thea arrived at the inn and was handed an envelope upon checking in at the desk. It was a note from Monty with clear directions on how to reach his ranch north of Taos. She was to dress casually and warmly, in riding clothes, if possible. He would see her soon.

Her room in the historic adobe inn was small but charming. Soon, dressed in layers of warm clothes and boots, Thea was once again on the road. Anxious as she was to see Monty, she barely took time to notice the quaint hamlet of Taos, much smaller than Santa Fe and higher in the Sangre de Cristo Mountains. She did, however, make mental note of the many art galleries scattered throughout the tiny town as she drove north.

She marveled at the magnetic effect Taos was having on her. But that had been true of New Mexico in general ever since her arrival. All around her stood the snow-covered mountains jutting against the brilliance of a cloudless blue sky. Enchanted by the countryside, she almost missed the narrow drive leading to Monty's property.

True to Paul's description, the ranch was a paradise. Thea emerged from the Jeep to gaze in wonder at the large, two-story adobe house, partially obscured by even larger evergreen trees. Horses were exercising in one of several fenced corrals.

She climbed the stone steps leading to the porch as an older man opened the front door to greet her. He stood tall and straight. His thick, silver hair framed a pleasant face, bronzed and creased by the sun. Astonishingly pale blue eyes twinkled as he bestowed a bright smile on her.

"You are Mrs. Kelly, of course. Welcome!"

"Thank you," Thea said, smiling and clasping his outstretched hand. "And you must be Mr. Johns. Please, do call me Thea."

"Only if you agree to call me Clayton. 'Mr. Johns' makes me sound old!" He laughed heartily. "This is my wife, Lydia."

Thea turned to greet the woman. Short and plump, her sweet face aglow and dark eyes shinning, she warmly embraced Thea. "So, this is the woman my Montana speaks of! Welcome, Thea, to our home!"

"Thank you both. You're very kind." Thea liked the couple at once. As they led her into the living room, she was reminded of the Ramirezes' home. The same Southwestern decor prevailed, and she soon felt at home. She was grateful for the constant chatter from both Clayton and Lydia as they informed her with obvious pride that Monty had designed and helped to build the spacious home.

"Of course, all the sculptures you see here and many of the paintings are Monty's," Lydia told Thea.

"You both must be so proud of him!" Thea said as she recognized the love the older couple had for Monty.

"Very proud of his talents, yes, but even prouder of the man," Clayton answered. "Ah, here we sit talking, when it's Monty you've come to see! He is at his studio today. He would like you to ride up, if you care to. We have a full corral of horses for your choosing."

"I'd love it! I haven't ridden in years, and I've missed it. How far is his studio?" The promise of seeing Monty again made Thea's pulse quicken, and she hoped she didn't sound too anxious.

"It's about a mile and a half up the trail. You can't miss it. As a matter of fact, if you allow me to choose a mount for you, I shall choose one who knows the way!" Clayton answered eager to be of assistance.

43

Clayton did indeed choose the perfect mount for Thea. Boots, the young gelding named for his distinctive markings, accepted her without hesitation. His keen animal instincts recognized her immediately as someone who not only knew how to handle horses but someone who loved them as well.

The ride to Monty's studio was pleasant. The A-frame log structure stood nestled among a huge stand of snow-laden fur trees, its front of solid glass basking in the southern exposure. Thea dismounted and looped Boots's reins loosely around the hitching post. She was immediately welcomed by the yipping of a small border collie, which proceeded to run circles around her, obviously delighted to have company.

"Sheba, stay down!" Thea turned at the sound of his voice to see Monty striding briskly down the path from the front porch, smiling as he neared her. "I'm glad you came. I hope you didn't mind the ride up here. I'm behind schedule for getting a piece to the foundry, so I'm doing a little overtime," he continued, taking Thea's hands between his as a way of greeting.

"I didn't mind at all, Monty. I love to ride. Your ranch is absolutely beautiful! And so are Clayton and Lydia. They made me feel very welcome. This is Sheba, you said?"

"Yes, I'm afraid she has me trained quite well. I got her to help round up stray cattle, but she's too smart for that. About all she does is lie by the fire and be a distraction." In spite of his gruff manner, Thea could see he adored the frisky dog.

They walked hand in hand to the open door with Sheba bounding happily in front of them. Impressed as Thea had been with Monty's home, as she entered the studio, she was overwhelmed. One huge room, giving rise to a twenty-foot ceiling, enveloped her. Against the wall, spaces between windows held shelves overflowing with books. Soft leather couches flanked the stone fireplace, and thick bearskin rugs dotted the Mexican-tile floor. A circular staircase led to what appeared to be a loft bedroom.

"Do you like it?" Monty asked almost shyly after several minutes of silence. He was obviously proud of the studio, and he should have been. His essence was everywhere. He belonged here, and Thea told him so.

"I don't know if I would have the discipline to work here," she commented, walking to the huge front window to gaze at the breathtaking mountains. "Why, I could just sit and enjoy the view!" She turned to face him now and found him grinning with delight at her compliments.

"You are welcome here anytime, Thea. Anytime." He spoke quietly, his eyes locking with hers, willing—no, commanding—her not to look away.

Finally, she was able to break the spell. She cleared her throat and drew a deep breath, preparing herself for what needed to be said. "Monty, I am so sorry for the way I acted last weekend. The terrible things I said to you can never be taken back, but I want you to know, you opened my eyes, and—"

"Thea," he interrupted her, "I had no call to chastise you the way I did. Sometimes, this hot temper of mine gets way out of hand. I, too, am sorry."

Thea felt the rush of relief. He was making this very easy for her. "You made me realize how self-centered I've become, Monty. What's worse is that I am finally able to see what a shallow person I was, even before Alexa's disappearance."

They both fell silent for several minutes. Thea, needing to purge her thoughts, struggled to find the words. After a time, she continued speaking.

"Even when my life seemed so flawless, I think I always knew that it lacked substance. Joe and I—we just breezed through life. We never had to struggle. We never had a *cause*, Monty, and people need causes! Oh, I certainly am not saying you need to lose a child to develop character, but I do know I'm a better person today. I've acted as though my grief is all that matters, and it isn't. You matter to me, and I hope you know that.

"Paul doesn't talk of your personal life," she continued, changing the subject. "But he did tell me that you, too, had suffered a great tragedy. I want to help." She had moved close to him now, and laid her hand on his arm. "Can I help?" she asked in a whisper.

Thea could sense the opposing forces within him fighting one another. He remained rigid for several minutes before he spoke.

"Do you feel like riding a little further up the mountain today? There's a place I would like to show you. It isn't far."

"Of course!" Thea exclaimed, once again buttoning her coat around her. Intuition was a strange thing, and hers was telling her at that very moment that their relationship was back on track.

44

"Sheba certainly seems to know where we're going," Thea said, her breath coming in gasps. They had ridden the horses farther up the mountainside and then tethered them to a small tree before proceeding on foot.

"She knows," Monty replied. "I haven't been up here this winter, but I used to come often. There's a well-worn riding trail; it's easy going when the snow's not covering the ground. We're here."

The moment they rounded the side of the hill, a view like none other took Thea's breath away. "This must be the most beautiful place on earth," she murmured reverently. Range after range of mountains spread before them, their snowy peaks rising to kiss the heavens.

The late afternoon sun glinting on the partially exposed granite caught Thea's eye, drawing her. For a long time, the two of them stood side by side, not moving, not talking. Finally, Monty broke the silence by reading aloud the words etched on the monument.

"Tondra Star Arroyo, born June 1, 1976, died June 13, 1997; beloved sister. This was always her favorite place. She would come here to think, to dream." His voice broke painfully as he struggled to speak. "I brought her ashes here."

"What happened, Monty?" Thea asked him quietly.

He knelt and proceeded to brush the drifted snow from the base of the marker. "Until I saw you, I thought Tondra the most beautiful woman I had ever seen. Of course," he smiled sadly up at Thea before continuing, "I suppose I was prejudiced, considering I practically raised her."

He stood up and dusted the snow from his jeans. To Thea's relief, he suddenly seemed anxious to talk. "We were so close all her life, much closer than most siblings. We hardly ever had a cross word. We were each other's best friend partly because we shared such a love for our arts. After Father died, our heritage was all we had.

"I soon found my niche in sculpture, and Tondra—she could have been world famous with her weaving. Authentic Navajo rugs bring high prices, and she had already won countless awards before she was nineteen. Everyone loved her and her work. She was well on her way toward achieving success in the art world—that is, until *he* came, with his lies and his poison!"

His last words were uttered with such hatred and venom that Thea shuddered involuntarily. "Who is *he*?" she asked gently.

"Jeb Collins," he answered her, his voice cold, his countenance dark and brooding. They had walked to a large flat boulder and, after clearing away the snow, sat side by side. Monty drew a deep breath and spoke again.

"Tondra wanted to move to Santa Fe after she finished high school. The move made good sense. She could take college courses in the evenings and have the days free to weave her rugs. She lived in your house, Thea. I bought it for her."

"And she was the woman in your fountain. Monty, I'm so sorry!" As her tears fell unchecked, Thea realized that for the first time in over two years, she was crying for someone else's pain and loss instead of her own. "Tell me what happened," she prompted.

"I had gone to visit her for the weekend, and I knew what was going on the instant she opened the door and I saw her face. She was in love. My baby sister was in love. I could see it in her eyes, the way they sparkled, and I could hear it in her voice. She sounded so happy, like a babbling brook. And I was right. She told me his name was Jeb, and he was going to join us for dinner.

"Well, my first impressions are rarely wrong. I knew he was no good the moment I met him. He and his group of friends were bikers from Los Angeles. They came to Santa Fe *sightseeing*, he said. I suspected from the beginning but couldn't prove that they were selling drugs."

Thea said, "Tondra fell under the spell of the unknown. Am I right?"

"Yes. You've never seen such a drastic change come over a young woman. Everyone noticed it. All her life, she had absolutely adored Paul and Elena. She thought Elena was the most graceful lady and said time and time again how she wanted to be just like her. But after only a couple of weeks of Jeb's influence, she stopped visiting them. She wouldn't even answer her telephone.

"He moved in with her right away. I didn't like it, of course, but I never said anything. After all, she was nearly twenty years old by that time, and, to tell you the truth, I figured he'd get bored and move on soon enough. I was a coward, you see. I didn't want to lose my temper and have Tondra end up hating me."

"It sounds to me like you tried to do the right thing, Monty, by letting her grow up and try her wings. How long did Jeb stay?"

"Too long! The worst thing about that bastard was the way he ridiculed her in front of his biker buddies, and everyone else, for that matter. He—" Monty's voice broke as painful memories enveloped him. "He made fun of the way she dressed and of her weavings. He called her his squaw! I couldn't even begin to know what kind of a hold he had on her—drugs, sex, whatever—but she stopped weaving her rugs. Thea, he made her ashamed of her people, of her heritage!"

"Where is he now?"

"Dead and burning in hell, I hope! In truth, I do not know. He stayed most of a year living off Tondra. The last time she and I were together was at her house—I mean, at your house. Paul and I had gone by to see her. She wouldn't open the door, so I kicked it in. Jeb was there, and I told him to get out. He opened his smart mouth, and I closed it for him. Thea, I hit him so hard that he was unconscious for twenty minutes!

"Then Tondra and I *did* fight. I said some horrible things to her, things that will always haunt me. I—I hit her, too. I told her how she'd shamed me, our parents' memory, her people, but mostly herself.

"We left then. Actually, Paul dragged me out the door. I came back to Taos the next morning and told Clayton and Lydia everything. They both cried like babies. They'd looked after Tondra and me after Father died and had such hopes for us both.

"Then, oh, about two weeks after our fight, I got a letter from Tondra telling me she was going to Los Angeles with him. She said she loved me and was sorry she'd disappointed me, but they were in love. *Love*! She was just a kid! What did she know about being in love? I never wrote her. I never even called. I guess my pride wouldn't let me. When I finally did calm down enough to go and try to find her, it was too late. Too late!"

Thea waited quietly until his emotions were once more in check before she spoke. "Was there an accident?"

"The worst part about losing someone who is practically your whole life is admitting that you are more than a little to blame," Monty answered, a faraway look clouding his face as the memory unfolded. "It was no accident, Thea. Tondra was murdered."

"Mur—oh, Monty, how horrible! But how can you blame yourself?"

"A few days before her twenty-first birthday, I decided to swallow my stupid pride, fly to LA, and talk to her. I missed her so much that I couldn't concentrate on my work. And with Clayton and Lydia worrying constantly about her welfare, this was a sad home for all of us. I needed to see her. I wanted to try and understand her feelings. It's hard for me to admit, but I do seem to have trouble understanding the opinions of others when they differ from mine." Monty said, smiling wanly at Thea, no doubt referring to his part in their earlier argument.

"So, you went to LA?" She prompted gently, anxious to learn of the young woman's fate yet dreading the details.

"I had hired a private investigator soon after Tondra left, so I knew her whereabouts. Jeb had apparently grown tired of her and had disappeared, just as I figured he would. The investigator found her living in a cheap apartment in a tough, inner-city neighborhood. He gave me the name of a bar she was working at—ahh," Monty groaned, again suffering from the pain his memories evoked.

Thea gripped his arm firmly and waited in silence until he regained his composure.

"When I got to LA, I went straight to Tondra's apartment, but she wasn't there. Another young woman, obviously strung out, opened the door. All I could see beyond her was a dark, smoky room. She said Tondra was at work, told me where the bar was located, and then slammed the door in my face.

"I found her about an hour later." Monty's voice dropped once again to its flat, toneless quality, and Thea knew that even as he related the story, he was trying to blot out the image.

"She was working as a topless dancer. She, uh, she was up on stage when I went in, wearing a G-string, boots, and nothing else. I'll never forget her eyes. They appeared glazed, like she was in a trance. And her face held no expression. She just moved to the music like some pathetic little puppet!"

"Did you talk to her?"

He shook his head. "I left without her ever seeing me. I couldn't look at her like that, and I knew she wouldn't have wanted me to. I turned and left that bar, and I had never felt so alone in my life, not even when Father died. That girl meant everything to me, almost like she was my daughter!

No, I couldn't talk to her. And because of my weakness and my pride, she's dead, and I have to live with that!" He spat out those final words, ridding himself of their vile taste.

"No, Monty, it wasn't your fault! What could you have done?"

"I could have climbed up on that stage, picked up my sister, and taken her out of that God-forsaken place! I could have brought her back home, cleaned her up, held her while she cried, and told her everything would be okay like I did when she was a little girl!"

Monty closed his eyes and took a deep breath before continuing. "I could have gotten her some counseling and told her I loved her more than anything. I could have saved her!" He wept then, and Thea joined him.

After a few minutes, he continued the story. "She was raped—raped, beaten, and stabbed to death in an alley behind that very same bar less than two weeks after I was there."

Monty's revelation took Thea completely by surprise, and an audible gasp escaped her lips. "Did the police catch him?" she asked in a shaky voice.

"The police caught *them*, and quite soon, too. There were four of them—eighteen, nineteen years old, high on drugs. They were members of a gang." Monty spoke slowly, in short phrases, measuring his words. "It was, they told police, an initiation!

"My name and address were found in her purse. I got a call the morning after they found the—after they found her. I flew back. I had to identify the body, you see. Strangely enough, it was easier to look at her lying there in the morgue, peaceful and scrubbed clean, than it had been seeing her up on that barroom stage. Is that crazy?"

"No, it isn't crazy. It's the way our emotions work," Thea answered. "It was easier for me after watching the man who took Alexa confess to all those abductions and the murders than it was before they caught him. Knowing made it a little clearer, I suppose."

"Ah, Thea, come here!" Monty pulled her to him with a force that very nearly made her lose her breath. She was held prisoner by his powerful arms but no more so than by his eyes that bored deep into hers. Even through the layers of thick winter clothing, she could feel the hardness of him pressing against her. Ever so slowly, she lifted her arms to encircle his neck, drawing his head down, wanting his mouth on hers.

But when his kiss finally came, it was not the gentle, teasing one she had fantasized about for so long. Instead, his lips met hers with a crushing fury, surprising her with their near-brutal force. His gloved hands roughly pushed back the hood of her parka, and his fingers entwined themselves in the thick fall of her hair. A small cry escaped her lips as he roughly tugged her hair, forcing her head further back.

Suddenly, the pressure of his arms relaxed; the intensity of his bruising kiss lessened. "My God, how I want you!" he said. "Since the first day I laid eyes on you!" Stepping back, he held her at arm's length, his eyes burning into hers.

"Forgive me, I didn't mean to be rough or to hurt you. I only—"

"Again, Monty," she demanded, her voice husky with desire. "Kiss me again!"

Slowly and with measured movements, he removed the thick gloves from his hands and pulled her gently to him. His fingers moved feather-soft over the contours of her face, stroking her swollen lips and moving down to gently cup her chin. All the while, his paralyzing caress was accompanied by soft, unintelligible murmurings.

Weakly, she whispered his name as lips cool and pliant descended upon hers. Her mouth opened to the gentle urging of his tongue, and she tasted the sweetness of him mingled with the salt of their tears.

"Stay with me tonight, Thea," he whispered against her ear.

"I—I shouldn't," came her fragile reply. Even as she protested, though, she knew her room at the inn would remain unused.

"Stay with me!" His breath was coming quicker and his embrace once again demanding.

"Yes." It was all she could say as his mouth silenced all but a faint whimper.

They were torn apart only by their realization of approaching nightfall and Sheba's impatient whining. But not even the sudden chill of winter's wind could penetrate the glow that blanketed Thea as they mutely made their way back to their mounts. Weak and trembling, she failed three times to grasp the horse's reins before Monty came to her assistance. After giving her a leg up and fitting the reins snuggly into her hands, he mounted his own horse and turned to look at her. His face was free of the gloomy mask he so often wore.

"I will try to never disappoint you, love," he vowed simply.

Love! The way he spoke the word was a caress within itself to Thea—a long-needed caress. "I know that, Monty."

45

"Clayton, Lydia, dinner was delicious!" Thea complimented the Johns several hours later after enjoying the veritable feast the couple had prepared in her honor. "Thank you. And the atmosphere was just as wonderful," she added.

The four of them sat before the crackling fire in Monty's living room, sipping brandy and talking easily. As a matter of fact, Thea found the Johns very pleasant companions, as if they were old friends.

"It was a pleasure, my dear," Lydia replied, happy with the praise. "Our Monty entertains so seldom these days, we don't often get a chance to prepare our favorites dishes."

"I have been remiss in repaying a number of social obligations lately," Monty said thoughtfully. "Perhaps Thea will agree to help us host an artists' reception in the spring. How about it, Thea?"

"Oh, well, I suppose I could." Caught somewhat off guard by the personal implication of his suggestion, as well as the casual presence of his hand on her knee, she found herself momentarily at a loss for words. "Of course, Monty. I'd be happy to help," she finally answered.

"Fine!" Monty said, grinning devilishly at the faint flush on her cheeks.

Thea realized Clayton and Lydia were beaming at her, too, and she was relieved when the conversation turned to business several minutes later. The two men began making plans to transport Monty's sculpture to the foundry just outside Santa Fe. Thea's mild embarrassment returned soon, however, as she found herself suppressing a yawn.

"My dear, you must be exhausted after your long drive and the ride!" Lydia exclaimed, rising to her feet. "And here we are boring you with talk of business!"

"No, Lydia, you're not boring me in the least. I just—" Thea's apology was gently cut short by Monty.

"Thea has accepted our hospitality to spend the weekend here. We'll retrieve her things from the inn tomorrow when we go into Taos," Monty informed the couple.

"Wonderful! Shall I make up the guest suite?" Lydia asked, obviously pleased with the news that Thea would be staying.

"We'll manage, Lydia. Thanks." Monty settled the issue.

"Well, then, we will see you tomorrow, Thea. Rest well," Clayton said as he rose to bid good night. Thea noticed that his blue eyes twinkled a bit brighter than before.

A short time later, she stood alone in front of the fireplace, staring at the flickering flames, her mind a jumble. She knew her life was moving forward and that after tonight, she would not be the same. While she wanted Monty in her life, at the same time misgivings gnawed at her. What if she suffered another failed relationship and another heartache? She did not believe she could survive another loss. This time things would be different, wouldn't they?

She was vaguely aware of Monty's movements in the kitchen as he spoke quietly to Sheba, settling her for the night and turning off lights as he made his way back to the living room. His moccasin-clad feet padded soundlessly across the floor as he came to stand behind her.

Strong hands gently encircled her waist as his head bent to nuzzle the hollow of her neck. Quietly, he spoke. "I hope I didn't make you feel awkward about staying here."

"Umm ..." she could hardly speak as the pressure of his hands and lips increased. "A little embarrassed, I suppose. Monty—"

Thea leaned against him now, her eyes closed, her senses ignited. His cologne, mingled with the faint scent of leather and clay, assailed her nostrils, intoxicating her. His hands left her waist and continued their upward trek. His open palms brushed feather-soft over the fullness of her breasts, causing her nipples to stand erect.

Finally, she found her voice. "Make love to me, Monty—slowly, and for a long, long time."

Her whispered desire caused him to shudder violently. She felt herself being lifted by strong arms. Effortlessly he carried her up the stairs, all the while whispering his words against her ear. They were unintelligible, foreign-sounding little words she did not understand—words she did not need to understand.

She lay naked on his king-sized bed, her skin prickling not from the sudden chill but from anticipation. The night's full moon shining through the windows and the glow of embers in the corner kiva illuminated the room as Monty stepped from the adjoining bath. His tall frame rippled with muscles as he walked slowly, catlike, toward her.

Without speaking, he lowered himself to the bed. His mouth met hers and then pulled away to leave its torturous trail over her entire body. As her soft flesh welcomed him, a rhythm as old as time itself took possession of the lovers. They moved together, each one giving and taking as their passions mounted.

Soft moans and whispered words crested in cries as their release came. A release that, for both man and woman, was as much emotional as physical.

~

Faint streaks of pink appeared like brushstrokes across the early morning sky. It was Monty's favorite time of day. He sat before the newly built fire in the living room and sipped his morning coffee. He'd risen well before dawn, easing himself from the still-damp sheets, being careful not to wake her. He had stood looking down at her image in the lamp light for a long time, drinking in the sight of her, then had dressed quickly and silently crept from the room.

He closed his eyes now, still seeing her sleeping form in his mind. How innocent she'd looked, almost childlike, and so different from the arduous woman of the night before. His belly tightened once again at the memory of their lovemaking.

But Thea Kelly was more than just a beautiful woman with whom he wanted to have sex—so much more. She was intelligent, talented, fun, and strong. The thought of her little girl passed through Monty's mind. He shook his head, unable to grasp the grief that had most surely overwhelmed the young mother.

"At least I have closure," he whispered aloud, letting his mind linger on Tondra's fate and on his own mourning. It was a mourning that needed to be laid to rest.

His step quickened as he climbed the stairs later, coffee tray in hand. There were so many places he wanted to take Thea, so many things he couldn't wait to show her. The sun was up as he entered the bedroom; it was going to be a beautiful day.

"Good morning, sleepyhead," he said. "Ready for some coffee?"

Thea stretched languidly before reaching out to him. "Maybe later," she replied throatily, her meaning crystal clear.

And crystal clear were Monty's thoughts at that very moment. He could not remember exactly when the first pangs of loneliness had surfaced in his life. It was early on, though, even before Tondra had gone away. The emptiness within him had been a void that could not be filled, until now.

Is this what it felt like to be in love? Maybe so, but he wouldn't tell her right away. After thirty-five years, he needed a little time to get used to the idea himself.

46

The mesh-covered opening in the metal door was narrow but afforded a full view of the kitchen beyond. "You 'bout done with them dishes, Dobbs?" the guard inquired gruffly as he watched the other man methodically wash and rinse the stacks of tin plates.

Hurley halted his progress just long enough to look at the guard with deadpan eyes and nod his head slightly.

W. D. Barnett certainly didn't expect a verbal answer to his question; everybody knew this crazy bastard couldn't talk. He wouldn't want the opportunity to lord his authority over a prisoner to slip by, though. The guard lingered at the window for several minutes, casually observing Hurley as he resumed his annoyingly slow-paced assault on the dirty dishes. Over and over, he scrubbed each plate with the soapy sponge before dipping it into the steamy rinse water. He wore no rubber gloves and didn't even flinch when his hands entered the hot water. *Probably doesn't even feel it after what he's been through,* Barnett reflected, as he thought of the several severe beatings Dobbs had received at the hands of his fellow inmates.

The seasoned prison guard had put in most of his twenty years overseeing the lifers in Huntsville before being transferred here to keep an eye on the loonies, as he and his fellow guards referred to the mentally ill inmates. He recognized that most prisoners, sane or not so sane, were all about the same. Except for the ones like Dobbs who were truly mentally deranged—and in Barnett's opinion, those were few and far between—prisoners had a code all their own. Whatever crimes they had committed, they considered themselves far superior to a child molester, not to mention a child killer. And to Barnett's way of thinking, Hurley Dobbs was just about as low as they came.

Generally, the guard believed himself to be a fair and compassionate man, but he really didn't give two hoots in hell if the others beat this son of a bitch to death! That, however, wasn't what the candy-ass lawmakers said, and they paid his salary. His job was to keep order and protect the inmates from one another and from themselves. He did his job. Right now, though, his back ached from being on his feet all day, and he needed to take a leak and smoke a cigarette.

"Hurry it up, Dobbs!" Barnett spat gruffly—for all the good it would do—and turned away from the window to stroll down the length of the hall. From what he'd seen, the guy was doing a pretty good job even if he was slower than smoke off cold shit. He'd take only a short break; surely Dobbs wouldn't be too much longer.

Hurley cut his eyes toward the door. The guard's words did nothing to speed up his actions. Instead, he ignored the man in much the same way he ignored practically everyone else. He had even managed to ignore his attackers while he was being beaten and kicked. It was easy. All he had to do was close his eyes and think about The Woman. Doing that always made him lose time, so he hadn't even felt their blows. Nor did he feel anything when he woke up in the infirmary.

Hurley didn't hear what people said to him very often. He was glad of that 'cause he didn't want to hear. All except for the young man with the tight collar—Hurley liked to hear him talk. He liked to look at him, too. The young man had smiling eyes, and he talked softly, not loud and screaming.

What was it the young man said his name was? Father Paul? Yeah, that's it. Hurley never quite understood how someone who looked so young could be his father, but that's what Father Paul said, so it must be true. It didn't really matter who the man was; what he said was what Hurley liked.

He started out when Hurley first came to live here, telling him that God loved him. Hurley had never thought much about God—didn't much care, either. The truly amazing thing was that a*nybody* would love him, God included! But Father said it, so it must be true.

Father never asked him questions. Hurley was glad 'cause concentrating on trying to answer made his head hurt. Father just talked low and soft, saying things like, "God loves you and forgives you, and so do I, Hurley."

The next thing Father talked to him about was heaven. Hurley liked to hear about heaven. That's where his little girls were. They were angels up in heaven with God and Jesus. He knew it was a wondrous place somewhere up above the clouds, but that was mostly all he knew. He wanted to ask Father more about heaven, but the words just wouldn't come out. So when Father had said he wanted to talk about heaven, Hurley simply nodded eagerly.

Father had smiled then and began to tell him about a place where everybody was happy and loved everybody else. That love part was just okay, but then Father said something about the streets being paved with gold, Hurley couldn't believe it! He'd spent most of his waking hours thinking about that and fantasizing about walking on streets actually paved with gold.

Lately, as images of heaven grew more and more real in his mind, Hurley began to believe that it was the place for him. He didn't actually hate living here, especially since they had put him in a room all by himself away from the others. He had no visitors—no one tried to talk to him except for Father—and that suited him just fine.

The doctors came to poke and prod at him every so often, and the guards said hateful things to him and gave him orders. He took no interest in their conversations until one of the doctors mentioned the pills he took. Hurley did listen to him then.

It was those pills that made him sleepy and forgetful, so he decided not to take them anymore. It was hard to do at first—to swallow them just a little and then gag them back up into the toilet when he was alone. He had it mastered now, though. Ever since he'd stopped swallowing the pills, he hadn't been so sleepy and had thought a lot more about heaven.

Hurley's thoughts had ceased to be a jumble of horrific images. He remembered his little girls and how soft and pretty they were. He missed being able to have other little girls but not nearly as much as he missed driving his truck. The only times in his life that he felt like he actually fit in with other people had been while he was driving.

The one question he wanted most of all to ask Father was if they had trucks in heaven. He just couldn't make his voice work. Somehow, though, he knew they did 'cause everyone was supposed to be happy there, right? Well, he certainly couldn't be happy without his truck.

Of all the things Hurley Dobbs hated—and that was still practically everything—making a decision stood at the top of the list. Thinking and trying to decide always made the buzzing start in his head. He'd put this off long enough, though; he had to decide about it soon. He might not know very much about heaven, but the one thing he did know for sure was how you got there.

Hurley finished the dishes and looked around the kitchen. Everything was gray. The walls and concrete floor were painted gray, and cold gray steel covered the counters and tables. Even the tin plates he had just washed were gray. He remembered his hour outside that morning; the day had been gray, too. Father came to see him a day or so ago and told him that it was the month of May. That was supposed to be springtime, but this morning hadn't looked like spring. It was dreary and gray.

Hurley's attention came to rest on the splashboard behind the huge stainless steel sinks. It was loose, and his lips parted in a mirthless grin as he carefully pried the piece of broken knife blade from behind the board. He wasn't as stupid as The Woman always said he was! Loathing filled him as her ugly face flashed before his eyes. Not stupid. No, sir!

Hurley was never allowed to wash the spoons and knives, only the tin plates, cups, pots, and pans. Cook had broken the big knife several days ago and gathered the pieces—all but one. Hurley studied the jagged piece of steel, turning it over and over in his hand. It was shiny, razor sharp, and gray. Slowly now, Hurley took stock of his surroundings.

He'd finished washing all the dishes, and he'd mopped the floor just like he'd been told to do. He could do a lot of things when he was left alone. He had done a good job when he worked for Mr. Santos; he had told him so.

Ahhhh! The pain was exquisite as the edge of the knife blade slid easily right on target—along the big blue vein in his wrist. Hurley became fascinated by the sudden flow of red that quickly covered his hand, his gray pants, and then the gray floor. He hurt, though, and his head began to spin. The floor was cool. It felt good to lie back and close his eyes. The kitchen had suddenly become very hot. Hurley was sweating; he could smell his armpits. There was another odor, too, a pungent odor.

His eyelids fluttered open. He didn't remember making the blade go on the other wrist, but he surely must have. The blood was coming from both his hands, making dark red pools on the gray floor.

Hurley yawned; he was getting so sleepy! He was dimly aware of the thin stream of saliva that had begun to trickle from the corner of his mouth. He should lift his arm and wipe it away with his sleeve, but the effort was just too much.

The pain was getting worse, but that was okay because he knew it wouldn't last long. Father had told him there wasn't any pain in heaven.

Nobody ever even got sick! That was all well and good, but the real question was, Do they have trucks there?

Ahhhh! Just imagine … driving around … in his truck on streets … of gold! Now, wouldn't that … just be something!

~

"No, no, no! Oh, Christ almighty, no!" Barnett's big hands shook, and his mind raced. He couldn't get the key in the goddamn lock—couldn't get the freakin' door open! Amazed at his presence of mind to hit the alarm button, Barnett finally managed to unlock the door and step tentatively toward the still form on the floor. He didn't need to even go into the kitchen, though, to know Dobbs was dead. He'd never seen so much blood in all his life.

"Oh, dear God, how, how—" his voice cracked as it echoed plaintively in the death-stilled room. Moments later, Barnett's ears detected the muffled sound of voices and the sharp clatter of boots on the concrete corridor leading to the kitchen. The blaring alarm was causing his head to pound. Blessedly, someone finally shut it off.

The kitchen area filled quickly with guards, and everyone was talking at once. Someone was barking orders on a radio. Soon, two attendants from the infirmary arrived carrying a stretcher. They knelt with stethoscopes, listening, shaking their heads.

Barnett watched the attendants from a distance. *Of course he's dead, you idiots!* He felt strangely detached from the chaotic scene before him. He thought of his wife, his daughter at Texas A&M University, his twenty years as a prison guard. He thought of how he would answer the warden's questions: *Yes, sir, I was watching him, sir! Only thing, I needed to go to the can, and, well, he looked okay!*

"He's deader than a hammer, W. D.," one of the attendants informed him as they lifted the blood-soaked, gray corpse onto the waiting stretcher.

"We'll notify the coroner. You call the warden, okay?"

"Yeah, yeah," Barnett muttered.

Numbly, his hands dialed the warden's night number. "Sir," Barnett said as his normally bass voice croaked. "Uh, looks like we got us a suicide. It's Hurley Dobbs, sir."

After a brief pause as the warden sputtered a series of inane questions, Barnett answered, "Yes, sir, I'm sure." He was sure, too, that his career was every bit as dead as child-killer Hurley Dobbs.

47

The clay was not cooperating. Monty tossed his knife aside in exasperation, a scowl shadowing his face. He hadn't been able to keep a steady hand all morning, and with little wonder, considering last night's argument with Thea. It hadn't been exactly an argument, he reflected—more like a clash of opinions. He was strongly opposed to having that Winslow character represent Thea, and he had told her so in no uncertain terms.

Was he wrong? Perhaps a little, he admitted, his temper having subsided over the course of a sleepless night. The man who had become the object of more than one heated discussion between he and Thea came to mind.

Monty had taken an instant dislike to Peyton Winslow, and this unaccustomed negative emotion bothered him. He had certainly experienced more than his share of prejudice, heaped upon him by small-minded people. It worried him that he, too, might be guilty of similarly misjudging first impressions of the outsider.

But, damn it, Winslow was being equally judgmental toward him by contradicting every word he said and putting him down, however politely, whenever Thea was present! Simply because Monty preferred the solitude of his ranch and studio and the mute company of his bronze creations to the phony facade of much of society didn't mean he was antisocial—just careful.

His spacious studio suddenly became confining. Monty paced like a caged animal. He finally collapsed on the leather sofa facing the fireplace and stared into the dying embers of his early morning fire.

He lit his pipe and continued to reflect upon this selective nature of his. It had served him well throughout his life. His rise to the top of his field had been swift, and he liked to think that he had dealt with fame and fortune admirably. Everywhere he traveled collectors and art patrons clamored, women gushed, and gallery owners vied for his attention.

But from somewhere deep within himself—a legacy from his father, perhaps—he had found wisdom enabling him to balance success and pride in his art with a sense of humility. Even though he'd been blessed with talent, he was, after all, only a man.

His thoughts came full circle, back to Thea. Oh, how he hungered for a mere glimpse of her! Lately, their time together had been scarce, and Monty chided himself for wasting even one precious moment arguing. Considering both their hectic schedules and the demands on them, this long weekend was likely to be their last one spent alone together for some time to come.

With the advent of spring, gallery owners were busily opening their shops in Santa Fe and Taos in preparation for the tourist season. The season promised success for new artists if they had the talent, and Thea certainly did. For weeks now, she had been busy at her wheel, turning out replicas of Pueblo vessels as fine as Monty had seen. Several galleries wanted to show her work, and he was sure her first full season in Santa Fe would be a successful one.

True, she would need representation in the marketing of her art. She would need an agent, in fact. Monty didn't argue with that fact, only with her choice of an agent. Oh, he would readily agree that Peyton Winslow had a certain charm. *Okay, the guy's got charisma. So what!* Monty conceded grudgingly, but those nagging doubts persisted. He had made subtle inquiries into Winslow's background, but no one seemed to know very much about him, good or bad.

He had made his appearance in Santa Fe rather flamboyantly a month ago at the meeting of the arts council, and to Monty's way of thinking, he had zeroed in on Thea immediately. Monty shook his head, recalling the previous evening's heated exchange.

"You're constantly finding fault with the man!" Thea had said. "Just what is it you find so distasteful about Peyton, Monty? I happen to find him charming, as do quite a few others in town. And he just may be the ticket I need to get my pottery recognized nationally. He has tremendous experience in marketing, and being from New York, he—"

"Why is being from New York so all-fired important?" Monty had lashed out uncharacteristically. "I should think a woman as intelligent and sophisticated as you could see through all the glitter, Thea!"

And that's exactly what Winslow symbolized—the glitz and glitter of an artificial way of life that Monty detested. However, he didn't deny the fact that the man stood out in a crowd. He was almost as tall as Monty. But the perfectly styled, collar-length curls seemed just a little too blond, the dazzling smile flashed teeth a little too perfectly capped, and that tan of his fairly shouted of hours spent basking in a Caribbean sun. Hell, everything about the man smacked of illusion!

But it wasn't only his ostentatious appearance that made Monty suspicious of Winslow. What was he doing in Santa Fe? And why bring his entire entourage of equally flashy city types here from New York, if they were from New York at all? Monty shook his head in frustration. He seemed all alone in his distrust of the newcomer. Even Paul and Elena seemed to enjoy Winslow's company and thought him rather knowledgeable on the subject of Southwestern art. They had certainly responded enthusiastically to his ideas for promoting young Santa Fe artists.

Monty turned his attention to the large block of clay on its stand awaiting his touch. He stared glumly at what was to be his finest sculpture to date, but this morning he had no desire to tackle what should be a labor of love. Thea had certainly given him a dressing down last night. Maybe she had a point.

"That's all you have against the man, Monty. You think he looks too slick, you say! I cannot believe my ears!"

"He wears too much gold jewelry, too!" Monty had shot back like a petulant child.

"Too much—I do not believe what I'm hearing! Go ahead, admit it. You are judgmental, you are narrow-minded, and, Montana Arroyo," she had paused, breathless, her eyes blazing. "You are jealous!"

Monty closed his eyes, mulling over past relationships. He would readily admit to having been somewhat casual in his love affairs. *Casual, hell. Arroyo, you were one cold, hard-hearted operator!* Love had not entered the picture, and he'd never expected it to—until now, until Thea had come wafting ghostlike into his life and into his heart.

Oh, he loved her all right, and he knew she felt the same toward him. They had not yet spoken the words aloud, face to face, calmly, in the light of day, fully clothed. Did he think the words, if spoken aloud, would dispel the aura? He knew they both feared what would come next. Advancing their relationship was a bit frightening for them both. Too many losses, too many wounds slow to heal still remained.

So, for the moment, they had only whispered their endearments to each other as they lay bathed in moonlight, amid a tangle of bodies and blankets. He closed his eyes and saw clearly her radiant face and shining eyes. He heard her soft voice call to him from the gauzy afterglow of passion: "Take me there, again, Monty!"

As if on cue with his thoughts, Sheba began barking excitedly and bounded from the sofa where she had been napping, her keen ears picking up sounds Monty had not yet heard.

"You left so early, I know you didn't eat breakfast. I brought lunch." Thea stood in the doorway and studied him guardedly, her unblinking eyes so big they seemed to fill her face. She hesitated before continuing, her voice uncertain. "Monty, please, let's not fight anymore. I—I'm so afraid of losing you!"

Funny thing, he didn't remember closing the distance between them, nor did he remember her setting the picnic basket on the table. But there she was, in his arms, arching her body ever closer to him. Her hands traveled over his back to lock themselves behind his head. With unrestrained abandon, she was kissing him, her mouth moist and open, and her soft tongue sliding over his. She tasted like honey. She smelled of soap mixed with the faint, not-unpleasant scent of leather and the horses.

His mouth left hers only long enough to nibble at her ear and whisper his wordless little phrases. Off came her knit hat, freeing her hair. Then came her jacket, and he could tell she was wearing nothing beneath the sweater. Her hands pushed his aside as she stepped back slightly and tugged the sweater over her head.

"My boots—" Her voice came in a hoarse whisper as she led him toward the sofa. Monty knelt to remove the riding boots, pausing to massage her feet, never taking his eyes off hers. *Jealous? Hell, yes!*

She was whispering his name now as she quickly slipped out of her jeans. She wore no panties, and as usual, the sight of her exquisite body fueled the fire within him to burn white-hot. He felt certain he was going to explode as she leaned toward him, reaching for him and kneading his rigid flesh, whispering his name over and over.

"Wait, my love!" he pleaded breathlessly, his desire for her making him ache. Restraint was not one of Monty's strong points where Thea was concerned, but at this moment he needed so much more from her than sex. He needed the essence that was her.

"Come, sit for me." Drawing her to her feet, he led her to the chaise lounge in front of the large windows. She allowed him to position her reclining on the long seat. "If ever an artist had inspiration—" His voice trailed off as he studied her, his eyes and heart brimming with emotion. "Do you mind?"

"I don't mind, not for you."

An hour later, Monty stepped back from his work and assessed his efforts critically. As he wiped his hands on a towel, he beckoned for Thea to join him. "What do you think of her so far?"

"It's going to be magnificent, Monty—your best ever!" She leaned against him and studied her clay likeness.

~

Dusk was gathering as Monty opened his eyes and realized he'd been dozing. He smiled at the trail of his hastily shed clothes, which led to the bearskin rug beneath him. His gaze traveled to the untouched picnic basket on the table. He was suddenly ravenous!

He listened for a moment to Thea's even breathing as she lay atop him. He lifted his hands to stroke her back, summoning a contented moan.

"Umm, am I heavy?" she asked, unmoving.

"A little," he answered. "Look at me, please."

She complied, stirring his heart with the tenderness he saw reflected in her eyes.

"I love you, Thea." He spoke the words slowly, amazed at how easily they had spilled from his mouth.

"And I love you," she answered.

She lowered her head once again to snuggle against his chest. The words were right; the feelings were right. Still, the thought needled him that they had not discussed Peyton Winslow. Nothing had been settled.

As with so many times before, she seemed to read his thoughts. Easily she lifted her body from his and looked into his eyes.

"Monty, I'm not some completely innocent young girl who's going to make a fool of herself. I do love you so, and I respect your advice, but—" she struggled for the right words. "Some decisions I need to make for myself. You're not going to lose me, my love. I'm not Tondra."

Could he possibly compromise his lofty ideals and give Winslow the benefit of the doubt? For her, he would try. Who knows? Maybe the situation would straighten itself out. Maybe the man would simply leave town. Maybe not.

48

"Why do we have to stay here? Can't you handle business from someplace like New York, for instance? You know, someplace that's actually civilized!"

Peyton Winslow chose to ignore the voice that had recently begun to grate upon his nerves. He stood on the balcony outside his bedroom, watching the setting sun slip magnificently behind the mountains.

He'd certainly have to get the boys up here with their high-dollar camera and lens to capture the moment, so to speak. A shot such as this accompanied by his very own glib descriptions would be just the ticket to selling property to jet-setters who were bored with making the scene and globe-trotting.

Yes, he could see the ads now: "Come, discover art that speaks to your soul! Gain spiritual reawakening by visiting mystical ancient ruins! Find your own enchantment in New Mexico! Experience the rich heritage of our Native Americans' way of life!"

Peyton scoffed; translation: "Come one, come all! Pay ten prices at Winslow's Arts and Crafts Center! Buy yourself a dream from Winslow's Land Sales Company! Enjoy après-ski activities at the Winslow Mountaintop Resort, the place to be and be seen! And don't forget your cameras, folks. The fat Indian squaws wrapped in blankets will gladly pose for you!"

Aspen and Vail were passé. Santa Fe would soon emerge as the fashionable place to be, and who would be the guru? He would, by God— Peyton Winslow Jr.! He didn't use the *Jr.* anymore, though, not since the old man had checked out. Peyton's thoughts wandered to his childhood and early adult years, being dragged from one dirty, one-horse town to another, pulling the same old tired scams.

What was it Pappy had said to him as he lay coughing and gasping for breath in the charity ward of a hospital somewhere in Alabama? "Don't forget our golden rule, Sonny: 'do unto others before they can do it to you'!"

The old man had given in then to the painful, bloody spasms that wracked his frail body. Peyton had signed the papers at the hospital stating that his father was indigent, and then he had left the hot and dirty little town with the name that eluded him. He'd headed north, to New York, and he had never looked back.

That was twelve years ago. He hadn't done too badly for himself, he reflected, "doing it to others." Pappy would've been proud.

"Don't you stand there ignoring me, goddammit! Answer my question, will you? Peyton, if you don't answer me, I swear I'll—"

"What was your question, Quinn?" Peyton reentered the bedroom in slow fashion, mentally preparing himself to remain calm in the face of her stupidity.

"My question *was,* Do we have to stay here very much longer?"

No, idiot, we can leave now and forget what could very well be a multimillion-dollar deal! "Yes, my dear, we have to stay here for quite a while—a year, maybe longer, in fact. You see, Quinn, in order to be able to buy up the land we need for condos and gift shops, not to mention enough for a ski resort, we have to meet the right people," Peyton explained calmly, as he would to a child.

"People like Paul Ramirez, right?"

Deal of the century! Tits and ass, and she's got a brain, too! "Exactly! And to be able to market true art, not just dime-store junk, we need to sign really good artists. More than anything else, Quinn, we have to get those artists to trust us. Art reproduction is big business, remember? We can't very well cultivate trust from New York, now can we?"

Quinn wasn't going to let it go. "Yeah, by really good artists you mean Thea Kelly, don't you? I've seen the way you look at her. Don't think I don't know what you're thinking!" She continued to bait him, her voice raising an octave to once again irritate him.

"I don't know what you're talking about, Quinn. How many times must I explain business to you before that pea brain of yours grasps it?"

He was tired of placating her. Damn, she was dense! Peyton turned to study his woman. She lay on the bed, naked except for the black garter belt, stockings, and black high heels. Of course, she wore an array of diamond jewelry he had given her over their years together. And she wore her makeup, too much of it.

There was a time—not too long ago, either—when the sight of her lying there looking vulgar and tawdry would have excited him. She knew this and was obviously expecting sex when he returned from his meeting with Ramirez. He had no desire for Quinn at the moment, though, and he wondered why. What had happened to the attraction she had once held for him? Had they simply been together for too long?

Peyton detested the thought of losing an investment, especially one in which he had sunk as much money as he had in Quinn Fallon. With her carefully dyed red hair and erect silicone breasts, not to mention the small fortune in designer clothes and jewelry, she didn't even resemble the skinny hooker with lifeless eyes who had propositioned him outside that Lexington Avenue deli.

She had told Peyton her price was fifty. He'd offered twenty-five, knowing all the while he only had ten. It was quick, in his cheap hotel room. She hadn't even gotten mad about the money, settling instead for a place to sleep on that cold New York night.

That was six years ago, and they'd been through a lot together. The money from his first big jewelry heist had gone for her methadone treatments. He'd been proud of her. She'd kicked her heroin habit completely; she hadn't slipped even once. After that, they had made their way west pulling scams mostly on old people, with Quinn turning tricks whenever they needed extra money. Peyton's really big hit came from a successful, if somewhat shady, land deal near Sacramento. That netted Quinn a boob job and a professional makeover. She'd looked good to him for a long time.

He turned his attention back to the bed. Maybe all she needed now was a few nips and tucks here and there, and he'd have that old feeling back for her.

She frowned under the scrutiny of his gaze. "You're doing it again, Peyton!" she whined.

"Doing what?"

"You're looking at me, and I don't know what you're thinking. Gives me the creeps!" she answered. "You got that rich bitch Kelly woman on your mind, I know it!"

Peyton rose and made his way toward the bed. "As a matter of fact, I was thinking of you, my dear," he said. "And I imagine that Ms. Kelly has her hands rather full at the moment with Tonto, don't you think? Maybe you'd like to try distracting him." He was making fun of her. It was ludicrous to think any woman could distract a man from Thea Kelly.

Quinn's smile was brazen. "I certainly wouldn't mind trying!" she answered, moving her hips suggestively. It was her turn to mock him, and it worked. Peyton found himself perversely aroused by the thought of her with another man.

Quickly he shed his clothes and went to her. His hands brutally slapped, pinched, and pulled at her. His thrusts were hard and brutal. His voice was hateful and vicious. That was just the way she always wanted it. There was never any tenderness between them, more like a mutual assault as her nails raked the blood from his back, making him groan.

"You whore, you like it like this, don't you?" he hissed. With his passion nearing its frenzy, Peyton looked at the woman beneath him. Her smeared makeup and twisted grin reminded him of a pitiful caricature. Suddenly, he envisioned another face looking up at him, one of erotic beauty—flawless, clean, and genuine.

"Admit it, you bastard. You want her!" Quinn's words spurred him on.

"Would you mind so very much?" Peyton asked, breathless, his hands pinning her shoulders roughly to the bed in preparation for his final assault.

She turned her gaze knowingly to the small red light on the far wall, the only indication of the hidden camera—one of several located throughout the condo. "Just don't leave me out," she hissed.

49

The Buick's speedometer rocked gently between eighty and eighty-five as Cal sped toward the New Mexico border. "Damn!" he said with a grimace, suddenly realizing how fast he was driving. He slowed the car to sixty-five before setting the cruise control. The last thing he needed was *two* speeding tickets on this trip, especially when he was this close to home.

He shifted uncomfortably, the car's seat cover chafing his backside. What a rotten waste of time this trip to Los Angeles had been! A disappointment, too; the photograph of the little girl had looked just like Alexa Kelly. The resemblance was so uncanny, in fact, that Cal had left immediately on the eight-hundred-mile drive. But the trip had proved utterly pointless, another dead end in his frustrating search for clues to the child's fate.

Cal's heart was beginning to rule his head. The one thing he wanted to do before he died was to find the girl and return her to her mother—if she was still alive, that is. That was looking more and more doubtful as the months and years slipped by.

He hadn't wanted to face the grim reality that Dobbs had most likely killed her and buried her body just as he had done with the other little girls. Maybe after this last wild goose chase, it would be best if he faced that fact. But how could he say that to Thea? He couldn't. He'd simply keep looking and keep responding to whatever tips he received.

His hopes, now dashed, had been fed a week earlier by the telephone call from LA. His brother-in-law had a number of informants throughout the Southwest, and one of them had responded to Cal's flier showing Alexa's picture. Yeah, yeah, he'd seen the kid, and recently, too!

The informant had told Cal that a middle-aged couple whom he knew to be childless had just enrolled a little girl into his daughter's school. After a bit of checking, he found that the couple had moved five times in the past year. The wife was extremely nervous, and the child cried the first few days of school. She looked exactly like the photo of Alexa. It had to be her, right?

Wrong! The truth of the matter was the husband had had a fling seven years earlier. The woman never made a fuss until she found out she had cancer.

"She couldn't take care of the kid anymore," Cal had reported to Sophie on the phone the night after he'd arrived in LA and checked out the lead. "So, she takes her to Daddy and tells him it's his turn. How 'bout that!"

"Why all the secrecy?" Sophie had asked.

"His wife forgave him and took the little girl in, but she was ashamed and didn't want folks knowing her old man had been screwing around on her. Anyway," Cal had answered tiredly, "it's all on the up-and-up. It ain't Alexa, hon."

"Come on home, Cal. Maybe—"

"Yeah, maybe," he'd muttered, interrupting her. Was it hopeless? Had it been hopeless from the start?

He'd be home in the early evening—*damn!* Cal had forgotten it was May 17! He coaxed the Buick back up to seventy-five. He'd try to get home in time to take Sophie out on the town for their anniversary.

~

"Hey, they're beautiful, hon. Thank you!" Sophie said, beaming at the roses a tired Cal handed her when he walked through their kitchen door several hours later. "I thought you might forget. And it would've been okay if you had," she added softly as she hugged her husband. He looked exhausted. Sophie shook her head sadly as she studied him. She'd been elated when Cal had chosen to take early retirement and leave Dallas. She was even happier to be living in Albuquerque near her brother. Now, if only her husband would concentrate on the other cases that needed his attention and stop chasing a ghost. But Sophie knew he couldn't forget her—or her daughter.

Cal's voice was upbeat. "Give me time to grab a shower, and we're going out on the town, Soph." He patted her generous backside as he prepared to leave the kitchen.

"Oh, Cal, before you do anything, you need to call Lois. She telephoned about two hours ago and said it was real important. I told her you'd call the minute you got in, okay?"

"Right away." Cal missed his best buddy; he wondered what was up. He'd call just as soon as he showered. It'd sure be good to hear her voice again.

~

The moment Cal emerged from the bedroom, Sophie knew something bad was afoot. He still looked tired from his days on the road, and the dark circles were still present under his eyes. Now, though, he actually looked as if he had been crying. His broad shoulders sagged noticeably.

"Cal, did you call Lois? What is it? What's happened?"

He stared into space for a long time before answering her. When he did, his voice sounded as tired as he looked. "I called. Hurley Dobbs committed suicide two days ago."

"How?"

"Got hold of a broken knife blade somehow. Son of a bitch slit his wrists." Cal lit a cigarette and walked outside to the patio. Sophie knew he loved to sit out there and look at the mountains. He did his best thinking out there, alone, smoking and looking at the mountains. She'd mix him a drink and take it out to him, and then she'd leave him with his thoughts. It was dark when she heard him come back inside.

"Sophie, would you mind if we did our celebrating another night? I need to sleep. And," he hesitated a moment before continuing, "I need to drive up to Santa Fe tomorrow. Thea, Ms. Kelly, shouldn't hear this news over the phone.

"One of the last conversations we had in Dallas was about the death penalty," he explained. "A lot of people would want to see Dobbs dead, but she didn't. Told me that as long as he was still alive, there was a chance he'd tell what he did with Alexa. I need to tell her in person, Soph. Do you mind?"

"Of course not, Cal. Go on to bed. We can celebrate anytime." She smiled at him. Loving him as she had all these years, his hurts were hers.

"Hellfire!" Cal exclaimed, turning to his wife. "I didn't even think to ask about the boys! Where are they tonight?" A look of embarrassment slipped over his face.

"The boys are fine. They're spending the night with their cousins. I thought we could use a night alone," she answered, not quite masking the hurt in her voice.

"Ah, Sophie, I'm sorry. Look, why don't you go with me tomorrow to Santa Fe? After I talk to Ms. Kelly, we'll take some time to look around. It's a great drive."

He was trying, and she knew it. "No, hon, you go on and tend to business. I've got a zillion things to do here. It's okay, really!"

"I love you, Soph. Happy anniversary."

"Happy anniversary, Cal. Now, you get some rest!" She barked the order at him good-naturedly and was still smiling when he closed the bedroom door.

No, she wouldn't go with him to talk to Thea. She'd never even met the woman, but she'd seen pictures of her and had caught a glimpse of her once at the station in Dallas. She felt nothing but compassion for her, but she'd noticed Cal's eyes all too often when he spoke of her. The last thing she wanted to see was that look when he talked to her face to face.

50

Thea was pleasantly surprised. It hadn't taken much arm-twisting on her part at all to convince Monty to accompany her that night. She knew he would make a genuine effort to be civil to Peyton, and she loved him all the more for it. While their weekend argument had not been resolved, their differences had certainly been put on hold for the moment.

"Can you help me with this cursed thing?" Monty said as he emerged, frustrated, from Thea's bathroom, tie in hand. "Formal dress was no doubt devised as punishment for some heinous crime!"

Thea smiled as she assisted him, thinking he did indeed look a bit out of place in the tux but resplendent none the less. "Max called. She's running late and will meet us there."

"Fine," Monty commented distractedly. "Let's get it over with, shall we?"

"Monty!"

"Okay, okay! I simply cannot wait to get there and hear more of Mr. Winslow's brilliant schemes—oops, I mean, plans! Equally enjoyable will be watching him circle you like a vulture!" He stalked from the room in a huff as Thea suppressed a giggle.

Elena and Paul were hosting a reception that evening to introduce Peyton to several local gallery owners. Thea was anxious to hear more of his plans to promote her pottery, even if it all did sound a little too good to be true. Monty kept telling her to be patient that recognition would come soon enough. Peyton's contention was just the opposite. She remembered his words to her the previous week during dinner.

"Thea, don't wait until another gifted potter emerges on the art scene. Make a name for yourself now! You should be the one to set a precedent for all others to follow."

She sighed. Peyton did have a point. What if someone else were to market a line of pottery similar to hers before she did? Why, then her pieces would be overlooked as mere copies! He was right; she needed to start an aggressive advertising and marketing campaign immediately.

Of course, she wouldn't mention this decision to Monty right away. Nor would she tell him of that dinner she had had with Peyton, innocent though it was. She would do nothing to further the rift between the two men. She'd only glimpsed the surface of Monty's temper and had no desire to see it reach its zenith.

Thea did agree with Monty on one point, though: Peyton's attentions were more than a little unsettling. She shuddered at the memory of being caught in that icy-blue gaze of his and made a mental note to avoid being alone with him again if possible.

~

The reception had, for the most part, been a success. Thea yawned and curled herself contentedly on Elena's couch. Practically everyone else had said their good nights some time ago. She, herself, had been ready to leave for an over an hour.

It was expected of Max to be the very last one to leave a party, but Thea was surprised at Monty's insistence to stay so late. He was usually uncomfortable in the midst of heavy drinking and boisterous chatter and always tried to slip away early. Tonight, however, he was right in the middle of things.

"If tonight were a chess game," she had whispered to him mid-evening, "I wonder who would be saying 'checkmate' right about now?" Her comment made reference to the forced politeness between Monty and Peyton.

Monty again voiced his concerns to Paul soon after the other guests' departure. "Paul, can you think of a plausible explanation for Winslow's wanting to purchase so much acreage here? And what do you make of his reaction to your offer? I know I would certainly welcome a group of wealthy investors willing to plunk down some big bucks to finance a plan of mine."

"Oh, Monty, you would not!" Thea spoke in amazement. "If you had an idea for something really grand, you would want the accomplishment to be completely yours. Why, it would be like selling part of yourself."

"Not if I didn't have any money!" Monty shot back, taking the defensive.

"Just how do you know he doesn't have any money? Admit it, Monty: you despise the man, and you have no intention of giving him a chance to prove himself. You won't even listen to what he has to say!" Thea was tired, both physically and emotionally, as evidenced by her sudden crabby mood.

"Now, now, let's not get upset with each other." Paul's deep voice eased the tensions in the room. "I believe Peyton spoke of his own investors, Monty. I didn't press him, but it seems to me he already has funds available to him for the land acquisitions as well as construction of the condos." He paused to sip his brandy, smiling patiently at his cousin. "Let's take things slowly and listen to his plans. Who knows? He might actually be good for Santa Fe. I know one thing for certain: his idea for an art exhibition arena certainly rang a few bells with the patrons tonight."

"Indeed," Elena responded thoughtfully, "but one does wonder where he could get his hands on so much money in so little time and on his recommendation alone. We haven't seen anything of formal projections—"

"Exactly my point," Monty interrupted, elated with even a hint of doubt cast in Winslow's direction. "Where would he get his hands on that much money? I believe he mentioned cash. Come on, Paul. No one has that kind of cash to funnel into a speculative deal—unless, of course, it's someone who needs that money laundered. And what about workers? You heard him say he would be bringing his own crews in. Oh, I can just about guarantee where *they'll* be coming from!" Monty finished in a huff to a suddenly thoughtful audience.

"I'm willing to consider all possibilities," Paul finally said, breaking the silence. "I'll have someone check Mr. Winslow out thoroughly. Will that satisfy you, my cousin?"

"I hope you have better luck than I had," Monty replied. "He doesn't leave much of a trail."

"You investigated Peyton? Monty!" Thea stared at him quizzically.

"I most certainly did!" He began to move uncomfortably under her wide-eyed gaze.

Paul noticed the tiny smile tugging at the corner of Thea's mouth. His pleasant chuckle was contagious, and soon the small group no longer felt on edge.

"I'm sorry, Monty. I didn't mean to be so cross," Thea said as she rose from the couch. "I guess I need a good night's sleep more than I thought." Suddenly very dizzy, she grasped the mantle for support with one hand as the other cradled her forehead.

Monty was at her side in a heartbeat. "Thea, are you sick? Here, sit back down." He guided her to a chair. "Why, you're perspiring! Elena, get her some water, please."

"No, no, I'll be okay," Thea said in a shaky voice. She opened her eyes slowly and looked into the concerned faces before her. "Really, I'm just tired, and I might have a migraine coming on. I'll be fine in the morning."

"It could be a touch of the flu, my dear." Elena clucked like a mother hen around the younger woman. "My goodness, you're trembling! Have you felt sick all evening?"

"No. Actually, I felt fine until a couple of hours ago. Then, I just suddenly began to feel so anxious. I suppose you could say I'm jumpy, you know—" Her voice trailed off, as uncertainty registered on her face.

Max knew that look. She'd seen it before on her best friend's face, and it worried her. Since the beginning of their friendship, Max had recognized the subtle qualities in Thea's personality to be evidence of a keen intuition that even she herself was not always aware of. It now became Max's turn to be anxious. "Get her home, Monty," she said. "I'll follow you."

"Call us in the morning, or before, if you need us," Elena called from the doorway as she and Paul watched the cars disappear down their drive. "I do hope she's not coming down with something."

"It's probably just the start of a migraine, as she said," Paul responded, closing the door. "Max was certainly worried, though. We'll give them until around ten in the morning, and if we haven't heard by then, we'll drive over and check on her."

51

"You're not asleep already, are you?" Monty asked. He supported Thea with one arm as he made the turn into her drive.

"No, I'm not asleep," she answered him quietly. "I just suddenly felt so drained, so empty. Look, there's a car in my drive."

Max turned into the drive immediately behind the couple and quickly exited her car. "Who's your company?" she asked as the three made their way toward the front door.

"It looks like—" Thea's answer was cut short by the creaking of the porch rocker. The tall man stepped slowly from the darkened recess into the moonlight.

"I was hoping you'd be home soon, Thea. Howdy, Max, Monty." Cal removed his hat and continued speaking in measured tones. "Thea, I need to talk to you."

Monty's arm tightened around Thea as he felt her sway against him. "Let's all go inside, shall we?"

Thea did not speak until the four of them were inside the house. With more calm than she thought she possessed, she turned to her friend. "What's happened, Cal? Is there news of Alexa?"

The investigator licked his dry lips and eyed the decanters on the bar longingly. Reading his thoughts, Max quickly poured him a vodka and waited in silence with the others.

"I have no news about Alexa. I—I do have some news, though. I wanted to tell you in person."

"Yes?"

"Thea, Hurley Dobbs is dead. He killed himself three days ago. I got the word last night." Cal took the much-needed drink in one gulp. "I'm so sorry to have to tell you."

"How?" Her voice came as a weak whisper.

"Guard wasn't watching him as close as he should, I guess. Dobbs had kitchen duty and somehow got a hold of a knife blade. Lois telephoned me, said they called her in Dallas." Cal paused, nodding to Max to get him another drink. "He slit his wrists and bled to death."

Thea accepted the news mutely, her expression never changing. After a while, she moved woodenly to her favorite chair by the window and sat staring out into the darkness, her eyes unblinking.

Monty knew what this bit of news meant. He ached to go to her and wrap her in his arms, but he let her be for the moment.

Max shook herself free from the shock long enough to mumble something about making a pot of coffee.

Cal had liked Monty the moment they'd met months earlier. He had seen honesty and integrity in him. He liked him more each time they were together. *Here is a man who loves her, and that's good. Let that love be enough to pull her through this*, he now silently prayed.

The minutes seemed to pass like hours. Max brought coffee and sweet rolls, which Thea silently refused and which Cal attacked ravenously. He hadn't had anything since breakfast, and the two quick drinks were making him woozy.

"Look, Thea, I'm going to get a room for the rest of the night. I'll be back in the morning and we can talk. If there's anything I can do, you let me know." Cal stood fidgeting with his hat, not wanting to leave but needing to. Awkwardly, he continued, "Monty, it was good to see you again. Max, it's always good to see you." He smiled tiredly as the two friends embraced.

"Cal?" Thea said.

Her sudden utterance of his name caused him to turn and hurry to kneel by her chair. "Yes, Thea, what is it?" He could see the shock was wearing off, and he knew the suffering would begin anew.

"Oh, Cal, that monster! He just keeps taking and taking from me! There's no chance now for him to tell us what he did with her! No chance!"

"This ain't the end, Thea, not by a long shot. I promise you I won't ever stop looking for Alexa. Somebody, somewhere, had to have seen something. We've got a network of guys—" Cal stopped speaking. He saw that his words were of little use. She didn't hear them.

Resignedly, Thea stood and headed for her bedroom. Monty said his good nights and followed to comfort her as best he could.

Her voice, fainter now, reached Max and Cal as they prepared to leave. "He just keeps taking!"

52

The breathtaking beauty of early summer in Santa Fe contrasted sharply with the wretched mood Thea found herself in day after day.

She had told herself that this morning would be different, that she would feel happiness again. After all, her dad had arrived yesterday, and the two of them had sat up until the wee hours talking together, almost like old times. She had so looked forward to showing him her new home, her town, and her pottery. She had written glowing reports of her new friends, especially Monty, but the excitement of his first visit to Santa Fe had been defused.

Nearly a month had passed since Cal had brought her the news of Dobbs's death, and the disparity she felt refused to pass. Having her dad there helped, of course. Her friends and her work helped, too. Monty helped most of all.

Thea knew how worried everyone was; she worried, too. She worried that she might never feel happiness or know fulfillment again. If she never worked again, how would she live? She couldn't simply allow the people she loved to take care of her. Sooner or later, she had to snap out of this depression. Oh, but it was just so easy to sit there alone in her garden, eyes closed, thinking of nothing—except the absolute, final, empty thought that her daughter was gone forever.

~

"How long will she sit out there, Monty?" Mike Chandler asked in a troubled voice.

"Until someone goes out and persuades her to get up, walk a little, perhaps eat something. I was hopeful that your coming here would be the spark she needed. She's talked about your visit for so long." Monty hung his head sadly as he spoke. "I wish you could have seen how she was blossoming before we got the news about Dobbs."

The two men fell silent for a time. Even though they had known each other for less than twenty-four hours, a comfortable alliance had been formed. Each man saw the other as a hero of the woman they both loved.

"I'll go out and talk to her right now," Mike said. "And I'll remind her that she promised me a tour of galleries today."

"I hope it does the trick, Mike. I hate to leave, but I've got my ranch to see to and a slew of appearances to make."

"Thea will understand. She loves you."

With that, Monty knew he had been given a father's blessing. "I hope the two of you have a good day, Mike. Tell her I'll call tonight."

Mike pondered his relationship with his only child as he strolled into the garden. He had been both mother and father to her for so long, and up until Alexa's disappearance, he had always known exactly what to say to comfort her. It was different now.

"Good morning, baby. Did you sleep well?"

"I guess so. How about you? I hope the small room is okay." Her reply was automatic and without emotion.

"The room is fine. It's the company that's lacking." Mike's tone became brusque. Thea had once referred to it as his military voice. "If you do not want me here, Thea, then please tell me, and I shall get out from underfoot."

The reaction he'd hoped for was immediate. "Daddy, you can't leave! You just got here! Of course I want you here!" In the blink of an eye, she was in his arms, her head cradled in the hollow of his shoulder, her tears wet and warm against his shirt.

Mike held her until her sobs subsided. "You never call me 'Daddy.' It sounds strange. Matter of fact, I kind of like it." He gently eased them apart and handed her his handkerchief.

"Yeah, well, don't get too used to it," she teased. A sad little smile showed itself as she dabbed her eyes. "'Big Mike' suits you too well."

"How about some breakfast and a tour of this town?" he asked as they made their way arm in arm back into the house. "That man of yours tells me you've got galleries clamoring to show your pottery. Is that true?"

Thea's smile was a little less sad this time. "Oh, isn't Monty wonderful? It's his work you need to see, not mine. Do you know that his bronzes bring the highest price of any Native American sculptor in the country? And wait until he finishes the one he's working on now—I'm the model!"

Mike smiled as he detected a faint blush rise to her cheeks. He held no illusion, though, that this sudden euphoria would last. He knew her emotional state would continue to teeter precariously between highs and lows. But for now, his Thea was back for a little while.

53

Under the watchful eyes of her father and friends, Thea's mood swings did, indeed, mirror emotions out of control. Throughout the summer, she exhibited energy and pride in her work one minute, despondency the next.

More than anyone else, Monty was aware of her erratic behavior. It was, in fact, her fragile state of mind that occupied his thoughts as he made his customary Friday morning drive from Taos to Santa Fe. Today, he did so automatically, his mind barely conscious of the physical movements necessary to navigate the familiar stretch of highway. Keeping his vehicle on the road was not foremost in his mind today; it was the conversation he knew he must have with Thea that caused him worry.

He had talked with Paul for hours the previous evening on the telephone, but the wisdom and support from his cousin did little to bolster his confidence level. In her present troubled state of mind, Monty wondered if Thea would give credence to the news he had to tell her.

He heaved a sigh as he neared the turnoff to Santa Fe. "She'll just have to accept it," he muttered aloud. "I've got the proof."

Still, the thought of further contributing to her depression worried him. And the thought of ever losing her purely scared the hell out of him.

~

Thea scanned the contents of her studio with a critical eye. Many of the vessels were not yet glazed, and many were simply not good enough. She shook her head forlornly, doubts settling in. Was she only kidding herself that her art had merit? Had she agreed to this showing too soon? Would the knowledgeable collectors be impressed with her talent, or would they merely smirk behind her back, mouthing "Amateur"?

Mostly, however, Thea's doubts centered on the decision she had made last night and the effect that decision would have on her future. Would what she and Monty shared together be jeopardized? Was she again being totally selfish? Into the wee hours of the morning, she had fought with herself, not only about her decision but about how to tell Monty.

Only Mike knew of her latest plan. During the three months he had remained in Santa Fe, he and Thea had spent hours talking, just like when she was younger and living at home. She realized just how heavily she still relied upon his advice as she recalled their conversation of the previous evening.

"Do you think it's a good idea?" Thea had asked her father.

"I think it's a very good idea. As a matter of fact, you should have done it a long time ago. I'm only sorry that I never insisted on it," Mike had responded positively. "But is your timing right? And, Thea, are you doing this for the right reasons, or are you simply running away again?"

She'd remained silent while Mike had continued speaking. "It must be your decision, my dear. But always know that I'll support whatever you think will be best for you. As I've told you before, the money's there. Just be sure you make a decision that you can live with."

Thea believed she had. She'd begun toying with the idea soon after Cal had come with the news of Dobbs's suicide, ever since she had admitted to herself the futility of finding Alexa. But admitting that hadn't made the pain go away. Would it ever?

Yes, Thea believed she had made a wise decision. All that remained now was to tell Monty and hope he would understand.

~

Monty entered the studio soundlessly and stood unnoticed, watching her from the doorway. "You're flitting around like a butterfly, my love. Can I help?"

"Monty, I'll never be ready for the show tomorrow night," she grumbled, barely taking notice of his arrival. "Why did I agree to this so soon after Market?"

The response to Thea's work had escalated during Santa Fe's peak season, thanks in no small part to Peyton Winslow's aggressive promotional campaign on her behalf. She recognized now that time was her enemy as she came to a standstill and stared forlornly at the shelves of pottery still needing her attention.

"There just hasn't been enough time to get everything ready, and I'm so tired!"

"There hasn't been time enough lately for a lot of things." Monty's voice was velvety soft and caressing. He moved close behind her and began massaging her tired shoulders.

"Mmm, that's nice," Thea murmured, closing her eyes and feeling herself relax against his strong body. Her need for rest was soon forgotten, only to be replaced by a different kind of need. It had been wonderful having Mike there for the summer, but his presence, coupled with hectic schedules, equaled precious few moments alone for the lovers.

"I do need to work—" Her feeble protests went ignored as Monty turned her to face him. The explosion of their first kiss took them both by surprise. She melted against his rock-hard body, her mouth meshing perfectly with his. His hands traveled down her back, cupping the round contours of her buttocks and pulling her even closer to him, but never close enough!

Locked in the heat of his embrace, the thought flashed through Thea's mind that last night's decision was the wrong one. But quick on the heels of self-doubt followed common sense. She would tell Monty tomorrow night and hope he would understand.

The sudden ringing of the telephone interrupted the couple's ardor. "Let it go!" Monty whispered.

"It might be important. I'll make it quick, I promise." Reluctantly, she tore herself from his embrace and made her way into the living room on unsteady legs.

"Hello? Oh, good morning, Peyton," she answered with a trembling voice. "Well, actually, I am a little busy at the moment. What can I do for you?"

Any interruption would have been unwelcome, she knew, but this one could not have come at a worse time. She cringed outwardly as the door leading into her garden slammed with a force that shook the small house.

"Monty, I'm sorry," Thea apologized minutes later. "He only wanted to read me the press release for my show and get my approval."

"I know what he wants!" His voice ground out the words abruptly. He hesitated. "Look, Thea,—" he began, but the words would not come.

She saw that his expression no longer held anger but worry. "What is it, Monty? You've been so distant lately. I know I've been preoccupied with Mike's visit and with this show, but I thought we had this thing with Peyton settled. You know my dealings with him are strictly business."

"I know that," he said quietly, keeping his thoughts his own for the moment. He couldn't bring himself to give her any bad news today, not the day before her first show. "I do need to talk with you about something, but it can wait."

"Oh? I need to talk to you about something, too," Thea responded. "We'll have some time alone tomorrow night. I'm still not sure a cocktail party after the show is such a good idea. If the whole thing's a flop, we won't have much to celebrate." Her misgivings surfaced again.

"Are you kidding? That party's the only good idea Winslow's had!" Monty's bravado made her smile. "This is just the beginning for you, darling. Believe it!"

54

Cal Evers patted the thick manila folder on the car seat beside him and thought of its contents. The dossier had taken him the better part of the summer to prepare. At first, the trail had been hard to follow. The more time and effort he put forth, though, the more information came to light. The facts were complete and accurate. The ramifications were damning!

He had talked at length with Paul Ramirez over the past few days, as well as with Monty. Both men feared that the information he had gathered would cause yet another setback for Thea. Cal didn't believe it and had told Paul so during their conversation the previous evening.

"Hell, man, with what she's been through, I doubt if this'll have much effect on her at all. Trust me!"

"I hope you're right, my friend," Paul had said. "At any rate, Monty doesn't want her to know until after her show. You're coming, aren't you, Cal?"

"I wouldn't miss it!" Cal had been witness to so many sad times for Thea; it would sure be good to be around for something pleasant. He just had a feeling her first show would be a success.

~

"Attention! Ladies and gentlemen, may I have your attention, please?" Peyton's honeyed tones reverberated throughout the rented gallery. The last of the customers had left, and the private cocktail party was about to begin.

As he waited for the ecstatic voices to soften, Peyton surveyed the room. What he had arranged was elegance, pure and simple. Each piece of pottery had been displayed on a pedestal draped with black velvet and illuminated by tiny individual spotlights. As the evening wore on and darkness fell, the entire gallery was bathed in starlight. Genius! It had cost a bundle for that lighting package, but Peyton figured he'd make it back in no time at all.

No one there was the least bit surprised at the positive reception that Thea's pottery had received, except maybe for the artist herself. *That's part of her appeal*, Peyton thought as he studied her with hooded, serpent-like eyes.

Why, she has no idea how talented she is, or how desirable! Well, he planned to make her know it soon—just as soon as he could get a couple of people out of the picture. Quinn, he could get rid of easily; Arroyo might be a bit harder. Putting his private thoughts on hold for the moment, Peyton again made a plea for the crowd's attention.

"Please, ladies and gentlemen, I have a short announcement, and then you may continue. As Thea Kelly's agent, it is my pleasure to announce that each and every piece of pottery exhibited here this evening has been sold!"

Thea was only dimly aware of the cheers, the embraces, the handclasps. She couldn't believe that her first formal show had been successful beyond her wildest dreams. She caught sight of Monty across the room, standing tall, smiling radiantly at her. He nodded his head, and she knew he was saying, *See? I told you success would be yours!*

"You did it, kiddo," Max said, her eyes tearing as the two friends embraced. "You're famous, Thea, just like we used to pretend! Remember?"

"I remember." *Memory: a gift or a curse?* "I couldn't have done it without you, Max. I'll never be able to thank you enough. You've always been there for me."

The two women embraced again as emotions that transcended words bound them.

Thea spoke. "Max, I need to talk to you. Come by the house tomorrow, okay?"

"Sure. What's up?" Max studied her friend's face. "Is something—"

"Sorry to interrupt, ladies," Paul said, "but the guests are starting to leave. After you've circulated a bit more, Thea, can you and Max come to our house? Mike, too, please." Paul spoke with a seriousness that belied his brilliant smile.

Neither woman answered but merely nodded her agreement. The mood of the moment seemed to demand quiet. Finally, Thea asked, "Where's Monty?"

"He and Elena have gone on ahead," Paul answered. With that, he walked away briskly, leaving the two women to ponder what the big mystery was.

55

"Unbelievable! How could I have been so taken in?" Thea said through clenched teeth an hour later as she sat in the Ramirezes' living room.

The confrontations she'd had with Monty over the past few months now came back to haunt her. Time after time, she'd ridiculed him in her defense of Peyton Winslow.

Not everything new is bad, Monty.... Give Peyton the benefit of the doubt, won't you? After all, he just might put your little town on the map.... If he's an outsider, then so am I. Is that what you think?

How she wished she could retract her words, but she couldn't. Nor was she able to say how sorry she was. All she could do was continue to stare at the thick file Cal had apologetically handed her earlier. It was all there: arrests but no convictions, suspicions but not enough evidence, inconclusive reports—no fire but plenty of smoke.

"A number of us were taken in, Thea, not just you," Paul replied. "Elena and I had high hopes that Winslow would establish a viable art center here. And another major ski resort would have meant more year-round tourism. We heard what we wanted to hear, I'm afraid."

"Hey, I never really liked the guy," Max interjected, "but I did think you were right to hire him to promote your pottery. Hell, he didn't do a half-bad job of that!"

Finally, Thea closed the file and handed it back to Cal. "You're quite an investigator, Cal. Monty couldn't find a damn thing on him."

Her comments and wry smile drew chuckles from the group. Monty had been sitting a little outside of the circle, but he rose from his chair and made his way to Thea. His arms encircled her protectively as he leaned down to whisper words for her ears only.

"If you think you're going to hear an 'I told you so,' think again. I am truly sorry it's turned out this way."

Thea hugged him back before addressing Paul. "What's going to be done now?"

"The district attorney will speak with Mr. Winslow tomorrow morning, bright and early. It's doubtful he'll bring charges, but several matters will be addressed. I'm sure you read Cal's notes on the construction workers that Winslow brought in—all of them illegal immigrants from Mexico. It'll be up to the DA to decide whether to push that issue. That would be the only substantiated charge we've got on him. The land-swindling charges stem from some deals in California several years ago."

"In spite of all he might have done wrong, I can't fault him for tonight," Thea said thoughtfully. "Tonight's show wouldn't have gone as smoothly as it did without his planning."

"Don't give him the credit, my dear. The praise goes to you," Mike said as he raised his glass to his daughter.

A chorus of cheers echoed as the evening's earlier joyous mood returned. "The success was, and will continue to be, yours," Monty said. His glass touched hers as their eyes met lovingly.

Thea accepted her accolades graciously. *Success*—the word tasted sweet, like caramels. It was sweeter still as she realized she would be putting it on hold indefinitely.

~

Mike elected to accept the Ramirezes' hospitality and stay at their home for the night. He and Paul—also an Army veteran—had developed a deep camaraderie during the summer months. With Mike's departure to Missouri scheduled in three days, the two men decided a night of recounting old war stories was in order.

Even though Thea took the news concerning Peyton in stride, she couldn't help but be a little upset and welcomed the opportunity of an evening alone with Monty. She wasted no time after they arrived at her house to break her news to him.

56

"You're sure this is what you want to do?" He reacted to her announcement stoically, showing little emotion.

"Monty, it's not only something I *want* to do; it's something I *need* to do. All my life I've wondered about my mother's family in Greece. But there never seemed to be a right time to go there. I was so young when Mama died that the thought never occurred to me. Then as I grew older, there was always something else I had to do; someplace else I wanted to go."

She took a deep breath before continuing, wanting desperately for him to understand. "I've let too much time slip by. My grandparents are gone now, and I never even met them. I don't want that to happen with my two aunts. They're old, and there's no way of knowing how much time they have left."

"Why didn't they ever come to America to visit?" Monty asked.

"There were hard feelings when my mother married Mike."

"Ah," Monty replied, nodding his head. "Cultural differences, I presume."

"That's partly true," Thea replied, "but there was more to the rift than that. My grandfather was a landowner and quite well-to-do. Great emphasis was put on preserving the old customs. Well, my mother was the youngest of the three daughters, so when she wanted to marry first, that broke with tradition. Her father forbade the marriage, and you can probably guess the rest."

"Yes. Mike and your mother eloped."

"My grandparents never spoke to her again. I can still remember Mama's tears when the letters she wrote to them would be returned unopened. But, Monty, she and Mike loved each other so much! It was all such a tragedy."

"Did your mother's sisters feel the same way?"

"They secretly wrote to her from time to time. They knew of my birth and sent a lovely gown for my christening." Her voice grew hushed, and her face became shadowed. "Alexa wore it for her christening, too. I still have it."

"You yearn for all that has been lost to you. I understand this, but are you going for the right reasons?" Monty asked.

She moved close to him, to touch his face, to look into his eyes. "Monty, I'm not running away this time. I am still searching—for what exactly, I don't know. Maybe I'll find it in Greece."

"How long?" It was all he could say.

"I'll stay until coming back feels right." She sighed deeply. "Can you understand? Can you wait?"

"Yes," he answered without hesitation as he reached for her.

Slowly, floating in a sea of desire, they freed themselves from the confines of clothing. Thea stood on her tiptoes and drew his head down until his lips locked with hers, triggering that familiar hunger. Her erect nipples brushed against his chest. Vaguely, she was aware of being carried to the bed, where she gently pushed him down and lifted herself atop him. Giddy from the success of her show and the wine she had consumed, she suddenly became the aggressor. She desperately needed the searing heat of sex to burn away her feelings of restlessness and to wipe the fiasco of Peyton Winslow from her mind.

Monty moaned from sheer ecstasy as her sweet, warm wetness enveloped him. She began to move with a slow, delicious rhythm, teasing him, urging him almost to the edge of endurance and then drawing him back, promising more. Her hair fell from its clasp. It hung thick and long, imprisoning the lovers within their own private cocoon, shutting out all the outside forces that threatened to pull them apart.

Since the very first time, sex between them had been intense, but never before had Monty experienced his passion soaring to such heights as it did through the remainder of the night and into the first pink light of dawn. When he could bear her sweet torture no longer, they moved as one, together, until she lay beneath him.

In the dim light filtering through the window shades, he opened his eyes and looked down into hers, into those wide and unblinking black pools. At that very moment, Monty knew that the true sense of belonging that had eluded him all his life was in his arms.

The passion he felt could no longer be held back, and neither could his heart's desire. "Marry me, Thea," he whispered, feeling every fiber of her body clutching his. "Marry me and let me take care of you. Let me make you happy. Let me give you children!"

The impalpable shift in her movements and the faint intake of breath were all that told him he had demanded too much of her. Caught within the moment's rapture, he had asked for the one thing she could not give.

They lay with their bodies entwined, drifting in the aftermath of their lovemaking. The silence was comforting. Finally, he spoke. "You know how much I love you, don't you?"

"Oh, yes, Monty, and I love you!"

"Then, must you go?" It was as close to pleading as he would come.

She hesitated, searching for the right words. "I don't know exactly what is happening to me, Monty, but I do know that I cannot bear to have you witness it!"

~

He stood, brushed the debris from his pants, and studied the efforts of his morning's work. The sun glinted brightly off the monument bearing his sister's name. Gone now were the weeds and briars that had been allowed to grow unchecked until they all but obscured the engraving. How long had it been since he'd been up here? Monty wasn't sure. He hadn't felt the need to come here for a very long time. It seemed the ideal place to be this morning, though, a place of mourning.

High overhead, the faint hum of a jet engine broke the silence. Maybe that was her plane. He hadn't wanted to go with her to Albuquerque. He hadn't wanted to see her board the plane. She hadn't insisted.

Sheba sat quietly some distance away, watching him. Perhaps she, too, felt his emptiness. It was the same emptiness that had lived within him before Thea had come into his life. It would remain with him until her return.

57

The psychiatrist pursed his lips together thoughtfully, delaying what must be said just a bit longer. He needed to be very careful with this woman. One wrong word and, he feared, he wouldn't be allowed to see the child again. The hardest part of treating children was gaining not their trust but the trust of their parents.

"Well, Dr. Leonard, can you help Reagan? These nightmares of hers are, understandably, frightening for my husband and me, but they absolutely scare her to death."

Dr. Abe Leonard cleared his throat and spoke in what he hoped was his positive voice. "Mrs. O'Malley, I've talked at great length with Reagan, and I do have a conclusion and a recommendation." He paused to smile at the beautiful little girl sitting patiently beside her mother. Abe loved all children, but this one was truly special. Those eyes of hers, so big and luminous, seemed to look straight into his soul, beseeching him to help her.

"Yes? Your conclusion, Doctor?" Peg prodded him nervously.

"I do not believe, Mrs. O'Malley, that the nightmares are the cause of Reagan's distress."

"But—"

Abe held up a hand to silence her interruption. "Let me explain, please. The nightmares are but a symptom of a more complex problem. In other words, Mrs. O'Malley, instead of her nightmares causing Reagan to be afraid, I believe a deep-seated fear within her is in turn causing the nightmares."

There, he'd said it. Now all that remained for him to do was wait for the denial he fully expected. He didn't have to wait long.

"That's completely absurd, Dr. Leonard," Peg responded curtly. She rose and extended her hand to him, indicating an end to the counseling session. "You see, Doctor, Reagan has no fears—none whatsoever!" She smiled with obvious adoration at the little girl.

"Before you go, Mrs. O'Malley, may I speak with you privately?"

"I suppose. Reagan, darling, wait for Mama in the playroom, okay? I promise I won't be long."

Abe couldn't let it go. He was certain that something, or someone, had instilled deep fear in this child. "Please let me explain my position here. When your family physician contacted me and suggested I speak with your daughter, I believed it to be just another case of childhood fears of things that go bump in the night. However, after a few sessions with Reagan, I have come to realize that there's more to it."

Abe took a deep breath and continued. "Mrs. O'Malley, your daughter is unbelievably intelligent, especially for a child of eight. Why, she carries on a conversation at almost an adult level! This sheds a positive light on her home life, to be sure. But—" Words failed him.

"But what, Dr. Leonard?" Peg's tone was cool, her manner guarded. Abe knew any attempt at further therapy was going to be met with strong opposition.

"I believe Reagan has suffered a trauma, perhaps very early in her life, even before she was old enough to remember. A trauma would not only cause her nightmares but would certainly explain the slight stutter she has. Is that possible, Mrs. O'Malley?" Abe asked.

He didn't wait for an answer before continuing. He simply had to make her see how important it was for Reagan to continue her sessions with him. "It could have been something that might not seem important now—oh, say, the violent death of a pet, for example. Or perhaps she saw a particularly brutal scene from a movie that she doesn't even remember seeing. Something has brought about fear within her, and that fear is manifesting itself through her nightmares."

She was silent for a time. "There was no trauma, Doctor. No violence. Nothing. I'm sure of it," Peg answered.

"Do you believe that my concern for your daughter is sincere, Mrs. O'Malley?"

"Of course, but I don't—"

"Then if you believe I have only Reagan's best interests in mind, I would like to advance my therapy one step further. I would like your permission to place her under hypnosis. It will be perfectly safe, and it just may tell us what's causing these nightmares."

"Absolutely not! How could you even suggest hypnotizing my daughter?"

Peg gathered her purse and coat and prepared to leave. This time Abe knew he could not stop her. Her hand was already on the doorknob as he made one final plea.

"Will you at least discuss it with your husband, please? Once we know what frightened the child so, then we can deal with it, perhaps put a stop to her nightmares completely. But the first step is to get to the root of the problem."

"Thank you, Doctor, for your time and your concern for Reagan. Good day."

Abe didn't have to hear Peg O'Malley's quiet voice instruct the receptionist to cancel all future sessions to know that he would no longer be allowed contact with the child. He shook his head sadly. It was times such as these that made him want to throw in the towel, to simply forget all the Reagans of the world and the monsters that lurked in the dark corners of their young minds. But he knew he could not.

58

"You did what? Peg, darling, is that wise?" Deep lines of worry creased Charlie O'Malley's face as he questioned his wife. "Reagan loves Dr. Leonard. She's sleeping better these days, and you said yourself her stutter has improved."

"Charlie, the man's obviously in over his head with Reagan's case. He's grasping at straws. We never should have taken her for therapy in the first place." Peg fell silent and turned her attention to the quilting loom before her.

Charlie watched her for a time, watched her nimble fingers work their magic with needle and thread. His voice was almost a whisper when he finally spoke. "What we never should have done was to—"

"Don't say it, Charlie. Don't ever say it!" Her eyes held that strange light he had seen all too often during the past four years. "Ridiculous—that's what it is to think a little child needs a psychologist!"

"Psychiatrist. I believe when they have a medical degree—"

Again, she cut him off. "Whatever!" She rose and walked briskly toward the kitchen, signifying an end to their conversation. "Reagan, come help Mama with supper, sweetheart."

Charlie stretched out on the couch and closed his eyes. How tired he was! As with everything else in their lives, nothing had been resolved. Problems could be dealt with later; decisions could be made down the road. What was it Peg always said? "Now, Charlie, things will work themselves out. You'll see. Come Sunday—that's what my mother used to say. Everything will be fine come Sunday!"

"Papa, are you asleep?" The tentative little touch upon his cheek brought him out of his daydreaming. "No, baby, I'm just resting and thinking about my pretty little girl."

She smiled at him then, a smile that could conquer empires. "M-Mama s-says come to supper, okay?"

"Okay!" Charlie followed the skipping Reagan into the dining room. For all his wife's delusions and fantasies, she'd done well by the child, he would readily admit. She was happy and knew above all else that she was loved, even when she was disciplined, which was rare.

Their mealtimes were quite the family affair, with the three of them sharing the events of their day with one another. Reagan usually dominated the dinner conversation, chirping happily about school and friends, but more often than not, about her arts class.

Tonight, however, Charlie noticed she seemed subdued. "You're very quiet, Reagan. What's on your mind?" he prompted.

"Why c-can't I see Dr. Abe anym-m-more?" she asked thoughtfully.

"Do you want to see Dr. Abe again?" Charlie knew his question would infuriate Peg, but he was past caring.

"Oh, yes! He's m-my very favorite person, 'cept for you and Mama," she added, her dark eyes dancing once more. "We talk and talk and talk!"

"You do enough talking right here at home, young lady," Peg said. "It seems to me you'd enjoy doing some other things after school besides sitting in a stuffy old office talking all the time."

"Things like what?" the child asked warily.

"Well, maybe we could go to the park more often," Peg began, "or you might take more art classes. Would you like that?" Charlie knew his wife was grasping.

"Well, m-maybe, but I really like talking to Dr. Abe." Her voice grew faint as disappointment registered on her face.

"We'll see, sweetheart. Now, go start your bath water." Peg's voice was kind but firm.

"I know what I want!" Reagan said, brightening. "Jason Miller's c-cat had kittens, and he said I c-c-can have one. Okay, Mama?"

"No, Reagan, you can't. I'm sorry, but Papa's very allergic to cats, remember? We've talked about this before. How about an aquarium with lots of pretty fish? We could go tomorrow after school and see what we can find. Yes, I think that would be lovely!" Peg stood and began clearing the table

"But we used to have a c-cat, didn't we?"

"No, Reagan, we didn't. Now please be a help to Mama and go get your bath ready."

~

The insides of our heads are strange places, Reagan thought as she lay tucked in her bed. Dr. Abe said so. He said there could be things in there we had forgotten about and then remembered again in our dreams. Reagan didn't like dreams, not the bad ones, anyway. Sometimes they were nice, with lots and lots of flowers and sunshine. But mostly, they were bad. Funny thing—she never remembered what happened in the bad ones, only that they were very, very scary. They scared Mama and Papa, too.

Reagan opened her eyes and looked around her room. The tiny night-light kept it from being dark, and she could see all her beautiful dolls and fun stuffed animals. She yawned sleepily. Maybe she should get up and get one of the toys to cuddle and sleep with. But which one did she want?

Her eyelids were growing heavy. It was just too much trouble to get up and get a toy. She didn't want one, anyway. What she *really* wanted was a cat to cuddle—a big fat one like Jason's, one that purred really loud.

"One like I used to have," she whispered into her pillow.

59

"I would like to talk to you when you are ready to listen, Athena." The old woman's voice rang out in clear, bell-like tones, a contradiction to her advancing years.

"Yes, Aunt Katrina. I'll be right in," Thea answered. She was reluctant to move from her comfortable chair on the hotel terrace. The view of whitewashed buildings clinging to the volcanic cliffs was well worth the day's exhausting walk through miles of winding cobblestone streets.

Since arriving in Fira, the capital of Santorini, that morning, Thea had barely stopped to catch her breath. Already, she looked forward to the next day's excursions to see nearby archaeological sites.

"Oh, Aunt Katrina, my head is spinning!" she said. "I have so many ideas for my pottery! Visiting the potters' quarter in Athens taught me more about vase painting than any classroom or book ever could. And to actually visit Akrotiri tomorrow—I can't tell you what it means to me! I've loved being here with you and Aunt Anna, although I don't think she likes me very much."

"Doesn't like you?" Katrina stopped her unpacking and looked quizzically at her niece. "Why, Athena, Anna loves you as I do! We have loved you since the moment you were born. We did not need to see you to love you. You are our Mary's child. And you are the image of her, my dear!" A rare smile tilted the corners of her mouth as she spoke.

Thea sighed. "Aunt Katrina, I've been in Greece eight months, now, and Aunt Anna has spoken barely a few words to me, and she never wants to go with us on our tours. I just assumed she didn't want me here."

"You assumed wrong, child. Believe me. I know my older sister better than anyone. She's exactly like our father. I do not speak disrespectfully but truthfully. He was a difficult man to get to know and an even more difficult man to love, our Papa."

The old woman stopped speaking and reached awkwardly for Thea's hand. "Come, let's go back to the terrace. You do not want to miss the sunset. We will talk there."

Thea was pensive. To hear her aunt speak of love seemed strange. She hadn't known what to expect in her aunts' home here in Greece. Certainly, she had held no illusion of being welcomed with open arms after a lifetime lived apart, yet Anna's aloof manner hurt.

Mike had warned her that the old ways still prevailed, and he'd been right. Thea's news that she and Joe had divorced was met with stoic silence from Katrina and a verbal rebuke from Anna: "You were not taught that the marriage vows are sacred?"

During her months here, conversation had been rare with her aunts. "I suppose I never thought about it, Aunt Katrina. Of course you love me, and I love you. I only wish we could have been close while I was growing up. My parents loved each other so much! But you know that, don't you?"

"Yes, child, I know that. The old ways—the old customs—were my father's way. They are Anna's way, also." She hesitated, and Thea knew there was something else on her mind.

"It is not the past that I need to speak with you about, Athena, but the future. It is your future that concerns me. Forgive an old woman for meddling, but I feel I must. There is not a great deal of time."

"Not time for what, Aunt Katrina? Of course, I'll be going home eventually, but there's no immediate hurry."

"Listen to me, Athena. I have regretted my entire life the rift that was between your dear mother and the rest of our family. I tried to talk to Anna, but the bitterness would not leave her. You see, she was the eldest, and it was expected that she would marry first. But, alas, Anna and I were plain. The young men did not come to call often."

She paused to take a small sip of wine before continuing. "Your mother's wanting to marry first was not the only thing that upset Papa. Mary was the beauty in our family and so full of life, as well. And she was Papa's favorite! Yes, it was obvious he favored her from the time she was born. You can imagine how it broke his heart when he lost her."

"But, Aunt Katrina, he didn't *lose* her!" Thea interjected. "She fell in love and wanted to get married. That's not loss. I could tell him what actually losing a daughter is like!" Angry tears sprang to Thea's eyes as she spoke.

"Yes, child, you speak of your Alexa. A tragedy it was and always will be. Michael wrote me when it happened, and I grieved. Both Anna and I grieved. It is about your loss that I will now speak. Dry your eyes, and listen to me."

Thea obeyed. She sensed, and rightfully so, that her aunt's words would hold little happiness.

"The doctors in Athens have told me I have only a little time left in this life." Katrina's grip tightened on Thea's hand as she continued speaking. "It is the cancer, the same that took your dear mother." Seeing the look on her young niece's face, she quickly continued. "It is not tears I want from you. I want instead your promise."

"My promise?"

"Yes. You must promise me that you will not waste your life grieving as I have done and especially as Anna has done. Oh, please do not think our lives have been completely empty. We have done fine for ourselves with investments and with selling Papa's lands. And we have our friends and our church. But, Athena, we have mourned our entire lives for what could never be!"

"How—how long, Aunt Katrina?"

"The doctors say maybe one year. But what do they know? I feel stronger since you have been here. So, I think maybe longer."

"I don't know what to say. I only found you, and now— Does Aunt Anna know?"

"Yes, I told her. She wishes it were her, instead, not only because she is older, but—I should not say this—I believe she would actually welcome death."

The two women sat in silence for a time, unable to enjoy the beauty before them but strangely content nonetheless. It was Thea who finally broke the silence.

"What do I do to keep this promise to you? No matter what I do, I cannot stop grieving for Alexa, nor will I ever stop trying to find out what happened to her."

"Of course you can't. No one would expect you to. But you cannot change the past, either. So, cannot this grief of yours have some purpose? Is there nothing you can do to help others who have lost a child violently? When I look at you, Athena, I see youth, beauty, and talent!" The old woman spoke now with passion "Use these gifts to help others. By doing this, you will fulfill your promise to me!"

Thea swallowed hard, choking back the tears she knew the old woman did not want. "I promise," she whispered.

60

"Saying good-bye to the two of you is one of the hardest things I've ever had to do," Thea said as she stood in the garden of her aunts' home in preparation for her departure.

The past year in Greece had done nothing but whet her appetite for her mother's homeland. She fully understood now what Monty spoke of when he visited the ancient ruins of his ancestors: "When I hear their voices, Thea, they tell me to be careful of what we leave behind, for it determines how we will be remembered."

Yes, she was sad to be leaving Greece, but at the same time, she couldn't wait to get back home to Santa Fe.

"We will miss you, child, so very much," Katrina said, embracing her warmly, surprising Thea once again with her strength. "You will write to us, yes?"

"Oh, yes, and I'll call you. Thank you so much for everything!"

Thea turned to Anna, who stood just out of reach, pretending to prune her roses. "And thank you, Aunt Anna, for your hospitality. I love you both."

"Have a safe trip home." Anna couldn't quite meet her niece's gaze. She spoke tentatively. "I was wondering if you would do something for us."

"Yes, ma'am. Anything," Thea replied.

"Well, I was wondering if you would perhaps send a piece of your pottery, one you've painted. I—I heard you talking with Katrina, and I thought it might be nice to have something you made. Our friends could see it."

Thea glanced at Katrina and saw the faint smile on her face. "Of course, Aunt Anna. I would be proud to make a vessel especially for you."

"God bless you, Athena," Anna said stiffly before turning her attention once more to her roses. The yellow taxi announced its arrival with a blaring horn and screeching tires, bringing an end to the difficult silence.

Katrina embraced her niece once more. "You should feel honored," she whispered into Thea's ear. "My sister calls upon God to bless few people!"

"Take care of each other," Thea said before climbing reluctantly into the waiting taxi. As they sped away toward the airport, she turned to watch the rapidly receding figures of the old women, the last of her mother's family. With a heavy heart, she wondered if she would ever see them again.

~

The flight from Athens to New York had been smooth and uneventful. The next leg of Thea's journey to St. Louis, however, proved to be horrendous. Unstable weather had made for a bumpy ride, and Thea's back ached. Still, she was glad she'd decided to stop over and spend a few days with Mike.

Slowly, she made her way through the milling throngs of people who crowded the arrival gate area and on toward baggage claim, where she and Mike had arranged to meet. Suddenly, her attention was drawn to the figure walking several feet in front of her. She could see only the back of the head and shoulders, but the resemblance was unmistakable.

"It can't be!" Thea whispered aloud. She increased her pace, elbowing her way through the crowd and excusing herself profusely. "Joe," she called out loud enough to be heard above the din. "Joe, is that you?"

Joe Kelly turned at the sound of his name. As recognition hit, his quizzical expression exploded into the same boyish grin she remembered.

"Thea! What in the world are you doing here?" He threw a protective arm around her shoulders and led her out of the jostling crowd to a small lounge.

"I can't believe it! Running into you like this—what are the odds?" Thea babbled, breathless with excitement. "I'm here to spend a few days at the home place with Mike. You look great, Joe!"

He was silent for a moment, his eyes drinking in the sight of her. "And you—you're even more beautiful! How've you been, Thea?"

"Fine. I'm really fine, Joe. I'm on my way back from a year in Greece. I visited my mother's sisters there. It was wonderful. And you?" She tried to sound calm, but her voice quivered, her mind whirled.

"Here, let's sit down. Have you got time?" He held a chair for her.

"Mike's meeting me in baggage claim, but he can wait a few minutes, I guess. He told me you'd moved back here some time ago. So, tell me. How things are going for you?" Her interest was genuine.

"I've been in St. Louis for almost two years now. I'm in business for myself. Matter of fact, I'm just coming back from a convention of architects in Atlanta.

"You, uh, probably remember Cassie Richards from high school," he continued. Awkwardly, he reached for his wallet and produced a small photo. "Cassie and I ran into each other at a reunion right after I moved back. We've been married a little over a year now. That's Joseph," he finished, proudly pointing to the infant held lovingly between the smiling couple.

Thea fingered the photograph, letting her eyes rest only briefly on the tiny head covered with bright red fuzz. "Congratulations, Joe. Of course I remember Cassie, and I'm happy for you both."

"How 'bout you, Thea? What's going on with you? And Max—how is she?" Joe rambled. "I ran into Mike once up at the lake. He said you love New Mexico and that your pottery has taken off like wildfire. That's great. I know it what's you always wanted." He put the photograph back in his wallet and turned to look at her once more. "Have you remarried?"

Thea laughed. "Now, let's see if I can answer all your questions in order! Max is wonderful. Judging from the letters she's written me during the past year, she's in love. I can't wait to meet this guy. He sounds really special.

"As far as my pottery is concerned, I'm still a little overwhelmed that it has been so well received." She hesitated briefly. "I have no plans to remarry, but there is someone very special waiting for me. At least, I hope he's still waiting," she finished.

"Did you ask him to wait?" Joe asked.

"Yes, I did."

"Well, then, there's your answer," he said, patting the back of her hand gently. "If you asked him to wait, believe me, he's waiting."

The lounge area had gradually grown quiet. Her eyes held his for a long time. "Joe, can you ever forgive me? God, I cannot stop thinking about how selfish and cruel I was and of the terrible things I said to you. I'm so ashamed!"

"There's nothing to apologize for, Thea." He smiled sadly at her. "We both reacted to tragedy differently, that's all. We did the best we could."

The tears were threatening to come, and she didn't want them. "I need to get going. Mike's probably thinking I missed my plane."

They rose in unison and began strolling down the concourse. "It was so good to see you. I'm happy for you, Joe. I'm really happy."

"Take care of yourself, Thea. If you ever need anything—anything at all—you let me know, you hear?" He was proud of himself. The practiced smile had remained perfectly in place as he watched her back away from him.

In his dreams, though, she never backed away but instead ran toward him, her arms outstretched, her eyes glowing with love. In his dreams, too, rang the haunting echoes of a little girl's laughter—

Thea's voice brought him back to reality. "You take care, too, Joe."

A crackling announcement came over the loudspeaker: "New York passenger, Thea Kelly, please meet your party in baggage claim." It brought chuckles from them both.

"What did I tell you? Mike's about to panic," Thea said.

"Go, then. Tell him I said hello."

"I will. Good-bye, Joe." It had been hard for Thea to meet his gaze earlier. Now, she found it equally hard to look away. She continued to back away slowly, thankful for the new tide of bodies that began to surge forward, coming between them and obliterating him from view.

"Will New York passenger, Thea Kelly, please meet your party in baggage claim?"

"Coming, Mike! Hold your horses!" she muttered, picking up her pace.

Joe did look well, and she was truly happy for him. What was it he had said? "If you asked him to wait, believe me, he's waiting."

Thea prayed he was right.

61

"Maxine Templeman," she whispered to her image in the mirror. Striking first one pose and then another, she studied herself intently.

"Hi, I'm Max Templeman." She moved closer to the mirror to examine the face looking back at her—a face that still glowed with the sheer wonder of it all. *So, this is what all the fuss is about! This is what it's like to be in love!*

"Hello, I'm Mrs. Aaron Templeman," she practiced once more.

"I hope it sounds as good to you as it does to me, my darling," he said quietly from the bedroom door. "How did I get so lucky?"

"I'm the lucky one, Aaron," Max replied. "I used to look at all my friends, Thea included, and think, 'That'll never happen to me.' I never thought I would feel that kind of love and commitment, that—" She stumbled for words. "Belonging—that's how I feel when I'm with you. Like I finally belong with someone." Max fell silent as she twirled the ten-carat diamond ring on her finger. She was still not at ease with the weight of it but was completely at ease with what it represented.

"I do love you, Aaron. I'll make you happy, I promise!"

"You already have, Max. I only hope all the differences between us— religion, age—" His words were not coming easily either. "Hell, Max, I'm fifty-eight years old, twice-divorced, and nothing to look at!"

"And you've won my heart!" Max said as she turned to embrace him. "It's right. We both know it. And the differences—they'll work themselves out. Now, we'd better finish getting ready. Thea's plane lands in a little over an hour, and I'm going to be there waiting! Oh, Aaron, you're just going to love her! I think I just heard a car. Yes, it's Paul and Elena, right on time."

Aaron reached to help Max with her jacket. "And I can't wait to meet your Thea. Have you told her about our wedding yet?"

"No, we'll tell her together. Trust me—she'll be thrilled. She's always told me what I needed was to fall in love," Max beamed. "How right she was!"

"Monty didn't change his mind about coming with us to the airport, I see," Aaron commented as the couple approached the waiting car. "I hope things are still the same between them. A year is a long time."

"It'll take more than a year's separation to end *that* relationship," Max assured him. With his gregarious, never-met-a-stranger personality, Aaron still couldn't quite grasp Monty's private, almost secretive, nature. "Just because he's not going to the airport doesn't mean he's not waiting for her. You'll see."

The late afternoon drive to Albuquerque was pleasant. Aaron's animated chatter with Elena regarding their mutual involvement in the jewelry industry allowed Max some much-needed time to reflect on the changes in her life that the past year had brought.

Although she would never have burdened Thea with her feelings, Max truly thought she might die of loneliness when her best friend left for Greece. Thankfully, Paul and Elena had recognized that friendship as being one of the few constants in Max's life and had swiftly intervened.

"Now, Max, you must go with us to San Francisco this weekend!" Elena had insisted a few weeks after Thea's departure. "We're meeting with the jeweler who'll be marketing my pieces in the Northwest. After that, we'll have a wonderful time sightseeing. Paul and I won't take no for an answer!"

Max closed her eyes, basking in the memory. That weekend had been the beginning of her transformation from cynical, liberated lady, who always managed to avoid that danger zone of commitment, into someone who now awoke each day to a world touched by magic. Had it really been just that easy for the barriers to fall?

Twenty minutes in Aaron's office had been all that Max had needed to know that behind his quick smile and incredibly kind eyes was someone genuine, someone different from all the others, someone who would instill in her the desire to love and be loved.

~

"We're here in plenty of time," Paul said. "I'll let the three of you out and then park the car."

"By the way, is Cal going to be here?" Elena asked as the car came to a stop. "I know he's looking forward to seeing Thea as much as we are."

"He told me last night that he'd meet us at the restaurant down in Old Town. Said he had some business to attend to for Thea. Apparently, they've been talking on the phone quite a bit during the past week. I'm sure we'll all find out the details at dinner." Paul waited as his passengers began to exit the car. "See you in a few minutes in the main terminal."

Max, roused from her daydreaming, smiled at Aaron as he helped her from the car. Soon, she would share this unbelievable happiness with her dearest friend. She twirled the ring again. Soon, the metamorphosis of Maxine Lindel would be complete—*Mrs. Aaron Templeman!*

62

Thea checked her watch again; time had never passed so slowly. The entire year in Greece seemed short compared to the flight into Albuquerque. Mike had even commented earlier at the airport in St. Louis how preoccupied she had become.

"Eager to be leaving, aren't you, baby?" he asked.

"Yes, I am. This week's been great here with you—the whole year's been great, in fact. But I'm ready to go home now."

"Miss, how much longer before we land?" Thea inquired of the flight attendant.

"Should be about twenty minutes, ma'am," the young woman answered, smiling. "Going home?" she asked. The words sounded so right.

"Yes," Thea answered, returning her smile. "I'm going home!"

~

She looked around anxiously upon entering the gate area. There! There they were! Of course, Monty wasn't there. It wasn't his way. But that was all right. She knew in her heart of hearts that he'd be waiting for her.

The flurry of embraces, tears, and everyone talking at once finally subsided.

"Just let me look at all of you for a minute! Oh, how I've missed you!" Thea dried her eyes and stepped back to study her friends.

Paul looked the same as he stood ramrod straight, his bearing almost regal. And the past year had done nothing but enhance Elena's exotic beauty.

"Oh, Max!" Thea whispered, marveling at the change in her best friend. Gone were the artfully applied makeup and the sexy clothing. Gone, too, was the aloof demeanor that seemed to say, "I don't trust you, so let me make the first move."

Thea saw before her now a woman who looked years younger. She saw a woman basking in the glow of love and trust and self-assurance. The reason for this transformation was obvious to Thea, and she turned to greet Aaron.

"Aaron Templeman," he said as he shook her hand. "What a delight it is to finally meet you, Thea! Welcome home!"

Exactly as Max had described him, he stood a full head shorter than she, balding, round of girth, and bursting with energy. Equally obvious was his adoration of her best friend.

"I'm so happy to meet you, Aaron. Max said your smile could light the darkest room, and she was right. It's good to finally be home!"

~

"The year did you good, lady," Cal remarked as he leaned back in his chair at the restaurant and studied Thea. She was exquisite! Even more beautiful than before she'd left, if that were possible.

"It certainly did, or rather, my aunt did. Aunt Katrina showed me what my life *could* be like years from now if I keep on brooding and grieving over something I cannot change. I want all of you to know that I won't let that happen." She continued speaking with conviction. "I'll never stop believing that Alexa is alive, and I can't stop hoping that one day we'll all know what happened. But it will no longer consume me. Cal, why don't you tell everyone my plan," she finished, eager to share the only positive outcome from her daughter's disappearance.

"Thea phoned me last week," Cal said. "She's come up with a great idea for her as well as for a whole lot of other folks, I believe. She's the one doing it. Me, I'm just putting her in touch with some really good psychiatrists, therapists, and the likes, as well as private investigators.

"She's going to use the proceeds from the sale of her pottery—and we all know that's going to be a lot of money over the years—to provide counseling for other parents who've had kids abducted, or worse." Cal paused awkwardly. "And funds would also be there to provide private investigative work for people who can't afford it.

"As I've told Thea before, in any disappearance, the first seventy-two hours are crucial." Cal chose his words carefully. "Okay, I'll just say it. In most instances, if we don't find the individual within that initial time frame, the chances of finding them alive are slim to none. Now, that's not always the case, of course, but it is the cold, hard fact that motivates police investigations."

"Many cases simply fall through the cracks, don't they, Cal?" Paul quietly voiced everyone's thoughts.

"Yes, they do. I can tell you for sure that Alexa's case did not. However," the veteran investigator said before he paused and shook his head, "with no clues for so long— Anyway, Thea wants to help other folks caught in that same situation. That's about it. Hell, Thea, it's your idea. You finish the story!"

"Yes, this sounds so wonderful! Tell us more." Elena's usual exuberance surfaced as did a chorus of excited murmurs all around.

"As I said, Aunt Katrina's the one who put this idea in my head. She made me promise to, in her words, let my grief have a positive path. This is what I've come up with. Maybe other families can benefit. It's all that's left for me to do."

"It's a wonderful idea, Thea," Aaron said. "I do hope you'll allow Max and me to be a part of it. It would certainly give us good reason to visit Santa Fe often, not that we'll need a reason since we both love it here. Oh, my. I've let the cat out of the bag, haven't I?" He grinned, red-faced at the look of surprise on Thea's face. "Forgive me, Max. You know my big mouth!"

"What do you mean, *visit*? Max, what's going on?" Thea asked even though she already knew the answer to her question.

"Well, kiddo, I'm living proof that it's never too late. Aaron and I are getting married!" Max beamed.

"Married? When? Where? I mean—well, that's wonderful!" Thea sputtered as she looked from one smiling face to the other before letting her eyes rest on her friend's left hand. "My God, I didn't know diamonds grew that big!"

The two women rose from their seats simultaneously to embrace.

"Soon, Thea. I've just been waiting for you. Can't get hitched without my best buddy standing by my side, now can I?" Max paused, dried her eyes, and went on. "It'll be a small ceremony, very private, at my house. Then Aaron and I will fly to New York for a week or so to visit with his son and daughter-in-law."

"And then, my friend?" Thea asked wistfully.

"Well," Max said as she drew a deep breath, "then we'll be leaving for San Francisco. That's where Aaron's business is. That's where we'll be living most of the time."

"But never fear, Thea;" Aaron said. He stood and placed an arm around each woman. "You'll see more of us than you think. Max doesn't want to sell her house here, and I don't want her to. Not only will my business keep bringing us here, but I feel as though I've found a family with all of you."

"Oh, Aaron, Max, I'm so happy for you both! I'm so very happy!" Thea said with genuine emotion.

"Now, Thea, Cal, please tell us more of your plans," Paul said, changing the subject after the excitement died down. "Will this be regional, or will you tie in with other support groups nationally? Could law enforcement agencies help?"

"For the time being, Paul, we'd be mainly regional," Cal answered. "Take it from me: the law can do only so much. If there are no clues to speak of, and in a lot of cases no suspects—well, you get the picture. What Thea has in mind is to provide the needed counseling and support for the parents and other family members. The timing is crucial, right, Thea?"

"Yes. You see, when a child goes missing, the best thing parents can do is get proper counseling to help them deal with the loss. Joe knew this, and I know it now, but I didn't always know it. I fought it. I fought the very thing that can help a person survive such a nightmare. What Cal and I want to do is to let people know that help is available to them without cost. They need to know that someone out there understands what they're going through and really cares. With Cal's contacts, he can line up private investigators. That can get expensive, and as he said, we'd help with that, too."

Paul spoke softly. "It's a wonderful plan, Thea. And Aaron's right, we are a family, all of us! Elena and I will be proud to be a part of this, if you'll allow it. Come to think of it, there's not a better person in the entire state to organize a fund-raiser than my lovely wife! How 'bout it, Elena?"

"Wonderful idea, darling! Why, charity work is what I do best!"

"No, Elena," Max said, "matchmaking is what you do best!"

"I'll drink to that!" Aaron chimed it, raising his glass.

Amid the clink of crystal, Thea smiled and added, "And to the future!"

63

"I'll have your car serviced first thing in the morning, Thea," Paul said as he pulled into Thea's driveway. "The mechanic will most likely have it brought over before noon. Do you want us to come in with you?"

"Thanks, Paul, but it's awfully late. I'll be fine. Gosh, my home looks good! I'll talk to you guys tomorrow." As much as she had enjoyed her homecoming party, she was ready to say good night.

"Fine, then. If you have everything you need for tonight in your overnight bag, why don't we just bring the rest of your luggage over in the morning?" Elena offered.

"Great idea. See you then."

Paul drove the car slowly out of the driveway, leaving her alone to absorb the stillness of the Santa Fe night. Her footsteps made a crunching sound in the gravel as she made her way to the front porch, and from somewhere nearby an owl hooted his lonesome greeting.

Moments before she saw the outline of the Jeep parked alongside her house and before the faint aroma of pipe tobacco assailed her nostrils, she knew he was there.

Soundlessly he stepped from the shadows and into the moonlight. "I've been waiting for you." His whispered words were like a caress.

"Monty!"

"It's late, and I know you're tired." He took a step toward her. "I could stay for just a few minutes and then come back tomorrow."

"Do I have another choice?" she asked.

He moved even closer until they were almost touching, their breath mingling, his eyes locked on hers. "I could stay forever."

"That's the one!"

~

Thea climbed gingerly from the Jeep, stretching and rubbing her back. "I always love the drive to Taos, Monty, but I gotta tell you—I've had enough traveling of any kind to last me for quite a while!"

"I shouldn't have insisted we come back to the ranch today, love. I'm sorry. It's just that Clayton and Lydia made me swear I'd bring you here first thing. And I have a surprise for you."

"Oh, what might that be?"

"You'll see soon enough." A mischievous grin spread over his face. "After we have bombarded you with questions about Greece and made you promise to never leave us again, I'll show you."

"That's a promise I'll gladly make, Monty. I won't leave again. And I just might have a surprise for you, too!"

The excitement of her homecoming was doubled when Thea told Monty and the Johns about her plans for a counseling and investigation service for the families of missing children. In fact, Monty responded with more animation than she'd ever seen him exhibit.

"Thea, what a wonderful idea this is!" He jumped up from the dinner table and began pacing excitedly back and forth. "This is something I can be a part of, something we can all be a part of! Clayton, Lydia, can you think of a better way to use the profits from her?"

"Who is *her*?" Thea asked, caught up in his excitement.

"Come, it's time for that surprise I promised you," Monty answered, pulling her to her feet. "She's in the den, waiting for you!"

Thea was speechless. As soon as the spotlight illuminated the life-size bronze, she recognized her own image. "You finished her," she whispered.

"It's truly the best work I've ever done," Monty said with quiet pride.

"I tried to persuade him to enter her in Market last month, but he said no, not until you saw her," Clayton added proudly.

"I wasn't sure I could bring myself to sell this one, even in a very limited edition. But now, after hearing your plans, I can. Yes, we'll release an edition of perhaps only twenty-five. And the proceeds, Thea, will go to help others who have lost someone dear to them, as you and I have."

"All you need do now is to name her," Lydia chimed in. "Monty could think of none suitable."

Thea stepped closer to study her bronze likeness. "I have a name for her," she said after a time. "She will be called 'Her Healing Spirit'!"

For this is Wisdom: to love, to live,
To take what Fate, or the gods, may give,
To ask no question, to make no prayer,
To kiss the lips and caress the hair,
Speed passion's ebb as you greet its flow,
To have, to hold, and in time, let go!
—"For This Is Wisdom,"
Laurence Hope

Part III

Part III

64

"Now, Reagan, what were we discussing during our session last week? Do you remember?" Abe Leonard smiled at the young girl sitting beside him on the park bench.

"Well, f-f-for one thing, I remember telling you how glad I was that Mama and Papa s-s-said I could come back to see you again. I sure missed you, Dr. Abe!"

Abe studied her animated movements as she spoke—kicking her feet in the sand one moment, smoothing her dress demurely over her knees the next. How he delighted in this lovely little woman-child!

The majority of girls her age were gawky, embarrassed by their budding breasts, the facial blemishes, and other horrors that nature heaped upon them, but not this one. Reagan O'Malley stood prepared to embrace the adult world with a sense of elegance and sensuality that would one day set her apart from other women.

"And I'm equally glad to have you back as my patient, Reagan. Although," Abe paused thoughtfully, "I don't think *patient* is the appropriate word here. More like friend. Yes, we're friends, and I've missed you, too!"

It was hard for Abe to hold his resentment at bay when thinking of the past five years, when he had been denied the opportunity to speak with this child. Five years that together he and Reagan could have broken through the barriers in her mind and driven out whatever demons lurked there. Enough recriminations—she was back in his care now, and that's what mattered. He decided to get right down to business.

"Let's walk down to the duck pond, shall we? I want you to tell me the very nicest thing about your whole life, okay?"

The young girl strolled along thoughtfully for several minutes before answering. "Well, the n-n-nicest *day* I've had in a long time was last S-Saturday. It was my birthday!"

"Yes, twelve is a wonderful age!"

She stopped dead in her tracks and, after tucking a wild strand of that glorious raven hair behind an ear, spoke with mock seriousness. "N-n-now, Dr. Abe, you know very well that I'm thirteen!"

Abe laughed heartily. "Yes, my dear, I know full well that you're a teenager now. Tell me, do the young men here in town know how lucky they are?"

"Lonnie Masters s-s-says he's going to m-marry me one day."

"What do you say about that?"

She sighed. "I'm not sure I w-want to get m-m-married. I want to be an artist. It's, it's all I ever t-think about."

"So, I suppose your art classes are the best thing about your life," the doctor said.

"Maybe the s-second best. The best is Mama and Papa. But—"

Abe's interest piqued. He allowed her a brief silence before responding. "But what, Reagan? You've no problems at home, do you?"

"I love them so much, and they love me;" Reagan answered. She stopped walking and turned to look up at him, those glowing black eyes beseeching him to help her understand. "Dr. Abe, do you ever f-f-feel like you don't belong?"

"Well, of course, Reagan. I suppose we all do at times." She'd caught him off guard, and that wasn't supposed to happen. "What makes you feel that you don't belong?"

"Secrets," she whispered. "S-s-sometimes I think there's a secret, one t-that everyone knows but me."

"Is that the worst thing about your life, Reagan?" Abe prodded gently. They had reached the pond, and he watched her as she began to toss bread to the gathering ducks.

"That, and this damned s-stuttering!" Her hand flew to her mouth in shock, and she was once again the little girl. "Please don't t-t-tell Mama I s-said a bad word, okay?"

"I won't tell her, I promise. See, now you and I have a secret. Secrets aren't always bad, are they?"

"I guess n-not. It's really hard to explain it when you just don't—" The child closed her eyes and groped for words. "It's hard when you just don't f-f-fit in!"

Abe skirted the issue. "How are the nightmares? I remember they used to give you and your mother quite a fright. Are you still having them?"

"Not n-nearly so much as when I was little. They're a lot like whispers now, like whispers in the dark," she finished thoughtfully. "Anyway, I know they're n-not real, right?"

"Umm, there's your mother." Abe didn't need to check his watch to know their appointed hour was up. It was obvious that Mrs. O'Malley's opinion of him and his counseling methods hadn't changed one bit during the past five years.

He had been delighted when his secretary had informed him the previous week that the O'Malleys would like an appointment for their daughter. In truth, it had been Reagan who'd insisted on resuming their sessions.

"Good day, Mrs. O'Malley. You're well, I hope."

"Fine, thank you, Doctor," Peg answered. "Reagan, your time's up, and Papa's waiting for us in the car." She turned on her heels, eager to be away.

"Mrs. O'Malley," Abe said again. "I know you have your doubts that I can help Reagan, but I assure you that I have only her very best interests in mind. Thank you for letting our sessions resume. I'm sure I can help the speech problem in time. She tells me the nightmares have all but stopped. I—"

She cut him off. "Dr. Leonard, my daughter outgrew the nightmares, just as she will the stuttering. 'Twas nothing you did. She simply outgrew her fear of the dark. And don't thank me for bringing her back to see you." Peg shook her head as she watched Reagan skip toward Charlie. "Her father spoils her; he gives her anything she wants." She paused, leveling her gaze on Abe. "Even when it's not what is best for her. Good day to you."

Abe made his way back to his office that overlooked the Delaney town square and small municipal park. He'd been depressed earlier in the day, but the session with his favorite patient as well as the spring weather had done much to heighten his spirits.

Favorite patient or not, others needed his attention. His secretary stood waiting as he entered the reception area.

"Doctor, Mrs. Sanders telephoned to let us know that Michael will be a little late for his session, and you just had a call from Dr. Pierce in Denver. Nothing urgent, he said, but give him a call when you have time." She lowered her glasses and continued speaking. "And I'm going to lunch."

"Sure, Mrs. Thatcher. Let me have Dave's number, and I'll call him right now."

Dr. David Pierce was Abe's best friend—had been since they were roommates in college. With so much in common, they'd stayed close throughout the years. Both of them had been basketball players, both chose psychiatry as their careers, and both of them had fallen in love with the same girl. Abe had moved to Delaney when she'd married Dave ten years ago.

His self-imposed exile had started out as some perverse means of torture, but as it turned out, he liked it in Delaney and had no intention of leaving. He liked it even more now that Reagan was back in his care.

Secrets? Not fitting in? That's a lot of weight for a kid of thirteen to carry around. "But that's what I'm here for," he muttered aloud as he punched in the phone number.

"Abe, you son of a gun," David began, "I thought you'd be here for the party. Grace was crushed! You're okay, aren't you?"

"Sure, Dave, I'm fine. I had a problem with a patient, that's all. I can't exactly run out on a suicidal high school kid even for a major event like your tenth anniversary, now can I?" He sounded chipper, or at least he hoped he did.

"Guess not, old buddy. But please know we missed you. By the way, when are you coming back to civilization for good? We do have synagogues here, you know. Wear that cute little beanie of yours, find a nice Jewish girl, and settle down—yadda yadda yadda."

"Screw you, Dave," Abe answered with a chuckle. "I happen to like it here in the boondocks. Besides, there's more to this business of ours than making money, but you wouldn't know that, now would you?"

"Abe, my man, that's cold! Money's not all I think about. I'll have you know I'm even donating six hours each and every month to a nonprofit organization. How's that for recognizing the important things in life?"

"It's a start," Abe responded. "What's it all about?"

"Some friend of a friend of Grace's turned us on to it. It's really a great idea. By *us* I mean myself and several other psychiatrists here in town. We set aside a few hours to give free counseling to parents who've had kids abducted or just disappeared, maybe victims of sexual abuse, that sort of thing. It's for folks who can't afford to pay. It's been around for several years now. You ought to look into it. It'll give you that warm, fuzzy feeling. You know what I mean?"

"Yeah, Dave, I know exactly what you mean," Abe quipped. "Half the patients I counsel now can't afford to pay me! Hey, I gotta go. Give Grace a kiss for me, and tell her I'm sorry I missed the party. Next time, okay?"

"Sure thing, pal. Now keep in touch."

"I will," Abe promised. "By the way, what's the name of this charity of yours?"

"It's called the Healing Spirit Foundation. Catchy, huh?"

65

"I thought that was the worst day of my life when she didn't come home from school," the young mother said through sobs that shook her body. "But it wasn't. The worst was when, when they found her! What he'd done to her, to my baby!"

The room at the foundation was pleasant and comfortable. The informal decor blended well with the neutral adobe walls and took a backseat to the panoramic view from the large windows. It was a quiet room, too, meant to encourage relaxation. The room was too quiet now, though, with the only sounds being the soft whir of the ceiling fan and the muffled sobs of the young mother.

Thea watched the woman, watched her thin shoulders tremble as she tried desperately to get the words out. And Thea knew her pain— remembered it, tasted it, smelled it. She knew pain as a separate entity, a presence that had lived within her for the past thirteen years. The only difference between herself and this poor, exhausted woman before her now lay in how they dealt with that pain.

"How do you stop the hurt?" The young mother looked pleadingly from her husband, who was trying to console her through tears of his own, to the psychiatrist who sat quietly, knowing it best to let her grief run its course. Finally, her eyes rested on Thea. "Ms. Kelly, how did you stop the hurt?"

Thea responded, "You don't stop it, Pamela, but you can control it. For years I didn't think that was possible. I pushed my husband out my life. I wanted to push away practically everything that reminded me of Alexa. One day, I realized that no matter how hard I pushed, no matter what I changed—surroundings, friends, occupations—that pain would always be inside me. But with the help of people who loved me, I managed to stop it from taking control of my life."

Thea smiled tenderly at the woman whose attention she held. "You see, dear, the pain is still in me, here," she said, her hand clutching her chest. "But it didn't grow any larger. It didn't smother the happiness I had left. Do you understand?"

Pamela Tremont remained silent for a few moments, mechanically shredding the wet tissue in her hands. Finally, she straightened her shoulders ever so slightly, leaned against her husband, and spoke.

"You people have helped me so much. Right after it—it happened, I wanted to kill myself. And I might have if Billy hadn't seen your fliers and made me come here. There's just no way we can ever pay you."

"Pamela, no one's asking for any money," Dr. Brighten said. "That isn't why we're here. And it isn't why Ms. Kelly and her friends founded the Healing Spirit Foundation. As you know, we like to make these counseling sessions very informal. With that in mind, does anyone have anything to add before we adjourn until next time?"

"Pamela, Billy, let me give you a mental picture that's helped me through the years," Thea said. "If the two of you ever garden, you know that in spite of all your efforts, those hateful weeds never go away. They constantly threaten the lives of your beautiful flowers. Well, there's not much we can do except keep them at bay while we nurture and feed the plants we want to survive.

"It's the same with that pain we were talking about. Keep it pushed back by nurturing the good things in your life—things like your love, your home, friends, and all the positive things that make life worth living. And Pamela, life is worth living!"

The young couple nodded as Dr. Brighten escorted them from the office. "You are amazing, Thea, and you make me a little more than ashamed. I'm supposed to be the expert here, yet you always seem to say the right things to these people. It's a pleasure to be part of this group," he praised.

"You *are* the expert, Matt," Thea replied. "Where would the foundation be without all our wonderful doctors and counselors like you and investigators like Cal who've given so many hours?" Thea looked around the room, one of many, and was touched by a deep sense of pride in what had been accomplished.

"We even have off-duty policemen donating their time to follow leads in some of these cases. Neither Monty nor I ever dreamed the foundation would grow to what it has become today. I'm not ashamed to tell you that it's been my salvation."

"I know that many of the disappearances of kids are the actions of noncustodial parents," Matt said. "That, I guess I could somehow accept, but not the others. Never the others! I cannot imagine what these parents and you have gone through!" He shook his head sadly.

"You make the world a better place. Don't forget that," Thea said as she glanced at her watch and prepared to leave.

"Monty and I are hosting a cocktail party and dinner at his ranch in Taos tonight, and I've got to get a move on. Cal's bringing some of his friends, so maybe we'll get more investigators signed up to give us some of their time, as well as some donations. I'll see you next month, right?"

"That you will. Good luck tonight," Matt answered.

66

The drive from the foundation's offices in Albuquerque to Taos was long and tiring but also pleasant and reflective for Thea. Her thoughts wandered back to that first time she made the trip to Monty's ranch—the start of what had been, through the years, the stabilizing force in her life. Monty was never far from her thoughts.

She appreciated full well how graciously the passing years had visited themselves upon him. To her, he was even more handsome than when they had first met. His hair, still worn long and braided, was now heavily streaked with silver, and the tiny lines that crinkled the corners of his eyes only enhanced the intensity of their smoky depths. Oh, how she loved him!

"And how unfair I've been to you, my dearest," she said aloud and with remorse at the thought of what she had denied her lover. She knew Monty's longing. She knew how he would have delighted in a little replica of himself to stand with worshipful fascination at his side while he practiced his art—just as he had done with his father.

He'd never mentioned marriage and children, not since that one time so long ago. Still, she knew that their love, as wonderful and lasting as it was, could never quite fill that void in his life. "Forgive me, Monty," she whispered. "Forgive me for what I cannot give you!"

Thea entered the outskirts of Taos and prepared to make her customary first stop. The dim interior of the tiny adobe chapel welcomed her. She was alone except for one old woman kneeling at the altar. Thea liked being there alone. She took a seat on one of the modest wooden pews, breathed deeply the slightly musty air, and waited for the peace and contentment synonymous with San Francisco de Asis Church to take possession of her.

It had become her practice to sit quietly there and gather her thoughts before driving the remaining distance to Monty's ranch. Today was no different. She closed her eyes and, for a time, allowed her thoughts to linger on the hectic schedule that lay ahead of her. In addition to tonight's dinner party, there were two more fund-raisers scheduled in the weeks ahead, and Indian Market was a scant three months away. As usual, Thea wasn't ready. Through the years, her work with the foundation had taken precedence over her pottery, and there never seemed to be enough time to do it all.

Time! It was hard to believe that eight years had passed since she and Monty had founded their beloved Healing Spirit Foundation. And eight years since Max and Aaron had married. Thea smiled at the happy memory. Sadly, though, the milestones that marked time's passage had not all been happy ones.

Nearly two years had passed since his death. He had slipped away suddenly, with no warning as he slept. Two years now, and she could still see his radiant smile, hear his robust laughter, and feel his strong presence at the very times when she needed him most. The pain of losing him still cut to the bone.

She had stood shivering, braced against the onslaught of winter's wind by Monty's strong arms and surrounded by the love and support of her dearest friends. Max and Aaron had come, and Paul, still weak and recovering from pneumonia, had insisted on making that long trip—dear Paul and Elena!

Most of her childhood friends had been there as well to stand with her to pay their last respects. Joe had come alone. "Cassie's due any day now, our fourth, but she sends her sympathy. He was a wonderful man, Thea. We're all going to miss him."

A single tear trekked its way down Thea's cheek as she relived that cold, gray day when Michael Chandler had been laid to rest beside his beloved Mary.

A myriad of other faces—many of them nameless, many of their features vague—flashed before Thea's eyes, the clearest of which belonged to Pamela Tremont. Such a lovely face she had, one that should have radiated with the wonder of youth and love but instead mirrored a horror.

"I—I keep Caroline's pictures everywhere in the house. Billy says I'm only getting myself more and more depressed. He says we ought to put them away. Ms. Kelly, what do you think? I'm just so scared that I'll forget what she looked like. Did you ever, you know, forget?"

Thea pushed open the heavy, old, wooden door and reluctantly stepped from the peaceful chapel into the late afternoon sunlight. She recalled Pamela's words and knew them for what they were—guilt and grief running its course.

Forget?

Once, her own memories of Alexa had triggered only sadness and had trapped her in that vicious cycle of loss, guilt, rage, and back to loss. ...*talking to herself as she made her way down the drive and around the curve* ...

Now, though, Thea's memories were a source of comfort to her. How many times through the years had those recurring images of her daughter come stealing softly and without warning from the cobwebbed corners of her mind? Sometimes she tiptoed in as the chubby-cheeked four-year-old, hair curling in damp ringlets, tiny hands clutching flowers she'd proudly gathered. But most times, Thea saw Alexa as she would be today—a teenager with childlike features melting into those of a beautiful young girl, poised on the threshold of womanhood.

Forget?

~

Twilight came quickly with the sun's descent behind Taos's looming mountains. Thea alighted from her car and hurriedly climbed the stone steps to the ranch house. Time had gotten away from her, lost in the past as she had been today. Now she'd have to rush to get ready when their guests arrived. Thank goodness for Clayton and Lydia!

The front door opened to Monty's smile and quick embrace. "I was getting a bit worried, love. Is everything okay at the foundation?"

"Everything's fine, Monty. I'm so sorry I'm late. I stopped at the chapel, and, as usual, I—" Her voice trailed off as she leaned against the porch railing, breathing deeply the pine-scented air.

"I know, I know," Monty crooned softly. "Tell me, love. Were they happy memories today?"

"For the most part," she answered him quietly, still somewhat detached.

He knew when she needed to be alone. "Lydia has the preparations well in hand. Stay out here a bit longer. You've plenty of time to dress before the guests start arriving." He tucked a loose tendril of hair behind her ear and nuzzled her neck. "I know how the night brings you peace."

"Umm, yes, I'll be in soon," Thea replied.

Darkness settled, and the chorus of night sounds began with the shrill cry of a hawk. She could not expel Pamela Tremont from her thoughts. She knew what torture the young mother was enduring right now. She was so wrapped up in loving her little girl as she'd been that she hadn't learned how to love herself. But Thea knew that would change. Time would bring peace to Pamela as it had to her.

Thea smiled, realizing that the yearning and the emptiness had long since left her. Gone, too, was that indefinable tugging that had once been so strong. Did every mother feel the need to pull her baby back inside of her, back to the safety of the womb, where it would once again belong to her and her alone, before it had to be shared with its father, its peers, the world?

True, the tugging was no more. Another emotion that was even stronger, though, had been allowed to take hold. A calm and ever-present knowing now soothed Thea. It was the knowing that, somewhere, her daughter lived.

Laughter erupted from inside the house, shaking Thea loose from the past. "No, Pamela," she whispered into the night. "You won't forget. You won't *ever* forget!"

67

"Stop it, Lonnie! I said no!" She pushed the amorous young man away and moved to lean against the passenger's door. "How many times do I have to t-tell you I'm n-not ready?"

Outside of waxing his precious car and playing football, Lonnie Masters's chief interest in life seemed to be pressuring Reagan to have sex. For months now, all of their dates had worked their way around to this, and she was getting tired of it. She didn't want to hurt him, though. With graduation only two weeks away, their separation would come soon enough.

The young man lit a cigarette, and Reagan turned to study his profile in the soft light. True, he was the best-looking guy in the senior class— okay, in the entire school. And he'd been in love with her since they were children. Her teachers, her friends, even Mama hastened to predict her future: "Now there's a match! Those two will be married the minute they get out of high school!"

But Reagan had always known differently. The task of convincing everyone else lay before her. "I'm s-s-sorry I'm so cross, Lonnie," she said softly, laying a hand on his arm. "I don't want to fight with you, but—"

"But what?" he snapped, unable to control his anger and frustration. "Why do you go out with me at all, Reagan? You don't care about me, about us!" He tossed the half-smoked cigarette out of the open car window and immediately lit another one.

"That's not true, Lonnie. I do c-care! It's, it's just that I'm not ready for a commitment, that's all. There's so m-much I want to do, so much I—" Reagan fumbled for the right words. What does Dr. Abe say? *Take a deep breath, relax, and the words will come.*

Her voice grew stronger. "Lonnie, there's so much I need to do. I can't stay here in Delaney. I've told you that all along. You just haven't heard me."

"Hell's fire, Reagan! Do *what*? And go *where*? And *why*? I'm taking over the business from Daddy just as soon as graduation's over with and we get back from the senior trip. You know that. You know it's a good, solid future, too! It's practically the only construction company for miles around—the best one, anyways. Look, Reagan," he turned to face her, his expression earnest. "You know I—I love you. I always have, since we was kids." His voice was soft, almost pleading. "I want us to get married."

There it was—what all the other girls whispered and giggled and gushed about constantly. Getting married was their dream, but it wasn't Reagan's dream. It was useless to try to make Lonnie understand her feelings. Even she didn't always understand them. For all of her eighteen years—at least the ones she could remember—Reagan had been searching for something just out of reach. She had tried only last week to explain these feelings to Dr. Abe. "It's like I'm searching for s-something that's just around the bend, Dr. Abe, something I c-can't quite reach! Does that m-m-make sense to you?"

"Well, Reagan, will you? Will you marry me?" Lonnie's hesitant voice brought her back to the present.

Suddenly, things began to focus. "N-no, Lonnie, I won't marry you. I'm not going to marry anyone, at least not anytime soon. It's not that I don't c-care for you, but we want different things, you and I. You want to s-stay here and take over your dad's business. There's n-nothing wrong with that, but I want a career in art. I know my paintings are good, and I'm going to pursue it. I've hinted to Papa about maybe going to school someplace like S-S-Santa Fe. Nothing's been decided yet." She took a deep breath; this was easier than she'd thought. "But one t-thing's for sure, Lonnie: I'm going to school somewhere this fall. I know you don't understand, but maybe you can f-find it in your heart to forgive me."

He looked at her for a long time, his face crestfallen. "There's nothing to forgive, Reagan." Mechanically, he turned the key and ignited the car's engine. "It's like you said: we just want different things, that's all."

A cloud of silence hung over the young couple during their ride. As he slowed the car for the turn into the O'Malley's driveway, Lonnie spoke again.

"My mama's always said you were different from other young folks around here. Guess maybe that's why I fell in love with you. Whatever it is you're looking for, Reagan, I hope you find it."

~

The quilt was taking shape nicely, its intricate double-wedding-ring pattern a difficult one indeed. Peg had a feeling she'd be giving it as a gift soon. Oh, Charlie tried to put a damper on her excitement, telling her not to get her hopes up where Reagan and Lonnie were concerned, but he never did have any faith in her intuitions.

She had been right all those years ago, hadn't she? Of course she had! She'd known what was best for all of them then, and she knew now. And what was best for her beloved daughter was to marry Lonnie Masters. His parents had a fine reputation in the community, and being the only son, Lonnie would do quite well in the family business. Not to mention the fact that he adored Reagan—that was obvious. June 10 was graduation day, only two weeks away. After a summer of trips and shopping, a fall wedding would be lovely.

Peg's dreaming ran its gamut. She rested the needlework on her lap, closed her eyes, and smiled. Charlie had retired to bed long ago, and the quiet time she spent waiting up for Reagan had become her favorite part of the day. Not that she didn't still love her husband and welcome his company, but Charlie had become so worrisome over the years. He was always harping on letting the child live her own life. Well, what did he think she was doing, living it for her? Of course not! But she knew what was best for her daughter. Why, who else but a mother could possibly know what was best for her child?

"Hi, Mama. You're still up as usual, I see." Reagan had entered the parlor soundlessly, startling Peg. "Is Papa already in bed?"

"Yes, dear," Peg answered. "You're home early. I must have been wrapped up in my sewing. I didn't hear Lonnie's car." She rose to embrace her daughter.

"Actually, I asked him to let me out at the t-top of the drive, and I walked on in. You know how I love the n-n-night. It's so peaceful being outside alone. That's where I do my best t-thinking. I'd just give anything if I could paint the night sky, you know? I've tried, but I just can't get the right s-s-shade of blue."

Peg listened to her daughter's idle chatter. "All this talk of art! Goodness, child, I'd think you'd have more than enough on your mind with graduation just around the corner. Where you get your passion for art is a mystery to me."

"I get it f-from you, of course," Reagan answered, giving her mother a quick peck on the cheek. "Just look at your quilts. They're beautiful."

"Thank you, dear. Look at this one. It's called the double-wedding-ring pattern. I don't suppose you can think of anyone who might be needing it anytime soon, do you?" Peg's eyes twinkled with mischief.

"No, Mama, I don't." Exasperation sharpened Reagan's voice more than she'd intended. "I just know *I* won't be needing it, if that's what you're getting at again!"

"I merely asked if—"

"Mama, I know what you asked. And I know you're having a f-f-fit for me to marry Lonnie Masters. And yes, he's asked me, and I s-said no, and I'll say no tomorrow and the next day and the n-next!" *Take a deep breath. Calm down.* "I'm going to go to art school this fall, Mama, s-s-somewhere!"

"This is getting out of hand, Reagan," Peg said firmly. "You're tired, so why don't we discuss this in the morning." Peg turned back to her sewing, dismissing the subject.

Tears of frustration stung Reagan's eyes. "No, M-mama. We'll discuss it now!"

"Reagan O'Malley, don't you dare raise your voice to me."

"The girl's right, Peggy. We'll discuss it now." Charlie's words silenced the two women. Wearily, he moved from the hallway into the living room for the confrontation he'd been dreading for months but now strangely welcomed.

"Now, baby girl, tell your mother and me what you want to do. Take your time. We've got all night to get this straightened out. Seems to me we're long overdue in asking you what you want to do with your life."

"For heaven's sake, Charlie, she's a child! How can she know—"

"Peggy!" Charlie O'Malley's voice boomed, and he could count on the fingers of one hand the times he'd raised his voice to his wife.

Reagan's eyes traveled from one parent to the other as an uneasy silence settled over the three of them. This was a turning point, and she knew it.

"Papa, you know what I want. I want to study art. My teachers, everyone, s-say my paintings are really good. And, and—"

"And what, baby girl? Tell Papa," Charlie's voice crooned.

"I w-w-want to go away to school. I c-could get a part-time job in an art gallery and take classes in the afternoons and at night." She hesitated, barely breathing, daring to hope they'd understand. "I'm thinking of maybe going to S-Santa Fe."

Peg sat rigid, unspeaking, her face a mask of dread. *She'll never forgive me for this*, Charlie agonized silently as he once again addressed his daughter. "Why Santa Fe? Have you talked with your guidance counselors at school or to your art instructors?"

"Well, there's s-s-so many art galleries there where I could get a job. T-t-there's other schools, but the college there has all the courses I want. My teachers all say it's w-where I should go. And I have a catalog." Reagan paused to catch her breath. "Papa, I'm not s-s-sure I can explain it, b-but I feel like it's where I n-n-need to be." She held her breath and hoped she sounded nonchalant. She waited.

"Very well, Reagan," Charlie replied. "Go ahead and apply. If you're accepted, you'll go with my blessing. All I've ever wanted was your happiness."

Reagan was immediately in his arms, covering his face with kisses, her tears of happiness mingling with his own. He was dimly aware of Peg's silent departure from the room. He'd talk to her later. Surely in time she'd come to see that it was the right thing to do. For now, though, he'd simply hold on with all of his might to this precious girl, this child of his heart.

68

The woman's dress shrieked with color. It hadn't looked nearly so bright when she'd tried it on in the department store's softly lit fitting room. Maybe it was the brilliance of a cloudless September sky that made the vivid peacock hues leap from the polyester fabric. *Surely, it'll look softer indoors!* she thought.

"Stop worrying!" she berated herself under her breath. Anyway, it was too late to walk the six blocks back to her apartment and change. Then she'd be late for her appointment. And what would she change into if she did have the time? Nothing much hung in her closet apart from the dozen or so black dresses, their dreary nature broken only by crisp white aprons and caps. No wonder the new dress had caught her eye.

She checked her watch and waited nervously for the traffic light to change. She'd been in Denver a little over a month now and was still leery about crossing the busy streets. She liked living in the big city, though. She liked stepping out on her small balcony and hearing the clamor of street sounds below. She liked shopping in the many stores, even if she wasn't sure what she should buy.

But most of all, she liked the anonymity of the city. How comforting it was to look into other people's faces and not know their names or their secrets. She drew equal comfort from the fact that those nameless people knew nothing of her life. She'd come to realize that knowing too much about someone could be a terrible burden to bear.

She rounded the street corner, and her destination came into view. The sight of the looming courthouse caused her to slow her purposeful gait, only to be jostled from behind by fellow walkers. Why should she suddenly feel so frightened? She hadn't done anything wrong—quite the contrary. She was there to right a terrible wrong.

She tried not to think of the multitude of lives that would be changed by her actions that day as she swallowed her fear and slowly began to climb the stone steps. Her mother had always told her to let sleeping dogs lie, but this time she couldn't.

Damn! Why did she always have to doubt herself? And why did her thoughts always go back to the mother who'd preached forgiveness but had been so quick to condemn her own daughter? Exactly what had been her sin, anyway? The woman remained mystified after more than thirty years. Was she to be forever condemned for merely loving and trusting the wrong man? She was guilty also of believing he loved her in return, believing he'd stand by her when she told him of the child she carried.

Even after all the years that had passed, she could still see the look on his face, a look that had told her all she had needed to know. She hadn't been surprised at all the following morning to awake alone in the cheap motel room. He'd gone, just like that, leaving no note. She supposed he had gone on to California as they'd planned, leaving her penniless in that hateful little town.

The doctors and nurses at the hospital had told her that worry had caused the miscarriage—worry and malnutrition. What in God's name would she have done if *he* hadn't taken her in and given her work? Gone back home to Kansas, to the mother who'd kicked her out in the first place? Hardly! No, her life had not been a happy one, the woman reflected, but there were worse crosses to bear—much worse!

Unconsciously, she clutched the worn leather tote bag tighter, her mind playing on its contents. She realized her palms were moist, and she smoothed them down the bright folds of her dress before turning the knob on the heavy office door.

"Good morning," she said as she tried to smile. But she felt her face twitch, and her voice broke, making a forced raspy sound. "I'm here to see, uh, is it *Miss* or *Mrs.* Vogel?"

The receptionist eyed her indifferently for several seconds before answering. "It's *Ms.* And you would be?"

She tried to clear her throat, but it came out as a hiccup and caused her to blush. "I'm Maddie LaCross," she chirped. "I have an appointment."

The receptionist continued to study her silently for several more seconds before dropping her eyes to the appointment book on her desk. "Have a seat."

Maddie knew she was being dismissed as someone of little or no importance. She nodded, accepting the treatment, and moved to a corner chair. She placed the tote bag on the floor beside her feet. Being overlooked didn't bother her at all. Very soon, she feared, people would be paying her altogether too much attention.

69

Fragmented images, like tiny specks of dust suspended in a lazy summer day's sunbeam, drifted in and out of her consciousness. Shapeless, but not lifeless, they searched for other bits and pieces to hook up with, striving for their elusive goal—memory!

Reagan stretched languidly, delaying the actual awakening process just a bit longer. When the dreams came as horrific ones, smothering her with fear, she found immense relief in opening her eyes to reality, to the familiarity of her bedroom and the promise of a new day. But when the veiled shadows of sleep had been hauntingly sweet, as with last night's, she resisted giving them up.

Reagan's dreams were different from those of most people. She'd had many a session with Dr. Abe on that particular subject. While actual conversations and events could be described in explicit detail and long remembered by other people, Reagan's dreams imparted only feelings—murky and vague. The bad ones would torment her with demonic whisperings that left her shaken for hours, even days, while the happy dreams filled her with euphoria, just as she was experiencing this morning.

Sleepily, her mind turned to the long-ago purchased journal on her nightstand, its pages still empty. How mad Mama had been when Dr. Abe suggested she write down any concrete images remembered from her dreams. "They're only dreams, child, nothing real! Why that man tries to make something out of simple childhood nightmares is beyond me!"

Mama needn't have fretted though—nothing remembered, nothing written. Oh, but even if none of the pieces fit, what a beautiful dream last night's had been! Reagan burrowed deeper into her down comforter against late September's chill. "Just a few more minutes," she murmured, prompting an immediate response from her bedfellow.

The first thing she had done since coming to Santa Fe, apart from registering for art classes and finding a part-time job, was to adopt Monet. The buff-colored kitten began his morning ritual, kneading her hair and purring loudly for his breakfast. Reagan loved the sensation of the tiny kitten's warm body nestled against the back of her neck. He was the one thing that belonged exclusively to her, something that took away the loneliness and isolation that she'd experienced on this, her first time away from Mama and Papa.

"I know, I know. It's time to get up." Reagan stretched again, throwing off the covers. "You want your breakfast, don't you, Peaches?"

Suddenly she was fully awake, the breath ripped from her lungs and every muscle in her body taut. "W-w-where did I get that? His name's Monet!" Her voice broke the morning's silence in a ragged whisper.

How long she laid there, eyes wide and unfocused, she didn't know. The kitten's worried mewing from the foot of the bed finally broke through. Reagan realized she needed to feed him and made her way to the kitchen on unsteady legs. Food for her was out of the question as nausea threatened.

70

From her vantage point behind the one-way glass, Kathy Vogel studied the older woman who'd just entered the reception area. Clearly, she was ill at ease, and Kathy felt the pangs of pity for her obvious lack of self-confidence.

Outwardly, she looked as though she'd just stepped out of the 1940s. Her hair, once dark but now graying, was pulled back into a severe bun on the back of her head, and she was devoid of makeup save for extremely bright red lipstick. She was tall and painfully thin and, judging from her careful steps, not used to the high heels she wore.

This would be Maddie LaCross, Kathy correctly surmised, the woman whose letter had intrigued the young assistant district attorney and prompted her to set up this appointment.

Kathy swung the painting back in its place covering the one-way window and moved back to her desk. Some people might consider this spying, but Kathy didn't. After all, she wasn't invading anyone's privacy; this was a public office. Observing people, especially when they were unaware of her scrutiny, provided her with valuable insight into their character and motives. Those with a genuine purpose for coming here were quickly separated from the ones who simply got off by being on stage. In the span of a few minutes, Kathy knew there were no hidden agendas with this woman.

"Rita," she called on the speaker phone, "send Miss LaCross in, please." Kathy rose, smiling, as the door to her office tentatively opened. Colleagues and adversaries alike had told Kathy countless times that her true talent in the courtroom lay in her ability to draw the witness out, to actually make people want to spill their guts, so to speak. She guessed it was her clean-scrubbed, girl-next-door looks that accounted for part of it. Whatever, she'd need the right stuff now for sure. This woman was scared to death.

"Miss LaCross, please come in. Let's sit on the sofa, shall we?" Kathy had to practically drag the reluctant woman across the room. She perched herself on the edge of the sofa, her back ramrod stiff and her butt barely creasing the leather cushion. Kathy watched silently as the face before her paled, and the huge, wide-set black eyes darted back and forth as if she were watching a ping-pong match.

Christ, I'm losing her before we even get started, Kathy fretted. She broke the silence. "Can I get you a cup of coffee, Maddie, or tea, perhaps? Oh, may I call you Maddie?"

"No. I—I mean, yes, please call me Maddie. And no, thank you, ma'am, I'm fine. I don't want anything." Her voice trembled.

"Well, then, if you'll excuse me for just a few minutes, I need to go to the ladies' room. I'll be right back. Please, make yourself comfortable. There are some magazines on the coffee table." Kathy hoped a little time alone to collect her thoughts would calm the poor soul down a bit.

"Now, thank you for being patient with me," Kathy said when she returned to her office a short while later. She was relieved to see that the mysterious woman hadn't bolted. "I can tell you're nervous, Maddie."

"Yes, ma'am, I sure am," Maddie admitted. Why did she feel the need to call this woman who was obviously young enough to be her daughter *ma'am*? "Actually, I'm just about scared to death!"

"Look at me, Maddie," Kathy said. Her voice was kind but firm. "This conversation is strictly confidential, off the record. Now, I'm not pressuring you, but you *did* contact this office, and, quite honestly, I was intrigued by your letter. I believe the words you used were 'A terrible crime's been committed.' Is that true, Maddie?"

For the first time since entering the office, Maddie did, indeed, look closely at the other woman. She hadn't known exactly whom she should contact with her story, so she had addressed her letter of several weeks earlier to the district attorney. Deep down, she hadn't even expected a reply, certainly not from a young woman. But this Ms. Vogel did seem like someone she might be able to open up to.

Maddie took a deep breath and squared her shoulders. She'd gone too far to back down now. "Yes, ma'am, it's true. A terrible crime has been committed."

This was going to be a long day, Kathy agonized—more like pulling teeth than getting information. "You wrote in your letter that you're from the town of Deer Run. I've never been there. In fact, it took me some time to find it on the map."

She scanned her notes and continued, hoping her chatter would put Miss LaCross at ease. "Now, let's see, you worked several years for Mr. Titus Peebles, correct?"

"Yes, ma'am. For thirty-one years I was his housekeeper," Maddie answered proudly. "I was housekeeper, cook, and his nurse after he took sick. I say *was* 'cause he's dead, now. Mr. Titus—that's what I called him—he died three months ago. He had cancer in his lungs. Smoked one cigarette after the other, he did."

"Well, I'm sure you miss him, Maddie." Kathy encouraged the other woman to continue. "Thirty-one years is a long time. The two of you must have been very close friends."

"Friends? Lordy, no, Ms. Vogel. We wasn't friends!" Maddie spoke with more emotion than the young attorney thought she possessed. "He was a godless man, that's what—a godless man!"

"I see. But your letter states that you uncovered a crime and that you felt that you owed Mr. Peebles. I'm afraid I don't understand."

Maddie hesitated several seconds before speaking again. "It's like this, Ms. Vogel. No, we wasn't friends. He was just my boss, that's all. Years ago, when I needed a job and a place to live, he gave them to me. I never expected anything from him beyond that.

"Then, when he took sick—well, there was no family, so I took care of him. I had no idea, but when he died, a lawyer from here in Denver came to Deer Run and told me that I was Mr. Titus's heir! He left me everything he had. He left me the house, the cars, and money." She paused and took another deep breath. "Ms. Vogel, he left me *a lot* of money!"

Still in the dark, Kathy prompted her. "And he told you about a crime?"

"Not in so many words, he didn't. Mr. Titus kept a journal. I knew he did. He was always writing in it. He kept it locked in the safe in his office, so, of course, I'd never read it until after he died and the lawyer came and all. Well, after I sold the house and was packing up, I had the safe opened, and—and here it is!" She handed the worn leather case gingerly to Kathy.

"I've wished a hundred times over that I'd never read it. Some of the things he wrote about—well, that's a person's private life, I guess. It's not for me to judge another person, right?" She waited for a response.

"Maddie, am I correct in assuming that this crime you speak of just might be someone else's business?"

"Yes, ma'am. That's why I'm here. See, Mr. Titus wrote all about it when it happened and about his part in it. You can read for yourself—I marked the pages—about how his conscience bothered him. He writes about it all through the years."

"Through the years, you say. Maddie, how long ago did this crime occur?" Kathy asked, her interest increasing by the minute.

"Thirteen—well, fourteen years ago come December. That's when he came to the house to talk to Mr. Titus. I remember it 'cause it was the first day in two, three weeks that folks was able to get out at all after the worst blizzard we'd ever had. Anyway, he came to the house that day to talk in private with Mr. Titus. Ms. Vogel, after that day, Mr. Titus never was the same! He was worried about something—I could tell. And he started writing more and more in this journal. And he would talk to hisself late at night in his study. I could hear him muttering, just sitting in there, sipping whisky and smoking them cigarettes. It worried him to death!"

"*What* worried him, Maddie?" Kathy asked.

"What they done, that's what!" Maddie leaned forward, her eyes large and unblinking, her voice barely audible. "What they done about the child they found!"

Kathy felt a sudden chill, as her own voice fell to a whisper. "Found? Who was it? *Who* found a child?"

"It was the chief of police and his wife! Pretty young thing, she was. Didn't mix with the townsfolk, though. I never even spoke to her. They don't live there no more. They moved right after that, but I know where they live."

The woman paused to catch her breath. "It's all there, right there in Mr. Titus's book, Ms. Vogel. I didn't want to get involved, but when I read about it, I could see how worried he'd been about his part in it. He writes that he wished he'd never got involved. I owe him, you know, him leaving me so much and all. Do you think I've done right, ma'am?"

Kathy rubbed away the goose bumps that had gathered on her arms. She needed advise on this one. She'd call her boss that afternoon. And Dave, she'd call him, too. He'd been working with families of missing children for several years. She might be in over her head, but she couldn't let Maddie know it. "You've done right, Maddie. Now, would you be willing to give sworn testimony if needed?"

"I—I thought that was what I was doing now."

"No, you're just discussing it with me, in confidence. How do you feel about speaking with the district attorney and giving us a sworn deposition?"

Kathy Vogel looked like a schoolgirl to Maddie, but something about her gave the older woman newly found confidence. "I'll do whatever you say," Maddie answered. After a thoughtful silence, she continued. "A lot of people are going be hurt by this, aren't they?"

But Kathy was too absorbed in the journal of Attorney Titus Peebles to comment.

"Yes, ma'am," Maddie whispered, answering her own question. "A powerful lot of people are going to be hurt."

~

Reagan felt a little better now. The long, hot shower had stopped her trembling, outwardly, at least. She'd even managed a light breakfast, but her plans for the day had changed. With art class now forgotten, she punched the familiar number on the telephone.

"It's Reagan O'Malley. Is Dr. Abe in, p-p-please?"

71

The funny thing about spending so much time alone was that it did wonders for sharpening one's perspective. Charlie O'Malley had always thought that the house was too small for his family until Reagan had left for school and Peg had begun spending so much time at the church. Now, it seemed that there was entirely too much empty space. He guessed he'd get used to the silence, but he'd never get used to the neatness!

Where was all the clutter? Charlie chuckled to himself. From the moment they'd moved into this house, he'd been tripping over something. First dolls and stuffed animals, then roller skates and other kids, and of late, canvases and easels. He'd voiced his gripes to Peg on more than one occasion that he didn't have room to walk through his own house and maybe they should get a bigger one. But his wife couldn't abide change and said they didn't need a bigger house.

"Turns out you were right again, Peg," Charlie said aloud. In the two weeks since Reagan had left for Santa Fe, he and Peg had barely spoken. Oh, she was pleasant when she did speak, but he knew something was lost forever between them. Or, had it slipped away years ago, and having the child around simply masked the loss?

The autumn morning was too beautiful for somber thoughts, he decided. Perhaps a long walk to the park would cheer him up. Or maybe he'd check his e-mail to see if Reagan had written. Charlie smiled. She'd sent detailed e-mails almost daily filled with glowing descriptions of Santa Fe, her job at the gallery, and her art classes. His smile faded as he recalled how he delighted in reading her messages over and over, while his wife barely scanned them, saying little.

The sound of the doorbell brought Charlie out of his absorption. "Now who could that be?" Maybe it was one of their neighbors coming to chat a while. Well, he'd sure welcome some company.

"Mornin', Charlie. I'm sorry to barge in on you, but these folks here—well, they need to talk with you." Police Lieutenant Jimmy Cahill stood at the door, nervously fidgeting with his hat.

Jimmy was Charlie's right hand as well as his friend. It was common knowledge in Delaney that young Jimmy would be the city council's pick to step into Charlie's shoes when the older man retired. He idolized his boss and would be the perfect choice to carry on the high standards of the office set during Charlie's tenure.

But this morning, Jimmy didn't look much like a potential police chief. Charlie's eyes narrowed as he studied the slender young man. "What's up, Jimmy? You seem mighty nervous. Nothing's wrong down at the station, is it?"

"Uh, Charlie, like I said, these folks here need to talk to you. This is Ms. Vogel, Assistant District Attorney for Denver County, and this is, uh, I—I forgot," Jimmy stammered, his apple cheeks blushing a bright red.

"Good morning, Chief O'Malley," Kathy Vogel said as she offered her hand. "This is Mr. Ben Rhymer and Mr. Horace Atkins, associates of mine. Sir—"

"Charlie. Call me Charlie, Ms. Vogel," he interrupted. "What's this all about?"

"It's complicated, Charlie. Now, I want you to understand that my associates and I are here unofficially. Lieutenant Cahill, on the other hand, is here in an official capacity. May we come in? We need to speak with you about your family."

Official capacity?

"My family? I—I don't quite understand, Ms. Vogel. My daughter's away at school and my wife's down at St. John's. She helps out in the church's day care center on Tuesday mornings." Charlie's curiosity was rapidly turning into dread. "Now, I'll ask you again, what's this all about?"

"We know where your wife is, Chief O'Malley," the short, fat man called Ben said. "It's the girl, Reagan, that we've come to speak to you about. May we come in, please?"

The girl, Reagan?

Charlie felt sick, like someone had punched him in the gut. He studied the faces before him. Those faces belonged to people who were there—how had she put it?—unofficially? The three of them stood with unflappable resolve, hands clasped behind their backs, their eyes on his.

"Chief O'Malley," the taller man said. What was his name? Atkins, maybe? Charlie tried to concentrate, tried to stay calm. "Sir," the man continued, "you used to live in Deer Run, didn't you?"

Charlie swallowed several times before answering. "Yes, I grew up there. Why do you ask?"

"And you were acquainted with an attorney by the name of Titus Peebles, were you not?" the tall man continued.

Time sure plays tricks, Charlie thought. Why, he could hardly remember what he had for breakfast that morning, but fourteen years ago—now that was just like yesterday!

He cleared his throat. "Ms. Vogel, gentlemen, come on in. I've been expecting you." He stepped back from the door and managed a tired smile.

"Oh?" Kathy shot the young lieutenant a withering look.

"Ma'am, I—I ain't said a word to nobody, I swear to God!" Jimmy stammered.

Charlie held up a big hand, silencing the young man. "Jimmy's telling the truth, Ms. Vogel. He hasn't said a word to me."

He turned and led them into the living room. "Have a seat, please," Charlie went on. "Truth is I've been expecting you for a very long time."

Abe Leonard unfolded his lanky frame from the confines of the rental car, stretched away the drive's stiffness, and took stock of his surroundings. In direct contrast to the bustling town square he'd just skirted, hardly a sound broke the stillness of the narrow residential street he now surveyed. A cracked and uneven walkway wound its way through tall evergreens and led him to a row of tiny tile-roofed casitas. Such an idyllic setting almost made his trip seem pleasurable—almost.

Abe smiled as the door opened to his knock. "The perfect abode for our budding young artist!" he exclaimed. Reagan returned his smile and hugged him fiercely. He felt the tremor and tried to forestall the tears that would sooner or later have to come.

"Let's have a look at you now," Abe said as he held her at arm's length and squinted through thick, black-rimmed bifocals in mock scrutiny. She looked tired, worried, and older. "I can honestly say you look none the worse after having been on your own for two whole weeks," he fibbed.

"Thank you for coming, Dr. Abe. I don't know w-what I would have done if you hadn't been in the office yesterday w-when I called." She led him into a small but comfortable living room furnished with overstuffed couches, small antique tables, and a profusion of canvases in various stages of completion.

"Well, I *was* in, Reagan, and I'm here for you now." Abe made himself comfortable on one of the couches and got right to the point. "What prompted your call?"

"I know you r-remember my adolescent paranoia about s-s-secrets. They can't be dismissed as childish fears anymore. And they can't be blamed on my nightmares, either. I haven't had a nightmare in m-m-months." She stood with her back to him and remained perfectly still. She breathed deeply and spoke slowly, just as he had instructed her to do. After a few moments, she turned and walked across the room to join Abe on the couch.

"Dr. Abe," she said before she cleared her throat and met his gaze levelly. "I—I have begun to remember things."

Abe had always let her do most of the talking during their sessions. He waited for her to continue, and when she didn't, he prompted gently. "Things, you say. What things?"

She exhaled. "Images, mostly. You know, shadows, whispers, the s-s-same old, same old. But since I've been in Santa Fe, some of those images are getting so much clearer. Like f-f-for instance, I remember a big swimming pool and a flower garden—so many, many flowers, acres of f-flowers! I remember being swung around in the air by a man, but he wasn't Papa. I—"

Her voice faded, and it was obvious to Abe that the struggle going on inside her mind was a powerful one. "Reagan," he said in barely a whisper, "don't try too hard. Just let the words come." He cupped her face between his big, gentle hands and met her somber gaze. "This is what you've waited for: memories!"

"I know. I knew it yesterday morning."

"What exactly triggered this?" Abe asked immediately before the answer to his question came bounding onto the couch and into his lap.

Reagan laughed at the startled doctor. "He did," she answered as she gathered the purring kitten into her arms. "His name's Monet and he triggered the m-m-most tangible memory of all. Dr. Abe, I had a cat a long, long time ago. It was a great big orange cat named Peaches. M-mama says we never had a cat 'cause Papa's allergic—that it's just a dream. But, it's n-n-not just a dream!" She was becoming anxious again.

"I'm s-sorry." She took a deep breath and continued. "This cat used to sleep curled up on the stairway banister."

Abe waited a full minute for her to continue. "Yes, dear? On the banister. Go on."

"Mama and Papa and I—well, we've n-n-never lived in a two-story house." She continued to hold his gaze. Abe knew he was witnessing a revelation, and he remained silent.

Her whisper was electrifying. "Dr. Abe, w-who am I?"

"Is *this* where you want the urn, love?" Monty grunted his question, straining under the weight of the heavy Grecian olive jar he held atop his shoulders. Thea could not have picked a worse day for her annual moving and cleaning spree, Monty decided. If Santa Fe had experienced a warmer autumn day, he couldn't remember it!

"Thea, please answer me before my back breaks! You want it here?"

"I won't know if that's where I want it until you set it down," she groused before turning her attention elsewhere, leaving him hanging.

"Admit it, love," Monty said after setting the olive jar on the floor. "You've outgrown this cottage. As a matter of fact, you outgrew it years ago. Why not sell it and move to the ranch?" He paused to wipe the perspiration from his face and drain a glass of water. "The two of us spend half our time on the road between here and Taos. Lord knows the ranch is big enough. And," he continued to build his case, "as far as your work goes, you could move to the moon and still have a market."

Thea listened as she always did to Monty's gentle persuasions and allowed herself a moment to daydream. True, with an ever-increasing demand for her pottery, location no longer played a key role in her success.

"You know you're always more relaxed at the ranch," Monty continued, his hands stroking her arms, bringing her back to the present. "Think about waking up together every morning in that great big bed of mine." His voice evaporated into soft kisses along the nape of her neck.

"Mmm, you'd make one hell of a lawyer, Mr. Arroyo," Thea said as she moved away from his caress and resumed her nervous rummaging through shelves jammed with pottery. She constantly rearranged piece after piece but accomplished nothing.

"Apparently, this one hell of a lawyer just lost his case. Any chance for an appeal?"

"Monty," Thea said without turning around, without looking at him, "ever since Max and I drove into the drive here twelve years ago, I knew this was where I belonged. Yes, the cottage and studio are too small and cramped, and you know I love the ranch. It's just so hard to know what to do!"

Monty watched her struggle with indecision, knowing he could not help. He'd spoken at great length the night before with Max in San Francisco, voicing the fear he would share with no other person. His fear was brought on by the change he saw in Thea as he helplessly witnessed depression worm its way into her soul.

"How long has it been going on?" Max had asked him. "I didn't notice anything wrong when Aaron and I were down for Market."

"Neither did I. It's always crazy here during that time, so who knew." He searched for the right words. "She's been this way for a couple of weeks. Her appetite's completely gone, she's cross and moody, and she can't sit still. She tears up at the drop of a hat. And she's incapable of making a decision. What's more, she wants to sleep all the time! Thea's usually so calm, so in control. Not now, though. Max, I've never seen her like this."

"Oh, yes, you have, my friend," Max had reminded him. "When Hurley Dobbs committed suicide, Thea knew it *before* she knew it!"

"You're saying something's about to happen?"

"Damn it! Damn it! Damn it!"

Jolted abruptly back to the present, Monty moved quickly to the studio threshold. Unbeknownst to him, Thea had abandoned her cleaning project and now sat dejected at her wheel. The misshapen mass of wet clay before her was all the explanation he needed for her uncharacteristic outburst.

"I can't do anything, Monty. I've lost it." Her voice was flat.

Of course Monty remembered. He hadn't wanted to remember, but Max was right. They had all seen her like this before.

"Come, love." He gently urged her to her feet and began to wipe the clay from her hands. "You go lie down, and I'll clean up here. It's only one pot, and you haven't lost anything. It's only one pot. The clay just got saturated and collapsed, that's all."

"Oh, Monty, if only that were all!" The tiny hint of emotion in her voice drew his attention. He turned to her, and this time, she met his gaze, imploring him to understand her plight. "I—I don't want to be like this!"

"I know that, my darling. How can I help?"

She smiled then, that glorious smile that always crippled his heart. "You can help me understand what's happening to me." She grew thoughtful. "I keep remembering something my Ozark grandmother, Mike's mom, would say when her nerves got the best of her. She'd say, 'Oh, child, someone just walked across my grave!' Isn't that a strange thing to say?" Thea began to absently shake her head. "But that's how I feel. I feel like someone just walked across my grave."

The best way Beatrice Thatcher could describe her boss's behavior during the week since his return from Santa Fe was that Dr. Abe Leonard was a man on a mission.

Bea had not been made aware of the details of a particularly official-sounding phone call, but she was sure that it had served as the catalyst for the current office upheaval. As instructed, she had cancelled all of the doctor's appointments indefinitely and had referred his patients to other counseling professionals—all but one.

She peeked warily at the doctor through his partially open office door. She'd been at her desk for just over an hour, and he hadn't even noticed her arrival, even when she set his cup of coffee before him. As usual, he was on the phone, saying very little—just staring into space and listening. Once in a while he would grunt an answer or comment, and whenever more input was needed from him, he'd get up and close his office door. Oh, well, he would confide in her when he felt the need.

But just look at him! In all the years they'd worked together, Bea had never known him to come to the office dressed in anything but a three-piece suit, immaculate dress shirt, and perfectly knotted tie. And he was always clean-shaven. This morning, however, he looked like a bum. His thick shock of black hair was standing on end, lending him an uncharacteristically comical look. And hadn't he worn that suit and shirt yesterday?

The doctor's voice drifted to the reception area, hinting at an end to his phone conversation. Even though his words were not fully audible, Bea mused at the upbeat tone of his voice. One would think that whatever duress the good doctor was under would've put him in a foul mood, but that was not the case. Bea had never seen him happier!

Abe leaned back in his chair and savored the brief luxury of closing his eyes. He kept his voice low. "Of course I understand your position, Ms. Vogel—Kathy. And believe me, I sympathize. Even with being so closely involved, I'm in way over my head here as well. That's why I've asked Dr. Whitfield to come here for a consultation. I've followed his work for some time, and I'm convinced he'll be a huge help to us. In spite of his youth, he's one of the country's most respected psychiatrists, and his research into dissociative disorders is cutting edge. I was lucky to track him down and even luckier to get him to change his schedule and consult with me.

"I know I'm repeating myself, Kathy, but our concern here cannot simply be legal issues. The emotional ramifications are going to be staggering! I want to thank you again for not jumping the gun on this one. After meeting with Dr. Whitfield, I think we'll all have a better idea of exactly how to proceed with this case. Thanks again."

Abe cradled the receiver and stared thoughtfully at the telephone. His voice had sounded raspy after countless hours of talking, and his eyes stung from lack of sleep. Mechanically, he reached for his coffee. Coffee—where had *that* come from? "Mrs. Thatcher, are you here?"

"Good morning, Doctor. You were so engrossed in that phone conversation, you didn't even know I came in," his secretary replied cheerily. "Although I don't know why I'm here so early. It's not like we've got a room full of patients to see."

Abe smiled inwardly. He knew that was as close as she would ever come to asking him what was going on. Had it not been for the top-secret label slapped on this case by the Denver DA's office, he would have taken her into his confidence immediately.

All in due time, Abe thought as he closed his tired eyes and rubbed his temples. He sorely needed a shower, a shave, clean clothes, food, and sleep—mostly sleep. Staying at the office all night had been foolish, but he hadn't been able to leave.

He'd finally tracked Eli Whitfield down to a convention in London, and the two psychiatrists had discussed the case and recent events well into the night. Whitfield was intrigued and would be flying to Denver directly from London instead of returning to his home in Boston. Abe would meet him in Denver, further brief him on the situation, and get his initial thoughts. They would then meet with Kathy Vogel and her colleagues prior to the scheduled meeting with the O'Malleys.

Of late, Abe had come to realize just how out of touch with today's technology he had become. He'd made his life in Delaney because of its obscurity; now he felt betrayed by it. Not so surprising was the fact that much of his information had come from his best friend, Dave Pierce. Dave was friends with Kathy Vogel, and he served on the board of the Healing Spirit Foundation. He had access to their sophisticated database profiling missing and abducted children. He had even shared with Abe the pending identity.

Abe felt both included and ostracized at the same time. After all, *he* was the one who had counseled her, soothed away her anxieties, and buffeted her against her nightmare world all these years. *He* was the one she called with her first tangible memory!

"Boy, you *do* need sleep!" Abe muttered aloud. He would not let his frustration get him rankled. After all, he had been consulted and had been given the go-ahead to bring another psychiatric professional on board. In addition, he knew that Charlie O'Malley had given, in Kathy Vogel's words, a very guarded statement to the DA's office. But, as yet, Abe didn't know the whole story surrounding the O'Malleys and what action might be taken.

Think about the important thing, buddy boy. Abe continued to keep himself on track as he finished his coffee, now cold, and prepared to make yet another phone call. The O'Malleys weren't his concern. The law wasn't his concern. And the media—oh, hell, the media! But they weren't his concern either. *She* was his concern, as was the shocking effect the truth was bound to have on her young life—a life finally stripped of all secrecy.

Her words haunted him: "S-s-sometimes I t-think there's a secret, Dr. Abe, one that everyone knows b-but me!"

75

The century-old Brown Palace hotel in downtown Denver had long set the standard for luxury in the city. Sleep deprivation had sentenced the two doctors to an early night, but after a generous breakfast, they settled comfortably into a quiet corner to get acquainted. Abe studied his young colleague and marveled at how he seemed to belong amid the elegance of the historic old lobby.

There was nothing flashy about Eli Whitfield. Conservatively dressed, he moved slowly, gathering attention little by little. In other words, he blended. He was of average height and build, with sandy brown hair worn short. His eyes, a startling emerald green, commanded immediate attention, but it was his ready smile and hypnotic baritone voice that conveyed trust. Abe decided he was looking at the total package. He liked what he saw.

"I gotta ask, Eli: what's next? I mean, Boston College, Harvard Medical, National Institute of Mental Health reviews, the lecture circuit, all before your twenty-eighth birthday. What's next?"

Eli accepted the praise with obvious pleasure and studied Abe thoughtfully before responding. "Thank you for saving me the trouble of submitting a resume," he answered. "Seriously, though, it's difficult for me to look beyond the present. When can I meet with Reagan?"

He got straight to the point; Abe admired that. "Ordinarily, we would be in my office, but Reagan is not to be anywhere near Delaney at this time. That's not only an edict from the DA's office but my recommendation, as well. I've brought her here to Denver since she'd have to be here anyway. A colleague and good friend of mine has given us full use of his offices for the time being. Assistant DA Vogel is calling the shots on the investigation.

In my opinion, though, it's a classic case of nobody knowing what to do next."

"Has Reagan spoken with the O'Malleys about any of this?" Eli asked.

"Has she ever," Abe replied. "Totally against my instruction, she confronted Peggy over the telephone yesterday with a barrage of questions, accusations about them deceiving her, demanding to know if she was adopted, et cetera, et cetera. Peggy blatantly denied any deception. Bottom line: Reagan's more upset than ever, Peggy had to be sedated, and Charlie O'Malley won't talk to a soul, not even his attorney. It's a mess!"

Abe paused to sip water and collect his thoughts. "The key here, Eli, is memory—Reagan's memory. That's where you come in. I know you can make the difference. You see, for years I've befriended her against whatever monsters she's hiding from in her mind. Now—"

"Now," Eli quietly interrupted, "it's up to me to lead her out of the darkness by finding out what sent a little girl there in the first place. And I will!" His green eyes misted as he voiced his pledge. He didn't try to hide the emotion.

Abe Leonard liked that, too.

$$\sim$$

"Dissociative disorders, thusly named because they are identified by an interruption in one's basic consciousness, come in many forms. The most famous form is known as identity disorder, which is what we used to call multiple personality disorder. We also see symptoms of these disorders in a number of other mental illnesses, such as posttraumatic stress disorder or panic disorder."

Reagan listened intently to the young doctor, absorbing his words like a sponge. "Is this what's wrong with me, Dr. Whitfield? Do I have m-m-mental illness?"

"Absolutely not, Reagan. Please believe me when I say that there is nothing at all wrong with you." As he studied the young woman sitting before him, Eli realized he had never spoken truer words.

Since their meeting the previous day, doctor and patient had spent few hours apart. Hers was a classic dissociative disorder, and Eli knew he could help her. He knew this because she so desperately wanted his help.

"Then, why have I started to r-r-remember things that—that maybe n-never even happened?"

Eli leaned forward, taking her hand in his and speaking calmly but emphatically. "Because, Reagan, these things *did* happen! I believe you suffer from dissociative amnesia. This condition usually results from a traumatic or stressful event. Actually, this disorder is probably the mind's defense mechanism, a way to shield the individual from the memory of trauma—" he hesitated "or abuse."

Abe Leonard sat in the elegantly appointed office that his buddy Dave had graciously provided. He was careful to sit just outside the doctor-patient space and remain silent, as he had throughout both days' therapy sessions. Abe marveled at how smoothly these two had navigated the initial adjustment period. Now, however, he was seeing a hint of doubt crease Reagan's brow.

"Not possible, Doctor Whitfield," she said as she shook her head. "I've n-never been abused! Mama and Papa, t-they love me—"

"Not you, Reagan," Eli interrupted. "I'm not talking about the Reagan O'Malley I see before me. It's quite apparent that she's suffered nothing of the sort in her life." Abe watched as her anxiety abated and she became once again receptive to Eli's voice.

"Then who?" she asked.

"The little girl, Reagan, the one you've been protecting all these years. The one you've sheltered from, from evil." He was whispering, now.

"Close your eyes, now—that's right. Lean back and relax. You've been protecting the little girl for so very long, and you did a good job. Reagan, your job's done now. She needs to come out. In fact, you've done so well that she doesn't need to hide any longer. She can come out now and play in the garden, among the flowers. She can play with her cat, Peaches, once again." Eli had done his homework.

"Mmmm, Mama?"

Abe chilled. It was the voice of a child.

"No, Reagan, you're not her." Eli continued his quiet direction. "You see her, though. She's coming out from her hiding place. You've hidden her well. Where has she been all these years—in a tunnel, in a fog, perhaps?"

The voice that answered was a monotone. "No, we don't see her."

"But you know where she is, don't you?"

"Behind us."

"Behind w*ho*?" Eli prompted gently. "Who is in the tunnel with the little girl?"

"She's behind us," she continued in the flat voice. "We haven't seen her for a long, long time."

"Will you turn around and look at her, Reagan? Will you do that for me and for Dr. Abe?"

"No."

"Then will you do it for her?"

"No."

Eli shook his head as he met Abe's eyes. "Just as I expected," he mouthed.

"All right, Reagan, let's leave the little girl where she is for the time being. Can you tell us why you had to hide her? Can you tell us her name?"

There they are again, trying to find out who we are and what we're doing here. Well, we're not going to tell! And we're not going to look back either! There's nothing back there anyway, nothing but the darkness and the fog. If we stay very quiet and very still, we'll be safe and warm, not scared anymore, not freezing anymore.

Abe didn't miss her increasingly rapid breathing and the occasional facial tic that broke her otherwise blank expression. "May I try?" he mouthed silently to Eli.

Eli nodded emphatically.

"Reagan," Abe said as gently as his croaky voice allowed, "it's Dr. Abe speaking now. I know you remember back when you were about thirteen years old and you and I used to have such fun walking and talking in the park. Do you remember?"

"Yes, fun—"

"That's right. Do you remember telling me that you thought everyone knew a secret, everyone except you?" A weak moan escaped her lips. Abe dared to speak a little louder, a little more forcefully. "The little girl, Reagan, the little girl behind you—does *she* know the secret?"

Her audible gasp brought both doctors bolt upright in their seats, their gaze riveted on her wide and unblinking eyes. "There is no secret." Her voice was normal. "Mama said so."

76

Sophie Evers sat at her kitchen table munching her second—or maybe her third—powdered sugar–covered donut of the morning and smiled as her husband's animated chatter carried from the bathroom down the hall.

"It's almost over, Soph. It's what we've always believed and now it's almost over!"

"I know, and I still can't believe it," she answered, rising to pour a fresh cup of coffee from the third pot of the morning. They hadn't slept all night, riding instead the wave of telephone calls that had begun yesterday afternoon and crested shortly after three that morning.

"Colorado, Soph. Colorado!" Cal said, padding barefoot into the kitchen, clad only in his shorts and with his razor in hand, his sun-weathered face still dotted with shaving cream. "She's been right there in Colorado all this time!"

Sophie sipped from her cup as she followed him back to the bathroom. She wanted to share her husband's exuberance, and a part of her did. But the countless crushing disappointments of the past fourteen years loomed.

"Now remember," she began, "Dr. Pierce only said they have reason to believe it *could* be her. Cal, you've been so sure before."

"No, babe," he said as he stopped his shaving and met her gaze in the mirror. "This time it's for real. This time there's no wild goose chases, no dead-ends, no mistaken identities. Dr. Pierce was merely quoting the DA. He's one of our foundation volunteers, and he's friends with the very doctor who's been treating this girl. Okay, so there are a thousand unanswered questions. So they're not 100 percent certain, but something's happened to make them contact me. It *has* to be her!"

Sophie made her way back to the kitchen. Cal was right—this *was* it. She felt it, too. Alexa Kelly had been found! Now the healing process could begin. Or could it? Had too much time passed? People change; their goals, desires, and needs change. Sophie's thoughts rambled. But not everyone changes; *she* hadn't changed. All Sophie had ever wanted—still wanted—was her husband, her boys, and that grandbaby that was on the way.

"A *housekeeper*, Soph," Cal said as he strode into the kitchen, fully dressed in his best suit and tie. "Hell of a thing, what with all the pros that have worked on this case over the years that the break comes from a *housekeeper*. Man, oh, man!"

"Does Thea know anything yet?" Sophie asked.

"No, but I've been given the go-ahead to talk to her. All I'm supposed to do is make her aware of the *possibility* that Alexa *may* have been located. But they wouldn't want Thea to come to Denver if they weren't sure, would they?" Cal paused and chuckled.

"I told Dr. Pierce that, by heaven, she'd better not hear it from anyone but me! I've made that clear to everybody. *I'm* the one who never gave up the search. I don't give a shit who they are or how high up the ladder they go, no one's telling her but me!" He paused again and continued thoughtfully.

"After all the times I've seen pain and suffering in her eyes, all the times I've had to be the one bearing the bad news, nobody's going to take this away from me now. Oh, I just can't wait to see the look on her face! Is that being selfish, Sophie? Am I thinking of just myself at a time like this?" He stopped his pacing, took a seat at the breakfast table, and looked to his wife for guidance.

Sophie didn't answer. Rising from her chair at the table, she began to clear away the morning's clutter. She stacked dishes in the sink and prepared yet another pot of coffee. She knew her rare silence perplexed him. Several minutes passed before he tentatively spoke again.

"What? You thinking 'bout something? Hey, Soph, why not go with me today? You never go, and well, don't you want to be there? Whatcha say?"

She dried her hands on the dish towel and smoothed the hair back from her face. She wanted to turn around and look at him, but she couldn't.

"You're in love with her, aren't you, Cal." It wasn't a question but a revelation. Strangely enough, finally voicing what she'd known for so many years gave her immense relief.

The chair creaked as he eased his large frame from it and moved to stand behind her, his hands resting on her shoulders. He gently massaged away the tension he felt there.

"Ahhh, Sophie." He whispered the answer she deserved—the truth. "Maybe just a little; not enough to hurt nothing."

Moments later, he closed the kitchen door softly behind him, and Sophie watched as he walked down the driveway to the car, lighting a cigarette on the way. As was his custom, he turned, waved, and flashed that brilliant smile of his—a smile she knew was meant for her.

She waved back and continued to stand at the window to watch as he backed the car out into the street and headed for Santa Fe. She worried about him driving without having had any sleep the night before, but that adrenalin rush of his would keep him alert for quite a while.

Sophie yawned and thought about her day. She'd wait a little longer and then call Gary to see if Beth had had a good night and find out how many times the baby had kicked. Then, she'd get some sleep herself. But for right now, maybe she'd have just one more powdered donut.

$\sim$

Cal made the drive in record time, which was surprising since weekends in late September usually brought the tourists to Santa Fe in droves. It was early, and he figured Thea might still be at home. He hoped so; this wasn't something he could tell her in a public place. He'd been rehearsing for years, playing it over and over in his mind just how he'd break the news to her. He wasn't sure he ever really believed the time would come—but he never disbelieved it either.

"This is a nice surprise," Thea said when she met Cal at the door. "You just caught me. I'm on my way to the gallery to set up a new display. Want to come along? Monty's already there."

"Uhhh, Thea, maybe we'd better stay here. I need to talk to you 'bout something. I'm glad Monty's in town. Why don't you call him and tell him to come on back here." Cal fidgeted with his hat. Getting started was harder than he'd thought it would be. He wanted to do this right.

"What's up, Cal?" Thea asked warily. "Is something wrong at the foundation? "Oh, no. Max—are Aaron and Max okay? What's—"

She stopped speaking midsentence, studying his face, her eyes boring into his. Moments passed. Ever so slowly, she began to smile. The lines of worry left her face only to be replaced by the light of hope.

"Oh, Cal!" she whispered.

"You go on now and call Monty;" Cal said, returning her smile. "We need to have ourselves a talk."

11

"Ladies and gentlemen, if this state learned anything from the Ramsey fiasco, it was how *not* to handle a sensitive investigation. If this situation should become a feeding frenzy for the media, I will hold each and every person here accountable, both personally and professionally. Is that absolutely clear?"

No one uttered a sound. Lincoln Reinhardt did not want an answer to his question. He prolonged the silence until butts shifted in chairs and eyes dropped to clasped hands.

Few friends and even fewer enemies could stand up to the withering steel in those gray eyes. No one, at least no one Kathy Vogel had ever known, could match Lincoln's zeal in the courtroom. She studied her boss. It was easy to see why the formidable district attorney had earned the nickname "Intimidator."

He broke the silence. "Now, Ms. Vogel, this is your party. Just don't let me read reviews in tomorrow's newspaper."

"Yes, sir. Thank you," Kathy responded as the door closed decisively behind the district attorney. She cleared her throat and spoke to her four staff members.

"As Mr. Reinhardt impressed upon you, this is sensitive and top secret."

"Will charges be brought against the O'Malleys?"

"Exactly where did the O'Malleys find the girl?"

"Was she abducted?"

"Please," Kathy pleaded, as she held up a hand to silence the interruptions. "Charlie and Peggy O'Malley and their attorney will be arriving momentarily to give their formal statements."

"I hear the mother—Peggy O'Malley, that is—has denied the statement made by Miss LaCross. Is that true?"

"How could she deny it? What reason would that old attorney have had to make up such a story?"

"Kathy, who's going to be present during the interrogation with the O'Malleys?"

"Finally, a question I can respond to!" Kathy smiled ruefully at her staff. "But before I do, I want to thank all of you. I owe you guys so much. I could never have compiled all the information in such a short time without your help. This story is going to make the front page, whether the DA wants it to or not. But we can keep the lid on until everyone connected has given their statements."

"Do we know the girl's true identity?"

"Not yet, but we are working with one particular foundation for parents of missing children. They've got quite a database—hey, we're wandering here, folks. I will conduct the interview with the O'Malleys, and that will include Reagan O'Malley as well. Their attorney will be present, of course, as well as two psychiatric professionals and a court reporter. I want this to be as painless as possible for Reagan."

Something Maddie LaCross had said that first day in her office gave Kathy pause: "A powerful lot of people are going to be hurt by this."

Kathy shook herself to clear away the dark thoughts and continued speaking. "We are looking at one possible identity based on photographs and timing but nothing definite. If it's correct, the mother's quite famous, as a matter of fact."

"Was this a kidnapping for ransom and they just kept the kid?"

"You've been watching too much television, Martha," Kathy said, dryly dismissing the rookie investigator.

"Who is the possible mother, Kathy?"

"I'm not saying, not until everyone has been interviewed and the whole truth has been told."

"But will the whole truth *ever* be told, Ms. Vogel?"

"Now, Martha, there's a good question. Sadly, I think we all know the answer."

~

Kathy had chosen the large, well-lit conference room for the gathering. Plush swivel chairs surrounded an expansive table, and the view through the floor-to-ceiling windows was spectacular. The soft whir of overhead fans cushioned the tension in the room somewhat.

"Shall I repeat the question, Mrs. O'Malley?" Kathy asked.

"No, I heard the question." Her voice quivered. "My name is Peggy Sullivan O'Malley, and I reside at 1520 North Eleventh Street in Delaney."

"Thank you. How long have you lived at that address?"

"Fourteen years come January."

"And before that?"

"I fail to see what relevance other cities I might have lived in has to these preposterous goings-on!" Peggy responded harshly.

"Mr. Cantu, please instruct your client to answer my question as asked." Kathy was determined to establish posture early on.

"Mrs. O'Malley, you must answer." Peter Cantu, the O'Malleys' young attorney, appeared as tense as everyone else—everyone, that is, except Charlie. Kathy had remained perplexed ever since their initial meeting at the O'Malley home three weeks prior. *The man seems almost relieved!*

"Very well," Peggy said reluctantly. "We lived in Deer Run, Colorado, prior to moving to Delaney. I'm originally from back east."

"Thank you," Kathy responded. "How long have you and Mr. O'Malley been married?"

"It will soon be twenty years." Peggy's eyes darted, Kathy observed, from her husband to the doctors to the court reporter's fingers. *But you never look at your daughter, Mrs. O'Malley.*

"How many children do you and Mr. O'Malley have?"

Silence.

"Shall I repeat the question, Mrs. O'Malley?"

"One. We have one daughter, Reagan."

Kathy continued her close scrutiny of the woman before her. Slender and petite, her pretty face was free of lines and framed by shoulder-length reddish-blonde hair. She didn't look much older than Reagan, Kathy mused. "Where was your daughter born, Mrs. O'Malley?"

Again, the silence.

"Please, Mrs. O'Malley." Kathy's voice was kind but firm. "Don't make me keep repeating myself."

"There, in Deer Run." Peggy's answer was barely audible.

"Mrs. O'Malley," Kathy said as she leaned forward and spoke softly, with compassion she truly felt for this woman, "the hospital in Deer Run lists only one recorded live birth to you and Mr. O'Malley—the premature birth of a boy who lived only a few hours. I am so sorry."

"M-m-mama?" Reagan spoke for the first time, her voice quivering.

Peggy's expression remained closed. "The records, Ms. Vogel, are wrong!"

The room was bathed in silence. Kathy waited.

"Everyone always wants to dwell on the past!" Peggy suddenly became anxious and defensive, her voice rising. "You," she said, pointing at Dr. Leonard, "that's all you ever did was to try and dig up the past! You never helped my daughter. You just wanted her to live in the past!"

She paused, breathless, tears threatening. "And now, we're here all because of the ramblings of some deranged old alcoholic!"

Kathy watched as the other woman's hands clenched and unclenched in rhythm. "Please, Mrs. O'Malley, stay calm," Kathy said soothingly. "We need to get to the bottom of this. Now—"

"Get to the bottom of what?" Peggy's fist pounded on the table. "You come into our home, disrupt our lives, and drag our daughter from her school based on what, Ms. Vogel?" She paused to catch her breath, her slight brogue becoming more pronounced. "The man you claim to have written this, this so-called journal is dead!"

Peter Cantu placed an arm around Peggy's shoulders in an effort to calm her. "Ms. Vogel, perhaps my client could have a short break?"

Kathy was about to agree when the strong, amazingly calm voice of Charlie O'Malley commanded attention. In contrast to his wife's, Charlie's eyes never left Reagan.

"It was the coldest night of the year—"

"No! Charlie, no!" Peggy cried out. Her face had contorted into a mask of fear.

"Mrs. O'Malley, I will have you removed!" Kathy spoke with authority, the kid gloves off. "Mr. O'Malley, please continue."

"It was the coldest night of the year," Charlie repeated, seemingly unaware of his wife's outburst. "According to the weather bureau, it was the beginning of the worst blizzard in thirty years. Peggy and I were on our way home from Denver. We'd spent the weekend here. Just outside of Deer Run, the weather broke a bit. It actually stopped snowing for a while, and the moon peeked through."

"Charlie, this is our *family*!" Peggy's pitiful plea was barely audible.

Kathy watched the man intently. Charlie winced but otherwise paid no attention to his wife, looking all the while at his daughter. *Eyes of love,* Kathy thought.

"In spite of the cold, I'll never forget what a beautiful night it was. We'd get a glimpse of the moon through the clouds ever' so often, and the whole world seemed brand new, clean, like Peg and I were the only people on earth."

Reagan could hear her own heartbeat. *Dear God, this is Papa talking!* Her stomach lurched.

"Just a few minutes more in that bitter cold and she would have died ..."

His voice was paralyzing. Reagan wanted to get up and leave, but she couldn't move. *This is Papa!* She must have tensed involuntarily. Dr. Whitfield's cool hand covered hers, and she tried to concentrate on Papa's voice.

"Soon she began to eat and move around. Wouldn't say anything, though, not at first. She didn't want Peg out of her sight."

This is what you've wanted as far back as you can remember, Reagan thought, coaching herself to remain focused. *You wanted to know the secret!*

"It wasn't my wife's fault," Charlie continued, his eyes locked now on Peggy's. "It was no one's fault, and yet, it was everyone's fault! You see, baby," he said as he turned and spoke directly to Reagan, "we, we thought you'd been abused and abandoned—God knows what else. You had bruises, you were dirty, and—"

No, no, no! They're just trying to get us to come out again! We don't want to hear anymore. We don't need to remember! We have all we need right here where it's warm, where we're not scared, not freezing, not hungry—

"Like I said, Titus Peebles didn't have a choice, not if he wanted to continue to have any kind of life in Deer Run. I would have exposed him for what he was in a minute!" Disgust crept into Charlie's voice. "You see, I would have done anything to make my wife happy." Charlie leaned forward, his eyes sweeping the room and imploring those present to understand.

Kathy watched as Peggy O'Malley sat motionless, her expression impossible to read. Kathy wondered, though, if she wouldn't be the survivor in this tragedy after all. Charlie would never be the same; this she knew.

"Mr. O'Malley, do you need a break?" Kathy asked.

"No, ma'am." He sipped water, took a deep breath, and once again turned his eyes to Reagan. "You," he said as he smiled at her, "you have been my life, *our* life! There's no one on earth who could have loved you more. But we had no right to love you, no right at all."

Reagan struggled. She wanted desperately to turn around and look into the blackness, to decipher once and for all the whispers that had permeated her dreams and choked her with fear. *All you have to do is turn around, you coward!*

"Nooooo!" Reagan's sudden outburst startled everyone, most of all her.

"It's all right, Reagan." Abe Leonard moved quickly to kneel beside her chair. He'd been relieved to turn his patient over to the care of the younger, more highly trained Eli Whitfield, but now Abe knew that their years together would be what she would cling to.

"Take a deep breath. Find your center," Abe crooned. "We'll get through this, Reagan. We'll get through it."

She swallowed several times. "W-w-who, Papa? Who—" She was crying now, and her tears tore like talons at the heart of everyone in the room.

Kathy didn't push. Instead she allowed all present ample time to wade through the quagmire of emotions. After a time, she spoke.

"Mr. O'Malley, you made mention in an earlier conversation to information you may have that would shed some light on this matter. Will you elaborate, please?"

"Information? What information?" Peggy asked, again becoming defensive. "I don't think my husband and I have any more to say!"

Charlie ignored his wife. "I've always been a big believer in fate, Ms. Vogel," he answered, smiling tiredly at Kathy. "Fate put me and Peg on that road at just the right time. That was good. We saved you, darlin'," he said with a nod to Reagan.

"But fate can be cruel, too. Yessiree, when fate put me in Dallas, Texas, eleven years ago—now that was cruel."

Kathy's pulse quickened as she looked from Charlie to Peggy. Clearly, from the puzzled look on Peggy's face, she had no inkling of what her husband was alluding to.

"Law enforcement seminars have never been my cup of tea," Charlie continued. "But that particular one sounded interesting. So, off I went to Dallas for three days."

"I remember. I didn't want you to go. I never wanted you to leave us," Peggy said flatly. "You were different when you came back. I used to think maybe there had been another woman. You were so distant—"

"It was the second day of meetings," Charlie went on as if his wife had never spoken. "And I just had to pick up that damn newspaper at breakfast! Headline was a story about an inmate at the prison, a mental patient who had committed suicide the week before. Pedophile, child murderer—"

Why is he telling us this story? We don't want to hear it! What does it have to do with us? We're not going to turn around. There's nothing behind us to see, anyway. Nothing but the fog!

"The *Morning News* ran a full section on the man, Hurley Dobbs—his life, his crimes. And, and they showed some—"

Charlie's voice cracked, and Kathy knew his calm bravado couldn't last.

"Mr. O'Malley, please. We can take a break and let you collect your thoughts."

"No need," Charlie answered. He swallowed hard. "You might remember the story. Dobbs abducted five little girls in and around Dallas. The police found two bodies buried behind his house and a third sometime afterward in a pond. At that time, they hadn't found any signs of the other two. According to the story, this Dobbs fella was crazy as a loon." Charlie stopped speaking and laughed a mirthless little laugh.

"Courts stuck him away with the criminally insane for life, disbanded the special task force, got on with other things, I suppose. And I just had to pick up that damn newspaper!" Charlie repeated tiredly. "Otherwise, I'd never have known."

"Known w-w-what, Papa?" Reagan's voice had lost its near-hysterical quality, and her large, dark eyes were now clearly focused for the first time that day, Kathy noticed.

Obvious to the assistant DA was the amazing turnaround in Reagan's demeanor since the beginning of the day's proceedings. Emotions, a desire to know the truth, perhaps even a smidgen of memory all battled the only reality the girl could remember. The winner was anyone's guess.

Kathy shifted her attention to Peggy. She sat motionless, no longer fidgeting, her eyes no longer darting but fixed on some distant, unseen object. *She's escaped*, Kathy thought, *into another time, a happier one before her family crumbled around her.* Kathy noticed the beads of perspiration along the woman's upper lip, and she wondered if the room had grown a bit too warm.

"It's all there, in a box in the old trunk in the attic." Charlie's voice, slightly hoarse now, broke the silence. "That newspaper story—they ran photos! I couldn't take my eyes off those pretty little girls, blonde hair, blue eyes …" He was rambling, staring off into space.

Kathy wanted to stop him, but she was powerless to do so.

"They all had blonde hair, 'cept for one. And the little clothes you had on—they're there, too, Reagan. I put them in the trunk so many years ago." Charlie had begun to slur his words slightly. He paused again, rubbed his head, and coughed hard several times.

"Had it in my mind to tell you when I got back home after that weekend, but I couldn't." He coughed again and turned to Reagan. "Darlin', do you remember what you said to me when I got home that night, when I came back from that trip? Do you remember?"

"I remember, Papa. I told you I didn't want you to ever go away again. I didn't like it when we weren't all together."

Not a stutter, Kathy noticed. She's in control now, and that's good. Or is it?

"So you see why I couldn't tell you! You see, don't you?" Charlie pleaded for understanding. "I always meant to, but the time was never quite right. And the years, they just flew by, and you were so happy." *cough, cough* "There's a letter to you, Reagan, in the box with the other things. I wrote it some time back." Charlie hunched forward and spread his big hands on the conference table. He looked older than he had just a couple of hours ago and very flushed. Kathy thought again about the room's temperature.

"I never knew." Peggy said, and her voice shook. "Reagan, my hand to God, I never knew!" She turned and directed a cold stare at Kathy and continued speaking. "And it wouldn't have mattered one bit if I *had* known!"

Kathy shivered in spite of the room's warm temperature. Peggy's left hand had begun to shake, and her wedding ring made a tapping sound on the tabletop. Reagan sat motionless, her eyes closed, her ragged breathing audible.

"It's too warm in here. I'll adjust the thermostat." Kathy spoke as much to herself as to the others as she rose from her chair and walked across the room.

She turned quickly at the loud *thud.*

She should have seen this coming! She was a professional and knew the signs! Kathy stood frozen in her tracks. In the span of a few seconds, the room had gone from virtual silence to chaos.

Her gaze swept the seven other people—four of them were on their feet, their faces registering shock; one was sitting ramrod stiff in the chair; and the other two were on the floor.

After a few moments, Kathy shook free from her paralysis and found her voice. "What is it, Abe?"

The psychiatrist raised his head from the still form on the floor. "Not sure. Could be a stroke. You'd better get an ambulance!"

Kathy quickly punched 9-1-1 on the telephone and waited. "Oh, Lincoln," she whispered under her breath. "This is not what you had in mind!"

78

Dr. Eli Whitfield believed in miracles. He always had. He believed in God, in the inherent good of mankind, and he believed that everything happened for a reason. Being a man of science and dedicated to the study and treatment of mental illness, Eli rarely shared this idealistic side with anyone, certainly not his peers in the psychiatric profession.

The young psychiatrist believed—no, he knew—that he and other professionals like him were the lifeline to which so many tortured minds clung, desperate to avoid perishing in a sea of depression and misery. Eli held onto his end of that lifeline tenaciously.

He believed that his patients wanted to be rid of their demons, whether they actually asked for his help or not. While many of his counterparts viewed their patients as little more than statistics, Eli became involved. His writing, the lectures, even his personal life took a backseat to the small group of patients in Boston who depended upon him. And now, he had one more.

Eli rested his head on the soft leather of Delta's first-class cabin seat. He was exhausted. How long could he keep up this pace? How long could he continue the weekly flights to Denver? His new best friend, Abe Leonard, had answered that question for him the previous week.

"You can do it for as long as is necessary, Eli," the older psychiatrist had told him. "I've seen how just one spark of memory from her gets you pumped up. You're doing an amazing job with her, and you can't quit now. You won't let yourself quit!"

How right Abe had been. Eli would work around the clock if necessary. He would juggle schedules left and right. He would do whatever it took to see her safely through the hellish transformation of becoming someone else—someone she still could not and possibly never would remember completely.

Of course, there were the sparks, as Abe put it. Quite often she would emerge from a session, her eyes bright and her voice bubbly with a tangible memory—the cat; details of rooms in a big, two-story house; a swimming pool; trips to the zoo; being carried by a tall, red-haired man; playing dress-up to the delight of a woman she as yet could not put a face to—memories that did not exist in Delaney, Colorado. Memories that did not include Charlie and Peggy O'Malley.

Thinking of the shattered O'Malley family struck a chord close to home with the young doctor. It was a source of profound sadness to Eli that he himself had no family, no close friends with whom he could expound upon the endless wonders of the universe. He rubbed his temples, willing the headache to remain at bay. He accepted the fact that his personal emptiness needed to take a backseat to more pressing concerns.

If Eli were asked to describe himself in one word, that word would be *focused*. He never lost sight of his goal, never allowed himself to become distracted. Hadn't he proved that by passing his college finals at the top of his class less than a month after losing his parents and twin brother in the auto accident? Then had come medical school, right on schedule, just as he and his family had wanted. His first attempt at being published had proved positive—success at every juncture!

So what was wrong now? Was he pushing too hard? Could he possibly be facing burnout at his young age? Eli tried to remain positive, but what other reasons could there be for his complete loss of concentration? He'd even been late for three appointments recently, which was unheard of in his structured life.

He turned his attention to the hodgepodge of papers that filled his lap, his own words now foreign to him. He'd never make his publisher's deadline at the rate he was going. Recognizing his problem was only a fraction of the solution. Eli had no idea how to stop the drifting, the wasted hours of building air castles, only to have them disappear in a poof of rationality. One thing was for sure, though: he needed to get back on track, and fast.

Eli adjusted his seat to its near-upright position and motioned for the flight attendant. "How long before we land in Albuquerque, ma'am?"

"A little less than an hour, Dr. Whitfield. May I get you anything?"

"Nothing, thank you," Eli replied, and settling into a comfortable position, he once again took up the thick sheaf of papers before him.

His notes during the past few weeks required the jumbo-sized clips to hold them together. Even though his sessions were always recorded, Eli took great comfort from paper and pen. They were a constant in his life, like brewing coffee and reading the morning newspaper before his regimented two-mile walk from brownstone to office.

Would he ever join his colleagues in their high-tech balancing act of Starbucks on one knee, laptop on the other, and cell phone glued to an ear only to arrive at their destinations hassled from their 'burbs-to-downtown commutes? He didn't think so.

Besides, his paper and pen provided a buffer for those patients who felt threatened by direct eye contact. They would at times be more forthcoming if they believed they were not under the microscope, so to speak. Even while committing every word to paper in his own style of shorthand, Eli studied his patients more closely than they could have imagined. He was indeed able to look into their eyes—especially if those eyes were big, round orbs of ebony, with quirky little silver motes dancing around the center, and eyelashes so incredibly long—

Good God, man, you're doing it again! he silently chided himself, troubled at how easily such sweet thoughts could lull him into believing that longing could one day become reality. He knew better. He was the doctor—the professional, for chrissake! And he was dancing across quicksand!

"Pardon me, young man." A gentle touch on his forearm jolted Eli from his drifting. "You've dropped your paperwork on the floor," the soft feminine voice continued.

Eli bent down to retrieve his notes before answering his fellow passenger seated across the aisle. "Thank you, ma'am. I'm afraid I'm quite distracted today. I didn't realize I had made such a mess." He finished gathering up the papers and began putting them away in his briefcase in preparation for the plane's landing.

"My goodness," the woman said. "You certainly have a lot of paperwork. Are you a writer?"

Eli smiled and answered her. "Occasionally, yes, ma'am, I am a writer. This mess, however," he said as he patted his briefcase, "is notes on one of my patients."

"Patients—you're a doctor, then?"

"Yes, I'm a psychiatrist, actually. I'm from Boston. At least that's where my practice is located. I've been traveling so much lately that it doesn't feel like home anymore."

"I'm from Chicago, and I'm visiting my granddaughter in Albuquerque," the woman informed him. "I've never been to the Southwest before, but my granddaughter and her husband tell me it's beautiful."

"It certainly is," Eli responded. "I find the area more appealing with each visit. In fact, I've been giving serious thought to relocating. That's always difficult to do in my profession, but I do have able colleagues in Boston." Eli paused thoughtfully. "And with this new patient in Denver, I'm spending more and more time in this area."

Why was he being so communicative with a complete stranger? Eli knew why. He was hungry for human interaction. He needed approval even if it came from a complete stranger with a sweet, grandmotherly face, whose interest was sparked by the boredom of a long flight.

"Pardon me for not introducing myself. I'm Eli Whitfield," he said, extending his hand.

"I'm so pleased to meet you, Dr. Whitfield. I'm Virginia Fowler." She shook his hand firmly.

"That's a coincidence. My mother's name was Virginia. Please, call me Eli."

"You say *was*. Is your mother no longer living?"

"No, she's been gone seven years now, as well as my father and brother. I have no family to speak of. I suppose that's why I get so wrapped up in my patients' lives," Eli continued, empowered not only by the basic human need to communicate but by the genuine interest he saw reflected in Virginia's face.

"I live alone," Virginia said. "My husband died many years ago, and my children are scattered to the four winds. I have my granddaughter, though, and we're very close. Tell me, are you married, Eli?"

"No, truthfully, I haven't had the time or the inclination. Again, my patients take the best of me, especially *this* patient!" He patted the briefcase once more.

"What makes this patient so special?" Virginia asked with interest. "If I may ask, I mean. I certainly wouldn't want to pry."

"You're not prying. Actually, I'd welcome the chance to chat with someone on the outside, so to speak. My patient is a young woman whom I have been treating for dissociative amnesia. In other words, she's blocked out the early years of her life due to her being—well, it's a long story. Let's just say she was separated from her parents at age four, raised by a couple who, other than keeping her true identity secret, seem to have been wonderful role models. Her birth parents have been identified. She's aware of her true identity, but she has only scattered bits of memory as far as they're concerned. She's the reason for my trip to Albuquerque today."

Eli took a deep breath and shook his head thoughtfully. "Today is the first meeting for the young woman, her birth parents, and the people she still thinks of as her parents, plus a few legal eagles thrown into the mix."

The bump of jet wheels meeting tarmac silenced Eli momentarily. When he again looked at Virginia, her knowing eyes met his. "What a tragedy for both the families," she said sadly. "I will say a very special prayer for everyone, you as well, Eli. God bless you!"

Eli took his leave of the plane and Virginia, feeling rather blessed indeed. The part he had played so far and would continue to play in the reshaping of a life was yet to be determined. But the knowledge that he had been instrumental in bringing her this far was exhilarating.

He made his way quickly through baggage claim and outside into the bright sun to watch for Abe. He closed his eyes and breathed the crisp, dry November air. His earlier apprehension gone, Eli now felt eager for the ten-minute ride to the Healing Spirit Foundation to be over. This was going to be a good day!

79

Reagan O'Malley slipped quietly from her room in the guest wing at the foundation. Her late-night talk with Dr. Abe hadn't helped, nor had the sedative he had given her. Sleep had once again proved elusive.

Her bare feet padded silently over the cool tile floor. Although it was not yet dawn, Reagan had no trouble making her way through the maze of hallways and offices and into the huge reception room. Soft, indirect lighting caressed the photographs and letters on display, marking the trail from despair to ecstasy for so many separated families. For others, only a sad closure marked the end of their search—but closure nonetheless—all brought about by this foundation.

Ever since she had been told everything, Reagan's curiosity had practically devoured her. She knew her nonstop questions of the previous day must have driven Dr. Abe to distraction. Instead of being permitted to relax during their flight from Denver, the poor doctor had been pummeled with a steady stream of *why, where,* and *who.*

Reagan smiled. Hadn't it always been that way between the two of them? She thought back to their countless sessions filled with little else but her obsession with the blanks in her memory—with *the secret.*

The questions had finally been answered, but those answers had brought her no closure. The only thing clear in her mind now was that nothing was clear. Her life was like a movie, with much of it running smoothly but with so many crucial scenes cut out that it was impossible to follow the plot or know the characters.

Reagan curled up on one of the overstuffed couches bordering the stone fireplace. The flames had died down hours ago, but the embers still glowed and helped to warm that part of the room against the predawn chill.

Thea Kelly! Reagan's amazement had not ebbed. Of course she knew who Thea was! Everyone even remotely associated with or interested in the art world had heard of Thea Kelly. What had captured the interest of both her psychiatrists was Reagan's admission that she had read none of the many feature articles written about the famous potter.

I never even looked at the pictures of her. Why is that? The question tore at her. Why, she had asked her doctors, would she purposely not purchase a magazine if the cover carried a photo or even a mention of Thea? Why had she not visited the galleries throughout the Southwest that presented Thea's work?

Neither doctor had given her an answer. Were they waiting for her to answer her own questions? Why, indeed?

Reagan was cold. She snuggled under the Navajo blanket from the back of the couch and continued to study her surroundings. The magnificent bronze in the center of the room commanded attention. She knew who Montana Arroyo was; he was legend. She knew, too, what he represented to the art world and to her—to Thea.

Reagan closed her eyes. The past two months had taken their toll. The endless questions, the attorneys, her own vague recollections, the constant stream of telephone calls, the tearful and sometimes explosive visits with Mama and Papa, the long days and nights at that hospital in Denver—all of it amounted to almost more than she could bear. But, as usual, Dr. Abe had come to her rescue with just the right counseling.

"You've been through worse, Reagan," he had said. "Although you don't remember it, you have been through worse."

The feather-soft touch on her shoulder jolted Reagan. "Are you comfortable here?" The woman's voice was a whisper.

"W-what?" Reagan was momentarily confused. "I didn't t-t-think anyone else was here this early." She struggled to sit up but realized her arms were caught in the confines of the heavy blanket.

"Don't get up," the woman continued to whisper. "I just wanted to know if you're comfortable here."

She stood between Reagan and the front lights, and Reagan couldn't see her face clearly. She knew who she was, though. "Yes, ma'am," she answered, "I'm very comfortable here. It's wonderful—this p-place, the art, the photographs—" she yawned.

Reagan still could not see the woman's face, but she heard her draw a deep breath. "It's all for you," she said. "It's all because of you."

"I don't remember you!" Reagan cried out, but the woman had disappeared.

Reagan's eyes flew open, and she sat bolt upright, her heart pounding. With shaking hands, she smoothed back her hair and tried to get her bearings.

The clock atop the mantle chimed in unison with her thoughts—nine o'clock. It was daylight, and from somewhere in the back of the building, she heard the faint sound of voices and smelled fresh-brewed coffee.

I've been asleep for hours! Everyone would be arriving soon for the eleven o'clock meeting. She wasn't ready for it. Would she ever be ready?

Reagan stood on shaky legs and began to fold the blanket. She had so much to do, and Dr. Abe would be leaving soon for the airport to meet Dr. Whitfield's plane. She had to talk to him before he left. This was a first for her, and she had to tell him about it. She had had an actual dream, a dream like other people have—one that she clearly remembered!

80

Thea would be late to the gathering on purpose. Not too late—not enough to appear rude or uncaring, but late nonetheless. She would be just late enough to avoid having to act as hostess to the group. That job had been bestowed upon Cal. After all, it had been his idea to hold the first meeting between both sets of parents and Reagan at the foundation.

"I want her to see what you've done and what you've given to so many people, Thea. I want her to see how you've honored her!" Cal's words had had their intended effect upon everyone concerned, the Colorado officials included.

"Is this late enough, love, or shall I make the block once more?" Monty asked, slowing the Jeep in anticipation of her answer.

"Once more around, please," Thea answered. "I want no time standing around making small talk. What I want is to walk in and see my daughter. I want to touch her and know she's safe. Cal will have everything well in hand, I'm sure."

"Once more, it is." Monty obliged by easing out of the turn lane and back into the light stream of traffic. More than most people, he appreciated Thea's aversion to putting this meeting on a social level. "Nervous?" He drew her hand to his lips for a caress.

"Very," she answered, smiling at him. "I'm nervous, excited, scared to death, still angry, and happy all rolled into one. But mostly, I'm happy!"

Monty and Thea had spent the previous night at a hotel in Albuquerque instead of in their usual suite at the foundation. Joe had arrived the day before and had accepted the hospitality of Cal and Sophie. Dr. Leonard had flown with Reagan from Denver, Dr. Whitfield was scheduled to arrive from Boston this morning, and the representatives from the Denver DA's office had been in town for two days.

Cal had informed Thea, Monty, and Joe at dinner the previous night that the O'Malleys would be driving from their home, accompanied by a nurse. Wanting to make sure her daughter was completely at ease, Thea had not offered guest rooms at the foundation to anyone except Reagan and Dr. Leonard.

Dinner the night before had gone well. Much to Thea's amazement and pleasure, Joe and Monty had gotten on fabulously and had had a great deal to talk about, due to Joe's having been awarded design contracts for two new art galleries in St. Louis and Chicago.

But the main topic of conversation hadn't wavered far from that of the past two months—Alexa had been found! Everything else that may have needed to be said—apologies that had been closeted for too long—paled in comparison to that one single fact.

Monty brought the Jeep to a stop in the parking lot. "Ready?"

"I'm ready," Thea answered. "The only thing that keeps this from being a perfect day is—"

"I know, love," Monty consoled her, reading her thoughts. "Mike knows, though, and he's with us right now, right here," he said, touching his hand to his heart.

Thea nodded, dried her eyes, and smoothed her hair. Alighting from the Jeep, she took Monty's hand, and together they walked into the small courtyard that led to the foundation's entrance.

"Will you tell me what you're feeling at this very moment?" Monty asked.

"I feel—well, I feel—"

She had buried Thea the victim long ago, along with her baggage of grief, guilt, and self-loathing. And hatred. She had smothered the images of birthdays, graduations, prom night, first love, broken heart, and all the other milestones that marked a life. And jealousy. She had won a clear victory over the wasted days spent in wretched yearning for what had been taken from her and might never be returned. And revenge.

Burial was supposed to be final, the end. Not so—not when the long-buried could be so easily exhumed and brought back to haunt her. Exhumed by cruel deception, those burdensome ghosts of the past weighed heavily upon her. Lately, she had been forced to carry them all over again—carry them, taste them, smell them, and stagger under the sheer weight of them. And almost be buried herself.

She had thought long and hard, but in the end the decision she had made was not a difficult one. Only Joe knew, and he supported her. Today, what had gone before would be laid to rest.

Then, she would bury them for the final time, those ghosts with their moaning placations of what-ifs, why-didn't-Is, and if-onlys. She would bury them deep this time, but with great care so as not to let compassion and patience and charity fall into the grave and become covered with dirt. And forgiveness.

"I feel whole!"

Thea opened the door and entered the Healing Spirit Foundation. Immediately, she was greeted warmly by Cal and Sophie. Sensing that everyone else had arrived, she purposefully walked straight ahead to where Abe Leonard stood admiring Monty's sculpture. The two had met on her initial trip to Denver and had talked often during the past few weeks.

"Abe, how is she?" Thea asked.

"Better than I have seen her in ages! You just wouldn't believe the positive effect your foundation has had on her. Your friend Cal was right in insisting we meet here," Abe praised. "As a matter of fact, Thea, you've got yourself another volunteer. I can hardly wait to become a part of your work here."

Thea thanked him and began a cursory examination of the room. Everyone had migrated to the sitting area in front of the fireplace. She glimpsed the slender woman with reddish-blonde hair standing some distance from the rest of the group, her hand resting protectively on the shoulder of the man in the wheelchair: The O'Malleys.

Thea did not dwell on them but studied for a few moments the young man standing alone by the fireplace. This would be Dr. Whitfield. She had not as yet been introduced to him but liked him already thanks to Abe's praises.

Kathy Vogel and her entourage sat apart from the group. Thea would deal with them later.

Then, there she was, sitting on one of the couches, her profile to the door. She was looking at Joe as he spoke quietly. Thea felt Monty's hand give hers a final, reassuring squeeze before he released it and stepped away. She took a few hesitant steps forward, not wanting to break the spell of the moment, wanting instead to savor it.

Joe's voice was low, but some of his words drifted to Thea's ears. "I was so afraid even to hope … guess I simply gave up. Not her, though …"

never lost faith … she always believed we'd find you … everything was done with you in mind …"

Thea stepped closer. She knew the dangers. The euphoric high she'd been riding ever since the day Cal had come to her with his news could easily plummet into despondency. She could not survive another bout of depression, nor could those who loved her.

She took another tiny step forward. It wouldn't have to be that way, though. After all, they were all adults here! If she exhibited patience, if she didn't become emotional, if she didn't push, and above all else, if she didn't expect too much, well, then—

But then she stood up from her seat on the couch, slowly turned, and Thea Kelly was face to face with a younger mirror image of herself, face to face with—

"Alexa!" She tried not to cry out, tried not to reach out to touch her, but she did both.

"I-it's Reagan. My n-n-name is Reagan." She took a small step back, just barely out of reach. Thea noticed the movement. She noticed, too, the disguise of calm that was unmasked only by the eyes. Her daughter was terrified.

"Reagan," she responded with a smile, willing herself to a level of composure she did not feel. "I'm Thea."

"I know. I m-mean, I've been told." She swallowed her words and then found them after a long pause. "This place is w-w-wonderful. You've done so much, and you're s-such a fine artist. I just don't—"

"Reagan," Thea interrupted gently, "everything doesn't have to be said today. We have all the time in the world."

"I r-r-remember things like the cat, Peaches, the big house, s-swimming pool." Reagan's brow furrowed, and her eyes welled with tears as she spoke. She was trying so hard. "But I don't remember you. I'm s-s-sorry."

The revelation seemed to suck the air from the room, and Thea couldn't breathe. Her ears rang. After what seemed like hours, she swallowed hard, managing to break the vacuum and find her voice.

"Your hair, Reagan—it's beautiful. May I?" Her hand hovered timidly, and at the almost indiscernible little nod of permission, she gently lifted the heavy raven curls away from the young woman's neck.

All the tests, the coinciding dates and times, and, yes, even the confessions be damned! Here was Thea Kelly's proof! "Do you remember," she began, her voice dropping to barely a whisper. "Do you remember a time long, long ago when you were 'Daddy's Berry'?"

Her shudder and sharp intake of breath brought Abe Leonard a step closer to the two women, but only a step. He waited. Thea waited.

"It doesn't m-matter what you c-c-call me," Reagan said, struggling to hang on to a thread of composure. "I don't r-remember you!" She turned and walked past Abe's awkwardly outstretched arms to the far side of the fireplace and to Eli's side.

Thea closed her eyes. Oh, those cloying images! They hadn't visited her in years, but here they were, back again. Back to tease her with sweet memories; back to taint those memories with the horror of reality. Was Joe ever visited by the images, or was it only her? Strange that the thought should occur to her at this moment, but she realized she had never asked him.

After several minutes, the shuffle of shoes on the stone floor and nervous throat-clearing permeated the deafening silence and finally drew Thea out of her daze. She realized that their saga was nearing its end. For the past two months, her imagination had worked overtime, writing and rewriting the perfect script for just such an ending. It would be a tearful but happy reunion; there might even be music playing in the background as mother and daughter were blissfully reunited at last. But life almost always refuses to follow a script.

She felt Monty's presence beside her. She smiled up at him. "I've done part of what I came here to do today, Monty," she said, surprised at how calm her own voice sounded, for she did not feel calm. "Now it's time to do the rest.

"Ladies and gentlemen, thank you for being here to share in the happiest day I've had in fourteen years. Some of you may need to leave, but please feel free to stay at the foundation as long as you wish." Thea cleared her throat.

"Ms. Vogel, thank you especially for your tactful handling of the situation. Families are sacred, and I, personally, will never forget the compassion you showed in keeping the outside world at bay. I do not think we will meet again, but I hope you know you have my sincere thanks."

"And thank you, Ms. Kelly." At once, Kathy assumed her courtroom posture. "We realize your need for privacy, but we will meet again. A crime has been committed, and the people of the state of Colorado intend—"

"The people of the state of Colorado, as well as any other state, have no say in this matter, not anymore." Thea's cool demeanor as well as her words raised eyebrows all around.

"Ms. Vogel, there will be no charges brought against anyone in this matter, at least not by my family. The only guilty party in my daughter's disappearance is dead."

After a brief silence, Kathy responded. "I'm confused. May I ask why, Ms. Kelly? A terrible wrong was perpetrated against you and your family. Again, I ask, why?"

"It's quite simple," Thea answered. "Enough has been taken from my daughter. I will not add to her confusion and sorrow by having people that she—that she loves taken from her."

Thea watched the two men with Kathy gesturing and whispering adamantly. Finally, Kathy shook her head and smiled apologetically as she spoke. "Ms. Kelly, it's not your decision to make."

"Oh, but it is, Ms. Vogel." Thea straightened to her full height and spoke sternly to the woman. "You see, if charges are brought against anyone in this room, I will use all my resources to fight you. And, I might add, those resources are considerable."

Joe moved to stand beside Thea, his arms crossed and his eyes on the assistant DA as he spoke. "Actually, I believe you could describe those resources as staggering."

"Practically limitless," Monty chimed in from Thea's other side, his stance and gaze equally intimidating.

Thea was not blind to the frustration that Kathy was battling. She wanted to save her further embarrassment. "Thank you again, Ms. Vogel," she said, her voice softened a bit. "And please, do one final thing for my family. Please make this go away."

Kathy knew when she was whipped, and she didn't much care. Take a mother's plea and mix it with the broken hearts of so many decent folks, and what have you got? A tragedy that had touched Kathy deeply, in a way she had not been touched before.

She took a deep breath and studied the three stoic figures before her. "I'll speak with the DA," she muttered. "I'll be in touch."

Eli had not taken his eyes off Reagan since she had run to his side. He had watched her intently while Thea spoke, and he could sense a rising current of apprehension begin to course through her body. "Reagan, tell me what you're feeling right now," he commanded.

~

"I've said this to you before, Thea, but I'll say it again: you're quite a woman!" Cal said as the two friends found a quiet corner.

"Oh, Cal, how can I ever make you know how much your friendship and your hard work have helped me over the years? Not only helped—" Thea struggled for the right words. "Because of you, I've kept my sanity. When everyone else gave up, you kept looking for her.

"And all this," she said as she gestured grandly. "There wouldn't even *be* a foundation without you." She paused, getting misty-eyed all over again. "You really did believe she was alive, didn't you, Cal?"

"Yep, I sure did. Many's the time I'd look at myself in the mirror and say, 'Evers, you damned fool, look at the evidence!' But then I'd see your face, hear the way you talked about her, and—well, maybe I just wanted to believe it so bad. But, yeah, I believed she was alive. Now, did I think we'd ever find her?" He chuckled. "I gotta tell you. I had my doubts!"

~

"W-w-what am I feeling? Dr. Whitfield, I'm not sure." Reagan sounded puzzled.

Eli wasn't buying her vague response. He could read her subtle nuances that signaled a memory. He also recognized the newly found sense of wonder that echoed in her voice—a sense of wonder still stained with fear. He knew, too, of the power struggle going on between the memories she actually sought and the ones that were bound to surface all on their own.

"Oh, I think you are sure, Reagan." Eli also knew when to push. "When Thea was speaking just now, something was waking up inside of you, wasn't it?"

She met his eyes levelly. She took a deep breath and exhaled slowly. When she spoke, her stutter was insignificant. "It's true what I told you and Dr. Abe weeks ago, and what I told Thea just now. I don't r-r-remember her. I've tried so hard, but I just don't see her in my mind. Sometimes I can remember images, places, and events, but I don't remember *her*!"

She stopped speaking, and Eli was deflated. Studying her facial expression and her body language, he had been certain she was on the verge of a memory breakthrough.

Reagan sighed heavily. "And yet—" She stopped.

Hopeful once more, Eli prodded. "And yet *what*, Reagan?"

She chose her words carefully. "Most people w-w-wouldn't understand, but you will. Even though I haven't been able to remember her at all, I *know* her!"

Her statement was emphatic and caused Eli's ears to tingle. "Go on, please," he said.

"I know her voice and her touch. I know her smell," she responded with little emotion.

"And you know this how, Reagan?" Eli asked.

"W-w-while she was speaking just now, I could—oh, how do I make myself clear?" She covered her face with her hands and began to cry once more.

Eli knew frustration as the enemy, and he was determined not to allow it in this time. He spoke calmly. "You're making yourself perfectly clear to me. Please go on."

"Okay. While she w-was speaking, I closed my eyes and s-suddenly the fog lifted. I could see the two of them in there together."

"Who did you see, Reagan? Where were they?" Eli whispered the questions.

"I could see them s-s-side by side," she answered. Then, her transformation lit up his world. No longer were her eyes glazed as if fixed on some faraway scene. No longer did her voice mimic someone in a trance. Animation danced across her face, and a near reverence filled her throaty voice.

"I saw through the f-fog, Dr. Whitfield. I saw them in the tunnel! It was the little girl and—and *her!*" She paused and then continued before Eli could respond. "It was her. It was Thea. She n-n-never left the little girl's side!"

They stood looking into each other's eyes for a long time, both of them absorbing her words.

"T-that's how I know her." She grinned up at him and gave a triumphant little nod.

"Well, then," Eli said, managing to swallow the lump in his throat and hoping his face wore its mask of professional detachment. "This is quite the breakthrough," he continued. "However, don't you think you should be sharing it with someone other than me?"

Reagan followed his gaze across the room to where Thea and Cal stood talking. "Oh, I wouldn't know w-what to say to her. I don't think—" Her head drooped as uncertainty crept back into her voice.

Eli gently lifted her chin until once again their eyes met. "You'll find the words, Reagan, just as you did with me," he said. "After all, you *know* her!"

"You're right, of course," Reagan agreed. "I'm going to talk to her now." In her enthusiasm, she took hold of his hand and held it to her cheek for only a second before releasing it and stepping away.

"Thank you, Eli!" She breathed his name and then turned and walked in Thea's direction.

Eli watched her walk with a newfound presence. The fortress she'd built so long ago had not fallen, but it had yielded. He poured himself an iced tea from the sideboard and settled comfortably in a large chair in the corner. He needed to relax and get a fresh perspective on the day's events. Contentment sat with him.

~

"What's next, Thea?" Cal asked her. "You must finally feel some closure at last."

"Actually, I feel as though I'm just getting started. I'm just getting started with our work here at the foundation and my and Monty's art. Of course, the biggest job of all lies ahead of me now—building a relationship with Alexa. I mean, with Reagan," she corrected herself. "Cal, I just have to believe that will happen!"

"That's my girl," Cal responded. He had expected nothing less of Thea. Even with Reagan's rejection of her, he'd witnessed too much of his friend's true grit to even imagine her quitting on anything or anyone. "I've got some plans of my own. We'll talk about that later."

"Just a minute, Cal." Thea broke in to speak to Sophie, who was standing by the door. "Sophie, thank you for being here today and for everything!"

Sophie smiled as she spoke. "God bless you, Thea! Cal, I'll be right outside. No rush."

"Okay, *plans*, you say?" Thea said returning her attention to Cal. "I want to hear all about them. But you've given me enough of your time today. Sophie's waiting for you."

"Uh-huh, and I do believe somebody's waiting for you, too." Cal smiled and gave Thea a conciliatory wink as he nodded in the direction behind her. "Looks to me like she's about to bust to talk to you."

"Now, wait just a minute. What exactly is happening here?" Eli pondered aloud, sensing a collective mood swing drift over everyone present.

During his quiet time, he had allowed himself to fall into a favorite pastime: people-watching. With everyone else in the room otherwise occupied, his keen powers of observation kicked in full-throttle. *How can so much tension that permeated this room earlier have vanished? Everything seems so settled!*

Matters had certainly been settled, at least for the time being, with the assistant DA from Denver. Ms. Vogel and her two cohorts had wasted no time in being the first ones to leave the gathering. Oh, Eli expected they would all have quite a bit more contact with the Colorado officials. But for now, he put them out of his mind and made room for more significant players.

The O'Malleys: Eli knew their marriage had been sorely tested during the past two months, and his heart warmed to see the devotion Peggy showered upon Charlie since his debilitating stroke.

Just look at them! Peggy had placed a shawl across her husband's shoulders in preparation for their departure and now knelt beside his wheelchair to tenderly dry the corners of his mouth with her handkerchief. Charlie reached out a shaky hand to awkwardly caress her cheek, and she smiled at him. Eli had not seen Peggy smile often; what a pretty smile she had. The couple would be fine, he decided. Actually, they would be better than fine.

Monty and Joe had been left on their own for the time being and appeared to have formed a comfortable alliance. Eli watched as Monty finished up the grand tour and the two men made their way toward the dining room for lunch.

Eli had to smile at Abe Leonard. The lively doctor practically skipped from group to group, bowing clumsily, greeting everyone in his comical style, and adding to the magic in the air.

"And here's to you, beautiful lady," Eli whispered under his breath. He studied Thea as she listened raptly to Reagan's words. "You look ten years younger than when you walked in this morning!"

Eli had properly categorized everyone in the room—well, almost everyone. Guilt stabbed at him once again, but not as deeply as before.

Perhaps the obstacles that earlier had loomed insurmountable in his personal life now merely presented a challenge.

What was directly or indirectly responsible for today's positive ambience, Eli realized, could be any number of factors. One thing was certain, though: he was among people who had put their own wants and needs second to Reagan's well-being.

Perhaps the wounds inflicted by the disappearance of Alexa Kelly could be healed through the manifestation of Reagan O'Malley. Eli's thoughts took a more simplistic turn back to his morning's flight. Maybe it was Virginia's "very special prayer" that had brought everyone together. Maybe.

He stood up, stretched, and walked toward the library, where he knew he would find his friend, Abe. Together, they had much to talk over and much to celebrate. Eli was through analyzing the morning's happenings, though. After all, it was perfectly clear to him what had occurred here today. Simply put, it was a miracle!

~

Cal donned his hat and closed the foundation's front door behind him. Sophie waited by the courtyard fountain, and he made his way toward her with the customary pack of cigarettes and lighter already in hand. He took a cigarette from the pack, fingered it thoughtfully, and placed it between his lips. Then, after a brief hesitation, he removed it and deposited all of it into the nearby trash receptacle.

Sophie's eyebrows shot up. "Quitting again?"

"Not *again*, Soph," Cal answered her with conviction. "I'm quitting *finally*!"

"Oh, looking forward to that!"

Cal ignored her sarcasm. "I'm quitting something else, too, Soph." He waited, and when she didn't respond, he went on talking. "I always promised you I'd retire by the time I was sixty. I aim to keep that promise."

"I'd never hold you to that, Cal," Sophie responded softly. "I know how much you love what you do. Besides, you'd be bored out of your mind around the house all day with me."

"Wouldn't be quitting the part I truly enjoy. I'd keep my directorship here at the foundation. I'd give advice and help out any time I could. It's the legwork I'm ready to pass on to the youngsters. As for all my other cases, hell, Rob'll just have to find himself another partner."

"You're serious, aren't you?" Sophie asked, half smiling at her husband. "How long have you been thinking about this?"

"Oh, for sometime, now," Cal answered his wife. He fished around in his jacket pocket, came up with a toothpick, and stuck it in his mouth. "Been studying on something else, too, Soph."

"Yeah? What's that?"

"Oh, just something I've been kicking around, something I think might interest you, too." He tried to sound casual and laid back. He knew he wasn't pulling it off.

"Tell me."

"Canada."

Sophie turned to look at him. "Well, go on," she prodded. "Canada is a country up north, cold sometimes, and pretty, so they say. What about it?"

"Been thinking how nice it'd be: just you and me in one of them motor homes—a big one, mind you, not just a camper. Anyway, we could turn a nice profit on the house here, and, and just think about it, Soph. The two of us heading out on a real adventure! It wouldn't be forever, of course. But you know I've always wanted to see the North Country, and—"

She cut him off and turned to face him squarely, her hands on her hips. "Cal Evers, if you think for one minute I'm gonna leave that new grandbaby, you've got another think coming! You know how I wanted me a little girl, and now that I've got one, you want me to just up and leave? Just, just—" she sputtered, and her voice caught in her throat. "Just to go traipsing all the way to hell and gone and leave everything we've—"

"Yessiree," Cal interrupted, only half hearing her tirade. "Just think about it—the two of us living with no timetable, no stress, just seeing the countryside and doing a lot of fishing. Hey, I might even get started on that book you're always on me to write." He finished to a cold silence.

The toothpick had lost its appeal. Cal popped a Life Saver in his mouth and waited. He waited for the signal that his wife's temper was cooling. After more than thirty years together, he knew the sign. She'd begin to sniff. That was the sure indication that Sophie was through quarrelling. Cal had expected her to balk at leaving the kids, but sooner or later he believed she'd some around.

"And you hit me with this today of all days!" she said, taking one last shot.

"I apologize."

Their silence lasted through two more Life Savers. Finally, Sophie turned toward him just a little, not quite making eye contact.

"So," (*sniff, sniff*). Her tone was sharp. "Canada, huh?"

Cal studied his wife for a long time. He reached out to tuck an escaped tendril of frizzy blonde hair back into its bun at the nape of her neck. Her skin felt soft to his touch. She smelled good. He smiled and nodded.

"Yeah, Sophie, Canada!"

Epilogue

"Whew! Where did all this stuff come from, Max?" Thea paused from her chore of packing to wipe the perspiration from her face and survey their morning's work. "I swear I don't remember half the things we're packing!"

"Never mind where it all came from. I can't believe you've managed to fit everything into this tiny house. It's a miracle the whole place hasn't exploded!" Max exclaimed between gasps for breath. "Honestly, when Aaron and I sold the house here last month, we didn't have nearly as many boxes, and I'm talking three thousand square feet," she finished, grinning at her friend.

"Still think you guys made the right decision to sell your house here?" Thea asked, taking a seat on a nearby box. "I mean, severing all ties to Santa Fe seems so final."

Glad for the chance to take a break, Max dropped to the floor. "See here now, kiddo. I'm not severing any ties. I mean, does anybody ever really *leave* Santa Fe? Impossible! This place," she said, growing thoughtful, "it haunts you. It stays with you no matter where you go. We take a piece of it with us when we leave; we leave a piece of ourselves behind. And don't forget, Thea," she said with a note of sadness creeping into her voice. "With Paul's health declining, Elena's going to need me back here more than she thinks, I'm afraid."

"You're right about that. He doesn't look well. She's going to need all of us to come as often as we can," Thea agreed.

"That'll be a snap for you and Monty," Max responded. "You guys have burned up the road between here and Taos for years! It's a little harder for us to do spur-of-the-moment trips from San Francisco."

"The ranch is wonderful. But I'm never going to sell this house. I just couldn't. It's been so much a part of my healing process. After all, it's where I met Monty. Speaking of Monty, he's supposed to be here in two hours, and he's expecting us to have everything packed and ready to load on the truck when he gets here. You know what a bear he can be when he has to wait."

Thea jumped up to resume packing, but Max would have none of it. The two women had precious few times alone these days, and she aimed to make the most of it.

"Hey, kiddo, remember the last time you and I stood in a house full of boxes? It seems to me you said the very same thing then: 'Where did I get all this stuff!'"

Thea smiled and responded, "Yes, I remember. Sometimes it seems a hundred years ago, as though it happened to someone else. Then, at other times, it's like only yesterday. What's that old saying about things being different yet the same?"

And some things never change, Max mused as she caught sight of Thea turning away to dab at her eyes. "So, what do you hear?" she asked the younger woman.

"Not much. Only two phone calls since Christmas, actually. But, hey, I'm not complaining. That's more than I had for fourteen years."

Thea moved aimlessly around the small room, absently fingering the contents of open boxes. "I do talk often with Eli—Dr. Whitfield. He no longer treats her, but he still flies to Denver regularly to consult with Abe regarding her therapy. He tells me she's making amazing progress. He's even talking of moving there. "

"Maybe the Southwest is working its magic on him, too," Max said.

Thea smiled thoughtfully before answering. "I get the feeling it's more than just the location that enchants him, and I think I like that."

"Let's get back to you and Monty. When's the wedding?" Max asked, hauling herself to her feet with a groan. "How about next month? You could be a June bride."

"We haven't set a date yet. Most probably we'll wait until after Market. Sometime in late September would be nice." Thea's mood brightened. "You know, I'd like a church wedding, but Monty insists on having it at the ranch house, and that'll be okay. I've always wanted to marry him, Max." She paused reflectively. "Now, I can finally let myself! I expect we'll both know when the time's right. Don't worry. You'll get plenty of notice."

"Wouldn't miss it! Now, who can that be?" Max turned at the sound of the telephone's ring.

"The question is not who, but where? I think we've packed the phone!" Thea replied as the two lost themselves in laughter.

"Here it is! I've got it! Thea's," Max answered, attempting to catch her breath. "Hello, Aaron, darling. I miss you, too!"

Thea studied her best friend. Her once-svelte figure had rounded pleasantly, and although the lines of age had begun to make their presence known, that look of wonder had not left her pretty face. Her marriage to Aaron was golden.

After hanging up, Max whirled around to face Thea. "He misses me!" She giggled like a teenager.

"I gathered that!" Thea said. "Our lives are blessed."

They stood looking at each other with hands entwined. "Our lives are blessed," Max echoed. "Now what?" she responded to yet more ringing from the telephone. "I'll bet he *still* misses me," she said, grinning as she reached to silence the ringing.

"Wait," Thea instructed. "I—I think I need to answer it this time." Her hand hovered briefly over the receiver before she picked it up. "Hello?"

"Uh, hi, Thea. It's Reagan."

Thea swallowed hard several times. *Alexa, baby, are you all right?* "Reagan! What a nice surprise. How have you been? How's Denver?"

"Art classes are good, my job's okay, but I'm having trouble painting. I just don't seem to have any inspiration, not like I had in S-S-Santa Fe. I'm in limbo! Do you ever feel that way?"

You are my inspiration! "Of course I do. Every artist loses direction from time to time. You'll work through it. You could always come to Santa Fe on weekends for inspiration. Matter of fact, if you do decide you want to spend some time here, I have the perfect house for you."

"I do have a trip planned, but t-that's not the main reason I'm calling. I mean, I just, well, I just—"

Will we always have to tiptoe around each other? "Reagan, is anything wrong?"

"No, nothing's wrong. I just wanted to talk to you about something, okay? I just need some advice."

And I need to see you, to touch you, to hold you! "How can I help?"

"Well, f-f-first of all," Reagan continued, the excited, youthful lilt returning to her voice. "I read the cover story about you in the *Santa Fe*

Arts magazine—wow! It said your upcoming show will be the biggest ever. Aren't you excited?"

"Excited and very tired," Thea answered. "I'm still not sure the timing is right, but Monty insisted that the week before Market would be perfect. I'm always nervous before these shows. That's something you'll experience, too, when you're a famous painter."

"I don't know why you're nervous. You're, like, totally the best and most famous potter in the Southwest!" Reagan praised. After a pause, she continued.

"Now, about that trip I mentioned. We, uh—Eli, uh, Dr. Whitfield, that is—well, we're planning to c-come to your show. We'll be staying for Market, too, and I want to come to your show," Reagan repeated herself nervously.

"That's wonderful," Thea responded. "However, I get the feeling that's not exactly what you wanted to talk to me about."

Reagan took a deep breath. "Thea, I—I wanted you to be the very f-f-first to know. Eli has asked me to marry him, and I've said yes. I know what Ma—uh, you know everyone, the folks—are going to say. Everyone's going to say I'm too young. W-what do you think?"

Of course you're too young! You're only four years old! "Reagan, I think you are incredible!" Thea chose her words carefully. "Everything that's happened has happened for a reason. This I believe. You are the sum total of all the people who have loved you throughout your life. Now, you want to experience a new kind of love with Eli. One day perhaps you'll become a mother; and then you'll know the greatest love of all." She blinked furiously against the tears. *You wanted me to be the first to know!* "You'll make the right decisions in your life. I have no doubt."

"Thea, I know who I am." Reagan spoke calmly but not without emotion. "I am Mary Alexa Kelly. That's *who* I am, but I can't *be* her, at least n-n-not right now. Eli has helped me so much—Dr. Abe, too. They've helped me to remember where I hid her and why I had to hide her. I know, too, that it was nobody's f-fault—" Her voice broke.

Alexa, you get back here this instant! I'll take the trash to the street. You come back! "Nobody's fault," Thea echoed. "Nobody's fault but—"

Why weren't you home on time, Joe? If you had only been there! Thea conquered the lump in her throat and willed her voice to remain strong. "Nobody's fault but a sick, depraved, tortured man named Hurley Dobbs."

What do you mean you have no suspect? No clues? You're the police! Do something! "Most of all, child, it wasn't your fault."

"I know that now." Reagan sniffed, laughed, and hiccupped all at the same time. "I can't wait to see you. Let's t-talk more about your show. What's the theme? How many pieces are you exhibiting?"

Thea laughed away her tears as she answered. "I've done thirty pieces so far, and we're calling the show New Beginnings."

"Perfect! Oh, just think about it," Reagan gushed. "Thousands and thousands of people will be there, and everyone will see your most beautiful creations!"

"Yes, Reagan, they certainly will," Thea answered her daughter. *They will see you, my Alexa. They will see you!*

~